GROUNDSWELL

THE DIVA BOOK OF SHORT STORIES 2

EDITED BY HELEN SANDLER

In the same series:

The Diva Book of Short Stories

First published 2002 by Diva Books,
an imprint of Millivres Prowler Limited,
part of the Millivres Prowler Group,
Spectrum House, 32–34 Gordon House Road,
London NW5 1LP UK

www.divamag.co.uk
www.divamailorder.com

Printed and bound in Finland by WS Bookwell

Distributed in the UK and Europe by Airlift Book Company,
8 The Arena, Mollison Avenue,
Enfield, Middlesex EN3 7NJ
Telephone: 020 8804 0400
Distributed in North America by Consortium,
1045 Westgate Drive, St Paul, MN 55114-1065
Telephone: 1 800 283 3572
Distributed in Australia by Bulldog Books,
PO Box 300, Beaconsfield, NSW 2014

Contents

Acknowledgements

Thanks to Julia Bell, Kathleen Bryson, Frances Gapper, Sue Harper, Jane Hoy, Cath Linter, Raj Rai, Gillian Rodgerson, Jane Scanlan, Bryony Weaver, the designer and the rest of the team; and to everyone who sent in stories and waited patiently for a reply, whether or not they ended up in this book.

Introduction

Welcome to *Groundswell*. Let me buzz you in. The tenants will take you into many different rooms. You will linger in some and be glad to shut the door on others...

The title was originally inspired by the description on the cover of the first *Diva Book of Short Stories*: 'a sea change in lesbian fiction'. (I had some notion that a groundswell might follow a sea change.) But one of the gifts of editing or reading an anthology is the enjoyment to be had from the links between pieces, and the feeling that each story here is another *storey* of a single building has grown stronger as the project developed. There are even links with the first collection, although where that book was anchored at the turn of the millennium, this one carries us from biblical times to the latest anti-war demonstration, via the suffragette movement and 1940s rationing. There are a few terrific north American contributions this time, and a broader range of styles.

The first tale, in fact, is a transatlantic one (from an American writer based in London). 'Trans' by Elizabeth Carola is a powerful story of crossing over. In this case, the transition is from being a Jew with certain allegiances to being a citizen of the world. While that story questions religious ties, the next goes back to the godly times of the Old Testament for a lyrical evocation of the love between Ruth and Naomi, by Virginia Smith. Although women then may have been better off with husbands to provide homes for them, those in the modern-day 'Jumping the Broom' by Denise

Marshall have plans to marry each other, if they can only find a ceremony that won't make a mockery of their love.

These first three stories lay out some of the themes of the book: the questioning that goes on in a life lived on the margins; the places where the personal is political – and the joint themes of religion and oppression, picked up in 'The Lost Seed' by Emma Donoghue. This is a historical story in which one man destroys the trust that binds his small community, all in the name of virtue. Hundreds of years later, not much has changed, as a young male-to-female transsexual is forced to learn 'the difference between Mark and Melissa' in the story of that name by Sue Vickerman. It shares with Kathleen Kiirik Bryson's 'Star Soup' an understanding of the pressure among young people to be 'the same' and the danger for those who are 'different'.

In Kathleen's story, a social *faux pas* of the highest order is turned to the narrator's advantage; whereas Clare Summerskill's adult protagonist gains nothing by making a fool of *herself* in the comic 'Maggie Maybe', as she pursues a crush on her old schoolteacher. Then 'Miss Manifold' by Christine Webb explores other barriers to love between women, in the postwar period when society was settling back into family units. A member of the Land Army is the 'extra' person in the house in that story, while in 'Looking for Aimée' by Polly Wright, it's an au pair girl who finds herself filled with longing in someone else's home.

Do lesbian and bisexual women spend more time in a state of longing than our heterosexual sisters? In Jane Marlow's story, a young woman goes to London to join the suffragettes, disappointed by her lover and obsessed with her heroine. By the end of the story she has witnessed a terrible sacrifice. And although Rosie Lugosi's 'The Purple Wallpaper' looks with dark humour at seemingly minor domestic disputes, someone may be asked to make the ultimate sacrifice here too, for the sake of a quiet home.

That is not the only household in trouble. Indeed, strange and beleaguered homes are a defining theme of *Groundswell*. In Louise Tondeur's haunting 'The House', memories are banned; in Jackie Kay's 'Making a Movie', a knife glints on the chopping board; and in both Frances Gapper's 'The Flood' and Carter's 'Hot', the words 'Don't go down in the cellar' resonate loudly up the stairs. In VG Lee's 'The Holiday Let', visitors are lured to Stoke Newington (for which Frances's narrator has already declared a deep hatred) by a campaign that claims it as the lesbian holiday capital of the world. And in 'Hunger' by the Canadian writer Jane Eaton Hamilton, a young woman lives in thrall to her older lover. All these houses have at least two things in common: the owner is not the only one with a key to the front door, and mental health cannot be guaranteed. Just your typical lesbian household, then.

Dykes, eh? If you're sick of the lot of them, if you're curling up with a good book as part of a strategy for getting over a breakup, then Robyn Vinten's instructions in 'How to Grow a New Heart' should bring some comfort. The experimental techniques of the narrator give a new meaning to the term 'open-heart surgery'. Another innovator is Jill James's heroine in 'Friday' who likes to write stories while sitting on the toilet at parties – but can spot a love interest through the keyhole. She happens to have her head turned by a woman; while the couple in 'May' by Ali Smith have an unusual dilemma on their hands when one of them falls for a tree. In 'Gasoline' by Susannah Marshall, there is a similar delight in the outdoors, but in a rather different setting – a gas station in the desert. The heat of the sun beats down on two bubblegum-chewing gals in this tale; then on Cameron McGill holidaying with her friend Becky, who urges her to solve a mini-mystery ('Pin Point') between tougher, novel-length investigations.

The link to the next story could be 'unusual viewpoints'. 'Hard Workers' by Kate Rigby is a tale that we can only assume takes place in Silicon Valley. Why? You'll see. And then you'll also see what delightful object 'Hard Workers' has in common with 'Suckling Pig', which follows it and features the trials of Androula and her butch lover. Readers of the first anthology will recall this couple – Cherry Smyth's creations – and their discussions about tying the knot. Now, suddenly, kids are on the agenda, with funny and poignant results. Watch out for a moving sex scene with echoes of a strangely similar moment in Jane Eaton Hamilton's story from earlier in the book.

Sex is also a factor in 'Border Women' by Norma Meacock, in which one individual's heinous sin of sleeping with a man gets her whole gang of rough and ready friends thrown out of the only women's disco in the county. It's a rather different life from that of the comfortable homebirds in Rachel Sutton-Spence's 'Small Change', but both groups put friendship above convention and pies above pounds. Finally, more friends gather together in Susan Stinson's evocative story, 'Crease', but it's an ending that's far from closed, that asks you to turn back and look again.

So, stick around, make yourself at home. Invite your friends. Join the groundswell.

Helen Sandler, September 2002

ELIZABETH CAROLA
Trans

ELIZABETH CAROLA
Trans

Maybe it does happen overnight: one day you're on one side of the equation, eating certain-coloured foods, having a certain-coloured family, standing, talking, dressing a certain way; being a normal dyke with a particular history. And the next, you're over a line, a line you didn't even really know was there before. You don't know if you stepped or were pushed.

But it is hotter and drier over the line. Sweatier. The goats are smaller. The cheese is different. There is only one true God and it's harder to get a beer. You feel normal walking down the street in your keffiyeh to get bread and yogurt. But the landscape inside you is different.

Take, for example, now. Ordinarily, this time of year, I'd be far away. I'd be sitting at big tables, doing seasonal things. Jewish things. There would be news, squabbles, ancient jokes. This would be family. Notions of freedom and slavery would be invoked, things would be eaten, bitter things, sweet, sour and salty things in symbolic honour of Our Story. Questions would be asked. Others wouldn't. References to friends, activities, lives, would be delicately tailored. Wars, divided loyalties, Muslim girlfriends wouldn't come into it.

The evening would end with a cheerful libation to a future in a mythical city. A holy city. A nice, clean, cleansed city. Finally, my uncle would cry, 'That's enough of that!' and close his book. 'Now for god's sake, let's eat.'

3

But I'm doing something different this year. I am here. I'm on my way to a demo. It's gonna be a big demo, I can tell from the Oxford Street approach. We didn't arrange a meeting point but I know I'll find my friends. A particular slouch, a gesture, a bright red John Lewis pram will alert me and I'll make my way through the crowd to them.

It is a cold day, a big spring day and this is a big, spring kind of demo. Seventy thousand people shouting and keening down the grand thoroughfares of central London. Bemused tourists. The usual.

There is a war on and this demo knows what it wants. And more and more, I want what it wants too, though wanting this, this desire, forms another splintery strand of my unbecoming. My transitioning.

The crowd hits its stride and the chants gain in rhythm and scansion:

> 2-4-6-8. *We don't want a Zionist State.*
> *From the River to the Sea, Palestine will be Free.*
> *From the Sea to the River, Palestine Forever.*

I pull my scarf around my shoulders. I wish Nurjahan was here. It feels cold without her, the chants feel louder. My friends, who spend the bulk of their weekends on demonstrations and are therefore oblivious to background noise, chat about their toddlers' teething problems.

'We're trying her on za'atar naan, and she loves it,' P'nina gushes to Sarah. They are cheerful in that Lifetime, In-It-For-The-Duration way of true revolutionaries. They are also polyglots, and patiently translate the Arabic chants for me. Occasionally, my friend Ben says, 'Hang on, that's a bit rich! Must have a word.' And wanders off to remonstrate with a megaphone-bearing group.

At one point, I pester him, 'What were they chanting?'

'Oh, they were going, you know, By the blood of Mohammed, we will Scourge the Jews from the Land...'

'And what did you say?

'I said, Hang on, comrades, that's a bit much, what you're shouting.'

'And what did they say?'

'They said, we're just chanting to get rid of Sharon...'

'And what...?'

'And I said, to the one with the megaphone, Oh no you're not, I speak Arabic, and you're going on about purging the Jews from the land, and I'm one of those Jews, and there are a lot of us on this demo, and as comrades we must –'

'So what did he SAY?'

'He couldn't bear my hectoring anymore and kind of slunk off.'

They're so great, this lot. They remind me of the poster we all had at Uni, the one with Che Guevara smugly intoning, 'The TRUE revolutionary is inspired by profound feelings of LOVE.' I forget if it was actually a bubble coming out of his mouth. But we all took it to heart and, really, it could have been *made* for my friends. When the crowd starts up with 'Long life HizBOLLAH! Long Live Ha-MAS!' P'nina smiles. I nudge her, 'What's funny?' And she says, wryly, 'At first I thought they were chanting, 'Long live Karl MARX.'

I'm not so cool. Shards of fear creep up my neck as we make our way through the surge and roar of the crowd, amidst Al-Aqsa, then behind Al-Awda, then beside Unison. A little voice somewhere behind my cheekbones, like a sprite, whispers threats at me. *'Watch your back,'* it murmurs. *'They hate you.'* I have to glance at my mates, laughing and relaxed. I have to remind myself: This is who I have become. This is my lot.

There is no place for fear in transitioning. There is no going back, there is only the road ahead.

Nurjahan is on an away-day break to Suffolk with her ex, Ruth. But as she pointed out yesterday, 'There will be other demos.' She sighed. 'Many, many demos.'

It was also on a demo that I met Nurjahan, last winter. She came up to me and said pointedly, 'I saw you at *grfft* last week.'

'Okay,' I said, noncommitally. I couldn't hear her over the crowd, but it was likely I had been at '*grfft*', whatever it was.

'I liked what you said about secularism. Give me your email.' It was a statement, not a question. I looked at her. She was my height, wiry and intense, with precise, quick hands. We chatted. She was so serious, so *to the point*. Her friends called her and she turned and said, 'We're having a benefit for *brrfft* this weekend. You'll be there.'

We got to be friends, talking for hours about the usual things, our horrible childhoods (until this became too much a source of competition – 'no, MINE's worse!'), the dearth of feminist politics, how to find good watercolour-painting classes. Sometimes I got this image, as if two little pots of identical protoplasm, in separate hemispheres, had begun bubbling simultaneously, brewing us until finally, across continents, we'd found each other.

She was still pining for her ex. I was going out with Sally, who was getting fed up with me. Maybe Nurjahan was one of the reasons. I couldn't sleep for thinking about her. I thought about her all the time. Something about where friendship meets sex and hovers. I needed to be physically near a phone just so I could ring her, hear her voice on the other end of a line. The phone would ring and I'd jump. Sally would mutter, 'I guess it's your Iranian girlfriend again,' and stomp off.

I would go round there and talk until it was too late to cycle home. So we'd just crash, on her small, hard bed. 'Revolutionary,' I teased her. 'Just like you.'

'Don't slag off my bed or you can sleep on the floor.'

I had no intention of sleeping on the floor. I'd fit myself alongside her, fling a close arm round her waist and we would talk more and breathe into sleep. Sometimes, lying there with Nurj, two storeys above the sounds of Hackney trunk-road traffic, hearing her heart beat and her sounds in sleep, it was as if the city had been evacuated and we been left, just the two of us, in a post... post-something, city. But we didn't do sex. In sleep I would wrap myself around her and we'd wake up, intertwined. But still clothed. We'd wake up, chat and argue, just like lovers.

'You should go for it,' friends said. 'It's obvious you're hot for her.'

'You're not going to find anyone with better politics.' (P'nina)
'It's over.' (Sal) 'So do what you like.'

It's not that I'm not hot for Nurj, it's just a different kind of hot. It's a wandering, refugee kind of hot. It's a hot that scares me, because we are so similar. But it is a hot that keeps me warm.

Last week Lotte and her girlfriend Sam came round for travel and fashion tips. Rich and intrepid, having done the rest of the world, they were now off to Iran, to the mountains, to make experimental films. Something about ice faces as metaphors of masked identities. Don't ask – we didn't. Nurjahan pulled out some old maps and told them about accessible bus routes to the mountains in the north; but baulked at chador-tying advice. 'Listen, I escaped just after the fundamentalist bastards took over. You expect me to help you with your romantic bondage. I will not' – and stomped off to make tea. I knew she'd be like that. I sidled up behind her and slid my arms around her waist, until I could feel her smile, relent. 'C'mon Nurj,' I cajoled. 'This is such a big opportunity for Lotte and Sam.' What I couldn't have known was my fingers' yearning for the smooth black cotton squares, my itch toward tying and twisting, smoothing over hairline, tightening under jaw. I sat down at Nurj's table and grabbed their training-chadors. 'Like this... here. There. I've done it! You'll look a treat on the bus to Demaverand.'

Meanwhile, across the desert, there's a war on.

Meanwhile, we are halfway through the demo. I've relaxed into it now, the swelling sound and excitement, the pain and warmth all mingled, like smoke.

> *George Bush, we know you. Your daddy was a killer too.*
> *Tony Blair, it's not fair. Our kids are dying everywhere.*

I've got to talk to Sarah, striding alongside us. Sarah just got back. She was out... there... doing solidarity work. I don't know what that means. She was travelling around, then staying with a family, then putting herself between them and the tanks. It was a martyr's family. She started spending some time with the fourth daughter, Suad. Suad had plans. Suad was going to do something that teenagers are doing. It did not involve school, exams, summer jobs in cafés. That was last month and now Sarah does not know where she is. Or if she is. If she's not around, there will be other people, other teenagers – two? three? five? more? – who won't be either. We heard about this in Sarah's cramped kitchen last week. And now I need to know more.

I wait for a pause in their chat and leap in. 'Hey Sarah. I need to ask you. When you were with the Nashibs, with Suad. What did you say? Did you... not... try to stop her?'

Sarah stares at me, startled, then looks down at the pavement as we walk.

'I didn't say anything. I had to respect the struggle. It's bigger than her, or me.'

There is no place for fear in transitioning. There is only the way ahead.

Maybe it does happen overnight: you wake up and you're in a different place. It's not that you know more. But something that was around you all the time, subtle as the backbeat rhythms of a dublek, has morphed into your body, your life. You can distinguish between the two local muezzins' calls to prayer (East London's high strident whine over Hackney's baritone). You crave za'atar, the astringent oiliness of olives and and pickled lemons. You are happy with the rich evenness of sesame and chickpeas and flatbread. You just don't want anything else.

At work, I haven't stopped wearing the standard issue youth service jeans and sweatshirt. But I take more care over my scarf, twisting it into different shapes: ulnah one day, a smooth dupatta the next. I find I can casually recite the five pillars of an Entirely Different Religion, when challenged by my Wednesday-night girls, while getting out the pots and tubes for their henna sessions.

'Here, Bea, do me,' they cry. 'You're good at it.' And they push up the folds of their khameez, thrust their hands and arms at me. And I love them, their eager, tough coltishness, the way they canter around the club, like teenagers all over the world.

The voice in my head, the sprite, pipes up: 'But these are the *wrong* teenagers. This is the *wrong* part of London. You're on the *wrong* side.'

But I'm too involved with what I'm doing. 'Whatever,' I tell the voice. 'Whatever.'

'Okay, girls, you do me now then.' And for the first time I offer my hands, my arms for the ancient ritual.

Nurjahan knows I am restless, that I want to do what Sarah and the others have done. She is distressed at this and shakes her head a lot. In the years she's been here, London has engulfed her, enfolded her in soft, dark arms. Safe but silencing. She sometimes doesn't want to even think about the war, the wars. 'Anyway,' she says, clicking her tongue, 'you don't know how bad it is. And not just one side. It's the whole thing, all those men with guns, going on about heaven.'

But I need to go. And if I'm honest it's not just about support work. It's about the pull towards something mysterious, new, forbidden.

Something big, scary, powerful. Old. The crowd as one. Half the world as one. Crouching under a fierce and unknowable desert sky. Feeling the weight of so many thousands of years around me, in the stones, in the markets, in people's expressions. Being the enemy. Hated, then loved. The tension between what people think they think and what they really think.

'It's like wanting to touch a particular cloth, a certain texture. I want to work with that tension. To feel it.'

'You are too romantic, Bea. It's what I have come from. It's not what you think.' She swats at the table with her dishcloth, peers at me.

'Maybe not. I'm not saying I understand it.'

We are nearing the end of the march. Swathes of people – families and congregations – pile into the Trafalgar Square rallying point to hear speeches, injunctions. 'Stop the insanity!' 'Will Sheffield Mosque make your way to buses numbers 6, 7 and 8, which await you.' 'Please everybody – pick up your litter!'

P'nina and Ben's toddler is getting fractious. We will head towards the church café for our post-rally ritual of coffee and civilised, exquisite cake. Kuchen and torte amidst the flagstones and chamber music. We will talk about The Situation, get out diaries to share meetings, vigils, meals. London will buzz with the rustle of opening diaries. Out there the tanks will multiply and advance like beetles. Some of us will walk out to face them. It is now March. Suad is still around, or maybe she is not. She has or has not done it. If she has, there are others, other teenagers, who are also not around. The men who gave her the gear, silently fastened it while her mother stood by, *those* men are still around. Like us, they're probably eating now, plates of lamb and rice. Nurjahan will be back on the nine o'clock train, I'll call her then. She won't carry a mobile. There is no heaven. There's only what is around you and the way forward, ahead. I'm going home to watch TV.

VIRGINIA SMITH
Ruth

VIRGINIA SMITH
Ruth

It's the light that wakes me, splintering through the narrow windows, stippling the bed with bars of bright and dark. Sometimes, it feels like a blessing, that light – as if it's worked its way clear from the mouth of God, as if he's spoken it.

If I turn on my side, I can see a corridor of olive trees outside the window, and a thin strip of road, baked bright yellow in the sun. When the merchants come, their horses stand in the meagre shade, fluting water into their mouths from the stone troughs. If the servant girls don't fill the troughs every hour, then the water evaporates. That's how hot is. Even if I wait for the relative cool of the evening before I bathe, as soon as I step out into the air again, pearls of sweat spring like tears to the surface of my skin.

Sometimes, I long for the blue waters of Beer-Sheba, for the green swell of the mountains of Moab – kind sunlight filtering soft over my father's vineyard. I can remember picking grapes from the vine when I was a child, biting into them, letting them burst wet and purple over my tongue. Here, those grapes would shrivel to dust and ash in a second. Here, everything has to fight to stay alive. The heat would blaze its way straight through to our bones, smoulder our marrow black, if we let it.

So, why do I stay? Because *she* is here, Naomi is here, simply that, and I have made my vow, before God, never to leave her. She tried to make me go once. We had set out on the road that would take us to the land of Judah, but she begged me to turn for home, to go back and find myself a man who would take me into his house, spread wedding blankets beneath my feet, lie with me in the redolent dark and slip himself inside me – make my body break into bloom with sons and silence. But I no longer wanted sons and silence. I no longer wanted wedding blankets and the redolent dark of a man inside me. I wanted only *her* – my mother, my lover, my sister, my bride. I said the words then, on the road to Judah. I made my vow. *Where you go, I will go, and where you stay, I will stay.* And she fell to her knees in the dust, took the dust into her mouth, crushing my hands in hers. *Your people will be my people,* I told her, *and your God will be my God. Where you die, I will die, and there I will be buried.* I knelt by her side and we held each other tight, and then we stretched ourselves out on the ground, and prayed, with the salt sharp sting of the desert searing our cheeks. We prayed to the one true God, the mighty God of Israel, and I bade him deal with me, be it ever so severely, if anything but death should separate me from her. Nothing but death shall.

We came to each other by chance, she and I, by the random crossing of paths. I was a business transaction – a sack of barley, a purse filled with silver, a finger of land. My father's hands pledged me into the hands of Naomi's husband, Elimelech, and he gave me to his son, Mahlon – a good man. His heart was pure. His beard was as black as molasses. He smelled of cedarwood, but when he touched me, my body had no answer for him. I pressed my palms to the clay of his thighs, his chest, the grey cave of his belly. I gave myself up to him. I did all of his bidding, but nothing stirred in me. The petals of my sex closed like a fist and would not open. Naomi came to me then. She smeared my cheeks with galera, my skin with myrrh, and she called me *daughter, beloved,* urging me to have no fear. She told me the Lord would bless me in time, as he had blessed her, with sons strong as oxen, tall as trees, and her touch was soft and steadying, and her voice was a benediction.

Elimelech died in the winter. Mahlon died in the spring. Naomi and I were out of favour with the Lord. She chose to return to her people and I went with her, and I made my vow on the road to the land of Judah, never to leave her, and we came out of one desert and into another.

Her kinspeople gave us shelter, but we were strangers to them at heart, pledged only to one another. At night we would sleep on the roof of the house, curled around each other under a map of stars, and sometimes Elimelech's name would spin from her lips while she slept, puncturing the dark. I held her tight those times. I moved my hands over her body, treading her grief to sleep with the tips of my fingers, and my touch soothed and smoothed Elimelech away. I shed no tears for Mahlon. Daily, my body forgot him, just as daily, it remembered Naomi, over and over, and the nights on the roof of the house were warm with the way our bodies dovetailed together, sweet with the crimson flash of wine in our mouths.

Her kinspeople were kind. We ate at their table. We drank water from their stone jars, but their home was not our home, nor ever would be. Our hearts looked outward, and then the barley harvest came, and I spent long days in the fields, gleaning behind the harvesters, gathering among the sheaves, taking home all that I collected to Naomi, and she called me *daughter, beloved,* and the words dropped like honey from her tongue, and I tasted them, savoured them.

One night, when she cried out Elimelech's name, I touched her as I always did – my fingers webbing calm across her skin, netting her grief into my palms, but she awoke, and her eyes were white with surprise. I thought she would take her blanket and climb down the steps to sleep. I thought she would be angry with me, and shamed, but instead, she took my hand in hers and pressed her lips to my wrist, touched her tongue to the blue tangle of veins, and my blood there ran hot and red as a sunrise. We only held each other that night, cleaving to each other, and a wellspring of longing sprang up in my belly. I remembered my father's vineyard, grapes bursting wet and purple. I thought I tasted them again, but it was Naomi I tasted – my mouth pressed to her forehead, her hair spilling like water over my breasts.

It began as all things begin, with need and with desire, but for a time, after that night on the roof, we were distanced from each other, she and I. I felt her turn her face from me, to Elimelech, to the crested memory of Elimelech, the father of her sons, and my heart was a rock split in two.

The barley harvest kept me all day in the fields, and some nights I didn't go back to the house of Naomi's kinspeople. Some nights I slept on the threshing floor, at the feet of the men, trying to fathom the musk of their bodies, trying to learn how to want what I did not want, but I learned only how it is possible to weep dry tears, pure salt, when the sun has sucked all the water from inside you, so you are just a husk, and your skin puckers and pinches, and there is only a howl of desert wind where your soul should be.

I worked in fields belonging to a man named Boaz, and, more than once, I caught him watching me, from the roof of his house: watching me stoop, over and over, scratching at the dirt with my fingernails, my blue skirts sticking to my thighs in the fly-blown air. More than once, he came down to speak to me, brought me water from a stone pitcher set in the shade of a sycamore tree. He bade me sit with him awhile in the shadow of that sycamore and when I did, he circled his hands around my waist, coiled me into his body, as pliable as rope. He told me I had found favour in his eyes, and that he would take me as his wife, if I desired it. I did not desire it, but he was a wealthy man and I'd heard people talking in the market, in the temple, of his kindness and his great mercy. I looked at his whitewashed house – an oasis of cool in all that heat, and I looked at his marble-heavy hands, folded like doves in his lap, and I looked into his eyes and I said yes, and he told his servant girls to bring bread dipped in wine vinegar then, and we ate, he and I, in the shade of the sycamore, with a ruby sun setting, and when I asked him if Naomi, my dead husband's mother, could find shelter under his wings also, a place in his house, he opened his arms and clasped me to his chest, and told me yes, and I ran through the streets to find my mother, my lover, my sister, my bride, thinking she would rejoice that our destitution was done with, but she only looked at me, and her eyes clouded dark with dismay.

That night, on the roof of the house, with the black sky heavy as death, *she* was the one to reach out for *me*, her soft hands diffident, timid as sparrows under my clothes. She spoke my name, and her voice was damp with tears. *Don't leave me*, she said, *daughter, beloved. Don't make me live the years to come without your love*, and I took her in my arms then, and I made my vow again, in a whisper, *never* to leave her. I told her I would rather die a beggar's death, out on the road, my bones burnt ochre by the sun, than ever be without her, and she kissed me – my mouth, my eyes, my hair – her hands discerning shapes and spaces, laying me open, finding me out. My body had been tight shut for so long, its leaves folded closed against the glare of the desert, but Naomi's touch was like rain, cool rain, and the blue waters of Beer-Sheba were in my mouth again. The green swell of the mountains of Moab lifted in my chest – coloured fruits bursting wet and purple inside me. My body gave up its treasures to the flood of her longing, to the flood of mine.

Boaz and I were married one year ago today. I live in his house, sleep in his bed. He is, as people said, a kind man and merciful. He spends long hours supervising the work in his fields. He wakes with the dawn and leaves me sleeping, until the white light strokes my eyelids open, and I see the road outside my window, with its corridor of trees. It is then that I slip on my robe and go to Naomi. Her room angles the corner of the house. It is cool there, all shade. She is always waiting: my mother, my lover, my sister, my bride. She reaches out her arms to me. She is the Black Sea tide that takes me, every time, down – her tongue, her hands, slipping me away into the shallows, to a different shore, a promised land.

Three months ago, I gave birth to a son. I named him Obed, which means *heart of my heart*. Boaz's seed gifted him to me, but Naomi sits with him in her lap, in the shadow of the sycamore, and rocks him tight as a clam. People say to me, *Sister Ruth. Look. The Lord, the mighty God of Israel has blessed your husband Boaz, and has blessed you, with a son.* I only smile.

DENISE MARSHALL
Jumping the Broom

DENISE MARSHALL
Jumping the Broom

'I want to get married.'

I can't see her face, it's hidden behind the newspaper, but her hand definitely twitches.

'I said, I want to get married.'

She puts the paper down, reaches across the table and wipes the remains of toast and peanut butter off my chin. Then she sits back, looks at me, shakes her head fondly and smiles.

'Any particular reason?' she asks.

Having broached the subject, I'm not quite sure how to proceed. 'Look, I know it goes against all of my principles, that I've always said it's a sad and pathetic thing to do, and I'm not even sure why I want to... but I do.' Not a good start, but perhaps she might interpret my inarticulacy as a sign that this comes straight from the heart.

She nibbles at her chocolate croissant, which, on another occasion, I would probably demand a share of.

'Wasn't it you who described marriage as a cunning institutional invention designed by men to keep women in their place?'

I nod my head. She continues, 'Correct me if I've made a mistake, but haven't I heard you say, many, many times, that women should think carefully, before tripping down the aisle, about all those women who are forced into marriage against their will? That anyone thinking of getting married should watch the documentary your friend made about dowry brides and women who were burnt to death because their husbands didn't want them?'

She stops, takes another bite and then continues, 'Isn't it also the case that you've been notoriously scathing about lesbian commitment ceremonies? Your views, as I recall, were that they aped heterosexuality, that they were unbearably naff and full of fashion sins, and that you personally would rather be dead in a ditch than ever attend such an event.'

I really hate it when she throws my words back in my face. It's not as if I've forgotten; in fact I still believe those things to be true – I just have an overwhelming desire to marry her and am prepared to make myself an exception to my own rules.

She picks up the newspaper and the bottom corner floats in her coffee. She deserves this so I stay silent, hoping it will drip on her white linen shirt before she realises. But if she thinks the conversation is over, she is mistaken.

'Look, sweetheart, I haven't developed Alzheimer's. I know exactly what I've said, but I do want you and me to get married. I'm definitely not talking about a phony commitment ceremony and I wouldn't want assorted family and friends witnessing the event under any circumstances…'

By now I'm furious that she's reduced me to having to explain. Why can't she just accept that I've changed my bloody mind? However, having started, I stand up and proceed to the heart of the matter.

'I want to wear a wedding dress, a big, fuck-off, lacy, trailing to the ground dress. I want it to be oyster silk, with a sweetheart neckline and short puffy sleeves. I want to wear it with stockings and a tasteful garter and white satin high heels. I don't care about a veil, but *I want the dress!*'

After this small outburst I need to sit back down and have a fag. I've surprised myself a bit – puffy sleeves? I think not. Sleeveless or long-sleeved but I have never seen myself as a puff-sleeved type of woman before. This anomaly worries me and I file it away for private consideration at a later date.

I'm not sure if talk of frills and flounces has now unnerved her but she runs her hands through her short hair distractedly and then adjusts herself through her jeans – not easy if you don't have gentlemen's arrangements but she carries it off with considerable aplomb.

'Dolly,' she says, 'if you really want to wear a dress like *that*,' (she can't bring herself to say the 'W' word) 'couldn't you wear one to Mardi Gras?'

This suggestion is typical – as always, she misses the point.

'Are you mad? I don't want to wear a wedding dress to Mardi Gras. I've seen other women do that and the trannies always look much, much better. I want it to be between me and you, I want us to have some sort of ceremony, to make some kind of statement that we are true soul mates, forever joined, that sort of thing.'

She considers this, then smugly asks, 'But if we have a ceremony or make a statement, what about the registrar? They'll be there and you said you didn't want anyone else around.'

Sometimes I find it hard to believe that the woman I want to live the rest of my life with can be so wilful or deliberately thick.

'The registrar person wouldn't count, because they'd be heterosexual and, as you know, in the grand scheme of things I have never considered *them* to be important.'

She laughs then and I am ready for her to start lecturing me about my attitude towards straights and how, if the boot was on the other foot, I'd be the first to start shouting about homophobia blah blah. But, snakelike as always, she slithers off down an unexpected path.

'So, along with the wedding dress and our declaration of everlasting love, will you be needing a piece of paper to verify we're committed? Will you want a wedding cake with two little mini-lesbians perched on top? Have you made plans for a honeymoon? Should we have a photographer so that we have a lasting memory of our special day?'

Before I can reply she throws in one last witticism. 'I am also concerned, my lovely, about your intention to wear white or even "oyster". Because, without wishing to cast aspersion, I think it would be fair to say you've had enough women to fill a small nunnery – don't you?'

'Piss off,' I say and leave the room with the sound of her smug chuckling in my ear.

I sulk magnificently for the rest of the day and am immune to the small treats she offers as consolation. Sadly though, my body lacks willpower and the promise of a late-night massage with orange-scented oil proves to be an irresistible temptation. She has the lightest touch, my lover, and even her incessant whispering, 'I do, I do,' does not detract from her consummate skills.

Two hectic weeks and no further wedding talks later, I am returning from a three-day conference, in a hurry to get home and see my woman. However, the rail company is clearly managed by homophobic conspirators and at the point when I should be wrapped in my baby's arms I am stuck in a non-smoking carriage on the outskirts of London with only a dead mobile phone for company. Time at last to ponder the doomed wedding conversation.

The thing about my girlie is that she rarely says no and so I feel, albeit reluctantly, that she might have a point. The puff-sleeve business has also continued to cause me angst. Am I unwittingly carrying some weird suppressed childhood memory in which my mother force-fed me pictures of catalogue brides? Knowing my mother, this is not too far-fetched. But, as she has said many times, I never showed my deviant tendencies in my formative years – a major factor, apparently, in her total shock when I finally announced that I preferred girls to boys – and so there would have been no need for her to undertake wedding catalogue brainwashing. Perhaps then the puffs are a fashion throwback to some happy time in my past... but I'm quite sure that now is my happiest time and I cannot remember ever wearing such horrors in my life. An enigma then, shrouded in mystery, a strange fancy that is destined to remain unresolved. Sitting in the smelly carriage it also occurs to me that if the puffs have worked their way into my femme fantasy then perhaps the whole dressing-up business should be dismissed as an aberration. After all, I am a feminist lesbian; in fact, the only reason I'm not a *separatist* feminist lesbian is that I know no men and hardly any straight women. True, I am a *femme* feminist, but that is no reason to start parading round in frou-frou, is it? Suddenly aware that the train is at last moving, I decide I have gone as far as possible with the whole wedding malarkey and am once again able to laugh directly in the face of brides, committed lesbians and any fool stupid enough to view puff sleeves as acceptable attire for an adult woman.

Walking up to the house I notice that something is different. Through the glass I can see that the lighting appears to be coming from hundreds of candles. A power cut probably, but why this has necessitated using the entire contents of an Ikea jumbo pack of tea-lights is beyond me. Tutting loudly at the waste, I've barely got my key out of the door when she appears, looking somewhat dishevelled, from the living room.

'Dolly, I didn't expect you back so soon.'

Hmm. Not 'It's fantastic to see you, honey.' Not 'I've missed you and your sweet kisses so much, baby.' Definitely not the reception I'd anticipated. She also looks distinctly shifty and my in-built guilt detector clicks into action. I move fast towards the living room but we end up doing a funky little dance as she quicksteps to stop my entry.

'You can't come in here for a while, babe.'

Oh really.

I glare at her but this does not have the desired effect so I flare my nostrils. She knows I do this when I am seriously pissed – the last time was when she wore my expensive suede coat out in the rain because she couldn't find her leather pimp mac. I flare away for a full minute before she realises and then, oblivious to the danger, she laughs and laughs until she cries.

'You silly bitch, I haven't got a woman in there!'

I really hate it when she knows what I'm thinking. I remain silent, scowling, but mute on the grounds that she has me at a disadvantage and I don't want to play my hand until I've got a clearer idea of the game that is unfolding. Wrong-footed already,

I'm not prepared for the huge hug that comes next or the shower of kisses.

'Listen baby, I want you to give me your bags and go upstairs to the bedroom. On the bed there's an outfit for you.' She laughs at this bit. 'Have a bath and then put it on and by the time you're ready to come down I'll have finished the preparation and we'll be able to move on to phase two of the evening's entertainment.'

My mind switches from suspicion to intrigue. Much as she is my true love, it is fair to say that she is generally too repressed for spontaneity or surprise – they are not her strengths – and so I am deeply curious as to what is waiting for me at the top of the house. Without speaking I move on up the stairs.

Laid out on our bed there is a dress, long and cream-coloured, with a train and a sweetheart neckline. It is sleeveless, not a puff in sight. I bend down and run my fingers over the material. Silk. It's a perfect dress, an elegant wedding dress that emanates class. Next to the dress lies a pair of white stockings and a frothy garter. A pair of strappy white shoes sit neatly at the foot of the bed. She's forgotten to buy a bra, but for a woman usually more interested in the cut of her jeans, she's done the business.

I walk into the bathroom and see a pile of new hot-pink fluffy towels on the side. She's filled the room with vanilla-scented candles and a bottle of expensive bubble bath, still in its shiny wrapping, sits on the shelf. I immerse myself in bubbles, singing favourite songs interspersed with the occasional humming of 'Here Comes The Bride'. I don't know all the words but am pleased with the lesbian version I invent as I soak. Having dried, moisturised, applied perfume and make-up, I slowly get ready.

The dress fits perfectly. A raw slub silk, with a satin lining to prevent itchiness, it moulds to my contours like a second skin. The neckline is incredibly sexy – with the help of a wired bra I have a bust for the first time, a cleavage to kill for. Walking in the shoes is a bit tricky: although never a Dr Marten girl, I haven't worn such high heels for at least a decade and have lost the ability to mince. However, after a few quick shuffles up and down the bedroom, I find I am quickly regaining the knack. After staring happily in the mirror for an age, I am finally ready.

Walking down the stairs it occurs to me that she might have barred me from the living room because she has secretly invited guests in a surreal Cilla Black *Surprise Surprise* scenario. If this is true, I will of course have no choice but to kill her and everyone else in attendance – halfway down I have to sit to contemplate life without her, locked up in prison with little hope of release. I've just got to the bit where my mother refuses to visit me on the grounds that it will make her asthma bad, when the door opens and about-to-be-murdered girlfriend hops into view. I take the bull by the horns.

'Please tell me there's no one else in this house.'

She stares blankly, her eyes revealing confusion rather than that 'oops you guessed' look she's mastered over the years.

'If you've invited guests, they need to leave now, and then I'm going to cut up all of your clothes into small squares and flush them down the toilet.'

She grins. 'Who d'you think I am, Cilla Black?'

I really hate it when she does that.

She stands at the foot of the stairs and holds out her hand. Together, we walk into the living room.

I'm relieved to see that she hasn't hung up Christmas decorations or a 'Just Married' banner. Everything looks as it should. Except, on the sofa there is a broom. Not any old broom – a customised broom. The mother of all brooms. You might even go so far as to say that it is a goddess of a broom.

It's painted fuchsia and has sparkly sequins all the way down the long handle. There are multi-coloured ribbons and glitter and what look suspiciously like some of my more decorative earrings attached. The bristles are a vibrant turquoise and she has attached sequins here as well. I am quite overwhelmed – all this from a woman who considers duck-egg blue too jolly for her wardrobe.

She sits down and pats the empty space next to her.

'Did you know that in America in the days of slavery, black people weren't allowed to get married?'

I didn't know this, although having watched *Roots* as a child it doesn't come as a great shock to me.

She continues, 'To white slave owners, the concept of marriage between a black man and woman was inconceivable, on a par with a horse marrying another horse, a cow marrying a cow. In their view, slaves were another breed of animal, there to work in the fields, carry heavy loads and breed to produce more animals which they could sell or put to work.'

She takes a deep breath and continues. 'So black people invented their own ceremony, made their own declaration of love. Think about it: two people fall madly in love, want to be each other's one and only, but according to Whitey up at the big house this affirmation of love is not permissible. No church, no officiate, certainly no bouquet of freshly picked flowers – what would be the point, they weren't human after all. But the black people didn't just lie down and accept this. They invented their own way of saying "I do," saying "I love you, sweetstuff, and I wanna spend the rest of my life with you." And late at night, when the white people went to their separate beds, the lovers came out of their shacks into the moonlight. Very quietly, gently, with the scent of mimosa perfuming the air, the moon shining down and illuminating their passion, they took a broom, placed it across the door of one of the huts and, hands entwined, they jumped across to the other side. This action, jumping the broom, signified their love. The act of jumping propelled them from two individuals to one united couple and no one, absolutely no one, could ever separate their souls again.'

She stops for a moment and gently kisses my hand.

'Dolly, my love, my mad, bad and dangerous woman, if I take it outside and place it across the door, will you jump the broom with me?'

So I did and we have both lived happily ever after... up until now, anyway.

EMMA DONOGHUE
The Lost Seed

EMMA DONOGHUE
The Lost Seed

In this world we are as seed scattered from God's hand. Some fall on the fat soil and thrive. Some fall among thorns and are choked as they grow. Some fall on hard ground, and their roots get no purchase, for the bitter rocks lie all around.

I, Richard Berry, make this record in the margins of the Good Book for those who come after, lest our plantation fail and all trace of our endeavours be wiped from the earth.

Shielded by the Lord's arm, our ship has travelled safe across the ocean through all travails. Today we stretched our legs on land again. The snow reaches our knees. We never saw stuff like this before. It is bright as children's teeth and squeaks underfoot.

On the first day of June came the quake. So powerful is the mighty hand of the Lord, it makes both the earth and the sea to shake. I was afraid, and I was not the only one.

But we keep faith with our Maker and our mission. We hack ourselves a space in the wilderness they call Cape Cod. The town we build is to be called Yarmouth, to remind us of what we left behind. May we cast off the old sins of England like dust from our boots.

I have written nothing in this book for years, being much occupied with labouring for the good of the Lord and this whole plantation. We have made new laws, and set down on paper the liberties of all freemen. The Indians have shown us how to bury dead fish with our seeds to sweeten the soil. We have sold them guns.

I am still unmarried.

Of late I have been troubled by a weakness of spirit. I think on my mother and father and come near to weeping, for I will never see them again in this life. But I must remember that all who till the soil beside me are my brethren.

There are few enough of us. A goodly number of us are in the ground, more than have been born. Edward Preston lost his wife this past winter. So did Teague Joanes, whose fields lie next to mine. He and I think as one in most matters; he is a godly man.

There are others in Yarmouth who seek to stir up division like mud in a creek. At meeting they grasp at privilege and make much of themselves. But our dissensions must be thrust aside. If we do not help each other, who will help us? We are all sojourners in a strange land. We hear of other plantations where there is not a Christian left alive.

Word comes that there is a new king in England, as bad as his father.

Our court sentenced Seb Mitchel to be fined three pounds for his unseemly and blasphemous speeches. He spoke against his Maker for taking all three of his children in one winter. He will have to sell his hog to pay the fine.

At least Seb Mitchel has a wife. God has not yet granted me one. I look about me diligently enough at the sisters in our plantation, but the greater part are married already, and others are shrewish, and still others have a barren look about them, or a limp, or a cast in the eye. I thought of Sara Jennet but she is young and laughs overmuch.

Our numbers are increased, yet I dislike these incomers, who are all puffed up and never think of our sweat that built this town. Hugh Norman said old ways should give way to new, and it was his first meeting. I pray these incomers be not like the seed that springs up quick and eager but is soon parched and blasted by the noonday sun.

*

These days some play while others work. Each man would go his own way. There is no concord or meekness of spirit. People forget that we are not separate, one from the other. In this rough country we stand together or we fall.

In the first days we were all one family in the Lord. But now each household shuts its doors at night. Every man looks to his own wife and his own children. I think on the first days, when there was great fellowship, through all trials.

Teague Joanes is the only man who says more to me than yea and nay.

Last night there was a snow so heavy that the whole plantation was made one white. I stood in my door and saw some flakes as wide as my hand, that came down faster than the others. Every flake falls alone, and yet on the ground they are all one.

I made addresses to Sara Jennet's father and he was not opposed, but she said she would not have me and he would not force her.

At sunset most evenings I meet Teague Joanes where our fields join. He tells me that though marriage be our duty, it brings much grief, and from the hour a child is born his father is never without fear for him.

Our court sentenced Joan Younge's master to pay her fine of two pounds, for she was rude to her mistress on the Lord's day and blocked her ears when the Bible was read, and he should have kept her under firm governance. I would have had the girl whipped down to the bone instead.

Good news on the last ship. The old King has been cast down for his Popish wickedness. Men of conscience govern England. Heathenish festivities no longer defile the name of the Lord and there is no more Christmas.

Here we work till the light fails. We have some blacks to hoe the land, but still too much of the crop is lost in the weeds, and strangled in rankness. I have no time to write in this book.

*

Our court sentenced Nathaniel Hatch and his sister Lydia Hatch to be cast out for unclean practices. He is to be sent off to the south and she to the north. We are not to break bread with them, or so much as throw them a crust. If we happen to pass either of them in the road, we are to turn our faces away. If either tries to speak to any of our community, we are to stop up our ears. No other Christian plantation will take them in.

I said in meeting that the pair of them should have been put to death, as a sign to waverers. (And after all, to be banished is itself a sort of death, for who would wish to roam this wilderness alone?) It has seemed to me for some time that our laws are too soft. If any man go after strange flesh, or children, or fowl or other beasts, it should be death. If any man act upon himself so as to spill his seed on the ground, it should be death. For the seed is most precious in these times and must not be lost.

I know I am a fruitless man. My grievous sins of pride and hardheartedness have made me to bury my coin in the ground, like the bad servant in the parable. I have begot no children to increase our plantation. All I can do is work harder.

Nathaniel Hatch is rumoured to be living still in the woods to the south of Yarmouth. I wonder if he has repented of his filthy incest. It would be too late to bring him back, even if the wolves have spared him. He has no people now. As for his sister, no one has set eyes on her for a long time.

My face is furrowed like a cornfield. The ice leaves its mark in winter, and the burning summer turns all things brown. But I will cast off vanity. The body is but the husk that is tossed aside in the end.

There is talk of making a law against the single life, so that every unmarried man or woman would have to go and live in some godly family. But I do not know any house that would take me in.

Sara Jennet is married to Hugh Norman these two years past. I forgot to put that down before.

Sara Norman – Sara Jennet, as was – is lightsome of countenance and speech. She forgets the saying of the Apostle, that wives should submit. If she does not take care, her behaviour will be spoken of at meeting. I passed by her house the other day, and she was singing a song. I could not make out the words, but it was no hymn.

Sin creeps around like a fog in the night. Too many of us forget to be watchful. Too many have left their doors open for the Tempter to slip in. I puzzle over it as I lie on my bed in the darkness, but I cannot tell why stinking lusts and things fearful to name should arise so commonly among us. It may be that our strict laws stop up the channel of wickedness, but it searches everywhere and at last breaks out worse than before.

I consider it my pressing business to stand guard. Where vice crawls out of the shadows, I shine a light on it. John Hammon said to Teague Joanes that Sara Norman told his wife I was an old snooping killjoy.

It matters not.

Death seizes so many each winter, we cannot spare a single soul. All must be saved for this flock to survive. Better I should anger my neighbour than stand by and watch the Tempter pluck up his soul as the eagle fastens on the lamb. Better I should be spurned and despised, and feel myself to be entirely alone on this earth, than that I should relinquish my holy labour.

They call me killjoy, but let them tell me this, what business have we with joy? What time have we to spare for joy, and what have we done to deserve it?

The Lord has entered into the Temple and the cleansing has begun. Let the godless tremble, but the clean of heart rejoice.

This day by my information charges were laid against Sara Norman, together with Mary Hammon, fifteen years old and newly a wife, the more her shame. I testified to what I witnessed. With my own eyes I saw them, as I stood by Hugh Norman's window in the heat of the day. His wife and John Hammon's wife were lying on the one bed together. They were naked as demons, and there was not a handspan between their bodies. They were laughing.

It is time now to put our feet to the spades to dig up evil and all its roots.

But already there is weakening. Our court was prevailed upon to let the girl Mary Hammon go, with only an admonition, on account of her youth. The woman's case has been held over until the weight of business allows it to be heard. But I have faith she will be brought to judgment at last after all these years of giddiness. In the meantime, Hugh Norman has sworn he will put her and her children out of his house.

Teague Joanes came to me last night after dark, a thing he has never done before. He would have prevailed upon me to show mercy to Sara Norman. He said, was it not likely the women were only comforting each other when I saw them through the window, and what soul did not need some consolation in these hard times?

I reminded him that consolation was not to be sought nor found in this life, but the next.

Then he asked me did I never feel lonely. In the depth of winter, say, when the snow fills up all the pathways.

I told him I never did. But this was akin to a lie.

Teague said he could not believe I was such a hard man.

I gave him no answer, for my thoughts were all confounded.

Then he said he would not part with me on bad terms, and came up to me and embraced me, and held onto me, and his leg lay against my leg.

All that was last night. And today charges were laid by my information against Teague Joanes for an attempt at sodomy.

These are bitter times. The wind of opposition blows full in my face, but I must not turn aside, for fear of my soul.

At last our court found Sara Norman guilty of lewd behaviour with Mary Hammon, but sentenced her merely to make a public acknowledgement on the Sunday following. She lives now in a mud hut on the edge of our plantation, and her children with her. With my own eyes I have seen some of the brethren stop to speak with her on the road. I ask why she has not been cast out, and there is none will answer me.

The case against Teague Joanes has not yet been heard. He is well liked among those who are deceived by a show of friendliness and Satan's own sweet smile. Many whisper that the charges should be struck out. No one says a word to me these days. But I know what I know.

Our paths crossed on Sunday, and he spat on my back.

I am not a dreaming man, but last night the most dreadful sight was shown to me. I saw Teague Joanes and Sara Norman on a bed, consorting together uncleanly, turning the natural use to that which is against nature, and laughing all the while.

And when I woke I knew this was no fancy but a true vision, granted me by the Lord, so that with the eyes of sleep I could witness what is hidden in the light of day. So I walked to the court and laid charges against them both.

The clerk did not want to write down my dream. So I took him by the collar and I asked would he wrestle with God's own angel?

In the whole town of Yarmouth there is none who will greet me. I hear the slurs they cast upon me as I go down the street.

I work in my own fields, though these days my bones creak like dead trees. I keep my head down if ever someone passes by. I wait for the court to hear my evidence. I must stand fast. I must not give in to the soft persuasions of Satan, who would have me show what he calls mercy.

Today I was called to the court. I stepped out my door and over my head were hanging icicles as thick as my fist and sharp like swords of glass.

There in the court were Teague Jones and Sara Norman and many others, the whole people of Yarmouth. And I read on their faces that they were my enemies and God's.

At first I spoke up stoutly and told of the wickedness that is spreading through this whole plantation, and of the secrets that hide in the folds of men's hearts. And then Teague Joanes stood up and shouted out that I had no heart.

It was quiet for a moment, a quietness I have never heard before.

Then I was asked over and over again about what I had seen, and what I had imagined, and what I knew for sure. But I could not answer. I felt a terrible spinning. All I could think on was the evening Teague Joanes walked in my door. Not of the words he spoke, but the way he stood there, looking in my eyes as few know how to in these times. The way he laid his arms around me, fearless, and pressed me to him, as one brother to another. And all of a sudden I remembered the treacherous stirring between us, the swelling of evil, and I knew whose body began it.

So I said out very loud in front of the whole court that I had perjured myself and that I withdrew all charges and that I was damned for all time. And when I walked to the door, the people moved out of my way, so as not to touch me.

I went home across the fields for fear of meeting any human creature on the road. And it seemed to me the snow was like a face, for its crust is an image of perfection, but underneath is all darkness and slime. And I wept, a thing I have not done since I was a child, and the water turned to ice on my cheeks.

Historical Note

This story is inspired by various documents collected in *Records of the Colony of New Plymouth*, edited by N.B. Shurtleff (Boston: 1855).

Richard Berry was a resident of Yarmouth, a town founded in 1638 on Cape Cod, Massachusetts. In 1649 and 1650, he made a number of accusations of sex crimes against his neighbours Sara Norman, Mary Hammon, and Teague Joanes. He eventually confessed to perjury and withdrew the charges.

In 1659 Berry himself was found guilty of 'filthy obscene practices' and was 'disenfranchised of his freedom', losing all his rights and being cast out of the plantation.

SUE VICKERMAN
The Difference between Mark and Melissa

SUE VICKERMAN
The Difference between Mark and Melissa

So I'm going, I've decided.

Promising myself I won't drink or smoke and I'll be home by midnight, but I'm going.

When Paul and Darren come round to walk down with me, I'm not ready, as per usual.

'Can't get my hair right! I'll be down in a minute.'

I hear my landlady asking them if they'd like a cup of tea.

Although it's only two days to my op, I think it'll be okay, going to this party. It's only close friends. Well, Paul and Darren's close friends. It's just, in the last few weeks and days, the waiting has become unbearable. It's now so big and real there's hardly space for it in my head. My landlady's been saying, 'Go on – go out. You'll only prowl around if you stay in. Take your mind off it for a while.'

I'm trying to get these hair extensions in that I bought on the market. One day, I want hair right down to my bum. For now, it's just long enough for two short, fat plaits. The extensions are for my fringe. Beaded ones. The beads knock against my nose. I've done eyeliner like an Egyptian – I'm going punky tonight. Straight skirt to my ankles with big pockets like on combat trousers. Cheesecloth blousy thing from Oxfam – a real find – drawstring neck, so you can bunch it up and it gives a nice puffy shape over your chest, very girly, but then later I'll be able to undo it, pull it wide open, off the shoulder even. Really revealing and sexy. It'll be great for after my op.

I can hear my brother laughing with Darren. They had their first GCSE mock today. That's why this party's on – everyone chilling out, trying to blot out the next exam tomorrow. Five years ago that was me. I've been there. I feel for them. Left school with nothing, went to school for no reason. All I got was bullying – and that was the teachers.

Bollocks to them.

Looking on the bright side, I'd probably still be on benefits, like I am now, even if I'd passed some exams.

'You ready? I don't believe it – she's ready.' That's Darren, supping tea, rollerblades round his neck. I love him.

'Heya Vicki. I'm definitely getting stoned tonight. Definitely.' That's my brother Paul, head in hands, looking morose, long hair – longer than mine – flopping over his face onto the table. I love Paul too. He's wearing strings of bracelets, like coloured sweets threaded on elastic – heart shapes, star shapes, glittery shapes. Him and Darren, they're really open-minded. They haven't succumbed to that skinhead haircut, the hard-man look.

They get bullied too.

'It was science. It was shit,' Paul says, nosing into his mug of tea. Darren leans across, ruffles Paul's hair then pushes his head roughly in commiseration. 'Ferguson was shit,' Paul goes on. 'Never learnt a fucking thing in science.'

'Ferguson was a bastard to me,' I say, putting my lipstick on in my reflection in the toaster. Just a touch; pale, not tarty.

'C'mon, you two – let's go. Forget it. School doesn't matter,' says Darren, putting his arms round both our shoulders.

I love Darren. I could marry Darren if he wasn't fifteen. He's so sensitive.

'I'm not drinking, you know,' I warn them as we set off down the steep hill towards Martin's at the bottom of the village.

'Course you're not,' exclaims Darren in a shocked voice. 'Not with your op in two days. You can't get so far, looking after your health and everything, and mess up your system now. I'm going to see that you act sensible.'

Standing on Martin's doorstep in the dark I feel for Darren's hand and squeeze it as Paul rings the bell. Darren gives me a quick, light kiss on the cheek. Then his face comes back close to mine, quickly before the shape behind the frosted glass reaches the door, and he kisses me on the lips. He's special, Darren. He understands. He thinks I'm beautiful.

Martin's living room is lit with candles, mellow, smoky. It's going to be one of those parties. Not a mad dancing session where people throw up and do wild stuff. More a talking party. Johnnie and Tariq are rolling up in opposite corners. There's already a long, fluffy-ended joint on its way round. The three of us shuffle off our coats and shoes in the hallway and pad into the kitchenette to pick up drinks. Darren hands me the sparkling mineral-water bottle. 'I know, Darren,' I say softly. 'I'm looking after myself. Don't worry.' He really cares about me.

In the living-room doorway I make my choice about where to sit. Gorgeous Melissa is lounging on a cushion looking quite out of it already. Mark, one of the ones trying to forget exams, is sort of next to her, but there's cushion space in-between. I make a beeline for this inviting spot between two people who I normally flirt with a bit.

Not that I'm bi. Or maybe I am. I don't know what I am – I'm just me. I could fall in love with anybody really, as long as they were attractive and sensitive.

Melissa's like Demi Moore in *Ghost*, sort of pure-looking. Her and me, we're probably the oldest in this room. She missed her GCSEs because of having baby Daniel. We're the same in a lot of ways like that. I mean, we've both been through a lot. We're mature.

Well, sort of mature. Only obviously she's got more sexual experience than me even though she's seventeen and I'm twenty. Melissa's told me everything. I've told her everything. She's one of the few who can really get her head around it. That last party, we got really close. I could imagine being with a woman. If I don't marry someone like Darren.

'This is really mellow, isn't it?' murmurs Melissa. The end of the spliff is ragged, glowing. We watch papery ash float from the end like a snowflake onto my skirt and we both giggle, then suddenly she's lying in my lap, eyes closed. I see some eyes on us, dead curious. Everybody's touching somebody in this room. It's one of those floor-level parties – bodies sprawling, intertwined. It's a party where everyone will gossip for weeks afterwards about who snogged who.

I pass the joint straight to Mark, whose shoulder I'm leaning back on, without taking a drag. 'Got to be careful,' I explain, looking into his eyes. 'I shouldn't be using substances just before my op.' Mark's smile is totally gorgeous. Even though I'm not stoned I feel like I'm melting. I think it's my hormones – I'm all over the place. Then he touches my back, secretly, where no one can see, and I nearly die. Melissa in my lap, Mark touching me in secret – after my op there'll be no stopping me.

That's why I don't feel old. Not twenty at all. People who were in my class at school, they're all married now. Divorced, even. Kids, council houses. And all I've been doing is getting through – getting counselling, getting attacked in the street, then getting abused by the police who get a kick out of using my birth-name even though I'm standing there in a dress torn by my attackers, my hair in plaits, crying my eyes out. I tell them it's been changed by deed poll to Vicki. They're not having any of it.

Of course, I've been falling in love since I was a kid, just like everybody. I've snogged people. But then I've been hurt because people have only snogged me for the novelty. I've been hurt because they wouldn't accept that I wasn't going to do it; go all the way with them. Not until I've got the body I should have been born with.

Melissa has taken my fingers to her mouth. I feel her lips under my fingertips. She's kissing them so-o-o-o gently. She's very open-minded, Melissa. We have those 'all men are bastards' conversations sometimes. She's certainly been fucked over by one. Sometimes I think – women are safer. Maybe I'll end up a lesbian, who knows?

Mmm. This night could go on for ever. Everyone's blissed out, saying daft stuff like it's something really significant, like you do when you're stoned. Paul and Darren are wearing silly grins, totally out of it, smooching with Karen and Philippa over on the couch. The music's soft, mushy – feels like it's coming up through the floor. Mark's been for another can and come back, and is sitting with one leg either side of me, making like an armchair that I'm leaning into. I can feel the seams of his jeans, hard against my thighs.

'Well, I think everyone's basically bisexual,' I say into the dense air of the room. From my lap, Melissa waves her arm vaguely in the air like she's answering a question at school.

'Yeah, so do I,' she goes, then lets her hand flop onto my knee. And then we're both giggling, listening to the grunting of uncomfortable males. Two guys choose that moment to sidle out of the room. Someone growls, 'Well, I'm not.' Someone else is going, 'Can't beat a pair of tits, though, can you?'

'What do you think, Mark?' I ask softly. He's fondling my neck under my straggles of hair. I feel his knees drawing tighter in, clamping me, his crotch bulging at the base of my spine. His breath is in my ear – quick breaths. When I turn my head he just looks at me with that smile again.

After a few people have already gone, saying 'see you in geography!' and 'I don't know anything, do you?' Melissa looks at her watch and sits up resignedly. Like me, she has to be sensible. She's got responsibilities.

'Told the babysitter eleven-thirty,' she sighs, getting to her feet. I must look a bit sad because she crouches again, looking into my face, and says, 'I'll come and see you in hospital.' Then she kisses me. On the lips. Not tongues or anything, but really slow.

Nobody sees (apart from Mark), because there's a general movement towards the door now. After a minute or two, it's just me, Mark, and the music, and the noise of male laughter in the kitchenette.

I check my watch. 'Have to be in bed by midnight,' I say, leaning my head back onto his shoulder one last time. Then I feel him gripping me closer than before in the circle of his legs, and his hands are reaching over my shoulders, moving downwards until they are close to my nipples. And I lean forward, reach my hand behind my back to find the tightness of his jeans, and lay my fingers there lightly. He groans, throwing his arms fully around my shoulders from behind, and presses himself into me. I finger his zip, tug it stiffly down, and feel between its raw edges until there's the pearl softness of underwear pulled taut. And we stay like that for – I don't know – for maybe five seconds, quivering, on the verge of something, until the lads in the kitchenette shout with laughter and we pull apart before they burst in.

The next day it rains again. It's still pelting it down at four in the afternoon when I find Paul and Darren on the doorstep, drenched, looking miserable.

'How was geography then?' I say, putting the kettle on. Their coats steam in the central heating.

'Shit,' says Paul in his usual way.

'And guess what, Vicki? It's all over the school,' says Darren.

'What?' I say, turning round with the teapot. He's looking really worried.

'You molesting Mark,' says Paul, scowling. 'The wanker. He's been calling you all sorts. The total wanking git.'

Mum always told me: never trust anybody ever again. Not after that last incident. Not when even teachers didn't back me up. Not when even the police have perverted little minds.

Later, Melissa is on the phone to warn me. Apparently Mark is going to tell his mum that he's been touched down there by a – a transvestite. 'Don't forget he's still a minor,' she reminds me. She then says every bad word she can think of to describe Mark. I put the phone down as my landlady bustles in, shaking her brolly.

'But you didn't do anything,' she says, exasperated on my behalf. 'Honestly. Some people. They're all losing their virginity at twelve these days and then there's you, all sweet and innocent. Is that tea still hot?'

So my landlady's really shocked when, at half past seven, the police are at the door.

There's graffiti – a penis – on the cell wall. My clothes are sticking to me. I did lie down to sleep, but my heart raced all night.

I'm due into hospital first thing tomorrow. I've got a new nightie. I always thought that today, the day before my op, I'd have one last, really long look at myself in the mirror with no clothes on. I never ever do that. I thought I'd have a long bath, write in my diary, walk across the fields, drop in on my grandma. I thought I'd have plenty of time to pack my little suitcase.

My poor landlady's face last night. Horror-struck. She came with me to the station, phoned my mum, phoned a lawyer, phoned everybody. Told the police about my op, but they're not bothered. And she really had a go at them for calling me Stuart.

KATHLEEN KIIRIK BRYSON
Star Soup

KATHLEEN KIIRIK BRYSON
Star Soup

The green M&Ms were the horny ones, the pervert ones. Carrie nearly always forgot.

Donna would dole them out by the junior-high lockers: 'Here, Shawna, these are yours.' Red, brown, yellow – and a couple of green ones, nothing to speak of.

M&Ms! Melt in your mouth, not in your hands!

'Here are yours, Rochelle.' Mainly orange.

If you sucked on an M&M until it broke and then licked the chocolate away inside your mouth, you were left with a little scooped-out sugar oyster-shell on your tongue, and if you put a finger between your lips and wetly picked it out, it would have faded to a pastel colour: beige instead of brown, pink instead of red, apricot instead of orange. Sometimes you could even still see the M letter on the shell, bleached like a newspaper left out in the rain.

'Here are mine.'

Red M&Ms were illegal through most of the 1970s because of the red food dye, but then they came back as you always knew they would.

'And here...' the giggling would start right about then '... here are yours, Carrie.'

Horny M&Ms equalled pervert M&Ms equalled the green kind.

Donna, little queen bee, always managed to pour out a pile into her own hand that had ZERO green ones. She always had LOTS of the red cancer ones, but that was because Donna liked to live on danger. She could eat hazards, swallowed threats right down her throat.

They had their lockers together right from the beginning of the eighth-grade school year, one-two-three, Donna-Shawna-Carrie. The gleesome threesome, the Three Musketeers, three peas in a pod. Rochelle's locker was further down towards the seventh-grader section, because they hadn't known she was going to be their friend when the school year started, hadn't known then she was going to be part of their group.

At Christmas break, Donna went to Hawaii and came back with a tan, orange-blonde hair from Sun-In and a new padded bra that probably had some Kleenex in it as well. It was cheating but it looked good anyway, and Carrie thought later that that was the day everything changed: the first school day after Donna came back from Hawaii, the day Donna became popular, the day Donna started playing games like the M&M game. Boys started to make hopeful allusions to 'going' with her – 'going' with a boy being as binding as a marriage contract in junior high – and Donna's newly tanned skin took on a sheen. Radiant, as if she had sprayed Sun-In all over her body.

Even the really popular girls like Violet Browne acknowledged that Donna was getting close to being one of them, and would smile and say hello in the halls during the five-minute breaks. They usually ignored Carrie, but would sometimes be nice to Shawna, who was known widely as a sweet girl: pretty, tiny, not a threat. Shawna's main distinction was that she had hair past her butt and even though she wore it in a virginal thick braid she somehow was always considered cute, never unfashionable. On the other hand, Shawna hadn't gone with any boys either. But you did get the impression that that was a matter of choice.

In the second half of the school year, Carrie's science teacher told the class that when you looked up in the sky and saw the stars there, well, by the time it took for the light to reach us, the stars would already be dead. And if there were aliens that far away and they saw our sun, we would all already be dead, including Donna and Shawna and Rochelle. When Carrie looked out at the stars she thought: 'What's happening now isn't happening; what's happening now is long past; by the time our light reaches those stars all this will have already happened, in reverse, just like those stars have already gone out.' It was like time was going backwards.

On the good days she would be part of the gang and they would forget all about the horny M&Ms, but once she made a mistake and wore green legwarmers that her grandma had sent her for Christmas and Carrie had thought it only counted for M&Ms, not clothing, but already before first-period language arts class the snickering had started.

'Horny green, pervert green,' said Donna. And Shawna laughed about it too and Carrie's ears grew hot and she wore the legwarmers throughout the whole day out of spite, but when she got home at 5pm after swim team she threw them in the corner and never wore them to school again.

In the second half of the year Carrie also took French I, where she found out that *vert* meant green. It was too bad that Rochelle, Donna's new best friend, was in the class too, because she giggled all the way through *bleu, jaune, rouge* and Carrie didn't know if Rochelle had GOT it and whether she would then report the perVERT connection to Donna at lunchtime, because Donna took Japanese and wouldn't know that in French horny pervert M&Ms were green too.

Since Rochelle was new that year and had real unpadded breasts, she was very popular and got a boyfriend right away – the one they all had a crush on, smart Joshua Lake, the preacher's son – and Carrie knew Donna was just a little bit jealous of Rochelle, even though Donna never said so. Mr Fuller asked Rochelle all the easy questions in French. Carrie stared at the clock as the minutes passed by, hoping that Rochelle wouldn't make the Carrie-is-horny-Carrie-is-green-Carrie-is-a-pervert connection because Rochelle was sort of pretty but kind of dumb and thankfully she didn't seem to pick up on anything.

Anticlockwise, the minute-hand swung past the seven towards the six.

10.35am, 10.34am, 10.33am.

At last it was 9.00am and they were free to go.

*

On St Patrick's Day, long-haired Shawna with the big brown eyes wore a bright green sweater.

'That sweater is SO cute!' said Donna, when all four of them – Donna, Shawna, Rochelle and Carrie – (the roarsome foursome, the Four Tops, four peas in a pod) stood by the lockers during second-period lunch.

'It's horny green,' Carrie said in a low voice. She didn't know how she dared. She closed her eyes, expecting a slap on her face, the world to fall apart.

'Oh, RIGHT,' said Donna in a scathing tone, 'like you even know what horny means.'

Carrie seethed but didn't answer, and stared at Joshua Lake sauntering past them. He had a swagger because he worked out and also had what Donna described as a tight butt. Rochelle detached herself from the group and said hi and then she and Joshua walked off holding hands. Horny meant pervert meant gross meant weird.

Joshua Lake's butt *was* tight, actually. It looked small yet muscular. Behind Joshua and Rochelle walked Missie McAndrews. Her butt was different from Joshua's – even though she was skinny it went out at the sides a little. Each side of her *Smile! Gelato* jeans looked like half of a pear.

'Oh my God!'

When Donna used that tone, you always knew you had done something wrong.

'You were staring at Missie McAndrews's butt.'

'I wasn't.' Carrie felt her cheeks go as red as red cancer candy.

'You were. You're a pervert. You are horny green.' Donna elbowed Shawna. 'Isn't she?'

Shawna snickered, but not too much, because it was easy to lose your reputation as a sweet girl. So she giggled softly, standing there in her sweater with a matching ribbon tied at the bottom of her goody-two-shoes braid, wearing much more of the colour in question than Carrie had dared to (only Carrie's socks, which were hidden). 'Yes,' Shawna decided, 'Carrie is horny green.'

Donna gave Carrie's outfit a once-over. 'You didn't even make an effort for St Patrick's Day. You're not even wearing green. You're not a team player, that's what I think.' (Donna had heard that last phrase from the school gymnastics coach, who thought Donna had a real talent on the floor routines and who was always mouthing such platitudes.)

Carrie pulled up her jeans to show her socks. 'See, I did too wear green.'

'Augh!' Donna shouted, and grabbed Shawna round the waist, like Carrie was contagious. 'Look, Shawna – Carrie is horny green!'

After PE on Monday afternoon of the next week, it became clear that Carrie had got her period, third time's the charm. Yet the first one didn't really count because it was just brown splodges on her underpants, so it was really only the second time. She didn't have any of the sanitary napkins that she was mortified her mother now had to buy for both of them and keep under the sink, so she approached the gym teacher. It was like approaching a policeman when you were in trouble: they would sort it out because they knew what to do.

Mrs Ham was truly unsympathetic. 'You're having your period, Carrie? So why aren't you better prepared?' She looked down at her clipboard with the basketball team line-up for next week and tapped her pencil in the metal part of the board. Carrie wasn't good at either basketball or volleyball and had never impressed Mrs Ham too much and now she could feel herself leaking even as she stood there, a running feeling, like she was dripping inside. 'Well, I've got the napkins, Carrie.' Tap, tap with the pencil. 'You got a dime, then?' A dime being the going price for a sanitary napkin in the metal machines in ladies' rooms, except for the unfortunate fact that the girls' locker room didn't have one of those machines installed.

'No, I only have my lunch money and I already spent it.'

'You're out of luck then, I guess.'

'May I *please* have a sani... a pad?' The words made her blush, blush, blush. (Tap, tap, tap.)

Mrs Ham tapped the pencil on the roster one last time and when she looked up, she was smirking. 'Sorry, Miller. No dime, no pad.'

Carrie's voice was nearly a whisper. 'But I don't *have* a dime.'

Mrs Ham rose from her chair, pushed open her office door and brayed out into the girls' locker room: 'Can anyone lend Miller here a dime? Miller's got a problem. Who's going to lend Miller a dime?'

Now all of them knew. Sarah Lovitch, always nice, said quietly, 'I can lend you a pad, Carrie.' Sarah went to her locker and took out a pad, handed it over, and Carrie folded it into her hands, so no one could see, and walked as quickly as she could to the toilet stalls. Her underwear was soaked through with blood. She crumpled it into a ball and threw it into the metal box where things like that went and tied her sweater around her waist, where she'd have to keep it for the rest of the day because she had been wearing white jeans.

None of the other girls would meet her eyes when she exited the stalls and went to the sink to wash her hands. They were all still changing and rubbing baby-powder-scented deodorant under their arms, white and creamy, fresh as a daisy, a thing women as opposed to girls did, like men-stru-ating (or *men-screw*-ating, as Carrie thought but never said in health class, because menstruation was all about getting pregnant, after all).

Not even DeeDee Tomkinson would meet Carrie's eye as Carrie walked back across the locker room to collect her bookbag, and no one was speaking to DeeDee Tomkinson much anymore, and there was a good reason why, too, because DeeDee Tomkinson had confided to her best friend Kim Wallace last month that if she were a boy, she would definitely like Monica Rebarchak or Shawna Hamlet, since they were the prettiest girls in the school, and Kim Wallace had blabbed it to everyone and DeeDee and Kim were no longer friends because it proved that DeeDee was probably a lesbian. In Carrie's opinion, it just proved that DeeDee had the worst taste ever because Shawna was not nice and not sweet and not even that pretty, and no one knew that better than Carrie. Shawna with her long brown braid was as bad a fake as Donna with her fake gold hair and fake padded bra and fake niceness to the really popular girls like Violet Browne. Even girls were fooled by people like Shawna and Donna. If you had to like other girls, like DeeDee Tomkinson obviously did, then why would you pick the safest, most predictable girls to like? If Carrie were DeeDee, she at least would like smart and interesting girls with strong opinions, girls who weren't total, total fakes.

In science class, last class of the day, Carrie knew everyone knew that she had got her period in gym and leaked through and that was why she had her sweater tied round her waist. Even the boys knew, because the girls would have told them. The one small blessing was that Carrie didn't have the same gym class as Donna, Shawna or Rochelle.

'Alpha Centauri is the closest star to our solar system apart from the obvious, and it is four light-years away,' Mr Lee said to the class. Four years ago backward and Carrie was ten years old and climbing in trees and playing doll games, not complicated games that involved a certain colour of a certain candy.

Horny wasn't a word that was in the dictionary. Well, it was, but it was just described as something with antlers or something hard, and Carrie didn't think that was what Donna meant. Dictionaries were useless. If you looked up 'masturbation', say, they only had 'the manipulation of one's own genitals' and then if you looked up 'manipulation' and 'genitals', you only came up with 'to handle' and 'the reproductive organs'. A dictionary never told you how you were supposed to manipulate your genitals or what was supposed to happen. If Carrie hadn't discovered, the nice way, all on her own, that manipulation meant rubbing just above her vagina for a long time, she might have believed Brandi Stevens when she said that masturbation was sticking your finger up your own cock, which was terrifying to think of, because first of all only boys had cocks and second, how on earth could they manage to stick a finger up that little slit at the end of their dicks? See, that was the type of situation where a good dictionary would have come in handy.

Maybe masturbation made you a pervert and somehow it showed on your face what you had done in bed by yourself last night, or maybe you smelled because of it, and that was why Donna and everyone else could tell you were horny green.

Maybe DeeDee Tomkinson was horny green, too. It was possible.

Math class was difficult and algebra equations didn't apply to real life. Equations ought to work like this: all Carrie's best friends were popular, so she ought to be popular too. But it didn't work that way. She wasn't even half-popular. She wasn't 'unpopular' either. She was a minus sign, not even a blip on the radar screen and, if equations worked the right way, then it bore repeating that she ought to be popular because she had popular friends.

'There are so many stars out there that it's hardly a Milky Way,' said Mr Lee in science class, 'it's more like a big star muddle, a big star soup, because space is uneven and unexpected things turn up, like black holes and anti-matter, just a proper soup like your grandma used to make, where unexpected things turned up.'

'Are there aliens?' asked Luke Kennedy, which was actually the question they had all been wanting to ask.

'According to Drake's Equation,' said Mr Lee, 'you take the total number of stars in the galaxy, around 150 billion, and then you reckon that the ones with planets will be around one billion, and then from those planets you take the number which would be able to support life as we know it. And even of these, only a small percentage will have intelligent life. And then this intelligent life has to be willing and able to communicate with other species. Well, Carl Sagan and Frank Drake estimated there might be as many as one million other civilisations out there not unlike our own. Pretty exciting, eh kids?'

'Cool,' said Luke Kennedy.

There was a big piece of white paper taped up on the wall in the commons where you could sign up for the games for Field Day, the last day of junior high ever.

Carrie looked at the list of names and squeezed her blue ballpoint pen hard in her right hand. She had always been really good at the three-legged race as a kid, back maybe five years ago and even before that, at the annual municipal Fourth of July celebrations. Someone had written 'Les Be Friends' in pencil after DeeDee Tomkinson's name where she'd registered herself for the obstacle course.

'Oh god, you're not going to sign up, are you? That's so nerdy.' Donna was tutting behind Carrie's shoulder, using exactly the same tone Violet Browne had used back in fifth grade towards those still wearing training bras when she started up the School Bra Club (three years ago, fifth grade, and Alpha Centauri still trucking along, destination Earth).

'So nerdy,' Donna repeated.

Slowly, Carrie put her pen back in her pocket. She saw Donna do the same with her pencil. Brandi Stevens had told Carrie a terrible story about a girl who reached into her pocket for a ballpoint pen and took out a tampon instead. And the girl had done it in front of boys, too.

'If you can figure out a star's proper motion across the sky,' said Mr Lee in science class, 'and whether it's moving away from us or towards us, you can also figure out its distance. You'll understand this better in two years when you study trigonometry in high school. There's another way of calculating distance – if stars are close, we can calculate their parallax from looking at them from both sides of the earth's orbit. Do you follow me?'

Nope, no one did.

'That's how far away a star will be in light years.'

The last day of school came pretty quick. All of a sudden finals were over (C-minus in PE) and the yearbooks had been printed and distributed and were being signed: 'Omigod! I can't believe it! High School next Fall! Lylas, Lana'; 'Your weird but your still cool, LYLAS, Sarah'; 'You're crazy. Don't eat green M&Ms, Lylas, Donna'; 'Miller, have a good summer, KH'; 'Frenz 4-ever, Lylas, Brandi'.

'Lylas' being, of course, Love Ya Like A Sis, which was nearly the same as the codicil you used all the way through elementary school: 'I love you, but in GOD's way.'

Rochelle and Joshua were caught kissing out behind the football bleachers and Mr Fuller said he wasn't tolerating any more of that behaviour. Like anyone cared what Mr Fuller thought anymore, because it was the last day of school, and they were all already fourteen years old, and they would all be high-school freshmen in September, so fuck off, Mr Fuller. No one actually said that last bit.

Rochelle and Joshua held hands defiantly through assembly even though they sat right in front of Mr Fuller and, because the second half of the day was a Field Day, there was excitement in the air and you could already feel summer vacation settling on your skin like perfume and, despite Mr Fuller's scrutiny, everyone who had a boyfriend was holding his hand and even DeeDee Tomkinson had a boyfriend today, although he was the short mean boy in band who played sax and liked to spit on the flute players.

Donna made it known that she was now dating a guy called Drew in the neighbouring town of Kometa who was a sophomore in high school, which impressed everyone, and Joshua's friend Scotty kept trying to hold Shawna Hamlet's hand while everyone was watching the three-legged race against the seventh-graders, and even Lana Lodge and Elizabeth Gershman were holding hands and singing I-love-you-you-love-me-homosexuality-people-say-that-we're-friends-but-we're-really-lesbians but that was okay because Elizabeth Gershman was the fastest runner in the whole school – she went to State for track & field and could run faster than the boys. Lana and Elizabeth were both really popular and Lana had huge grey eyes and had had a boyfriend every school year since she was ten or so and of course holding hands and singing was okay because it was just on the right side of a joke and everyone knew it and Elizabeth's brother David had been one of the fastest runners ever in the history of the school and the dusty glass trophy case in the commons was crammed full of his awards.

A seventh-grader called Ronald Pickson won the egg & spoon race, but he threw his egg in the air after his victory and it came down on top of his head. All four of them (*un-deux-trois-quatre*, Donna-Shawna-Rochelle-Carrie) sat superior in the bleachers counting the splattered egg messes along the asphalt track that circled the football field.

'We can have lockers together in high school too, if we all register at the same time in August,' Donna was saying.

And Carrie was just thinking of an eternity of horny-green, Four Peas in a Pod, one-two-three-four, as sure as autumn follows winter, as sure as winter follows spring, when Shawna kind of cleared her throat and said, 'My family's moving to Kometa and that means I'm attending Kometa High School, not Sequel City Central.'

Carrie shut her eyes and envied Shawna's new start so hard she was afraid it would show, but Donna was nearly crying and saying, 'But that's SO unfair! They can't just split us up like that! What about the Roarsome Foursome? Did you tell your parents about that?'

'I did,' Shawna looked guilty but Carrie thought she also seemed rather excited, 'and they said of course I would make new friends, but they knew it wouldn't be the same, and so they said I could have a slumber party for my birthday in July as a kind of goodbye to my best friends in the whole world.'

'Too right,' said Donna, who was picking at the REO Speedwagon glitter decal on her Pee-Chee folder.

Carrie got the invitation in early July.

So far she had spent vacation hanging out at the video arcade playing Ms PacMan and Centipede with Erin, her old best friend from before junior high, and the summer had been going all right for the most part, aside from the dread she felt every morning when the mail came, waiting to see if today would be the day that the invitation to Shawna's slumber party arrived.

The weight of the already-sodden sanitary napkin was heavy in her underpants as her dad drove all the way to Kometa to drop her off at the party. She wondered if he knew when she was bleeding; whether he paid attention to the curious snails of rolled up pads swaddled in toilet paper that she had been told by her mom to deposit in the bathroom trash.

'Here you go,' said her dad as he pulled the truck into the driveway of the house which Shawna's family had not yet finished building. 'What time do you need to be picked up tomorrow?'

'Shawna's mom is driving their Suburban back into town tomorrow afternoon and dropping everyone off at their houses.'

'Well.' Her dad didn't know what else to say. 'Have a good time.'

The floor of Shawna's new home was plywood and there were huge gritty pink rolls of insulation still stacked in one of the corners. It was exciting, all of Shawna's family living there in the summertime, moving in before the house was completely finished. It was like going camping.

But Shawna's mother was apologetic. 'We've only got the plumbing working in the downstairs bathroom,' she said, 'but you're in luck, it's where you girls will be sleeping. Put your sleeping bag in that corner.' Mrs Hamlet pointed to the far end of the bare living room where it was swept clean from sawdust and where there were already three navy-blue sleeping bags rolled out and lined up perpendicular to the far wall. 'Shawna and Rochelle and Sarah are all outside listening to the radio.' Sarah was Shawna's sister, only one year younger, and often hung out with Shawna's friends. 'There's potato chips and Fritos and some Coke out there too, Carrie. I think the party's already getting started.'

'Hi.' The radio was playing that new song by Spandau Ballet that Carrie had heard before on Casey Kasem's American Top 40.

'Have some Fritos.' Shawna was lying on her stomach while Rochelle braided her hair, and didn't get up, but she shoved the big metal bowl of corn chips towards Carrie.

'Thank you.' Because maybe it was going to be okay.

Things continued peacefully for the next hour of early evening, with the braiding and unbraiding of Shawna's hair; the braiding and unbraiding of Sarah's hair, which was almost as long as Shawna's; the braiding and unbraiding of Rochelle's hair. There was a bowl full of cinnamon candy red-hots as well as the corn and potato chips but no bowls full of M&Ms, for which Carrie silently blessed Mrs Hamlet. No one offered to play with Carrie's hair because it wasn't too long, but she felt proud that Rochelle had allowed her to do a French braid in her curly dark hair and it wasn't such a bad one, either, and both Sarah and Shawna seemed impressed that she knew the group that sang 'One Thing Leads to Another' when it came on the radio (The Fixx) – thank god for Casey Kasem, that's what Carrie was thinking.

When Donna arrived, and after they ate as much microwave pizza as they wanted, they started calling up boys. First they took out the phone book and called up Mark Franklin in a funny voice and told him that they knew someone who had a crush on him and hung up, and then they called up Joshua so Rochelle could talk to him because they'd broken up the last day of school and then Donna called up her boyfriend and talked for almost half an hour and then after Donna hung up with kiss-noises she called up Luke Kennedy, who Donna said was a nerd but who Carrie thought was kind of cute, and Donna told him that she was DeeDee Tomkinson and Luke said hi and then Donna-as-DeeDee said that she had a crush on him and then Donna burst out laughing and hung up the phone.

'Excuse me,' said Carrie, and she went to the bathroom with her purse, and she had nearly forgotten about her period and now she was almost leaking through. The door didn't have a proper lock yet, just a hook and a nail, and maybe Shawna's little brother Todd who was eleven would be able to see through the crack of the door while Carrie detached the pad from her underwear.

It was then that she realised there was no place to put it. In this new bathroom, there was no trash can where you could hide the sanitary napkins rolled up in the wads of toilet paper. Carrie knew from experience though that you could flush them down the toilet and this was exactly what she did. She removed a new fresh pad from her purse and pressed the glue bit into her underwear and there was no evidence at all; the toilet-bowl water clear not bloody, a cotton-white lump of a pad fresh between her legs.

'Hurry up,' said Donna, sitting cross-legged on the deck outside when Carrie returned, and Todd the little brother was there now too sitting with Sarah and Shawna and Rochelle. And Donna had an empty plastic Coke bottle that she was holding between her index finger and her thumb.

They made Todd kiss Carrie on the cheek in the spin-the-bottle game and then when Donna spun the bottle it landed on Rochelle, and Donna and Rochelle French-kissed. There were parallel universes that Mr Lee had told the class about, where everything was the same but somehow different, like you would all be the same people but maybe your skin was purple or maybe your aunt's name was Jeanette instead of Linda and maybe there were slumber parties where no one was playing games of spin-the-bottle, and maybe even places where you could like both Joshua Lake's butt and Missie McAndrews's butt and it wasn't such a big deal, maybe that was all part of Drake's Equation too, but also maybe that wasn't the theory at all.

When Carrie spun the bottle, it landed on Shawna.

'I don't want to,' Carrie said.

'You have to,' Donna said, but then she got bored and changed her mind about which radio station they had to listen to and put on WHQ instead – 'WHQ... ROCKS the Peninsula!' – and ate all the rest of the barbecue potato chips, which was really rather selfish. They had now stayed up past midnight and Donna pointed to her watch and they all cheered, but according to Carrie's timepiece it was quarter to twelve and moving towards eleven-thirty with every second that passed.

Todd shook up one of the cans of 7-Up and everyone called him immature.

Carrie went in the bathroom and changed her pad. She had stuffed her pants pocket with a new pad earlier when nobody was looking, so that no one would ask or guess why she had to keep bringing her purse into the bathroom with her.

When she got back it was time for truth-or-dare and they made Todd run around the whole house naked and Rochelle tell whether Joshua had put his hand down her shirt yet (he had) and then they got in trouble with Shawna's parents because of Todd being naked and Todd had to go upstairs so it was just Donna, Shawna, Rochelle, Sarah and Carrie downstairs and they were also told to keep it down a bit, because people were trying to sleep upstairs.

They probably went to sleep around 2.00 or so, except it was hard to say because they turned the lights off and the giggling echoed all the way around the bare big room, and because Carrie didn't have a light-function on her watch. But she counted on her fingers: 4pm drop-off tomorrow, that was fourteen hours back to now, give or take a few, and by 4pm tomorrow she would be back home safe and, like starlight, all the time between now and then would have already happened.

Shawna's dad, saying stuff like hell and fuck and other things he shouldn't be saying, was what woke them up at some point later in the night when it was all still dark and he was standing in rubber boots and there was a light on in the bathroom and there was water going everywhere and he was holding one of those plunger things and Shawna's mother was there too in a bathrobe, saying 'Never mind, girls, go back to sleep,' and Shawna's dad was saying 'Disgusting! Disgusting!' which was more emotion than Carrie had ever heard him express because he was as tight-lipped as her own quiet father.

And then Shawna's mother said, 'Girls, if you're awake, we could use some help after all,' and they got up and helped mop up all the toilet water that was now flooding from the bathroom all the way across what was going to be the living room when it was done being built.

'I don't know, I swear it was fixed,' Shawna's father was saying to Shawna's mother, 'it must have gotten plugged or something.'

Carrie slept hard and unbending with dread the rest of the night, like she was a frozen fish-stick. When she had to get up and go to the bathroom in early morning because the pad was fat with blood and gunk again, she took her purse with her and rolled the used pad up in as much toilet paper as she could and shoved it in the bottom of her purse so she could take it home with her, but she was also grateful that nothing had been revealed, and now there were fewer hours left until four in the afternoon when at last it would be over.

And the next morning after the pancakes and maple syrup Mrs Hamlet made for breakfast, Carrie rolled another dirty pad up and stuffed it away, and she did the same thing right before they all got in the Suburban to be dropped off back in Sequel City.

Rochelle was dropped off first and then Donna and that was

good, and Carrie even managed to tease Todd a little bit and make him laugh before finally the big car pulled into her own driveway and she stepped out and said goodbye to Shawna and thanked Mrs Hamlet politely and the Suburban pulled away and drove off with a rumble and then Carrie let out the biggest breath of her life, because she'd made it. Then she had to run inside the house, because she was leaking through again.

'Hi honey,' said her mom when Carrie exited from the bathroom, 'I didn't know you were getting home this late. Did you have a nice time?'

'Yeah,' said Carrie.

'Where's your purse?'

Carrie's limbs froze like she was a fish-stick again, or maybe like she was floating in terrible cold outer space, yeah, that was a better description.

There was an up-side to the whole thing. Shawna would probably never call again and not just because she was starting at a new high school either, and Shawna would tell Donna and Rochelle too, who would have to be coolly polite in the future but also somehow embarrassed when they saw Carrie because she had done something so gross and shameful that she couldn't even be teased for it because it would be cruel, like teasing someone who was blind or in a wheelchair.

But that night, six more hours forward past the time she had been dropped off at home and left her purse behind in the Suburban, the nondescript purse that would have to be gone through in order to figure out whose it was, Carrie went outside and stood on the grass barefoot and looked at up the stars and felt nothing but freedom, freedom that she had done the unforgivable and that Donna would never let her in the group again.

Out there were constellations full of white and silver and yellow giants. They looked like a big star chowder, a thick star soup. Out there, dotted through the universe like an economy pack of M&Ms, were other stellar systems. You could see the white and silver and yellow giants, but there were other colours too – mainly cherry-sparks of light from the red dwarf stars like the cancer ones, just like the packets you bought at the store but, if you looked very, very hard at the Milky Way and even further, you could see blue stars twinkling out there and, yes, even green ones. It made you think about big things, looking at the sky like that; it made you think about what would happen next.

The next thing happened: Carrie looked up across the sky and now there were only the green dots of M&M candies, strung across the heavens like Japanese lanterns, green dot to green dot to green dot; inside the stars was Milky Way chocolate, creamy and sweet; the outside shell of the stars was brilliant hard green shining all the way to earth, faster than the speed of light. Carrie closed her eyes once and then opened them again quickly to see other colours joining the green ones: red cancer, blue, lemon-yellow, orange, brown, filling up the sky, shining like anything. The M&Ms multiplied and grew brighter and brighter in the faraway galaxies, green-red-blue; moved closer and closer to Carrie until light-years became light-months and then light-minutes and then all of a sudden the M&Ms went SNAP! and for a moment candy showered down from the sky. Carrie felt the light hit her bare arms and bare legs like rain, as the starlight of Alpha Centauri, Fomalhaut, Betelgeuse and even Deneb reached her at last.

She looked at her watch. Next September would be a new fresh start at a new school and everything would be different, as sure as autumn followed summer, as sure as summer followed spring, as sure as a minute-hand moved from a six clockwise towards a seven.

CLARE SUMMERSKILL
Maggie Maybe

CLARE SUMMERSKILL
Maggie Maybe

I have fancied older women all my life. In kindergarten I used to wish I could stay behind after school with Miss Cooley, who I assumed lived in the classroom. When I was ten I remember crying when my games teacher told me that she was going to leave at the end of the term to get married, and when I was fifteen Miss Boxall became my history teacher. Miss Boxall was the greatest love of my life.

After I left school I continued to be attracted by older and usually wiser women on whom I could develop a crush and if they looked anything like Miss Boxall, well that was an added bonus. Tutors at college, directors in acting jobs and inevitably in later years any therapist who would take my money.

But the one thing that all the women I love have in common is that every single one of them has shown absolutely no interest in me. As an adult I can now see that this makes perfect sense since I know that unattainable love is and always has been a lesbian's trademark. And at school you couldn't get more unattainable than Miss Boxall. She was a teacher, she was straight and she was completely unaware of my existence. The perfect lesbian crush. I probably still love Miss Boxall more than I've ever loved any other woman since.

Which is partly the reason I had arranged to meet my best friend, Annie, at a somewhat chic and overpriced gay restaurant in west London on a rainy night in February. Not, I hasten to add, to discuss my embarrassing behaviour in the presence of my history teacher two decades ago, but to update her on the latest news about my ever-disastrous love life. I'd finally split up with Steph: 'late forties, professional woman, good sense of humour, wants to share fun times out and quiet nights in' – but obviously hadn't wanted to share the fact that she already had a girlfriend whom (I'd since found out) she carried on seeing throughout our relationship.

So I had to talk Annie through the latest events of the little lesbian drama that I call my life. The screaming rows, incriminating accusations, hysterical sobbing followed by a leaden heartache and a very slight flutter of relief when Steph gave me back the keys to my flat, which hopefully meant that deep down I'd done the right thing by finally telling her to get lost.

Once I'd finished my initial rant and got Annie up to speed on the latest developments, I paused for a while to throw some much needed wine down my throat, which gave Annie the chance she'd been waiting for to start her 'I told you so's. They were as predictable as usual and annoyingly accurate, but since I couldn't remember one time when she had ever approved of anyone I'd ever been out with (since her), I took them with a pinch of salt.

Still, over the years it wasn't just Annie who had continually worried about my choice of girlfriends. To be perfectly honest I too was beginning to doubt my own judgement in that area. Once again I found myself coming back to that inescapable question: 'Why can't I find someone normal?'

As I polished off the garlic bread and Annie polished off her third cigarette, I found myself looking around the restaurant to see where the waiter might have got to with our main course. I noticed that most of the customers were gay men with cheeky smiles and perfect pecs. There were two women on the table next to ours who looked decidedly straight but hey, what do I know about these things? And a couple of dykes over at a window table near the door. One of them caught my eye because, even though her back was turned to me, I thought she looked a little bit like my old history teacher. Well, about twenty years older than she was then, of course. Now *there* was a woman I would have stayed with forever.

Suddenly she turned round and I saw her face. My heart quite literally stopped. Oh my God. It was her. It was Maggie Boxall! There was no mistaking it. There she was, my old, supposedly straight, married, mother of two, history teacher, in the flesh and only a few yards away from me.

There was nothing for it, I did what any other self-respecting besotted, love-stricken lesbian would have done under the circumstances. I dived head-first under my table and hid from her sight under the safety of a large white tablecloth.

My mind swirled back through time to my adolescent years when I had last seen her. Those days when everything I did or said around her involved some odd, embarrassing behaviour on my part and resulted in weary, bemused looks from Miss Boxall. Or 'Maggie' as I was later to call her…

I'd known that Miss Boxall's first name began with an 'M' but it wasn't until I got her to sign my rough book so that I could get a new one from the stationery office that I found out the 'M' stood for Maggie. I copied her signature out several times just for the thrill of it and then I went down to the shops and bought 'Maggie May' by Rod Stewart. After three days locked in my room, playing truant from school and listening to the song several hundred times through, I was convinced that it was in fact Maggie Boxall who had led me away from school, because she didn't want to be a fool, she stole my heart and that's a pain I could do without.

Miss Boxall never actually told me which road she lived in but she obviously wanted me to visit because during one of her lessons she mentioned that she had a stream at the bottom of her garden. Well, I knew that she lived in a certain village in Kent, which for the purposes of protecting her anonymity shall remain nameless… (Kemsing).

So that night, Ordnance Survey map in hand, I cycled there, traced the routes of any rivers and streams within a six-mile radius of the village until I finally came across a likely road… and saw her car parked in one of the driveways. I have a very vague memory of it now. I think it might have been a blue Mini, registration number XPR 482G. I was the original lesbian stalker.

After that discovery there was no turning back. I had found a shrine at which to worship and night after night I would cycle there and position myself across the road from her house. Looking at her car, her driveway, her windows. Looking for what? Well I suppose just a passing glimpse of her would have been thrilling to the extreme but there seemed little chance of that. It was, after all, evening time and dark and winter, and the curtains were always drawn. But every once in a while someone would brush against them and they would move ever so slightly and my heart would leap into my mouth.

Perhaps she might look out now. Perhaps she might see me in the shadows. Perhaps she might enact the little script I had going around in my head that went something like this:

MAGGIE: *(Drawing curtain)* Is that Clare Summerskill from Lower Five B? What on earth could she be doing outdoors on a night as cold as this? I must go and talk to her... Hello, you poor little thing, what in heaven's name are you doing out here in the rain?

CLARE: *(Shivering slightly)* Hello Miss Boxall. I hope I haven't disturbed you from your book marking?

MAGGIE: Not at all! I'm just glad that I saw you. Now I insist that you come into my house immediately and I'll make you some hot soup and dry your hair with a towel by the fire. It's quite apparent to me that you must come from a totally dysfunctional family who neglect you terribly. I see that I shall have to apply for adoption papers first thing in the morning and then tell my husband to move out while you come and live with me instead.

Well, that's how the script ran. But spoilsport that she was, Maggie Boxall never played along. And as you might already have guessed, she never adopted me either. She never so much as opened the curtains.

And now, under the restaurant table, I was trying desperately to gather my thoughts. I might have been vaguely aware of Annie's concerned voice asking if I was okay, but all I could think about was what I'd say to Maggie Boxall once I'd summoned the courage to get up.

For twenty years I'd dreamed of this very moment when I would meet Maggie as an adult. And in my head I had a little script we might enact, that went something like this:

MAGGIE: Is that really Clare Summerskill from Lower Five B, over there in this gay restaurant? I must go and speak to her. Hello. Fancy seeing you in a place like this!

CLARE: *(Trembling with excitement)* Is it really you, Maggie, after all this time?

MAGGIE: Yes, and you were right all along, I am a lesbian, but it just took me a while to find out. But I'm single at the moment. I don't suppose luck would have it that you are too?

Well, that's how the script ran, and now was the time to try it out for real. I decided to bite the bullet, face the music, screw my courage to the sticking point and use as many metaphors as I could in one sentence. I stood up abruptly, momentarily forgetting about my foetal position and banging my head quite violently on the underside of the table, screaming loudly as I did so. The crockery and the glasses on the table clattered their way to the floor and spilt their contents over me as they went flying.

But still my resolve to speak to Maggie held firm and, visibly shaking, my shirt and trousers now drenched in wine, I stood up and started walking over to the window. As I did, I noticed that her table was being cleared. Both the women had disappeared. I ran to the door and looked up and down the street. I rushed back to my table and asked Annie:

'Did you see her go?'

'See who go?' Annie asked.

'The woman by the table at the window.'

'Erm... yes, I think some women did leave around the same time as you got up and knocked the table over. I expect they probably went to find somewhere a bit quieter.'

I'll never know if Maggie left because she saw that it was *me* making a spectacle of myself – yet again – or if that was just a coincidence. Annie says it was probably never Maggie in the first place, just wishful thinking on my part. Annie thinks I should learn to live in a more reality-based world and start looking for a girlfriend who isn't a) totally unattainable or b) non-existent; but more importantly is c) my own age and d) someone she can get on with.

So I have told Annie that, as usual, she's right, and that I'll try my best to find someone fitting that description.

But I hate to make promises I know I can never keep.

CHRISTINE WEBB
Miss Manifold

CHRISTINE WEBB
Miss Manifold

Miss Manifold looked at her visitor.

The child was about 13. She had tow hair tumbled anyhow round her face, and a challenging stare. She held a notebook and a pen.

'I've come to see you about the Landarmy,' she said in a rush. 'My teacher talked to you. She said it was all right... D'you want me to come back another time?' she added, suddenly losing her poise and beginning to back away.

'No, this is a perfectly good time,' said Miss Manifold gravely. 'Please come in.'

She turned slowly and stumped in front of her visitor back to the room overlooking the garden. Faint scents drifted in – cut grass, lilac. Please let me not fart, thought Miss Manifold. The young still trust the treacherous body, and are easily shocked.

She indicated a chair at a diplomatic distance.

'I ought to offer you some tea, but I expect you'd prefer Coke. I didn't think, I'm afraid.'

The child shook her head, muttered something that sounded like 'S'all right' and poised herself, clutching the pen. For an instant she was unable to begin.

'I expect you have some questions prepared,' suggested Miss Manifold.

'Oh. Yes. What sort of work did you do in the Land Army?'

They began. Miss Manifold dutifully remembered details about uniform, money, discipline. Fields, weather. Time off. The cinema. Transport. She tried not to say too much. It is so very easy to bore the young. But the child did not seem to be resenting this – presumably – imposed task. She wrote steadily and neatly. Half an hour passed.

'I think you should probably stop now,' said Miss Manifold. She spoke mildly, but the habit of authority is strong, and the child nodded, running a line under her last sentence.

'Thank you very much,' she said punctiliously. 'Can I come again?'

'Yes, of course, if you're sure you want to.'

'I've got some more questions – shall I leave you a copy?'

'That would be very nice. I could get my ideas in better order.'

They went together to the door. The child shrugged on her jacket, then turned.

'Have you always lived here?'

'No,' said Miss Manifold. 'I've moved about a lot in my life.' (More than I'm going to tell *you*, she added silently.) 'But I stayed for a time in another village near here when I was in the Land Army, many many years ago. Now, did I get your name?'

'Lisa,' the child said, half over her shoulder, and set off down the path at a run. Miss Manifold watched her, before limping back to her room. She looked at the list of questions, then sat for a long time, until the lilac faded in the spring night and a huge moon rose over the garden. Silver shapes like paper cut-outs jigsawed across the carpet.

Where did you live? Was it a nice billet?
It was a cottage with a spare room, just on the edge of the village.

The kitchen door was open when I wheeled my bike round and swung down my bag, and the girl was standing with her back to me, bending over a table. I glanced at the paper in my hand, wondering where Mrs Thwaites was; I'd been told her husband had had an accident, so she would welcome a bit of income. They'd said nothing about a daughter, but this young figure couldn't be more than my age. She had a long thick plait of fair hair – not coiled up as the fashion was but swinging across her shoulders. She was slim and lithe, and I caught a glimpse of her face as she moved, the expression both tender and laughing, wholly absorbed in the other person in the room. He was sitting on the table, naked.

She had just finished washing him after his afternoon nap. He was clean and rosy, and she was tickling him while he struck out with his fists and squealed with delight. The fat legs were kicking and his willy, disproportionately large it seemed for such a small body, wagged pinkly. I wanted to avert my eyes, but her intensity of concentration was arresting. She folded and pinned a clean nappy and swept the child high up into the air.

'Little pidgy-pie, my darling little manny!'

I must have made a slight noise, because she looked round sharply.

'You made me jump.'

'Sorry,' I said gruffly, and after a moment, 'I'm – I've been told I should come here – I think this is my billet. I was looking for Mrs Thwaites.'

'That's me. I'm Sarah Thwaites.'

'Oh. Well – good afternoon. I'm Susan Manifold. I'm starting work at Bridge Farm.'

She set the child on his feet and came across the kitchen.

'I'll show you your room. It's all ready.'

At the child's pace, she climbed the wooden staircase and pushed open the door of a small room overlooking the garden. A bed, a small alcove with hooks and shelves for clothes, a stand with a washbowl and ewer, a wooden chair with a cushion. Under the bed, a chamber pot; on the wall, a small mirror; on the deep windowsill, a mug with a few sweet peas.

'There,' she said, and before she turned back to her son I got a small share of her smile.

*

What was the food like in those days? Were you on rations?
Yes, we were still rationed, but I was lucky in several ways, and my landlady was a good cook.

I tucked into bread and a boiled egg: I'd only just given her my ration book, but there were hens at the foot of the garden, and the egg was beautifully fresh. The table was only set for two, with the child in a high chair beside her, eating soldiers dipped in her egg. He would be two in a few weeks' time, she said.

'Your husband had an accident, I was told?'

A look came over her face that I couldn't interpret. Its planes hardened very slightly, and the open expression of her eyes was replaced by a guarded coolness.

'Yes.'

'I'm sorry.'

'The tractor – Phil's bike collided with the tractor. In the lane, a fortnight ago. It broke his leg in two places. He was – we were lucky it was no worse. But he'll be in hospital for some weeks yet, and on crutches for longer. So I'm glad you needed a billet, you see. We should be on short commons, Tommy and me, shouldn't we, my darling? Short commons!'

'Comma,' said Tommy.

She wiped egg from his chin, popped in another mouthful and the life came back into her face.

That evening we listened to the wireless while she knitted and I mended a split in one of my working shirts. From time to time I glanced round the room, looking for clues about my landlady. No photos – not even a wedding photo. Our conversation was friendly but not intimate: I told her about my previous postings, the sort of work I'd done, and she filled me in on the neighbourhood – where the cinema was, what places were within cycling distance and, when I mentioned sketching, the nearest shop for paper and materials – but she showed no curiosity about whatever I chose not to tell her. And she said nothing about herself. There was a combination in her of cordiality and privacy that made it impossible to intrude. I went to bed intrigued.

What did you do? Was the work very hard?
I started at Bridge Farm the day after I'd arrived, potato picking, and after a week the haymaking began.

Nineteen forty-seven was a hot fine summer, and the long days with the hayfork were backbreaking – raking and pitching. We worked on into the evening, while the air that had been like a sweet-scented furnace gradually cooled around us, the wood pigeons crooned, and the blue shadows stretched across the field. By the end of the day the little hayseeds had got inside everyone's breeches, shirts, underwear and socks. Each night I sat picking them slowly out of the fibres of my clothes, while my head ached from the heat and my face burned. Then I would flop into bed and fall asleep within seconds, waking up only occasionally for a drink of water, or a pee. Working in the fields makes you permanently thirsty.

Sarah worked just as hard. She cleaned the house, hauled great quantities of washing in and out of the tub and made good meals for us from our rations, supplemented by her own produce. As well as the hens she had a big vegetable garden, and with no one to share the work she just buckled down to it – hoeing and weeding and, in the long hot weeks of that summer, carrying water. And she had Tommy. He spent his days speeding about at a stagger, climbing into or under every stationary object, clucking to the hens, trying to put peas or pebbles up his nose; he had a small vocabulary, too, which Sarah claimed to understand. Even I, who liked neither boys nor babies, grew fond of him and watching Sarah, I could see he was the most important person in her world. Twice a week, taking Tommy with her, she caught the bus to visit her husband in hospital, five miles away, and always returned quite serene. I'd expected her to show signs of anxiety, but she did not seem to worry about him between visits. Nor did she complain about her life or its demands, although everything about her – her accent, her manner, her indefinable style – showed that she was neither a local girl nor one who would have expected to marry an agricultural labourer.

After the first few days it seemed natural to be a household of two women and a child. Natural to me, at any rate. But then Sarah was by no means the first girl I'd lusted after, or lived with. Never, however, in quite these innocent circumstances.

Did you make friends? Do you still keep in touch?
I seem to have lost touch with the people from that time in my life.

The gang of girls at the farm were good sorts. There was Freda from Lincolnshire, with a rollicking infectious laugh. She kept a snap of her fiancé in her dungarees pocket, between her packet of Players and her heart. There was Mavis, who'd joined the Land Army in 1940 and had worked right through the war and on to today. She'd taken exams and got certificates, and she was going to get married too – to a cousin who was a farmer. She had her life planned. And there was Lorna, and Betty, and Eileen. I spent many more hours with them than in Sarah's company. We went cycling together occasionally on a Sunday, or to the cinema on a Saturday afternoon. We shared a lot of laughs, and the camaraderie of the work held us together.

Still I couldn't disguise from myself that the times I spent at home – I had begun to think of it as 'home' – were what I enjoyed most. I'd done some sketching and bought some watercolours; I did a picture of the cottage, and was trying to do a pencil sketch of Sarah and Tommy, for her to take to her husband. I'd done one for each of the girls, but somehow the one of Sarah was more difficult to get right. I had two versions of it on the go, and thought that if they both worked out I'd keep one for myself. I knew I was on dangerous territory, and tried to keep myself busy: there was always mending or ironing, or the evening watering once the heat had gone off the garden, if Sarah hadn't done it first. But I kept having to swallow down endearments or restrain affectionate gestures.

*

Do you have any special memories?
A few.

One day Sarah came back from the hospital looking agitated. It was very hot again, and I'd cycled back for a bite to eat before a last session in the field. Haymaking was nearly over, and with the moon at the full we hoped to finish in the extra light. As I set out again we passed in the doorway. Cheerio, I said automatically as I ran for my bike; I was going to be late. She scarcely answered. All that session, her sad face swung in front of me as the pitchforks rose and fell and the haycarts were heaped higher and higher. The moon rose above the elm trees and seemed to take on her features. I sneered at myself: she was just worrying about her bloody man! Why should that matter to me?

When I got home she was sitting by the window looking out into the breathless night. I wheeled my bike up the path, and we looked at each other across the sill. The intense domesticity of our positions caught me by the throat. Oh God, to be a man and marry a girl like this! Something of my feeling perhaps showed in my face, for she said suddenly, 'Are you all right?'

'I'm fine, just tired – but we've got the last load in.'

Suddenly it was possible to add, 'But what about you?'

Her lips began to tremble. I propped the bike against the wall and came in. *Tell me, sweetheart,* I said in my head, but out loud: 'What is it, then, old girl?' And greatly daring I reached out and touched her shoulder.

She cried then as if she would never stop. I found a ragged handkerchief and pushed it into her hand. Then I just sat waiting for the storm to give over. I was uncomfortably aware that my concern for her was mixed with rising excitement.

'It – it's a long story,' she said at last.

I waited.

'Phil. I – I didn't want – didn't mean to – to marry him. Marry anybody. I never really thought about it. Not really. You know – when you're a kid you think one day you'll be married like everybody else, don't you? But somehow as I got older...

'I was only really close to one person. Joyce. She was on my corridor at training college – I was going to teach – but she joined the Wrens just before the end of the War and – she was drowned in an accident in the Solent.'

She went on again in a controlled monotone.

'I went really wild for a time after that. Phil – was a sort of misjudgement. I met him at one of the college hops – he's a cousin of one of the girls – and we were a bit careless. He's a decent bloke and he really cares about me, and Tommy. We settled down here in the village – it's where his work is. Where his life is. My parents are disappointed, of course. They put up a good show on my – my wedding day. But all I could think about at the end of it was how I wished Joyce was still there. That she hadn't died. That it was Joyce I was going away with.'

There was a long pause.

'Then – today – Phil was so pleased to see me when I got to the hospital. He says he should be home in another ten days. And I – I was so relieved when I came away. And disappointed that I've only got ten days left. It's terrible. How can we go on like this? All our lives? You've no idea how good it's been having you – being just two women in the house.'

'It's been good for me, too,' I said.

She looked at me properly for the first time.

'Has it? Really? Susan – or do you prefer Sue?'

'My girl friends call me Manny,' I said.

This time the silence was different. We had reached a precipice. I held her gaze, and waited to see if we should go crashing down. Then – 'Oh,' she said softly, and at last looked down again, at her hands and at the scrubby handkerchief I'd given her.

'You've been so kind – not just this evening, but ever since you've been here. I hope you don't think...'

Her voice trailed away.

'I think you are the most beautiful girl I've ever seen,' I said, 'and since I've been here you've made me love you.'

I didn't dare say any more, but got up and went out in the clear evening air, round the corner of the house to the little limewashed lavatory. I tried not to think at all, but came back and washed my hands under the kitchen tap. Then I went upstairs. If she wanted what I wanted, she knew where I was. If she didn't, there was no point in pushing it. I'd have to find another billet, though: I couldn't live in the house like this. I found I was trembling as I undressed and had a late, scrappy wash in cold water.

The stair creaked. A foot brushed against my door and my heart began to bang so loud I was sure she'd hear it outside. Then the door opened.

'You forgot your glass of water.'

She'd undone her hair, and it swung silver as the moon poured in through the window. Our fingers met sweatily round the glass. It slipped and fell, and an age passed before it hit the edge of the bed with a soft thud, then rolled unbroken across the floor. Cold water splashed down on to my foot.

In the silence my indrawn breath sounded like a shriek. But there was no answering cry from Tommy across the passage, and I let go the breath I'd been holding. Beside me, I felt her do the same.

We were standing so close that I hardly had to move to take her in my arms. The square of moonlight we stood in showed her eyes closed and her lips very slightly open. Then we fell back together on the bed, and the reality of her body against mine drove out of my head all the words I'd dreamt of saying to her. I found her mouth, her breasts, the cream and ivory of her belly and thighs, the soft nest of her secret hair, the hot wetness of her secret sex, the endlessness of her skin. She was not ignorant – how could she be? – and I had been in bed with women before, but I felt as if we were making new the meaning of making love. This, then, was what had been waiting for me in this undistinguished village – waiting for me all my life.

Twice during the night she went to check on the child. Waiting for her return, I leaned out of the window and sniffed the scents of the garden. A breeze got up, and the branches of the trees moved in the faint moonlight, curving and tossing like limbs.

*

Christine Webb

What's the hardest time in the farming year?
Harvesting is certainly one of them.

The days that followed were hot and endless – thatching the ricks, balancing on ladders and feeling the coarse hot slippery hay pressing against my body. Through a fever I watched my hands manipulating, pegging and tying; through a fever I felt my legs moving up and down the ladders or tramping across the farmyard. At the end of every day I carried this aroused, fragile self back home.

We were both exhausted: the work we were doing cried out for sleep. But this was the only time we were ever going to have. We didn't speak about it – we never even mentioned the phrase 'ten days' after that first evening – but we never forgot it for an instant. Sometimes we fell asleep for a few minutes after supper, or after putting Tommy to bed, or after watering the vegetable rows. Then we would stagger into the kitchen – where previously we had politely alternated each evening – and lovingly wash together. Once we boiled kettles and unhooked the big tin bath; it must have been a Saturday. And then bed. We continued to use my bed, leaving Tommy in the bigger room. He was a mercifully peaceful sleeper, tired out every day by his discoveries of the physical world. And across the landing, his mother and her lover continued their own exploration, rapt, drenched, tangled.

There was a night when Sarah told me an ancient rude story and the bed rocked with our laughter. There was a night when we thought we were too tired for love – until we woke in the small hours, our hands unconsciously locked between each other's thighs. There was a night of tales, when Sarah told me more about the 'madcap' Joyce and her passion for motorbikes and I wept in her arms for my family, dust under the dust of Coventry four years ago. Each night had a small solid identity, a bead on a string of beads. But the string was so short.

The day before Phil came back, we began the main harvest at Bridge Farm, using a combine harvester. I'd worked on one before, and learnt to respect it. The machine has its own language of noise

90

and heat, and as time passes you become part of it, a slightly more flexible, infinitely more vulnerable part. You must never trust it, though you get to work so closely and know it so intimately. One wrong step, and the moment it is waiting for will have arrived. Its teeth and its dark throat are on the watch. It has swallowed stronger and more experienced mechanics than you.

Afterwards, the pounding continues in your head for hours, and your muscles can't forget their tensions. That night I was tense for other reasons, too, and for the first time our lovemaking failed. I think we both lay awake, achingly quiet, trying not to disturb each other. Then the early light came into the room, the wood pigeons set up their crooning, and our bodies suddenly relaxed. Sarah turned her head and smiled, and we forgot everything except the joyous surprise of love: at the end I realised we had both cried out together, and that our cry had been echoed by the clatter of a blackbird's alarm-call as it rocketed across the garden. Sarah laughed, and a little sound set up another echo: Tommy had staggered in, and was sitting on the floor chuckling to himself.

'Mumma laugh,' he said. 'Mumma kiss Pidgy-pie?'

We swept him into bed with us, and he put out a fist to beat us gently on the face and shoulders, still laughing.

I went to work, Sarah's kiss tingling in my mouth, and worked all day like an automaton. For once, the prospect of the long day was a relief; I dreaded the moment of arriving home to confront Phil, and to see Sarah tending him with the hands and arms that had embraced me. When I finally swung in at the gate it was past eight o'clock, and wheeling my bike round I saw Sarah bending over among the peas. Then she straightened up and saw me, and just as on the afternoon I'd met her I got a share of her smile.

'Phil's home,' she said, and there he was, sitting in a chair just outside the door, shelling peas, his plastered leg stuck out in front of him. He was dark-haired, with a small moustache and – even after several weeks indoors – the permanently reddened leathery skin of the farmworker. He smiled too, but shyly, and putting down the pan of peas held out his hand.

'Pleased to meet you. It's – Miss Manifold, isn't it?'

'Oh, it's Susan,' I said hastily. 'How are you?'

'Getting on,' he said. 'All the better for being home.'

'Yes, I'm sure.'

'Reckon you'd like to wash, after your long day. Sarah and me'll be busy outside for a bit, so you just make use of the kitchen.'

'Thanks very much.'

I washed in furious privacy. He was friendly and thoughtful, despite his shyness. If he'd been brutal or hostile I could have hated him. I hated him anyway, but I knew it was wrong. He had more right to hate me.

I went to bed as soon as I could, and lay like a child hearing the murmur of talk downstairs. I even dozed for a time, then woke with a start to hear the uneven thump of the plastered leg dragging up the stairs. I stuffed my head under the pillow, swallowing rage and jealousy like nausea. At least, I thought, he can't do *that* with her. Not yet.

Two more days passed. I began to think of ways I could reasonably leave. There was a space in the hostel a mile away: Mavis's father had died suddenly and she had gone home to her mother. I could give Sarah and Phil the grace of their own home again. I could hardly bear it, but I couldn't stay either; I felt sick all the time, and whenever I looked at Sarah her face seemed thinned with strain. Didn't Phil notice?

On the third morning I packed my bag early and stripped the bed, then came down to the empty kitchen and had a solitary breakfast. The high arched sky was as clear as all the rest that summer, but as I looked out at the garden the weight in my chest nearly bent me over. When the others came down I explained briefly that a vacancy had arisen at the hostel.

'So you'll be able to have your space back.'

Sarah stared at me.

'I'll get your ration book,' she said after an instant, and went into the sitting room. I heard the rattle of a drawer.

'It's all fixed up, then?' said Phil.

I nodded, trying to look cheerful, and bent to give Tommy a

hug. He clasped me round the neck, gave me a sticky kiss, and said in his loud pipe:

'Where sleep night? Not sleep Mumma now?'

In the total silence that followed I set him gently on his feet. Sarah came back in, I took the buff ration book from her outstretched hand and hurried out of the back door. I loaded the bags on to the bike and rode precariously away. As I turned into the lane I thought I could hear Tommy crying, and then realised that I was crying myself.

The morning seemed endless. Without Mavis we were short-handed, and I was slow and clumsy. The tractor engine, the roar of the combine and the thudding and rattling of the cut wheat swirled into a pattern of brain-battering noise. We had a short mid-morning break, then went on again. At lunchtime I said I'd turn the machine round, while the others walked over towards the shade. It was a relief to be by myself even in the noise for those few moments, hauling the machine round, making its great voice echo my own internal beat. 'Sarah,' it said endlessly, 'Sarah, Sarah.' I felt a sob heaving up in my throat, and for an instant my arms and shoulders went slack.

'Hey! You there!'

The rhythm splintered as I spun round. Across the field a figure came limping towards me, gesticulating and mouthing something inaudible – but the engine was roaring and something was tilting the platform. For a split second I hung there looking down into that dark throat. Then the knives were eating up my leg, and I was screaming and screaming.

This, too, then, had been waiting for me.

Did you move away after your job ended?
Yes.

'Miss Manifold, you have visitors.'

They had all come – Sarah holding Tommy's hand, and Phil following them with only the slightest of limps. The plaster had gone, and as they approached down the long ward I had time to appreciate all the different ways of walking, none of which I would ever know again, and to arrange my face in an appropriate expression. They came up to the bed.

'We brought you these,' said Sarah at last.

'Out of the garden,' Phil added.

'Thanks.'

They were dahlias, wrapped in damp newspaper, their autumnal scent reminding me sharply how long I'd been here.

'How – how is the garden?'

'Oh, fine,' they said together.

'I expect you've got tomatoes by now.'

'Yes, lots,' said Sarah, and Phil added, 'Real good crop.'

As if the word 'crop' were taboo, Sarah gave a sharp intake of breath. We fell silent again. Then Tommy piped – 'Wanta wee!' – and Sarah turned to him with relief.

'I'll take you.'

We watched her walking slowly down the ward, bending over towards the child. Then we only had each other to look at.

'She's been worrying,' he said. He didn't say what about.

I didn't answer.

'They said you didn't want to see anybody.'

'I didn't.'

He cleared his throat.

'I – was trying to warn you,' he said at last, 'but I was too far off. That corner of the field, it's on a bit of a slope – I could see the combine was going to tilt over. But you couldn't hear me.'

'You made me jump,' I said – and remembering that these were the first words Sarah had spoken to me, suddenly couldn't say any more.

'Another thing,' he said, studying his knees in their shiny serge. 'What Tommy said, that morning. She didn't hear him, and I've not said. And he seems to have forgotten. So I think it's best if you and I do the same.'

I looked down at the dahlias. Red, with small tight yellow centres, they seemed almost unbearably real and fresh. A crumb of soil rested on one petal. I touched it, but found nothing else to say. Sarah reappeared, leaning down and talking to Tommy; she had found a vase, and he ran forward to take the flowers from my hand.

'Mumma get water.'

'Good boy, Tommy. Help put the flowers in. That's right.'

She took him on her knee and held the vase so that he could reach. We watched him, absorbed in his new dexterity. His parents' eyes met above his head. They were going to be all right, I suddenly thought: the child they had made by accident was bringing them together in a bond neither of them would choose to break. There would be more children, too. I felt very tired, and longed for them to go.

Tommy pushed the last stem into the vase and looked up triumphantly. He leaned across and gave me one of his smacking kisses.

'Come soon?'

'Not yet, Tommy. I've got to go away. They're going to make me a nice new leg.'

'Why?'

'Well, mine got broken, you know.'

'Like Dadda?'

'A bit more than Dadda,' said Phil, lifting the child up. 'Time to go, now.'

He walked away quite smoothly carrying Tommy, and Sarah and I were for an instant alone in the buzz of the ward. Then she too leaned over and kissed me – a sisterly kiss – but as her hands touched my shoulders and moved away, they left prints on my skin I could feel for half an hour afterwards. Then she was gone.

*

'Miss Manifold.'

Lisa stood rather uncertainly at the open door.

'Oh… come in. I've just got back from the hospital. Have you been waiting?'

'No. Are you – shall I come back another time?'

'No, we'd arranged this, hadn't we? Don't worry, I'm not ill. Been for the final check for my new leg.'

'Your new *leg*?'

'Yes, the old one didn't quite fit any longer. They don't, as you get older. Of course – we hadn't got on to your question about accidents, had we?'

As she sat down, Miss Manifold stretched out both legs. Lisa looked down at her ankles. You could just see that the colour of one ankle between the trouser cuff and the shoe was slightly different from the other.

'Good, isn't it? And much better than they used to be. Mind you, they thought that was a technological marvel in its day.'

'How did you...'

'Lose it? Fell into a machine. Not thinking what I was about. Now, I found a few old photos: your teacher said you were going to have a display.'

'Oh, thanks.'

Miss Manifold got up and bent over a desk. She shuffled papers and photos, while Lisa tried not to giggle at the broad tweed bottom presented to her.

'Here you are.'

She handed Lisa an envelope, and a small sheaf of photographs.

'This one as well?'

'What? Oh, not that – it's only a sketch.'

'It's really good,' said Lisa, studying it before handing it back.

The sketch was of a young woman holding a child. He sat on her knee, leaning back drowsily into the crook of her arm; her head was bent towards him, and a long plait curved down over her other shoulder.

'Did you do it?'

But Miss Manifold was on her feet again, and leading the way quite briskly to the door. You'd never imagine she only had one leg. How much of her leg was left? Lisa wondered suddenly, then found herself unable to speak as the idea of Miss Manifold's legs became, briefly and ludicrously, real to her. It was safer not to think of old people's horrible bodies.

She felt vaguely disappointed. The answers to most of her questions had been very short, and the photos were tiny grey oblongs. How could anything interesting ever have happened to the people in those faded images, wearing their ridiculous clothes?

POLLY WRIGHT
Looking for Aimée

POLLY WRIGHT
Looking for Aimée

Angela is sitting on the edge of my bed. She wears a lemon-yellow towel wound round her head in a turban the same colour as the bedspread. She runs her hand down the length of my body, feeling the curves and crevices beneath the blue checked nylon.

Why are you wearing a J-cloth? she laughs. When she gets to my feet, she bends to kiss them. I try to sit up to stop her looking at them. I haven't cut my toenails for weeks. She pushes me back down again and her turban falls off, but her hair isn't wet. It is backcombed and stiff and the colour of cake.

I whisper, *I'm sorry about Marie* and she doesn't say anything. She makes her way up my body again with her hand and a flame snakes up me as if I am laid out to be lit like a firecracker. When she gets to my shoulders she rocks me in her arms and I can smell talcum powder and soap and lemon.

And I can feel her skin, soft as her own baby's.

When I wake, I hear Mum coming up the stairs. She'll try to persuade me to come downstairs for supper. I can't get up. I have to lie still so I can get my breath properly. I have to concentrate. If I go down they'll both watch me while I hold my rib cage and gasp my breath. I can't bear their anxious, kind faces.

She taps at the door.

'Rachel. Are you coming down?' I lie very still and watch the sun sink behind the bristly horizon of trees and telegraph poles.

I need to gulp air, but I can't. She might hear, and know I'm not asleep. At last, I hear a bump as she puts the tray down outside my door.

'Don't let it go cold.' *Oh go away, Mum. Leave me alone.*

'It's spaghetti bolognese.'

At last she goes. I listen to her soft steps on the stair carpet and then the clip clop of her shoes on the parquet floor downstairs. The dining-room door opens and closes and I can hear low muffled voices start up again and the high squeak of knives and forks on plates.

I lie flat, put my hands on my sides and open my mouth for air. Like a fish.

The next day, Mum wakes me. I have known it is morning for a while, but I hold on to sleep. As she sits down on the bottom of the bed, I shift my feet out of the way. The sheets in the new place are cold.

'Doctor Swain's here,' she says. 'He's talking to Dad in the front room. Politics, of course.'

Mum never allows Dad to get on to politics if she can help it. She's playing for time to get me to have a wash. I'm not sure I can get to the bathroom without passing out. I gulp as much air as I can and pull myself out of bed. The spots come and my heart flutters. I fall heavily onto Mum.

'Just a little wash, darling, please.'

She fills the bowl for me, still with her arm around me, and when she has finished with the taps, she uses her free hand to rummage in the airing cupboard to get out one of her clean nighties. The material is like the stuff they make J-cloths with and it has a broderie anglaise flounce at the top.

'*Mum.*'

'*Please,*' she whispers, unbuttoning my stinking grandad shirt. She has to leave me to it as she can hear the doctor on the stairs.

'Hurry! He's coming up.'

The doctor is standing at the end of my bed with his back to me. He turns round as I come in. He has a sad face, but nice. Like Trevor Howard in *Brief Encounter*.

I can't tell him I'm dying. They said it was nothing at the hospital. He'd probably say the same.

'Just been to the toilet,' I say and he nods, implying he understands bodily functions. I fall heavily into bed and try not to look at Mum. She's furious that I'm not wearing her hideous nightie. Nobody says anything for a minute. He breaks the silence.

'Well, let's have a look at you, shall we, young lady?' He already has his stethoscope round his neck. He doesn't look at me. That's understandable. It must be embarrassing looking at young girls' breasts in front of their mothers at three o'clock in the afternoon. But he still doesn't look at me when he takes my pulse and feels the glands in my neck. He stares out of the window at the beech trees with such intensity I am sure he is going to say something about them when he shifts his watery eyes back to me.

But he says: 'Everything shipshape there.'

Perhaps they suggested nautical phrases for certain bedside situations at medical school. I can't imagine he's ever been on a boat.

'There's nothing wrong with her heart.' He clicks open his briefcase and rummages for a thermometer.

'Let's pop that in, shall we?'

Now we all look out of the window. After a moment he takes it out and looks at the silver line without interest.

'A little above normal. Nothing to worry about.'

'I get dizzy. I get black spots in front of my eyes when I stand up.'

'I thought, perhaps, anaemia?' Mum says hesitantly. He sighs.

'She'll have to come into the surgery so I can take some blood.'

He gets up and stands by the other window – where the blind is still down.

'May I?' he says as he pulls it down so it will go up. 'Pity you've no view of the cathedral from here.'

'No, but we've got a good one of the water tower.' Mum giggles as she says this. *Does she fancy him?*

'How old are you?' There is a pause and then I realise he's asking me.

'Nineteen.'

'You'll be going to university soon, or something?'

'Art school. I hope.' Why is he asking me all this? There is another long pause, while he steadily looks out of the window. Is he determined to see the cathedral?

'What were you doing before... you got...' He can't say ill.

'I was an au pair.'

'She was living abroad?' He turns to Mum for explanation.

'Oh no. Here. Well, not here – in Littlebourne with a woman called Angela Didier. She was looking after two children. She was going to go to Paris but – well – it didn't work out.' Mum is nibbling the back of her hand as she talks.

Hearing Angela's name makes me suddenly feel like crying.

'It didn't suit me.' My voice is shaky. Mum looks at me sharply. The doctor still keeps his eyes on the water tower.

'Is there anything troubling you?'

'I don't think so.'

'Is there anything you'd like to tell me?' He clears his throat. '*Alone.*'

'Oh, yes,' says Mum. She gets up, fussily, picking up a pair of dirty tights from the floor as if she has only just spotted them.

'No.' I'm almost shouting.

'All right.' He sounds a bit relieved and puts his briefcase on the end of the bed to open it. The catches click.

'Don't keep it to yourself. Talk to your mum about it.'

I feel hot with embarrassment and mumble, 'Okay.'

He lifts the stethoscope from his neck as if he is removing a garland, folding its tubes carefully. He puts his thermometer in its silver case and fits it somewhere into the briefcase's padded lid. A place for everything. Shipshape.

He takes his prescription pad from a fold in the lid, and a pen from his jacket pocket, but he doesn't write on it. He still looks sad. I feel responsible, somehow. As if I should have cheered him up.

'You say there was a man. French, you said?' I hear him asking Mum, as they go down the stairs.

*

Madame Didier was not at all what we expected. For a start, she wasn't French. Mum and I had imagined a thin, stylish woman with dark hair, cut sharp along the chin, getting English phrases wrong and shrugging a lot. In the letter arranging the interview she had signed herself 'A Didier'. We decided that this probably stood for Aimée.

So, when this big blonde woman waved her rolled-up *Kent Messenger* at us in the Koffee Kup, neither Mum nor I took any notice. We hovered in the doorway, looking for Aimée.

The Koffee Kup was on the top floor of a department store in town – next to the beauty salon. It smelt of perming solution and nail varnish and was packed with women. They sat in pairs or threes at tables on spindly metal legs, their stilettos digging into the zigzag black and white lino, trying to drink their frothy coffee without spoiling their lipstick. They all had either honey blonde or chocolate-coloured hair backcombed high off their scalps and plastered into huge flick-ups.

In the end Madame Didier had to come up to us and virtually shout over the clatter to get our attention. She had a posh English accent.

'Mrs Walker? Rachel?'

Mum twigged before me. 'I'm sorry... we were expecting...'

'A French woman? Sorry – no. I'm Angela. My husband is French. Gide – Gide Didier.' She added his full name proudly.

Mum was overcome with confusion, and kept on apologising as we followed Madame Didier back to her table. She strode through the groups of people quickly and cleanly, while we stumbled over bags of shopping and feet.

She motioned us to our seats and put the newspaper down on the table between us. For a moment we all looked at it, as if to remind us of what had brought us together: *Au pair required – to look after two children and some household duties. Required two months trial period in The Old Rectory, Littlebourne, Kent, followed by nine months in Paris.*

'So, Rachel. Tell me why you want to do the job.' To my surprise, she was looking at me with something like approval. But then I remembered – Mum had got me out of my usual rugby shirt and jeans into costume: brown velvet skirt, neat white shirt, American Tan tights and shining shoes.

'I want to go to Paris,' I said.

Mum looked horrified. 'She loves children. Don't you, Rachel?'

'Oh yes. I love children. And cleaning. I love cleaning, too.' Mum stared at the floor. Madame looked suspicious.

'I *am* very houseproud,' she said.

I nodded. As if I too polished and sprayed my house and body until everything was lacquered and nothing stank or moved.

My first night in The Old Rectory, I couldn't sleep. I got up at about two and laid all my jumpers and shirts on the bed. I folded the arms behind the torsos like they did in shops. I wished I had tissue paper to make a really good job. I laid them back in the drawers again. The insides were lined with waxy paper and smelled lemony. Mum always lined ours with newspaper.

The next day, I missed the alarm and was up late. Madame had started making breakfast and from the way she was banging around it was clear she thought it was my job.

'Wash this lot up, will you? I'm late and I still haven't done my hair.'

Her hair flopped disobediently over her eyes. She was a large woman. Like a Rhine Maiden or a grown-up Heidi.

'And, in future, you should be down at seven,' she tossed over her shoulder as she went. She always delivered judgements on the hoof.

I piled up the dishes and poured away orange juice from the kids' plastic beakers. I turned on the transistor on the window sill. 'Hey Jude'. I stood for a moment with my hands in soapy water, humming the tune.

Suddenly I was aware of Madame behind me.

'You should rinse after washing. That's what the other sink is for.' I had noticed that there were two sinks, but I hadn't thought to ask why. I just thought it was part of being rich – like having two cars and two bathrooms.

'Look.' She pushed me out of the way. She demonstrated – using one of the children's Beatrix Potter cups, lifting it out of the bubbles and filling the other bowl with clear water to plunge it in.

'See?'

I nodded dumbly. She turned to the mirror and applied her orange lipstick. When she finished she blotted her mouth on a tissue. Mum hardly ever wore lipstick and when she did she was always in a hurry and it smudged.

'The kids are in the playroom.' She kept her eyes on her reflection as she turned her head from side to side and patted her hair. 'Make sure you never let them out of your sight. And they're not to have their elevenses till eleven o'clock.'

I smiled. She looked at me sharply. It wasn't meant to be funny. 'Understand?'

Mum's planning something, I can tell. She and the doctor have been talking. It's about six o'clock and she comes in with her sherry. No knocking, again, I notice. I seem to have forfeited all rights to knocking now. She plonks her so-called sewing basket on the end of the bed and plunges her hand into the tangle of cotton and loose needles. Mum never looks for anything – she just feels. Eventually she pulls out the wooden darning mushroom and stretches Dad's sock tightly over it. The way she does it, it reminds me of Danny pulling that slimy membrane over his thing and I feel sick.

'Shall we have some music?' she asks, after a moment. I don't answer. All the same she puts the radio on.

'Hey, you... get offa my cloud...' she twiddles the controls till she gets what she wants. 'Ah, *The Messiah,* how lovely.'

I lie, curled up, staring at her cream sherry. It is ruby red in the lamp light. In the shadows it is the colour of dried blood.

'Darling. This man. Madame Didier's husband. What did he *do?*'

'Some sort of business.'

'Rachel! You know what I mean. You said – in the hospital. He came back for the weekend and he... did something.'

'He... just... you know.'

'Made a pass?'

I watch her pushing her needle hard through the grey woollen sock.

'I don't want to talk about it,' I say.

The children's playroom was as big as a primary school classroom. Neither Peter nor Marie looked up as I came in.

'Your mum's gone out for the morning,' I said.

'We know. She told us,' said Peter. He was playing with his cars and Marie was taking her shoes and socks off.

'Would you like me to read you a story?' I asked Marie feebly.

'Shoes off!'

'I think you should keep them on,' I said.

'Off!' She stuck her chin out and kicked her fat peachy legs at me, as if she wanted to get rid of them as well as the shoes.

'She should keep her shoes on, don't you think?' I appealed to Peter, who was six.

'Keep them on, stupid.'

'No!' She managed to work one of her sandals free. The force of her kick propelled it across the room into a plant pot. The sock went with it. I gripped both her ankles.

'No. No shoes off,' I said. She screamed and kicked.

'Let her have her shoes off,' said Peter without looking up from his Dinky cars. I put her down and let her kick the other sandal and sock off. She stopped crying and started to run round the room on tiptoes.

I couldn't think what to do with them.

Then I remembered elevenses. Although it was only half past nine, I let them eat and drink as much as they liked. When they had finished, Peter asked for cake. I said I hadn't got any, but he led me into a sort of larder and showed me a yellow sponge with pink icing and drifts of hundreds and thousands all over its top. It had a silver frill with a frayed red border round its waist. Peter and I stood in the cold room and shivered.

I knew it was not for eating now.

'We can't eat that now,' I said.

'Just a little piece,' he whispered, touching my shoulder seductively.

'Another time. When Mummy says so.'

He looked at me, coldly. He seemed to be planning what he was going to say next.

'You're ugly,' he said.

It was as if he had hit me.

'You shouldn't say that sort of thing to people,' I said in a shaky voice.

'Why not?'

'It hurts their feelings.'

He shrugged. I squeezed his arm very tight and yanked him off the chair. He cried out.

Back in the playroom, I sat dully on one of their little chairs. I knew I wasn't beautiful but no one had said I was ugly before. If it was true, there was no hope. No one, apart from Danny, would ever fall in love with me and my life would never change. I wanted to squeeze the breath out of Peter.

When Madame came home, Peter ran up to her and whispered something. She looked at Marie's feet and her face distorted.

'*Where* are her shoes?' she bellowed.

Mum pulls a plastic tube triumphantly out of her cardigan pocket.

'Dr Swain left this.' She gives it to me. I turn it over. It has a label wrapped round it and a screw top.

'You know what it's for, don't you, darling?' I shake my head although I do.

'You do a pee into it and Dad will drive down and drop it into the surgery.' I see Dad getting into our rattly van, holding the bottle upright in one hand and driving with the other. I feel hot and my ears burn.

'Doctor says we need to take a urine test, you see.' Because he thinks I'm pregnant. 'Pop into the loo now and do it. There's a good girl.'

'I don't want to go. I've just been.'

'You haven't, dear.' Does she know everything? 'If it's difficult to go, run the cold water tap. The sound will make you.'

In the bathroom I sit and stare at the running water while I hold the bottle under me. I can hear the 'Hallelujah Chorus' from my bedroom, with Mum joining in, in her high quivery voice. At last, warm liquid gushes over my hand and misses the tiny mouth of the tube – which is, in any case, pressed up against the wrong place.

'I told you. I can't do it,' I tell Mum when I snuggle back into my warm bed.

'What happened?'

'I missed.'

'I'll come in with you.'

'No! Mum!'

Back in the bathroom, she firmly plumps me onto the loo seat. She turns her back and rummages in the corner cupboard.

'Yes. I thought so!' She almost falls over in her effort to reach something at the back.

'It's still here.' She turns round, red-faced. She is holding a powder blue plastic potty with a picture of Peter Rabbit on the front.

'This should do the trick. Pee in here, and I'll transfer it to the tube.' She is looking pleased with herself.

'Mum, no! I can't,' I shout.

'Yes, you can, my girl. Now, I'm going to go and make us some tea – and when I come back I want that potty full.'

After she has gone, I lock the door and slowly lower myself onto the cold plastic.

Angela was girlish in the evening. After her bath she got out of her smart day clothes – a polo-necked jumper and slacks – and put on a sort of Indian kaftan affair which she told me Gide had bought for her in Paris.

'Just slipped into something more comfortable,' she giggled. We were sitting on her huge flowery sofa and eating our dinner on our knees. I heard Dad's voice, scoffing: *TV dinners. So American.*

We watched the news.

'Holding the country to ransom,' she said when a man from the unions came on. 'Listen to that accent. I can't understand a word he's saying, can you?'

I concentrated hard on not spilling my tomato soup.

'Really, you'd have thought she'd have done her hair before she went on television,' she said about a woman whose house was flooded.

The phone rang. She skipped out into the hall like a big schoolgirl. Angela never walked.

'Ah, *mon cher*...' She obviously thought my French was much better than it was, because her voice suddenly became muffled. She must have stretched the cord into the broom cupboard.

When she came back, her mood seemed to have changed. She turned the TV off and sat, looking at the fire. Then she picked up a magazine and flicked through it aggressively. I finished my dinner with relief, and sat back so I could take a good look at her.

She had what Mum called English Rose looks. Pink and yellow, like Battenburg cake. I felt an incredible urge to stretch out and touch her golden haze of hair. I had to grab my left hand by the wrist to stop it moving.

'Have you got a boyfriend, Rachel?' she suddenly asked, without looking at me. I supposed everybody else thought Danny was my boyfriend, so I said that I had, while reminding myself to chuck him.

'What's he like?'

'He's okay. Just someone I knew at school.'

'Is he good looking?'

'Not really.'

She laughed. 'Why d'you go out with him?'

'Because he asked me.'

She turned and looked straight at me. 'You could do better than that.'

I was dumbfounded.

'You'd be quite pretty really, if you did something with your hair.' As she said this, she leant towards me and pushed my fringe aside. I froze.

'Let me do it,' she said, standing up.

Angela's bedroom carpet was white and there were drapes all round her bed like an old-fashioned four-poster. She motioned me to sit on a white and gold seat in front of the mirror which was designed so you could see yourself from three angles. I couldn't meet my own eyes while she picked up handfuls of hair and dropped it, rubbed it into a fringe right over my eyes, then gathered all of it in both hands and pulled it hard off my face so it hurt.

The circle of gold hairspray cans was multiplied three times in the mirrors. Angela picked out the tallest. Then she shook the can, which rattled as if there was a single bead inside it, and made huge circles with her arms as she sprayed my head. She stepped back, like an artist, to judge the effect.

Suddenly she seemed to come to a decision and frantically backcombed my hair. She sawed away until it was sticking out round my pasty face like Struwwelpeter. The hairspray smelt like aniseed and I struggled not to sneeze.

'Much better,' she said, through tight lips, full of grips. She crammed my hair into a French pleat, the way she sometimes did hers. When she finished, she picked up one of her hand mirrors and showed me the back, like they did at the hairdresser's.

'Very nice,' I said, wanting to cry. I couldn't believe how old and pale I looked underneath my hair, which had become a wig.

In my room, I tore out the grips and brushed and brushed till my scalp hurt. Afterwards, I lay for hours, looking up at the shadowy triangles of the attic ceiling, unable to get the sweet synthetic smells out of my nostrils. At last, I drifted into sleep.

Angela and I were staring at our multiple reflections, while she brushed my stiff hair. Sparks of static electricity crackled and flashed. Suddenly she lifted it all off and, underneath, my head was bald and wooden, like a puppet. Then I was lying in bed, with the bedspread pulled right up to my mouth like a security blanket and Angela was leaning over me – like Mum used to when I was ill. She pulled me up and rocked me. She smelt of lemon and aniseed and her skin was as soft as a baby's.

'Angela,' I whispered. And she kissed my forehead and my nose, like a mother. And then my mouth, like a lover.

The kiss was the kiss I had lain awake and dreamed of, before my first kiss.

When I awoke, I couldn't breathe. I couldn't get enough air in my lungs. I pushed the bedclothes aside and lunged towards the window. I wrenched the handle off its spike and pushed myself half out. I gulped and gasped air into my lungs, as if I had just been underwater. Deep breaths weren't enough – so I snatched lots of shallow ones. Then I felt so dizzy, I thought I might fall out of the window. I gripped the flaky frame until my hands hurt.

When at last I got back into bed, numb with cold, I couldn't sleep. Afraid of what I might dream.

After that, we settled into a sort of a pattern. In the day Angela chided me like Cinderella, but in the evening, she confided.

Gide never came home, all the time I was there, but he rang every night. One time, after the call in the broom cupboard, she came into the sitting room, crying. I sat back in the armchair, stiff with embarrassment, longing to disappear into the blowsy pattern. Eventually, she stopped and slopped wine into her glass. I hoped for a refill, but didn't like to ask.

'He's having an affair,' she said. I could not believe that she was talking to me as if I was one of those women in the Koffee Kup. 'Occupational hazard of being married to a Frenchman.'

'Are you sure?' I had seen a picture of Gide and thought he was very lucky to have anyone as pretty as Angela. He was losing his hair and seemed to be shorter than her.

'Oh, of course, he doesn't tell me in so many words.' She adopted a sort of ironic nasal tone, like they did in television plays. 'He doesn't say, *I'm having an affair*.'

'No, of course,' I said, not knowing at all.

'You just know, don't you? Woman's instinct.' She knocked back the wine as I'd seen Dad do with spirits. *Don't let it touch the side of your mouth – straight down the hatch.* A trick from his Navy days.

'Who...' I trailed off. I couldn't think how to phrase the sentence.

'Oh, his secretary, of course. Who else? Little tart. Don't trust them an inch.'

'Who?'

'Men. What about Danny?' She was suddenly looking at me. 'Your boyfriend.'

I was amazed that she'd remembered.

'What's he up to, while you're here?' I had no idea – and cared less.

'I...'

'You watch him. He'll be off – soon as your back is turned.' She sloshed more wine into her glass and fumbled for her cigarettes. I hadn't seen her smoke before.

'Men. They're all the same.'

The cigarette packet wasn't made of card like the Embassy and No. 6s we smoked at school. It was floppy and blue. I watched as she tapped the end and a fag popped out, smooth as a dispenser. She inhaled glamorously. The exotic smell filled the room. It was as if a fox had entered a perfumed bedroom.

'I love her,' I thought, and tried to breathe.

That night she was there. In my dreams. This time she was more bold. Her hands stroked my breasts and my thighs. She didn't seem to need to breathe – her kiss was continuous. Her breath tasted of wine and musky smoke.

When I woke, I ached between my legs and I could feel how wet I was without touching. She seemed to have sucked the air out of me. Clutching at the frame again, the cold night jabbing my lungs, I thought: 'I am probably dying.'

Then I thought: 'How can I tell her? How can I go downstairs and part the curtains on her four-poster to say: *Please, Madame. I am dying. Get me to hospital now.*'

'She had long, long silver hair and was sitting at a spinning wheel. And when the princess looked up she saw that the blue ceiling was painted with millions of tiny stars. But then she realised that there was no roof and she was in fact looking up into the sparkling night sky.'

Marie's eyes widened. I held my breath. How long would she be like this?

'Draw me. Draw me stars...'

I put my lips to her plump arm and made a sort of farting noise so the gesture was funny rather than affectionate. I couldn't risk displays of love in case she pushed me away again.

'Don't you want me to finish the story?'

'Stars!' she demanded.

I got out their paintbox and glue. I didn't have any silver so I slapped blue and grey and white onto some roughly drawn stars.

Peter was running round the room with his arms stretched out, making loud aeroplane noises. He stopped and looked at what I was doing.

'That's rubbish,' he said.

Marie started to lose interest. 'Want Mummy,' she said.

'No, stars,' I said urgently. 'Look – look at this.'

I drew two people as fast as I could – a girl and a boy. With underwear, to avoid awkward questions. I was good at drawing – I could get likenesses really well. I did cartoons for people's birthdays at school.

'This is Peter and this is Marie.'

Even Peter stared. The pictures really looked like them. He had a boy's haircut and sturdy legs and she had a chubby face and wispy curls.

'Shall we make some clothes for Marie and Peter?'

I drew trousers and a dress with cut-out tabs like I'd seen in *Honey* magazine.

'Now, you colour them in.'

To my amazement Peter was excited. He sloshed his brush into the jam jar of water and scrubbed it into the thin paints. Soon his hands and face were spattered with every colour in the box.

Meanwhile I stuck the paper figures on cardboard and made them stand up on a little table holding hands. I lay down to make myself disappear, like a puppeteer, so they saw the dolls without me:

'I say, Marie. Let's go for a walk, shall we?'

'Oh yes, brother Peter. It's a lovely sunny day.'

Now, I'm good at voices. At school I was always picked to play men or old people or characters with strong accents. I could just think hard about the person and the voice would come.

I couldn't see Marie's face, because the puppets were in the way. Peter came and lay down beside me.

'Say, "Let's go into the woods",' he whispered conspiratorially. 'And say, "We're going to find the gingerbread house."'

'Let's go into the woods, sister Marie. Ooh and look, there's the gingerbread house,' I said in Peter's voice.

'And the wicked witch,' he hissed.

'And here's the wicked witch – and you children look good enough to eat...' I put on an old hag falsetto voice.

I could hear Marie whimpering. I looked up, over the puppets' heads, and saw that she had tucked both her wrists under her chin and was clenching her fists.

'No wicked witch! Want Mummy!'

She started to scream and kicked the jam jar. The water went flying all over the beige carpet; the plastic paintbox was kicked into the air and landed face down on the carpet. Peter stood up and put his hand over his mouth.

'Ummm...' he said.

'No wicked witch!' Her face was screwed up and bright red. She lay back on the bed, thrashing her bendy legs and arms. I bent over her and tried to grab hold of her wrists and ankles to get some stillness.

'There, there,' I said hopelessly.

'Hate you! Want Mummy!'

She was tiny. A bundle of plastic and cotton. Squealing like a pig in a frock. Like in *Alice in Wonderland*. I put my hand over her mouth. Not hard. Just to stop the noise. 'Shut up! Shut up! Fucking shut up!'

Madame was at the door, with Peter. Her face was crooked. She pushed past me, knocking me so I fell over. She lifted Marie onto her shoulder and rubbed her back, making cooing sounds.

'Pack your things,' she snarled, without even looking at me. 'Pack your things and get out.'

I held my ribs and tried, *tried* to fill my lungs, but I could not get enough and then my heart started to do jumpy things like a trapped bird in my chest and I saw black spots ringed with light like a kaleidoscope and I said:

'Please, Madame Didier. I am dying. I need to go to the hospital now.'

The room tilted and went dark.

Clouds move fast. I never noticed before. This one coming at me is going really fast. It's huge – like a deep-blue ocean liner. The cream puffy ones behind it are stiller, though. They seem painted on, like a stage set, lit from below.

Mummy is different now she knows I'm not pregnant. Neither of us has said anything but we both know that was what the urine test was for. She comes and sits with me every day and I like it. She doesn't ask me questions any more.

Yesterday she brought a bottle of pills with my tea. She shook out two blue and red capsules onto her palm and gave them to me. She said the doctor prescribed them. I took them. I don't ask questions now, either.

Mummy brings me special things to eat. Like today she brings Battenburg cake. I love the crumbly pink and yellow squares and its heavy marzipan coat. It reminds me of Angela.

Angela came to me again last night, though I wasn't quite sure it was her. She seemed thinner and her hair was dark and well cut. She still smelt of lemon and aniseed but she tasted of French cigarettes.

This time I made love to her. She whispered to me what to do.

I don't get any of the breathing now, when I wake up.

Mum asks me what I am smiling at. I say a private joke. She looks worried.

Today there's a letter on my tray. I can see it's from the art school. I don't open it. She asks me if I want her to do it. I say okay.

'They're offering you a place,' she says.

'Oh,' I say. 'Put the radio on, Mum.' She lets me listen to Radio Luxembourg now. It's 'In Dreams' by Roy Orbison. *Only in dreams.* Like me and Angela, I think.

She turns it down.

'D'you want to go, darling?'

'Where?'

'Art school.'

I don't answer.

'In *London*?' she says, very quietly.

I still don't say anything. I'm too tired. I'll have a little sleep first.

It's getting dark. Mum puts the light on, but doesn't draw the blind down, so you can see the whole bedroom reflected in the window.

She's cutting up last year's Christmas cards and sticking them onto new cards to send this year. I think how shocked Angela would be if she sent one to her.

'Madame Didier rang while you were asleep. You left your red jumper there. She's sending it.'

I picture the jumper, nestling in the lemony drawers, and I wonder if she was surprised by how neatly I folded it. I think about whether I would like to see Angela again. In the flesh.

'She was pretty icy. I suppose she's embarrassed about her husband's behaviour.'

I pull myself up and lean against pillows. I watch the raindrops sparkle like thin strands of tinsel on the window and the street lights hanging like orange lozenges in the blue night sky.

'D'you want to talk about what happened, darling?'

'No.'

My face is reflected in the window. And now I see Angela's spectral face on top of mine. Like a doubly exposed photograph.

We both smile.

JANE MARLOW
The Suffragette

JANE MARLOW
The Suffragette

'Can't you see it would be torture for me to stay here now?' Clara hurried down the iron steps and onto the station concourse.

'But why can't you see sense?' pleaded Isabelle, as she chased after her, cursing the billowing fabric of her own skirt.

Clara stopped, turned and put her small brown suitcase down next to her. 'You're the one who's being unreasonable, Issy. I have never felt as foolish as when I opened my heart to you. I truly wanted us to be together – I wanted this adventure for both of us – but you've made it perfectly clear how you feel. How could I possibly stay here now?'

'I have never said I wanted you to go –'

'And yet, it has to be. In London, there will be no reminders. I can immerse myself in my work and forget this ever happened,' said Clara, as she pulled herself up defiantly. 'You have done me a service. I've realised what a complete idiot I have been. I'm not going to wait around for other people to make things happen any longer, and dedicating myself to the cause is a perfect place to start. I want to make a difference –'

'Make a difference?' tutted Isabelle. 'You think throwing stones, setting fire to letter boxes and committing acts of arson are the way to make a difference? Just because that woman engages in such antics, doesn't mean to say you have to run off and do the same.'

'Don't start that –'

'But it's as if you've become spellbound by her. You've lost the ability to think straight.'

Doors slammed and voices rang out around the station as trains came and went.

'The 9.35 to London will leave from platform four in two minutes!' declared a station official with his cacophonous hand-bell. Clara stooped to collect her case and opened a carriage door.

'It's not even as if she's in favour with the WSPU,' continued Isabelle. 'You won't be part of her set –'

'I'm sorry if it makes you jealous that something other than your wellbeing might absorb my attention,' said Clara calmly.

'It has nothing to do with jealousy,' snapped Isabelle, the muscles in her jaw rippling as she turned away. 'Why must you insist on misinterpreting my words?'

The couple was split by passengers intent on boarding the train. They stood in silence, each wordlessly examining the other's expression.

Clara reached out to touch Isabelle's arm, in one last attempt to rekindle the intimacy she so wanted to be part of her life. Her suitcase felt like a dead weight swinging from her hand: it could conspire to root her to the spot, or it might provide her with the momentum to leave.

'If you were to stay, it should only be a couple more years before we could be together every minute of the day,' continued Isabelle. 'Father is sure to marry again and then I will be free to follow you wherever you desire. We're still so young.'

'I'm twenty-one, Issy. And besides, one year will become two and then three… Please don't patronise me. Can't you see how difficult it is for me to accept that you have obviously made your choice?'

'How can you think it's a choice? I can't leave the family now…'

Clara turned to look inside the carriage and then back at Isabelle. A long, piercing whistle occupied the space between them.

She climbed aboard the train and stared at Isabelle's face through the window. Tears were spilling out of Isabelle's wide, brown eyes and her nose and lips were red and quivering. Clara would write to her when she had settled into her lodgings in London. Isabelle would be left in no doubt about the wondrousness of the life she had so brutally rejected. She would take care to report every detail of her enchanting new friends, her work. Her happiness. Her success.

'I do love you, Clara,' mouthed Isabelle as she reached up and placed the palm of her hand on the glass.

What was love if all it consisted of was false hopes and unkept promises? Worse than nothing.

The train lurched as the engine heaved its load out of the station. Slowly it moved forward until Isabelle became nothing more than a dot on the Newcastle townscape, like a full stop, marking the end of Clara's old life and the beginning of her new one as an employee of a London branch of the Women's Social and Political Union.

The bustling, vigorous office Clara had imagined was actually a quiet, small set of rooms populated by herself, Nell (another helper), and Mrs M, a tall, rather matronly woman in her middle-to-late fifties, who was in charge of them both.

Clara was shown to her desk and invited to make a pot of tea.

'If you could lay the tea cups out on the large table, Clara, perhaps we could have a discussion about our contribution to the Union's summer festival,' instructed Mrs M. 'After all, we do only have a week left to prepare.'

Clara looked at her employer with disbelief and glanced over at Nell, who had already registered her incredulity and was trying to hide her smile.

'I'll show Clara where the stove is,' said Nell, guiding Clara in the direction of the kitchen.

'The festival is like a fête,' explained Nell as they waited for the water to boil. 'You know, with stalls and games and amusements.'

'Yes, I understand that,' replied Clara. 'But, to be honest, Nell, I thought we would be occupied with more serious matters.'

'I suspected as much.'

'I've read newspaper reports about all manner of activities. Had it been made apparent that I would be involved in little more than trivial pursuits...'

'I take it you're referring to demonstrations and such like?'

'Well, yes.'

'You thought we would be sitting round a table, talking in hushed voices and hatching plans like Guy Fawkes?' Nell laughed again and shook her head.

Nell poured the steaming water into the chipped teapot and Clara watched the steam creep out of the tiny hole in the lid. Nell loaded the tray and handed it to her.

'Clara, you've hardly been here two minutes. You can't be so impatient. You'll get involved soon enough, once you've met the right people.'

'But I have to do something soon or else it will all have been for nothing.'

Nell held the door open. 'What do you mean, "it will all have been for nothing"?' she hissed as Clara brushed past.

Clara did not reply. How could she explain that she had to show Isabelle she had left her behind? Even though she did not speak Isabelle's name out loud, she felt the flush of anger and determination it inspired in her.

At the office table, Mrs M was already poised to make notes. 'Now, girls, pay attention. I have nominated you both to ride on the haywain that will travel through the West End on the day of the festival to announce the opening of our event. You will be allocated sundresses and bonnets, and flowers to distribute to passers-by. You must be friendly and genial at all times...'

One more minute hanging around in the boiling heat with the hay scratching her legs through her linen frock and the ribbon of the sunbonnet irritating the underside of her chin, and Clara would have leapt off the cart and made her way across town to the festival on foot. The two cart-horses were harnessed, the yokel and the driver were standing next to them chatting, mopping their brows and pointing at the sun at regular intervals, but Clara couldn't fathom what was holding them up. She flopped back into the hay and tried to concentrate on the peaceful blue of the sky. The fact was, though, that the longer they dallied at Lincoln's Inn, the longer it would take to get to Kensington. The longer it took to get to Kensington, the less time she would have to find Miss Davison.

Clara let her head go limp and breathed deeply. She hadn't come to London to sit on haywains and be paraded around like a mannequin. How Issy would laugh if she knew! She balled up her fist in anger and frustration and punched the hay with all her might. Her fist made contact with the bag she had hidden, and she checked its contents once more: white shirt, green skirt, purple neckerchief. All the suffragette colours were present and correct and Clara sighed with relief. The mere thought of introducing herself to Miss Davison wearing little more than a linen skirt and sunbonnet made her tingle with shame.

The cart stirred and Clara looked up to see Nell, who made a hollow in the hay and settled down next to her friend.

'You've really made your mind up to slip away at Hyde Park Corner?' asked Nell, her eyes sparkling with admiration.

'I really don't have much choice,' replied Clara. 'Miss Davison is due to arrive at the festival at four o'clock to lay the wreath at the bottom of Joan of Arc's statue. If I don't leave then, I might miss her.'

'What are you going to say to her when you find her?' asked Nell eagerly, as she pulled her bonnet lower over her eyes to protect them from the beating sun. 'You've got a nerve, there's no question about that!'

'I still haven't worked out quite what I'm going to do,' she confided. 'Something will come to me when I'm there, I'm sure.'

'Lord above,' laughed Nell. 'You militants are all the same: so much passion, so little planning!'

'I don't know how you can say that, Nell! Meeting Miss Davison and being part of her campaign is the only thing I care about.'

'And you think it'll be as easy as that? I can just picture you marching up to Miss Emily Davison and saying: "Excuse me, Madam. I've been a great admirer of yours for many a year now and would love to be involved with your next incendiary campaign".'

Nell laughed at the ridiculousness of the idea. 'She'll think there's a Yorkshire terrier snapping round her ankles, demanding attention!'

Clara's riposte was jolted out of her as the haywain surged forward. Laughing and clinging on for dear life, they lurched into the Holborn traffic in the direction of Oxford Street. They took much amusement from frightening amazed omnibus travellers with their high spirits and enthusiasm for the 'magical kingdom' that was waiting for anyone who would make the trip to the festival at the Empress Rooms. Clara was half tempted to do the full route and return with the others to Holborn. This would have delayed her arrival at the festival by a good three hours, however, so when the cart rounded the west side of Hyde Park Corner and started up Park Lane, she threw her last rose at her last blushing passer-by and slipped off the cart into the crowd below.

'Cheerio, Clara!' yelled Nell. 'I hope you achieve your aim!'

Clara waved at Nell. Her heart was thumping with anticipation. This time tomorrow, when she was writing to Isabelle with news of her meeting with Miss Davison and outlining her involvement in the campaign, her aim would, indeed, have been achieved.

The first thing Clara noticed was the smell. Roses, dazzling in their beauty, covered every inch of the garden. Their perfume drenched the atmosphere and hit the back of her nose like a waft of smelling salts. People were crammed into every nook and cranny, talking, drinking, eating, reading, laughing, carrying items they had purchased from the myriad stalls that filled the space. The noises and activity continued, unaffected by her entrance, and she felt as if she was spying on the scene through a knot-hole in a fence.

'You can't stay there blocking the doorway, my love,' said the woman who greeted her. 'Why don't you go and find the lucky-tub in the barn?'

She wanted to say she wasn't interested in the childish presents a lucky-tub would have to offer, but by the time she had formulated the sentence, the woman was talking to another visitor, so she heeded the advice and made her way further into the garden.

Coloured lamps nestled among the pergolas of roses and lay at the base of the fountain in the middle of the lawn. Instead of settling her, the water and light and the statue of Joan of Arc that dominated the scene simply enhanced the air of mystery and trepidation that had been with her from the start of her journey. It was anathema to her that women could be so composed that they were able to play golf on the putting green, or recline while their children enjoyed the Punch and Judy show that clattered away in a booth next to the fresh-produce cart. She was weaving in and out of the stalls, pausing to pick up a book or examine an item of clothing, when a voice attracted her attention.

'How about sending a postcard to a loved one?' enthused the owner of the stall, who led her over to a table where an array of different pictures were exhibited. An image of Eros at Piccadilly covered in snow was thrust into Clara's hands. Icicles clung to his bow as make-believe people rushed about his feet, collars up, heads down. It looked so magical, so exciting and such a long way from home. She paid and felt the corners of her mouth twitch into an involuntary smile as she tucked the piece of card carefully into her bag. Already she was enjoying the look of wonderment on Isabelle's face when it arrived at her front door.

'We have our own letter box!' Laughing, the woman pointed at a bright red box with a sign hanging under the slot declaring that it was 'guaranteed safe'. There could not have been a more effective reminder of her reason for being there.

Her priority had to be to find Miss Davison. Without her, there would be nothing to write home about. It wasn't quite four o'clock yet, so she decided to retire to the refreshment room upstairs to collect her thoughts and compose the words she was going to say when she finally met her.

The tea tasted as if it had been maturing in the urn for days and, with two heaped spoonfuls of sugar, was exactly how she liked it. It swirled round after her spoon as she mixed the granules into the liquid and tapped the spoon on the side of the cup. The familiar sound helped steady her nerves and enabled her to concentrate on the task in hand. Perhaps she should just be honest and tell Miss

Davison she had been following her activities in the papers, that she admired her immeasurably and desperately wanted to be involved in her future campaigns. Maybe she could enquire about the time she hid next to the heating system of the House of Commons in an attempt to see Mr Asquith and ask him exactly why he would not give votes to female taxpayers. That was a particularly favourite tale but it did have the potential to appear somewhat fawning. It might be better to buy a book from the stall downstairs – a classic work of literature – and affect an incident whereby it fell at her feet. Emily would pick it up and, such was her love of literature, a conversation would strike up. It wouldn't be too difficult, given the event they were attending, to progress to a discussion about the strategies of the suffragettes, whereupon she would have the chance to impress her with her own experiences. The trouble with this scenario was that she didn't have any experiences to speak of. Among all these upright, self-assured, strident women, Clara suddenly felt incredibly small and otherworldly, like an unwritten character at the Mad Hatter's tea party. She took a deep breath, made herself sit up straight and promptly got the fright of her life.

It was a loud brassy blast that interrupted her thoughts and she hurried over to the balcony to see what was going on below. Random activity stopped as the mêlée of women turned to look at the holder of the horn, who declared the wreath would be laid at the base of the statue of Joan of Arc in five minutes' time. Clara leaned over the rail even further to try to catch a glimpse of the speaker. Her hands gripped the brass more tightly as her eyes fell on Emily Wilding Davison for the first time.

Clara stood and stared, her eyes consuming the vision of her heroine. She was taller than Clara had imagined, but slighter. Her hair was folded up underneath her hat and her dress looked almost severe, but her gestures were animated and her smile infectious. Surrounded by a group of friends she laughed and seemed to be enjoying the spectacle. Without altering her gaze, Clara glided down the stairs and edged her way over to the Yankee Notions Stall. A women told her about the benefits of the superior bodkins they had to offer, but these were of no interest. Instead, she loitered next to the millinery table where Miss Davison's group had gathered. Miss Davison turned to look at something her companion was pointing out. Clara watched her laugh and throw her head to one side as she did so. She noticed her eyes were green. Wide and bright and breathtakingly green.

'I have the prettiest hat you have ever laid eyes on, young lady. It would suit you down to the ground,' declared the proprietor of the stall. Clara stood passively as the woman fixed the wide-brimmed hat onto her head and adjusted its floral decorations. Guiding her over towards the mirror, the saleswoman cooed over her client's reflection. 'No rush to decide immediately,' she explained, warming to her task. 'You take your time. I have plenty of styles that would be exquisite on a pretty little thing like you.'

She left Clara in front of the mirror while she went in search of bigger and brighter hats. Onlookers might have thought she was transfixed by her own image, but in reality her only fascination with the looking glass was that it gave her the opportunity to examine Miss Davison's group without detection. A party of women surged across the lawn, forcing those in their way to move aside. The ebb and flow of the crowd brought Miss Davison even closer. It would have been so natural to simply turn around and say hello, but excitement kept Clara's feet planted on the floor and the air that might have breathed life into her voice trapped in her lungs. As a result, the image she saw was a mere facsimile, but the words she heard were real enough.

'Will you be helping out here for the duration of the festival, Emily?' asked the first woman.

'Indeed I will,' she replied. 'Except I'm not sure what time I shall be here tomorrow, as I plan to go to the Derby.'

'The Derby?' repeated the woman.

'Yes,' replied Miss Davison.

Clara watched as the women exchanged glances and closed the ranks. Her eyes remained fixed on the mirror.

'What are you going to do?' asked another of their party. Her voice was breathy and excited.

Miss Davison smiled and cocked her head to one side. 'Ah!' she teased. 'Look in the evening paper and you will see something.' As soon as the words had left her lips, an organiser appeared at her side and reminded her about the laying of the wreath. Now that she was swept off to another part of the garden, Clara chided herself for lacking the conviction to take her chance. She listened to the voices of Miss Davison's companions.

'There has been talk of a protest at Tattenham Corner,' said the second woman. 'All very hush-hush. Flag-waving and the like.'

'Really?' prompted the other.

'It appears that the idea is to distract the King's horse and put an end to the race. Imagine the furore! It would be news all over the country...'

Slowly, Clara took off the hat and returned it to the milliner's table. That was it. It was perfect. The Derby. It could not fail to be national news.

The train to Epsom was crammed with the most diverse collection of people imaginable and all of them but Clara were united by one common goal: picking the winner of the Derby and making their fortunes.

Clara hugged her bag to her chest as they clattered through the suburbs towards the racecourse. She had packed a bundle of leaflets taken from the office, an apple, some bread and cheese and, of course, a purple, white and green flag fashioned out of material her mother had unknowingly donated.

As she emerged from the station, the vast, undulating Downs stretched as far as her eye could see, yet everyone headed off in the same direction. She took her lead from them and together they swarmed over the landscape like the King's troops at Agincourt.

A woman walking a little ahead of her stopped abruptly to tend to her child and Clara nearly tripped over her crouching body. The male companion bellowed: 'For gawd's sake woman, it's five and twenty to three. We're not going to see any of the races at this rate!'

'All right, all right!' the woman barked back at him. 'You go on ahead. I'll see you at Tattenham Corner.'

The man waved and hared off over the Downs. Clara quickened her pace and set off after him, relieved now she had a guide.

When they approached the railings, mounted police were clearing the course and Clara gleaned from the pattern left in their wake that it was constructed in the shape of a horseshoe. The man pushed his way through the crowd that had gathered in front of the Grandstand and headed up the course towards the final bend. Clara gave chase. The angle of the bend looked formidable from her place on the flat – it had to be Tattenham Corner. A man's voice announced the start of the Derby Stakes and people began to cheer and shout. Individual names of favourite horses and jockeys became a blur of noise as she used her elbows to paddle her way through the crowd. A gunshot cut through the din. The race was on.

At the corner, however, there was no sign of Miss Davison nor any hint of impending subterfuge. She had expected to see the group of women she'd come across the day before, waving flags and shouting slogans, but there was nothing except anxious spectators waiting for a glimpse of their horse as they stampeded towards the finish line. Drained by disappointment, Clara was on the verge of retreating from the jostling crowd when at last she spotted Miss Davison, right at the front by the railings. Unlike those around her, she looked unruffled, disjointed from the hysteria. Her coat swung open and Clara caught a glimpse of a tell-tale purple, white and green flag secreted in its folds.

'Miss Davison!' she cried out as she realised she had arrived at precisely the moment of action, but her voice was no match for the crowd. She could feel the pounding of the horses' hooves rippling through the earth as she pushed rudely past onlookers, determined not to miss the moment when the horses came into view and the protesters produced their flags and disrupted the race. Reaching into her bag, she drew out her own bedraggled flag and clutched it to her tightly. The horses rounded the corner.

'Votes for women!' she shouted, willing Miss Davison to turn round. One final row of people stood between Clara and her destination.

Pushing a jeering man to one side, she lunged forward to touch

Miss Davison's shoulder, but instead of catching the coarse fabric of her overcoat, Clara's hand cut through thin air. Miss Davison had disappeared... she had ducked underneath the railing. Clara's pulse thumped in her neck and she felt bile tickling the back of her throat: Emily was on the course.

Momentum carried Clara forward and she lurched into the space occupied by Emily only seconds earlier. Her ribs crushed against the railing as people swarmed forward, trying to make out what was happening. Fear squeezed her heart as she watched Emily venture further onto the course. The horses rounded the corner, nostrils flaring, lips rippling, eyelids forced back by the speed at which they were travelling. The noise of their hooves was as thick and deliberate as the pounding of her own blood. Their power vibrated through the earth and paralysed Clara's body.

The first group of horses thundered by, throwing up great clods of earth in a frenzy of whips, colour and sweat. Emily was unscathed but she didn't retreat. More horses followed, muscles strained, sinewy frames stretching forward towards the finish. 'No!' screamed Clara, as Emily ran in between their thrashing hooves.

When Emily grappled for the reins of one of the beasts, Clara lost all sense of sound. She heard nothing, not the crowd, not the horses, not even her own breath. She saw Emily's body take the full force of the careering race horse and buckle as if it were a bundle of straw. The impact lifted her off the ground and sent her flying through the air. Her coat was forced over her head and flapped in the wind, making her look like some exotic, flailing bird. The horse lurched forward, trying to pull up, but instead threw the jockey over its head. Like a multi-coloured ball, he twisted in the air before rolling to safety. But the horse didn't regain its balance. Its thin legs were unable to support its huge, falling body; it staggered and fell on top of Emily's lifeless form.

Clara felt as if someone had punched her in the chest. For a second her senses intensified. Vivid green grass. Screaming voices. Brilliant blue sky. Cigarette smoke. Sparkling white railings. Cheap sickly perfume. Bright red blood. Fresh, bubbling, bright red life-blood.

'She's got the king's horse!' shrieked one flabbergasted onlooker. 'She got hold of Anmer!'

Making sense of these words was the last coherent thing Clara's shocked brain did that day. The colours faded, the noise muted and the world fainted into blackness.

'Have you finished typing that letter? Clara!'

'Excuse me, Mrs M. What did you say?' Clara awoke from her daydream with a jolt.

'We need to make sure everyone knows exactly where they will be standing in the funeral procession and what function they will perform. I've been entrusted with this task and I'm asking for your assistance.' It was hot in the office and Clara's superior looked flustered as she barked her orders.

'And we need to make sure we've got enough copies of The Suffragette to go round, Mrs M,' added Nelly, who had popped her head round the door to check up on Clara.

'It's a funeral, not a rally!' The older woman's tone was even sharper than before.

'Can't you see that it's both?' exclaimed Clara, angrily. 'Do you think Miss Davison ran in front of that horse as some kind of lark? If the King wouldn't receive our petition she was bloody well going to make sure his horse did! Don't you see – this is what she wanted – everybody's talking about it.'

'You think she meant to kill herself?' asked Mrs M.

Clara shook her head and turned away. She could feel the tears welling up in her eyes again and didn't know if she could hold them back.

'All I know is you don't go running onto a racecourse without believing you might get roughed up a little,' piped up Nelly.

'Yes, but to sacrifice one's own life…' Mrs M's voice tailed off. She pulled out her handkerchief and dabbed at her forehead. 'Please excuse me, girls.'

Clara slumped back in her chair and wrenched the letter out of the typewriter. It was littered with mistakes. She would have to start again.

'How are you bearing up?' asked Nelly, as she perched on the end of Clara's desk.

'I just can't help thinking, what would have happened if only I'd arrived a moment earlier?' Clara's voice faded as she went over the scene once again in her mind.

'You have to stop thinking like that,' soothed Nelly. 'There wasn't anything you could have done to change things.'

Clara picked at the dust stuck between the keys of her typewriter. Occupying her mind with such inconsequential tasks seemed to help somehow.

'Oh, by the way, this came for you today.' Nelly placed a letter in front of her and waited, then nudged it further towards her. 'Aren't you going to open it?'

'It's from a friend back home – Isabelle.'

'Don't you want to find out what she's got to say?' encouraged Nelly.

Clara shrugged and wished the heat would stop making her heart thump so loudly.

Nelly picked up the letter and turned it in her hands. 'Do you want me to open it?'

'No.' Clara's voice was shrill and concerned. 'We left on bad terms. She didn't want to come... She didn't me to come here; become involved in all this.' Clara's gesture took in the whole office. 'I know she thinks that now Emily is... is no longer with us, that I will be content to return home and everything will be just as before. She'll only have written to say "I told you so".' Clara snatched the letter from Nelly's hands, tore it into pieces and threw them in the waste-paper basket on her way out of the room.

To be among that number of people and not hear one human voice was eerie. If you closed your eyes you would hear the band playing Chopin and Handel, the rhythmic thud of the drum, the gentle creaking of the banners, the slow steps of fellow marchers and even the crunch of the hearse's wheels, but you would not have had a clue about the enormity of the six-thousand-strong funeral procession.

Men removed their hats and women threw the occasional flower as the mourners walked from Victoria to Piccadilly, up Shaftesbury Avenue and on to the church in Bloomsbury. For two hours Clara was alone with her thoughts. She knew now the meaning of true commitment, selflessness and gratitude, and her determination to dedicate herself to the struggle for justice grew with every grief-laden minute. The person she had been in Newcastle must never be resurrected. It was true that she'd used her enthusiasm for the cause as a way of forcing Isabelle's hand, putting her feelings to the test. But it was real now. She might have lost Isabelle, but she had gained a genuine purpose, based on living people, not romantic images concocted out of newspaper reports. As she stared glassy-eyed in front of her, she ran her hand over her ribs, which were still bruised from being crushed against the railing at the racecourse. She wondered if the feeling of responsibility would subside like the pain of her injury.

When they reached Bloomsbury, those invited filed into the church as the crowds and mourners waited outside, and Clara took her chance to slip away.

She had only taken three steps out of line when she heard someone call her name.

'Clara, wait!'

Even in such a crowd there was no mistaking Isabelle's voice. Clara paused for an instant before giving in to her urge to bolt into the crowd. She rounded the corner of the square and heard footsteps following her. Looking over her shoulder she could see Isabelle gaining ground. Weaving in between pedestrians, Clara hared down an alleyway. Her legs felt heavy and tired, tears streamed down her cheeks, but she wasn't able to shake off her pursuer. She felt a hand grab her shoulder and the sudden break in momentum flung her round so her back thudded against the wall.

'Why are you running away from me?' Isabelle's voice was broken and desperate.

'I can't let myself be tempted to go back. You have to understand, it's not a game any more,' gasped Clara. She paused as she tried to order her muddled thoughts.

'I haven't been playing any game.'

Clara averted her eyes from Isabelle's confused, penetrating gaze; her knees buckled and she slumped onto her heels.

'I was there when it happened,' she confided.

Isabelle crouched down beside her lover and ran her fingers through her hair. No words came out of her shocked, open mouth.

'I wanted to be involved because I knew you would see me in the newspapers and be reminded of your choice. I wanted you to be jealous, to miss me, to feel regretful and miserable.' Clara sobbed and finally raised her head. 'But the moment Emily Davison stepped onto that racecourse, everything changed.' She drew her sleeve across her wet nose and sniffed loudly. 'I feel ashamed that I was so selfish and naïve. But it's real for me now. So Issy, I have to warn you that whatever you've come to say, I can never go back.'

She looked at Isabelle's bewildered expression and felt soft hands gently cup her face, guiding it upwards.

'I haven't come to ask you to go back, my darling,' said Isabelle, as she kissed Clara's tear-streaked cheek.

Note

Although the inspiration for this story came from actual historical events, all the characters – with the exception of Emily Wilding Davison – and their experiences are entirely fictional.

The following sources were invaluable: *The Life and Death of Emily Wilding Davison* by Ann Morley and Liz Stanley; the WSPU magazine *The Suffragette*, 6–20 June 1913; and *Laugh a Defiance* by Annie Richardson.

ROSIE LUGOSI
The Purple Wallpaper

ROSIE LUGOSI
The Purple Wallpaper

The day I fixed the roof it started raining. Real rain, not that pathetic half-damp, half-dry stuff. Rain like Manchester's never seen before. Let me tell you, Mancunians know nothing about rain compared to the water that came down that afternoon.

I was on the roof, sitting on the pitched point with one leg facing east and the other facing Asda. I'd worn my strongest roof-fixing pants, the ones Ma handed down to me from Gran. Not the one who eloped with the sergeant from the Liverpool and Scottish; the other one. The one who sank the *Titanic*. That's what Ma said, and Gran wasn't around to confirm or deny. However, Gran, coming from a family of inveterate liars such as ours, would no doubt have winked a shrunken eyelid and told me how salty the water tasted in the North Atlantic as she swam to America leaving the stricken ship in her wake. Ma kept quiet. She was good at it. Had to be. I'm coming to that.

I had a satisfying stack of roofslates tucked under my armpit and was munching on a chew I'd fought the dog for. Fortified with minerals. Ma fed me them as a kid. I've teeth like marble slabs and is my hair shiny! Like you wouldn't believe. I was gazing in the direction of my left foot to where the sun goes down behind the gas works. And we say, there's no views left in this country.

There was a shout from the front yard below. My girlfriend Mimi was standing there, planting footprints in the sand I'd raked so carefully the night before. *Japanese sand garden*, I'd said.

We're laying flags, she'd said.

'Wallpaper!' she shrieked, and meant it. Jabbed her weeding trowel at the jut of the bay to indicate where the offender hung, on the other side of the windows. 'I've had enough. Of it. Have you any idea?'

She flicked her hair off her ears, whimpered to her gardening boots. 'It's 1970s. Decades out.' I heard her.

'And what about the fireplace?' I shouted from where I was spending a day on the tiles. 'It compromises my historical sensibilities.'

She looked unappealingly blank.

'It's decades out too,' I said, very slowly.

She frowned at my unreachableness for a good slap. I took her dislike of heights as an opportunity to continue.

'This house was built round 1915. George the Fifth,' I intoned, patting the exposed roof beams with heavy emphasis. 'Ypres, Loos. No later than the Somme. Here you are, obsessed with buying up Victorian Original Features and nailing them to the walls. Victoria shuffled off her mortal fifteen years before this house was built. You're the one who's out of date.'

I slapped one of the chimney pots, but Mimi had had it cemented in too firmly for my ministrations to take any effect. The fireplace was at issue. It skulked indoors, dominating what she had taken to calling the Front Parlour on her weekend pilgrimages to architectural antiques warehouses.

'So how many years is the fireplace out, eh?' I bawled, knowing the answer. The lace nets across the road shivered. 'Got to be sixty years too early. Capture of Sebastopol.'

'And the wallpaper's not sixty years too late?'

'The difference is I *like* it. You hate that bloody fireplace.'

Her look calculated the correct angle of an airborne trowel in order to make contact with my head. Then she brightened and disappeared back into the house, slamming the door. I hate it when she smiles. She's not a liar, so it always means she's happy about something. Me? I'm far too clever for that. It's the secret of our relationship. I lie, she doesn't. Eight happy years to date. And eight more, judging by our success rate.

*

I like the wallpaper. Hanging it was the only honest thing my mother ever did. I sat in my grey pleated skirt on top of the TV where she perched me, tapping my heels against the screen, gently so as not to incur a paste-spattered telling-off. Watched her slap the garish paper into submission to the tune of 'Windows of your Mind' till it surrendered, gasping defeat on the dungeon walls of the lounge. Mauve interlocking blobs like stained chloroplasts – a word I'd lifted from a biology textbook she'd stolen at a parents' evening. Far more obscene to my ears than *labia* and *clitoris*, labels for things I knew at age seven.

'Stop that,' she growled through the Pall Mall jammed into the right side of her grin. 'You'll get chilblains.' Even more dangerous than old men with sweets. I stopped kicking, held my breath to see if I could faint.

'And that, and all.'

Pathological lying had invested her with the ability to see out of the back of her curly perm. I attempted to remember what honest breathing was. Marvelled at the plumbline accuracy of the drop of each roll, the way she lined up every purple cell with its neighbour.

Dad had been papered into the walls years ago. 'Did it myself,' said Ma. 'So I could be sure. Otherwise I'd never know if the bugger would turn up again unexpected. Charlotte Perkins Gilman, they called me then.' She coughed through swirls of fag smoke, tapping the paper where it swelled mysteriously. 'Before ready-pasted or blown vinyl. Before you were born.'

Around six years before, when I worked it out on my fingers. 'I had a long pregnancy,' was her answer. It could have been one of her pathologicals; but with Ma, I never knew for sure. On bad days, she would attack the wall with a broom, screaming *you bastard, you bastard*.

She left me the house. By mistake. Swore to her last hacking bloodied breath that it was going to Cats' Rescue, but if she'd planned it that way she never wrote it down. After a brief tussle with lawyers it was mine. No siblings to share it with; Ma had seen to that. 'One kid's enough: strangled the rest,' she'd said, pulling smoke into her shattered lungs. If she'd ever had them. She wasn't the maternal type. By the time she was dying, and she took a long time about it, I'd got better at spotting when she was lying. Which was all the time.

Mimi moved in with me a year after we met, which proved the trueness of our love. We had our lovers' wrangles: she'd laugh at the wallpaper and tickle my feet, saying she loved me but not the paper. I'd laugh right back and say she'd better consider Oscar's last words: *If the wallpaper goes, I do*. She'd hoot and say I didn't mean it, and wasn't I a tease.

She sat on Ma's sofa, ate off Ma's dinner plates (five remaining) with Ma's Viners stainless steel as comfortably as she could, but not as comfortably as me. I had cultivated my own patch of grease on the wall above the bed where my head rested on Sunday mornings and had done so for the decade since she'd gone. Ma, that is. Mimi wouldn't leave me.

Of course, being in love made me stupid. First, it was the windows. I wanted UPVC. Guaranteed a lifetime. Never need painting. Sounded like a good deal to me. Instead, we got wood, mitred and dovetailed to look like sash windows. *It's in keeping*, Mimi said. Then the picture rails went up.

'Ma and I spent a week pulling them off twenty years ago,' I remarked through a Bonio as she teetered nervously on her stepladder, brandishing a hammer at the wall. She looked at me affectionately. It was our fifth anniversary.

'More nails,' she said sweetly. She always said the right thing.

And she never threw anything of Ma's out. I chucked *her* stuff all the time. She couldn't hang on to a wallpaper scraper for more than forty-eight hours. She had a pained understanding (as she never called it) that my mother's death had been messy and agonising. True. So disposing of any of Ma's knick-knacks would be messy and agonising for me. Course it wouldn't. But pretending made for a quiet life.

Eyeing the Formica, she'd ask me, *Could we maybe get a different dining table?* I'd only need to say, *But it was Ma's* and she'd flush; say sorry. Sometimes I'd say, *Yeah, sure, why not?* And Christ, she'd be so grateful. It was so embarrassing I preferred to say, *It was Ma's*. Made me horny.

I knew she hated all of it. She was clever enough to appreciate the attraction of valuable Seventies kitsch, but Ma's stuff was neither kitsch nor valuable. It was cheap and ugly. A wakeup call that the Seventies weren't a riot of technicolour glam excess. Maybe for Marc Bolan and David Bowie in their bisexual coke-snorting fairyland they were, but not for my ma and me in Levenshulme. She worked hard to buy the plates from Woolies. One at a time. Pale green stripe bordering spindly flowers. *Quality*, she said, and she was right: broke only one in thirty years. Bit it in half when the morphine ran out one Bank Holiday weekend.

Eight years of teeth-gritting hasn't done Mimi much good. She's made herself into a miserable bint, contorting herself into a granny knot over Ma's bequests. I can smell the repressed dislike on her. *If only I'd throw out just one thing.* See what I mean: horny. She's spent years and large chunks of her wages (not mine) on making the house look (what to her is) lovely. Genteel. Picture rails, stained glass panel in the front door, cornices, stripped doors. It's all Victorian window-dressing. And all the wrong date. Like icing slapped on a cake it wasn't designed for. Happy Birthday on a Three-Tiered Wedding.

The fireplace was different. Even I couldn't avoid the stink of the old one, yellowish flames licking round disintegrating fibre-glass logs. *I'll sort it*, she said, happily. *Okay*, I said. She was happy. I missed that red light.

By the time I got home from work the next day, Ma's faux-slate feature surround had disappeared and the Victorian had taken up residence, filling the chimney breast three-quarters of the way to the ceiling. Mimi's eyes were shining.

'It's real,' she said. 'Not replica.' She wrapped the fingers of her right hand around those of her left. 'And the chimney's fine. Had it swept. We can have a real fire.'

There were oily smears of soot on Ma's Ribbed Cord.

'Sorry about that,' she murmured. 'We'll have to get a new carpet too, I guess. I've got some swatches.'

'Whatever,' I said, and went to get a beer out of the fridge. Drank it in the kitchen. She was on the phone for hours. She pays the bill. That's love.

I'm wiser to her dangerous good moods now, so I shifted the slates onto my shoulder and slid down the ladder to investigate. She was singing. I hate that even more than when she smiles. She'd locked the door on me so it wasn't until I climbed in through the side window of the bay, fighting the nets and winning, that I saw her raised arm and what it was doing. A long rind of lavender wallpaper hung halfway to the floor. She must have bought a scraper and hidden it. I reflected on how heavy the slates were, how sharp their edges against my palm.

'Dado rail,' she chimed, face beaming with the beginnings of guile. She pointed to a stack of orange pine strips leaning casually against the wall. 'Just what the room needs. Of course, we'll need new paper. I thought I'd get started. Darling.'

Outside, I could hear the rain start, hissing against the windows. Lucky I'd got all the roof felt nailed on. As I watched Mimi flay the walls it occurred to me how nicely she would fit alongside Dad. I still had all of Ma's wallpapering gear, under the sink. She never trusted Dad wouldn't come back, tearing himself free through Lincrusta woodgrain and foamed polyethylene. Taught me to keep a keen eye on the bulge above the radiator. There was plenty of room. The rain was hammering down now. With Mimi gone I could rip out the Crimean fireplace and put in a beaten copper flame-effect with red lightbulb and painted coals. And yes, some new paper. Time to move on. Years of sitting on TVs has given me just the right wrist movement, the proper stretch. Something cheerful; buttery. Yellow. Hawaiian Primrose. I'm following in my mother's footsteps. Just call me Charlotte Perkins Gilman.

LOUISE TONDEUR
The House

LOUISE TONDEUR
The House

She was going to the House to burn the body of her friend. Before she left, the woman with the green eyes reached into her bag for an omen. Bones and Death and the Tree of Fingers. The black bag was like night time inside and like the night time it was full of shapes and spirits. The spirit of the moon, she thought, thinking of the night creatures, voles maybe, badgers, owls with big yellow eyes swooping, inside the bag it was like that. She picked out the three stones as if she were playing Scrabble and wanting to make words. She put them down one at a time on the table in front of her. The omen wasn't good. The Finger Tree meant danger, the Death stone meant a new beginning and Bones meant that something would affect her deeply or to the core as if she were an apple and she carried around pips inside her, which were waiting to take root in her stomach and would do if she ever ate enough soil.

On the day of the burning, before the fire was started, Rachel sat at the brown wooden desk in the library, which had marks etched into it from scratching with a pen on thin paper. If she put her palm on the desk she could feel the indentations of the words she had made earlier. She looked up from the book she was reading to help her forget about the body waiting to be burnt, and gazed through the window. She looked out into the garden where the leaves, green and red and heart-shaped, spiky even, climbed up and over the white gate. Beyond the end of the garden she could see the thin line of grey that meant the sea was there in the distance. The land was flat but the sea was a while away from here, especially when she followed the winding paths with the hawthorn hedges which she couldn't see over. When she stood still she could imagine the bushes and the thorns closing in over her head and, if she stayed longer, lacing themselves into two locked hands. Rachel thought about the woman with green eyes who would come to light the fire. She had shiny green eyes, almost like glass; or like two drops of the sea, scooped into the palm and left to drip from the hand onto the woman's face. They were like drops of seawater. Water containing monsters, because the woman looked as though she had seen things before and new things wouldn't surprise or frighten her. Rachel wondered whether there was anything at all that would frighten the woman; perhaps there was one thing that scared her, nothing else. If only I could find out what it is, she thought, the thing that frightens her. Then she saw the woman come through the white gate and she knew that it was nearly time. She left the book of adventures on the desk and went to get ready.

Benny was the oldest member of the House. She had white hair around her face, which looked like feathers. Her face had become as lumpy as an old mattress and, now that she hardly ever left her chair, Benny was as soft and as uncomfortable as that. Although the woman with the green eyes brought her stones with her, Benny had her own set, inside a wooden box that she kept on the mantelpiece and which she took out and shone with the corner of a scarf or the edge of her dress, and lined up in front of her.

Rachel knew them off by heart like a promise, because she had seen Benny set them out carefully like dolls night after night and, although she wasn't supposed to remember, she did. Bright red with grey marble flecks just under the surface, with three marks like someone counting to three quickly. One was green, but not shiny, pastel-coloured like a crayon, with a star in a circle. One was light brown. It had no markings and, although the top surface had been polished, the underside was still partly rough and randomly smoothed by sea water and sand, and Rachel liked to imagine it at the bottom of the sea being thrown about by currents. There was a small white stone and a flat dark brown one, like the moon and the night. The white stone had a mouth carved on it and the dark brown one, an eye. Another was yellow with a curvy cross etched onto it and the final stone was purple and was quite round, the same size as a sprout and with the same cabbage-leaf-like indentations on the surface. Sometimes Rachel thought it was like a planet with countries marked out on it.

When Rachel first arrived at the House she had been frightened of Benny, or rather, of the music that she played. When Rachel first arrived she picked up the paperweight in her room and felt frightened of being trapped like the yellow and white flower in the glass, but the music that she heard Benny playing frightened her more than anything, more than small spaces or the yellow flower. Benny's room was on the ground floor of the House, because she was too old to climb the stairs. After her first lesson in forgetting, Rachel came along the ground-floor corridor past Benny's room. The music made her run quickly towards the stairs. She couldn't find the light switch, so she went up in the dark, all the time thinking that there were fingers a few inches away from her, waiting to close around her face. Although she could no longer really hear it, the feeling the music gave her followed her along the landing and into her room and so did the fingers, until she had turned on the lamp and got into bed with her pillow over her ears.

When Rachel first arrived at the House, she went straight up to her room and she thought that she would never get used to all the things that were kept there, but now she couldn't imagine being without them. The objects stood in for memories and helped her to forget the things in her head. Rachel's room was on the left side of the building at the top of a winding stairway. It was painted dark bluey green which made it feel smaller than it was. It would have taken a Stranger a week to remove each object from the room, to wonder at each one and then take them out of the House into the gardens. Once all the things from Rachel's room were lined up outside the House then the Stranger could look at them one at a time, in detail: chipped paint, dyed feathers, dark wood, green fabric. The wooden parrot hatstand. The paperweight with the perfect yellow and white flower inside it. A book of photos of the moon, a green chair covered in tapestry, musty books about Greek adventurers, candles in candle holders, pots, one with dried oregano inside, one with 'mustard' in grey letters printed on it. A jar of earth with a miniature garden. A scrap box full of recipes and another with fabric pieces. A crate of old dolls. Scarves and three hats, a fountain pen in a stand, a comfortable old armchair, so old it was haunted by hundreds of stains and spills and hundreds of people who had fallen asleep in it. Buttons in a jar too and a rubber plant with large flat leaves in the corner. None of these things were hers. They all belonged to the House.

'Objects just are,' Benny told her. There was Rachel's bed next to the window with enough space on it for her to lie down and next to it for her to stand up. There were clothes discarded on the end of the bed and on the haunted armchair, mostly versions of the hooded tracksuit tops that all the members of the house wore.

It seemed like a long time ago that she arrived, but she couldn't remember how long ago it was. The House was a healing place, that was one thing she knew; and two, a peaceful place. They grew herbs and vegetables and they sat in the sun in garden chairs. She had been there a year at least, she thought, because it was autumn when she came and it was autumn again now. Calendars and clocks weren't allowed at the House and the members never mentioned the time. Now is important, one of the members would say if she talked about yesterday. Writing was allowed, so was cooking and flowers. Most things apart from talking about the past were allowed. There were some things which were the same every day. They washed their hands in bowls of water next to them at breakfast and ate lemon and cream, then bread, then more fruit of some kind. They kept their hoods up outside. The food was always good and there were books and the sound of the sea was brought in on the wind sometimes. They could go out when they wanted to. There was nothing to stop you leaving by the white gate and following the winding path and going on and on until the House was far behind, and starting somewhere else. One or two had done it. They had no car. All money had to be given in for the good of the House. But one or two had stolen money or had walked the miles to the main road and hitched and it didn't matter because they were yesterday and that was gone and it was the only way for a member to leave after all. No one made you stay. Rachel walked the roads around the House often, after she had finished her jobs for the day. It was her job to write letters asking for donations to the House and other letters about business like selling honey and vegetables at a new market. She wrote letters at the desk in the library on thin pieces of paper, until her words became etched on the desk, one line of words over another.

Now that Rachel had been in the House for a while, she had got to know Benny and her music, which sounded like a woman crying. She often took her tea and biscuits and went to sit with her in the long room downstairs.

When the woman came to do the stones, Benny liked to narrow her eyes and fix her with a stare as she waited for the reading. Then Rachel would have to pick up the tea tray and leave the room, even though she wanted to stay and watch the woman with the green eyes. Afterwards, Rachel was sometimes allowed back in to stand and look out of the window at least, and Benny would rise up straight in her chair, play with her feathered hair and smile. Then the woman with the green eyes would pick up her black bag and go out into the garden without saying anything else and Rachel would watch her cross the grass with big strides.

On the day of the burning, Rachel was sitting at the desk in the library writing letters, but she had stopped to look at the stories in her favourite book. It was an illustrated copy of the adventures of Odysseus. The story of the Cyclops, the giant with one eye, had a picture of a green giant and a flaming torch. The drawings were hand-painted and Benny had told her that the book was very valuable. She had seen the woman with the green eyes arrive and she knew she would have to go outside to the fire soon. The words of the book stopped her thinking about the flames of the fire which already leapt about in her head.

Rachel picked up the paperweight from the edge of the desk. She had brought it with her from her room to stop her letters flying around in the draught from the library window. She held it above the words of the book and looked through it. The letters turned big and upside down, as if it was a word crystal ball. She imagined that the paper wasn't there and that she was looking into magic glass at the end of her stories, but they ran away from her like streams. The yellow flower in the paperweight could have been a spider, when she turned it on its side, with eight fragile legs and a white eye. When she held the paperweight just above her own words written in blue ink across the page, it magnified them until they looked like the tracks of a strange blue sea creature or like electricity and not like words at all. Or maybe the paperweight was like a large glass eye. A giant's eye watching her. Spinning it made the giant giddy. Nobody is killing me. Spin it and it makes the magnified words spin too. When it stops, tip the giant eye this way and that and you can sometimes make out the words. She lifted the paperweight. The words became the right size again. Nobody is killing me, the words said. Spin the word crystal ball around and it will pick up a word or two and spit them back up to the surface. Green, sent, understand.

The woman with green eyes came to make bread every Tuesday. She did flowers too. She brought in bunches and laid them out on the table, naked without a vase, with the stems pointing towards the door. Then she would sieve flour and weigh the bowl in her hands. She made dough that made the whole House smell of yeast. Rachel stood in the hall from where she could see a slice of the kitchen through the half-closed door. Every Tuesday, she watched the woman kneading and stretching. As soon as Rachel heard the taps run, she knew that the woman would emerge with red wet hands to chop the stems of the flowers to the right height for the vases, and then she would retreat silently.

Once in mid-autumn, just after Rachel had first arrived, the woman came to make a bonfire, after she had swept up the apple-flavoured leaves and the twigs in the garden. The flames were blue and orange and lit up the woman's face, but she didn't smile. She looked sad as if she was remembering things. Rachel watched her then and thought that her face looked beautiful in the firelight, but she went back to her room without speaking to her.

Members couldn't talk to Strangers, unless it was business talk about apples for the market or selling herbs from the garden. A Stranger was someone from outside, who had memories that they had not forgotten. The woman who made the bread and did the flowers and the stones was a Stranger. The House paid her to help in the garden too and she took vegetables and herbs to the nearest town to sell for them.

If you leave the house you can't come back again, because you are past. The Stranger who made the bread was the only member who had left and been allowed back into the house. She was allowed back because of her talent with the stones. But she wasn't a member anymore. She found it difficult to forget things. She was a Stranger now and no one was supposed to talk to her about anything other than business. Only the one or two who had been at the house the longest spoke to her more than that. Like Benny, who couldn't remember her past before the House. She refused to remember and now the past had actually left her.

'The past is a different place from now,' she said, when Rachel asked her where she came from before, and she smiled to herself. Then Benny put on her music and Rachel wasn't frightened of it any more. She had been at the House too long for that. She let the music into her head and closed her eyes.

Rachel told Benny that she thought the woman who read the stones was beautiful.

'She is, yes,' said Benny, stirring the tea that Rachel had brought for her.

'She reads other things too,' Benny said when Rachel asked her about the stones. 'Bodies.'

'Dead bodies?' said Rachel. 'I know.'

'Live ones too,' said Benny and she smiled.

When a member died, it was the woman who read Benny's stones who lit the fire and then stood back while the members held hands in a circle with their hoods up and waited. A day later, when the bones that were left were cold, she read the head, naked of flesh, and told the members that their friend had been reincarnated to a place of peace or war or into a tree, or perhaps she said that the spirit waited at the House unable to leave, Rachel had forgotten which. A tree should be planted where the ashes are, the woman said. And someone said that because the woman wasn't a member she shouldn't be allowed to talk about trees, but Benny told them all to listen to her and the tree was planted. Later, a member saw a dead face at the end of a corridor and they gathered again and covered their heads and sent the spirit on with a broom and sprinkled water.

'She reads bodies. Live ones,' Benny told Rachel as they listened to the sad music.

'What about mine?' said Rachel.

'Come down to the library tonight. I'll arrange it,' said Benny and she chuckled to herself.

It was the first time Rachel had spoken directly to the woman with the green eyes.

'Take off your top,' said the woman, like a doctor would have said in the time before the House, Rachel thought. She took off her hooded top and stood in the middle of the library, with the moon shining brightly through the window at her. She reached out the hands she used to break branches and arrange flowers and knead bread. She picked up Rachel's arm and saw the scars crisscrossed over it in patterns, and here and there burn marks too. The woman touched her arm and looked into Rachel's eyes. Rachel tried not to think about the knife she had used because it was gone like a leaf from an autumn ago. Or the blood, which was bright and proved that she was still alive. In the House she could remember doing it once – or was it twice? – although she was supposed to forget. The time she remembered, there had been no cigarettes so she used a match from the kitchen. The flame was pretty. If she had done it more than once while she had been in the House then she had forgotten it. Now the pen she used on the paper, which was thin like skin and rested only on the wooden desk, was like a knife or a flame – the way the words got into the wood.

The woman ran her fingers over Rachel's arms and then her neck and face. Then she made her put her hood back on and sit down. The woman offered her the bag of stones. Rachel took three of them as Benny had told her to do. She laid them out in front of her. She felt the knife feeling come back in her stomach as she did so, even though it was past. Then she felt warm and safe, knowing that the scars were under her sleeves.

'Close your eyes,' said the woman. 'Put your hand above the stones. Now move them into a shape.' Rachel felt the stones under her hand – the rough parts and the smooth parts. Her hand was like the sea, she thought. She moved the stones into an upside-down triangle slowly, one at a time, rubbing each one in her palm as she did so.

'Open your eyes.' The woman looked at the stones in the moonlit library and stayed silent.

'Tell me,' said Rachel. The woman got out a notebook instead and drew the triangle of stones quickly, then she wrote in spidery writing underneath each one.

'Tell me,' Rachel said again, but the woman refused.

'Go to bed now,' she said.

The next day Benny was dead and her life, the other members said, was past like a blown-out flame and didn't matter because it was gone. But Rachel knew about flames and scars. She held her sleeves in her hands and thought about Benny's life and what it was like even though she knew she was breaking the rules and that if she remembered one thing she might begin to remember others too.

When the woman came later to light the fire, and the ceremony began, she looked at Rachel for a long time, as she stood in the circle. It was as if she was thinking about the night before, which didn't exist any more, just as Benny didn't. They couldn't talk about it when the other members were around. Rachel was thinking too, about Benny and how the woman's bread hands had touched her. The woman, who was no longer a member, could think about the past as much as she wanted to. Rachel could see that it worried her, like a page in a book that made no sense. Then Rachel began to feel bits of her memories that she had forgotten come creeping back into the corners of her head, and she decided that it was the woman's hands and thinking about Benny that did it.

After the burning, the woman said that Benny had been reincarnated in a place of peace, had been made into a tree and would live for six hundred years. The members continued as before and forgot the past that had Benny in it.

But while the fire was still lit and the other members were just beginning to go back inside after the hand-holding, and the head was too hot to go near, Rachel ran into the library and sat at the desk again as she had earlier, reading anything to keep the story of the past coming back in with the knife and candles and cigarettes. She had found the story of Odysseus killing the Cyclops in the painted book again. She was reading the page where Odysseus tells the Cyclops that his name is Nobody and the Cyclops shouts 'Nobody is killing me' as he is blinded with a fiery stake. Rachel read and read, not seeing the words, until the woman with the green eyes found her and took her by the arm and led her outside, so that they could talk. It was dark. They moved across the gardens quickly, towards the fire where the remains of Benny's body lay. Nobody is killing me, Rachel said to herself, over and over. Nobody is killing me. If she stopped, she thought of the knife feeling in her stomach, which had her old memories in it.

The woman took her over to a tree near the herb garden and she could smell the sage and the night air. The flames were lower now than before, but they still burnt strongly.

'One of the stones last night said death and I was frightened,' the woman told Rachel.

Frightened of the stones, Rachel thought, now she knew what

frightened the woman – the stones that she carried with her all the time.

The woman put her hand under Rachel's hood and touched her face, then she put her hands on her waist under her top and they kissed each other slowly. Whenever she kissed anyone after that evening, Rachel remembered smoke and sage.

'What were the other stones?' Rachel asked.

'Sit down and I'll show you.' They sat on the grass, which was damp, and the woman took out her stones again and handed the three which had frightened her to Rachel.

'This is death.' It was the yellow stone with the cross. 'Because it was this way up.' The woman turned it over. 'And at the top of the triangle. This one is ink and this one is memories. Together they mean fire.'

'Benny's fire?'

'Yes.'

'Memories aren't allowed.'

'I know. It frightened me. Death, memories and fire together.'

'And ink?'

'Write.'

'Write what?'

'Your memories.'

'I don't have any. We're not allowed. That's the point of being here.'

'I used to be a member. I know what the rules are.'

'No before or after.'

'What about Benny?'

Rachel didn't answer, instead she thought about the knife in her stomach. When the woman was gone, she thought, she would have to go to the kitchen to find a knife. She would be safe. Everyone was asleep. The woman touched her face again.

'Can I stay with you tonight?' she said.

'You're not allowed,' said Rachel sharply, thinking about the kitchen. 'You're not a member. Strangers who haven't forgotten can't sleep at the House and sex can only be with other members.' So the woman went back over to the fire and didn't say anything else.

Rachel went and found a knife. She was going to take it up to her room, where there were so many things that no one would notice one more, but she couldn't wait so she went into the library where the desk with the word marks was and sat down. She rolled up her sleeve and ran the blade over her arm. There was her blood, singing and whispering. But just a few memories trickled out onto her arm, the rest stayed inside. She wanted to get rid of them all, to cut and cut until they were gone. She raised the knife again. But then the door to the library opened suddenly. There was no one there although Rachel felt cold as if there were a spirit in the room. Benny's spirit, she thought, and she put down the knife. But then there was the woman with the bread hands in the doorway looking at the blood on Rachel's arm and on the table and the knife. She didn't say anything at first. She went and got damp tissues from the bathroom and mopped up the blood. The cuts weren't deep and they stopped bleeding quickly. Then she went and got some of the thin sheets of paper that Rachel used for writing her letters and a blue pen and put them on the desk.

'Go on,' she said. That night the woman watched while Rachel wrote down her memories which had flooded back into her stomach when she saw Benny on the fire and when the woman touched her arms. The woman sat next to her and watched, while Rachel wrote page after page in blue ink. She wrote quickly as if she couldn't stop, but when she did, the woman undressed and told Rachel to do the same, as if it was a normal thing to undress in the library with the books watching. Rachel sat on the woman's lap and they kissed again in different places and twisted around each other, until they were on the floor next to the desk, turning over and over, with the memories on the paper above them. Rachel could smell smoke and sage.

In the morning, one of the members found Rachel's memories, remembered and on the desk in the library. But Rachel and the woman with green eyes had gone through the white gate and along the winding paths towards the sea and they were past and gone like leaves. The spaces that they left closed behind them and the members of the house forgot about them and did not remember.

JACKIE KAY
Making a Movie

JACKIE KAY
Making a Movie

Opening credits. My enemy makes movies. She is tall with a sharp nose. She's paranoid and thinks that everything is about her when everything isn't about her at all. I used to love her. She used to make me her own chapatis and this particular dish that I liked. I forget what it was now. It is a long time ago. It involved an aubergine. The time that she cooked it best she was wearing white jeans. I remember that like a flashback. In her kitchen waving a wooden spoon with white jeans on. It was impressive. The glorious ghee. Bringal bhaji! That was it. I loved then to see unfamiliar things in a kitchen. The sight of fresh ginger, fresh coriander, long linked bulbs of garlic, I found exhilarating. I was impressed because I can't cook, not to speak of, not to remember. People who went to dinner at my enemy's house always spoke effusively about her food. 'Isn't she a good cook,' they'd say. Others in the know would nod greedily. It was an interesting house with a large conservatory at the back of it that her lover had built. Her lover was good with her hands. My enemy grew tomatoes there. I liked watching them turn from fairytale green to red. They had the kitchen and living room upstairs and the bedrooms and workrooms downstairs, which I thought odd. Her lover was an electrician and quietly spoken with a Geordie accent and had more beautiful eyes than the eyes of my enemy.

She didn't make movies back then, but now she does. Back then, I went round to her house often and ate and confessed to various emotions and then we discussed them and she'd pull me apart, dipping her chapati in the curry, or eating her basmati rice with her fingers and telling me that I was unbearably honest. Perceptive. She loved me. She said this with burning eyes. 'I love the way your mind works,' I remember her saying. 'It's strange.' Her monosyllabic lover nodded, chewing slowly, picking up some raita with her chapati. My enemy had taught her Newcastle lover how to eat like her. When I left I was always aware of sex, even before I'd finished climbing down the bare wooden staircase, the spices still in the air. The complicit smell of cardamom and cumin. It was something to do with the food, the confession. Something to do with me leaving.

Where did I go? I went home and slept. Often I dreamt of my enemy and her lover – the most vivid and frightening dreams of my life. I remember some of those dreams even now – me up on a red roof scrambling. Me in a wedding dress with a thick, swollen tongue unable to speak to my mother. The fascist golfers in their red pullovers climbing up my drainpipe to bang on my bathroom window. And through every dream, my enemy and her lover making a sudden appearance like Hitchcock in his own movies, as if they were the creators of my dreams. They would be getting on a bus, or rushing out of a shop, or waving from one of those electric caddies at the golf course. The lover with the premature grey spiky hair, my enemy with her jet-black hair. Or they would be cleaning my windows.

The two lovers liked to be extremely affectionate to each other in my presence. I don't know why. My enemy would run her hand down her silent lover's back; or she'd rub her thigh and say, 'You rewired this whole house, didn't you, you clever thing?' But when she was touching her, she was looking at me and it was a queer feeling I found in myself. A sort of flipping over inside. Like a fish.

I don't know what made me do it. It is not something I would imagine I would ever do. But then certain types of people cause you to surprise yourself. It is something about them and something about you, the side of you that you were not fully aware of till they revealed it to you. If my enemy were not so obsessed with screen life versus real life, things would have certainly turned out differently. Well, I suspect they would have. Then again, when jealousy is involved, there is no telling the depths, the sinking. No telling, none. I can see that now. It is not regret that has allowed me to see or even guilt: it is hatred. Cool, hard hatred can afford honesty, generosity. I don't need to misread the truth. I have no passion left for my enemy. She is my enemy; it is simple and it is clear.

Perhaps there is an element of sorrow. I used to love her. I used to love my enemy. Isn't that an awful thought? Doesn't it make you sway and sink, remembering, all those intimacies, compliments, revelations? All that time we shared. All those long, held, meaningful looks. All that laughing, those tight over-long hugs. I looked right into the depths of her eyes and I thought I loved her. I really did. I thought I could see her soul.

It all started on a wonderful summer's day. A glad to be alive kind of day where the sky had never seemed so generously blue, or the sun so happy. Everything was good. The trees on the streets looked lit up from the inside, holy. I even had clean clothes to match the weather. Cool blue jeans and a white T-shirt. Close-up. I looked at myself in the mirror and wondered if my enemy would fall for me. I put on dark glasses and then I pulled on a cream-coloured cap over my dark curls. I put on some lipstick. It was in the days when lipstick was frowned upon by feminists. I wasn't interested in looking beautiful for men. I wanted to look beautiful for my enemy. Of course she wasn't my enemy then, but the present has tainted the past and I can't bring myself to use her name. I can't trust myself. I might hear love in my tone of voice. I might find myself saying her name in the old way. I loved the sound of her name. Foreign and strange on my tongue. I often felt as if I was singing, just saying her name.

So there was the sun, the heat. And there was me stepping down the three steps from my front door and out into the sweltering street. Wide angle. Money in my pocket. Those were the days when no feminist would be seen with a handbag. I admit I found it quite difficult going without a handbag, but liberating too. When you carry a handbag around with you, you might as well carry your own house on your back like a tortoise. A woman's handbag is her house. The keys, the tampons, the lipstick, the fat, spilling purse, the photographs, the pen, the shopping list, the electricity bill in the side-zipped pocket. Loathsome, really. I was happy to be stepping down my three steps with a twenty-pound note in the back pocket of my Levis.

Longshot. I passed the Italian delicatessen on my street – closed with a note on the door saying, 'Gone to Sicily for six weeks,' and I felt pleased Lorenzo was getting his holiday. Last year, money was tight and he'd stayed in London all summer. And I never saw a sadder, longer, Italian face. It seemed as if his homemade special pastas and breads and pizzas tasted homesick too that summer. I passed the vegetable shop where Mrs and Mr Khambatta had just come back from Calcutta. I passed the barber's where several black men were getting their heads shaved for the summer. And all of London looked wonderful to me in all its glory and difference. It made me happy to walk down an ordinary street and see so many vivid, compelling black faces. It made me happy to have my eyes looked into and to look back and to feel part of it all, London, the summer, this day in June.

Cut to me with the flowers. I stopped at the flower shop to buy her flowers. For a moment I briefly worried whether her lover might mind. Then I thought I could buy the flowers for both of them, but she would know they were really meant for her. I bought a bunch of pink peonies whose buds were closed tight, closed terribly tight, I imagined, in a kind of sexual spasm. I pictured them bursting open in their house, with the light coming in on the light wood table and the flowers – stunning – standing at the bottom of the wooden staircase. Like a beautiful still life. She would think of me every time she passed them, how could she not? I breathed in the cool, damp sweet flower-shop smell as the floral woman wrapped my beautiful bunch of peonies. Her thick bare arms, her face red and vibrantly, viciously healthy.

Everything appeared bigger to me, more important, magnified. I was still slightly hungover from the night before. That might explain some, not all, of it. The pavement itself sank and came back as I walked upon the hot asphalt. I set off with my peonies and walked as far as the number 73 bus. I loved London buses. I joined the bus at Tottenham High Street outside Tesco. I climbed up the top so that I could see everything. Another longshot. The bus travelled down through Stamford Hill where I saw the Hasidic Jews out in their black hats and ringlets. I felt an odd protectiveness every time I saw a Hasidic Jew, as if the difference was so strong, stronger than my own. More visual, more vivid somehow than my black skin. They looked mysterious to me as if they walked through another time. I could imagine them appearing through mist or fog. I wondered if the clothes, the black hats, the ringlets, the white shirts protected, or not. Through Stamford Hill, down past Stoke Newington's tiny common, round past the fire station and on down Church Street, past the Abney Park Cemetery, where my enemy and I had had many a walk and talk, where we enjoyed spotting many a man hastily pulling up his fly behind some gravestone, and on down Albion Road onto Newington Green where there was a wonderful Turkish bakery. I stopped there and bought some baklava, some olives, some spinach and feta cheese triangle things – spanakopitas, I think they were called. It's years since I bought them. But I remember everything from this day. Perhaps something in me already knew. Perhaps you anticipate disaster before you are anywhere near it. Surely you must. Why else remember everything in such heartbreaking detail? It can't be the detail of retrospect, of hindsight, can it? Does trauma highlight every moment beforehand with a vivid startling colour, so that you can go back and say, 'And then this happened. And then this.' Like a path lit up from behind.

I cut through the back streets of Newington Green into Islington, down Canonbury Park South, Canonbury Place through to Upper Street, right down Islington Park Street, straight across Liverpool Road and into Barnsbury Square where my enemy and her lover sumptuously lived. It was a fifteen-minute walk if I walked at a pace. I did that day. Here's me walking. Cut to my feet, my black boots, walking quickly. As usual, I was anxious to see her.

I carried the flowers in the crook of my arm. I felt fairly self-conscious carrying the flowers out in the open streets of London. I thought that they forced people to imagine things about me, to ask questions: Who were the flowers for? What was the occasion? The flowers were for my enemy who I then adored. The occasion was a party my enemy was throwing for a black American filmmaker from New York. I wasn't a great one for independent arty films but my enemy assured me I was missing out. When she showed clips to me, pointing out the way the film was edited, the techniques, the effect of the music, the atmospheric soundtrack, the choice of lettering for the credits, I loved the whole experience, not because I liked the films (they were often quite dire) but because I was in love with my enemy's voice, and more than that I craved the intimate act of her attention. To sit with her side by side on the sofa while she pressed rewind, then pause, then play, was something, it really was. To watch her lovely fingers move swiftly and expertly over that remote control. To watch her move the image along, bit by tiny bit. It was so good I was convinced every film she showed me had been made by her.

The film, what was it called, *Lianna's Fish*, was to have a private screening at the house of my enemy. She had twelve Key People coming, she said. They had a small screening room in their basement, which the lover had created herself. The screening was to be at seven, but I had said I'd come early to help with the party that was to happen after the screening. So I got there around 5pm. I was then – I am not now – the sort of person who went early to help, who brought a dish and flowers, who stayed late to clear up. I was creepy; I can admit that now. Very helpful people are creepy, no doubt about it. Why the hell go to someone's house and rub and scrub and make things nice and sweat and cook and put finishing touches on the table? In mitigation, I suppose I was lonely. It was only my enemy who found me riveting and she had a lover. I flattered myself in thinking that my enemy found her lover dull, and only enjoyed her lover's rather basic touches in bed, but infinitely preferred my consummate intelligence, my sudden leaps of imagination.

So I arrived early, even earlier than they were expecting me. I let myself in with the spare key. I used this key when they were away, to water their plants and check on their conservatory. I liked sitting in there, when they were travelling, with my feet up and a cup of freshly ground coffee and a newspaper, admiring my enemy's green fingers. I liked looking in their cupboards when they were away. I liked pulling drawers open and looking in. You can tell a lot about people looking in their cupboards. It's like a sneak preview.

As soon as I opened the front door, I heard it. Laughter, if you are not involved yourself, is a terrifying sound. It came from their bedroom. I was going to shout 'Hello', but for some reason I didn't. I just crept in. Their bedroom was second to the right as you came in the front door. The hall was fairly long and narrow, like so many halls in London houses. The door to their bedroom was open. I knew they were expecting me. I mention all this in mitigation. The silent lover was dressed in a sailor suit. Her father had been a sailor man. There was a photograph of the father from Newcastle on their mantelpiece in the living room, dressed up in all his naval regalia, with badges of honour and such pinned to his breast. There were five pound notes by the bedside and my enemy was dressed in a red dress, her head back on the bed, laughing. Her dress was pulled up and the sailor's trousers were pulled down. Something was sticking out of them. That was all I saw. In a split second perhaps. There was a lot of quite aggressive movement from the taciturn lover, and a lot of silly laughter coming from my enemy who was perhaps having trouble taking the whole thing seriously. Her lover was having no such trouble; I caught the side of her face: it was dark and serious.

I don't remember the next bit properly. I know I went to the kitchen, climbing softly up the stairs. I know I started cooking, chopping like I'd been taught to chop when I worked in a restaurant; fast, keeping the sharpest of knives close to the wood board and moving along from the front to the back viciously, expertly quickly. Greek parsley shattered into tiny pieces. Quite a deep, almost a jade green. I tried not to listen. I put the radio on low, Radio 3. Their radio was permanently tuned to Radio 3.

Someone was singing some sad opera song. The voice took me away from their noise for a few moments.

They came into the kitchen with completely different expressions on their faces at 5.30. My enemy looked ashamed and soft as if she knew she had hurt me. She ruffled her hand through my hair and said, 'Oh thanks, Beverley, for getting started.' I loved it when she said my name. Although she had lived in England for most of her life, her accent had something extra, her stresses and intonations were slightly different. She stressed the last bit of my name.

Her lover picked up one of my spinach and cheese triangles and ate it in one bite. 'Nice. Did you bring these?' she said. Then she stuck her middle finger in the bowl of hummus that I'd sprinkled with paprika, and licked her finger. The gesture was really saying *Fuck you*. She stared right at me as she did it and then she said, 'All right?'

'You're cutting it a bit fine if people are arriving at 6.30,' I said.

'No sweat. Everything's under control,' the lover said looking over at my enemy with the sailor's stare on her face. 'Isn't it, sweetheart?'

I think that was it. That was the final blow. I exploded. 'What do you two think you are playing at! Do you think I'm your skivvy, come to get your party food ready while you two play at sailors? Don't look shocked. You meant me to see.' I was shaking with anger.

My enemy put her arm round me and said, 'Come here.' And I went. I followed her through to their living room where Nina Simone was singing *Oh Baltimore ain't it hard just to live*. I sat down next to her on the sofa and I laid my head on her breast. 'When is Beverley going to get a lover?' she said.

I got up, calmed for a moment by that superior closeness, by feeling her breath on my neck, her hands on my shoulder. I didn't really want more than that. That was enough. But it was clearly too much for the lover. She looked as if she would like to get me on my own in one of those narrow Islington mews one night.

As I left the room, I saw the pair of them exchange a look. I remember it because it puzzled me. What were they saying to each other: she's tougher than we think; she's crazy; we've gone too far; let's play some more? Whatever it was, they were in complete agreement. I went back into the kitchen and continued making tabbouleh the way a Lebanese friend had taught me. I chopped the parsley and the mint. I soaked the bulgur wheat. But I couldn't get the image out of my head. The lover in the sailor's suit. It all seemed obscene to me. It seemed disrespectful to her father. My enemy was too innocent for all of that. She needed a nice girl like me.

At the party that night, the Key People appeared to me like an odd cast of characters full of poise and presence and posture, talking a language I didn't understand. I fought with myself not to feel stupid, but I stayed in the corner and said very little to anybody. I sipped at a glass of wine and tried to look interesting, but nobody was drawn to me. I didn't even eat any of the food I had prepared though I noticed it was going down well. I overheard my enemy say to one of them, 'Don't mind Beverley, she's always like that. A bit shy.' And I fumed. They were mentioning names of people and films I had never heard of. I liked thrillers, *films noirs*, spaghetti westerns. I liked Bette Davis, the Godfather movies and *Calamity Jane*. I loved Julie Andrews. I loved the scene in *The Sound of Music* where Captain von Trapp tells her she can stay and she claps her hands to herself three times on the stairs. I didn't imagine anybody would want to talk about any of these people to me. I did try. I said to a woman with very dark dyed-black hair, 'Do you like *Calamity Jane* at all?' and she sort of stared at me and said, 'She's fun. Look, I have to get a refill,' and never came back. All this was out of my depth. I couldn't wait for them to go and for me to have my enemy to myself. I noticed Lover Girl was getting drunker and drunker and her Geordie accent thicker and thicker till she sounded like someone out of *When the Boat Comes In*. I could hear it like a soundtrack inside my own head. Finally they all left, in twos or threes. Nobody else offered to help clear up. The very idea! The lover was stoating about the place, unsteady on her pins. I watched her clumsy movements in slow motion. Then she passed out on the sofa. That left me and my enemy, washing plates, glasses, putting drinks away. I was standing at the sink washing the dishes when she put her arms around me from behind and turned me round. She pulled my hair towards her and kissed me, passionately.

It was like the kiss in *Double Indemnity* when they first fall for each other. It was risky. Dangerous. Then she took my hand and led me downstairs to their bed. I did not initiate anything. I swear on my mother's life I didn't. The film she made was a lie. I didn't even have a part to play when I look back on it. She wrote the script and she directed. I think it was her idea of fun.

We went to bed and she took off all my clothes. Pulled my jeans down, took off my pants, my bra, till I was completely naked lying next to her fully clothed. I went to say something and she put her finger to my lip and said, 'Sssssssh. Don't talk, my darling, don't spoil it.' Then she took off her red dress, slowly. Oh god, very slowly. She bent down and put her fingers in my mouth and moved them out and in, so so slowly. I didn't speak. I collapsed into her, I pulled her towards me. I couldn't stop myself. I had been waiting too long.

It was only when we had finished that I noticed her lover standing by the door, watching. I broke out into a cold sweat. I pulled the white sheet around my naked body. I felt so revealed. Captured in the one shot. The expression on her lover's face was not what I would have expected. She looked excited, not angry. Aroused, not agitated. It came to me in a flash that they had planned this whole thing. That the lover had pretended to fall asleep. That she'd wanted to watch. That my enemy had made a total fool out of me. She didn't love me. She didn't care about me at all. She just wanted to humiliate me.

I saw myself get up, pull on my jeans, pull on my T-shirt. I saw myself walk up the bare wooden staircase in my bare feet. I saw a close-up of my own feet on the top stair. As I turned the corner towards the kitchen, I swung around and saw the two of them standing at the bottom of the stairs. The lover had my enemy pushed up against the wall and was kissing her violently. The kitchen door opened and I walked through it. The mugs were swinging from the rail. The pans and pots were shaking from their silver hooks. The terracotta tile floor was too damn red. I picked up the small sharp vegetable knife. I saw my hand do it. It is true. My own hand. It looked to me as if for a moment there was nothing on the Formica except my hand and that knife. I remember all of this too vividly. I remember the strangeness of carrying out actions without any feelings. I remember how heavy my feet felt as I walked slowly down the stairs. One step at a time. Absurdly, I noticed the sheen on the pine staircase.

I told this in court and it is true. My enemy saw me coming downstairs with that knife in my hand. She did nothing to protect her lover. I saw her look up and see me and almost look excited. I couldn't go as far as saying she gave me an encouraging look, but she certainly didn't look horrified or terrified or any of those other words she used in court. Perhaps she wanted us to fight for her in an old-fashioned kind of a way. I found out later that she and her silent lover had set up the video secretly in the bedroom to watch later. I can't remember who told me that. Though apparently all they kept in was the kiss, that first kiss. They must have edited the rest out.

My enemy was vehement in court that nothing more had taken place between us than a kiss and that I was infatuated and unstable. It was rich coming from my enemy. Who does what she does? Who likes their lover to sleep with other people and watch it. How sick is that? Or am I just too prim and proper? I should have known I wasn't their type and they weren't mine. I was trying to be someone else by the friends I kept. I needed to get a life.

This was all an interior. Strange headache lighting. There were no external shots. There was very little dialogue. It was mostly action. It went like this: I had the knife in my hand, close up the blade was very sharp, stainless steel. It didn't stay stainless for long. My enemy had her back to the wall and was facing me. She saw me coming. Her lover had her back to me and was still messing around with my enemy, making grunts and noises and saying very rude, filthy things into my enemy's ear. I heard them quite distinctly as if they were playing inside my own head. I couldn't understand the use of the language, for so-called feminists. The lover was calling her for everything. By now I knew that she had not meant a single word of anything that she had said. I was not perceptive, sympathetic, understanding. I was naïve Beverley; a toy. I could easily imagine the laughs the two of them would have had when I left their house. The tears pouring down their cheeks.

My hand was shaking by this time. I watched it – the odd business of involuntary shaking. How demeaning it is. Impossible to believe that your own hand can do this, let you down in this way. My enemy was moaning, 'Don't stop, don't stop,' to her lover but I knew it was a message to me. I hadn't planned it, of course I hadn't. It wasn't premeditated, manipulative. It was spur of the moment. Fast as a dark horse bolting. There was nothing I could do about it. It was all impulse. It was real life. I didn't put gloves on. I didn't try and cover my tracks. I didn't pretend I hadn't been there. I didn't run away afterwards. I waited with my enemy for the ambulance and the police.

Strange how big moments are always very fast and very slow simultaneously. Looking back at them, you can see yourself doing every single thing as if in slow motion, yet in reality, in the heart of the terrible moment, everything happens too swiftly, so fast as to be out of control. I have never worked that out.

I must have rushed at her with the knife. I could not stick a knife in her back; my upbringing wouldn't allow that, too cowardly and underhand. I grabbed the lover and swung her round. 'Take this!' I said and stabbed the knife straight into her side. Then the moment rewound itself, a screaming whirr backwards and I saw myself stabbing her in her side. She grunted and moved her hand to the wounded place and then fell onto the floor. She lay on their Turkish carpet with the blood seeping out of her. It worked beautifully, it hurt her, but it was not lethal. All flesh, no organs. I got a suspended sentence for mitigating circumstances; being previously so clean, so law-abiding, helped, I think. It was quite a cause célèbre, our little trial. It attracted headlines that made it very difficult for me to bring my pint of milk in or to go to my corner shop. *Lesbian Love Triangle* and such awful headlines. Do people really *think* like that or is it just the tabloids?

I let the knife fall out of my hand and onto the floor. I felt like collapsing myself from the effort of it all, from all that love and emotion. I couldn't credit myself. I was the last person in the world to pull such a stunt.

The lover had a minor stab wound and recovered quickly. A few years later when their movie came out, *All About Beatrice,* I went along and was horrified at how they portrayed the character that was clearly myself. They had got me all wrong. They really were stupid. It infuriated me that they were still playing around with me in this way, that they underestimated my intelligence. They had me down as some geek, some weirdo, some lonely lesbian that had tried to come between them in an *All About Eve* kind of a way. In their movie, the character that is so obviously and revoltingly me tries to contrive a whole relationship out of one drunken kiss. She reads too much into things. She is pathetic, clumsy, dyslexic, lonely. The other two feel sorry for her and she takes advantage. She starts to creep in and tries to take over their lives. They kick her out after the kiss.

They would never have dreamt that I would get my revenge. It is private, my revenge. I would never show it to the public. But it is sweet. I know they have seen me once or twice hanging outside their house with my camcorder, filming them going in, filming them closing the curtains of 10 BARNSBURY SQUARE. I know they suspect it is me who rings, then hangs up. Once I heard my enemy say, 'Beverley? Bev, is that you?' She sounded really quite unnerved. Of course they could try and do me for stalking them, but I'm quite clever. I'm not the total imbecile they thought I was. And I could sue them for libel. If I was ever to make a movie, I would call it that, 10 BARNSBURY SQUARE. It would be about three women. It would attract controversy. It would not be your wishy-washy arty lesbian movie. It would be a huge and unexpected hit. I quite fancy trying my hand at it. But I've heard you need contacts for such things, to get started. You need Key People.

It astonished me that, although they changed their locks, they didn't change their secret hiding place for the spare key. There it was still under the empty flower pot. Once or twice I've risked going into their house when I was sure they were out. I've gone in and I've watered the plants. I've left the jug in an obvious place. I'm sure they know I've been. Once I took an age making their bed. I stripped it of the dirty sheets and shoved them in the laundry basket. I chose some fresh sheets from the airing cupboard. I put the bottom one on carefully, folding under the mattress as I'd been taught to do when I worked in Homerton Hospital. Smoothing out all the wrinkles. I put the duvet on, corner to corner, gave it a good shaking then whoosh onto the bed. I put on clean pillow cases and rested my head for a second on one, bending over, not trusting myself to lie down. I must have looked awkward. I have always had an awkward carriage.

I enjoy returning to my room and playing over that camcorder footage of 10 Barnsbury Square on my white bedroom wall. I have got a good sense of strange angles though I say it myself. I know what makes a good shot. The pair of them look at a loss without me. Fame seems to be boring them to tears. Sometimes I'm sure the expression that I've caught on my enemy's face is wistful. I pause and hold it for a long time. I know they know I've been. They move the plant I've moved back to its proper place.

Strange though, how that sentence of hers still rings. *When is Beverley going to find a lover?* I still haven't found one. Not yet. Before that night I had never had sex with anyone. I don't know if she knew that or not. I was always waiting for the right moment. Since that night, the right moment has never come again. Her lips were so very soft, so surprising.

FRANCES GAPPER
The Flood

FRANCES GAPPER
The Flood

I've always hated Stoke Newington, N16, a precious enclave in the London Borough of Hackney. Alternative healing, psychotherapy, gift shops, an obsession with house prices, an aspiring Notting Hill. It's the people who live there, including several of my friends or ex-friends, who I really can't stand. The people who wouldn't live anywhere else, despite the area's incredibly high levels of burglary, street crime, drug dealing and Stoke Newington Police Force, ha ha, a byword for corruption. The people whose faces divide between frozen horror and polite sympathy on learning you live in Tottenham, although in fact Tottenham is just up the road, it practically *is* Stoke Newington.

I did live in Tottenham, a quiet place apart from the riots and unpretentious, until 1988, when I became a house-price refugee. Unnerved by the Nigel Lawson effect – though being partnerless, his deadline for the abolition of double tax relief on mortgages didn't even apply to me – I'd grabbed a one-bedroom conversion on Downhills Park Road, a cut-through from the A10, for a bargain price, only about twice what I might have paid the previous year or the one following. Then I got a tenant to help pay the mortgage and went to live in my friend Nina's spare room, in her Victorian house in Merde Crescent, Stoke Newington, near Abney Park Cemetery. On a temporary basis, or that was the understanding.

Trapped now in my least favourite place on earth, I became withdrawn. Nina's training to become a psychotherapist involved many workshops on Greek islands. One day a burglar entered the front room behind the overgrown privet hedge. 'Hello!' I cried, hearing the sound of breaking glass and running downstairs. His face looked honest, or at least professional, webbed with anxiety lines. 'Please go,' I said and he climbed out backwards through the window.

Nina began dropping hints about me moving on. I attacked the privet hedge with giant blunt shears. Also I helped out by opening the door to her clients. They trooped past me, looking depressed. It was 1995, my seventh year of residence. Next door's overflow pipe splashed continually onto a lower roof. The former occupant had died, a fine old woman who used to piss in her back garden in the moonlight, a true native Hackney-dweller. The house, council property, had been boarded up for two years, although temporarily squatted by young people who asked Nina for permission to run a line off her electricity supply.

I heard Nina talking in the kitchen – '... how to get rid of her... friends once, but... she's become a monster!' Surely she wasn't referring to me? I knew I should challenge her to define her terms of reference, but instead I scuttled back upstairs, like Quasimodo seeking the grateful shadows, the high solitude of his belltower. A stair creaked under my foot: the voices hushed. I should leave, but the simplest actions – packing a suitcase, walking through the front door – seemed beyond my capability. I felt like the sarcastic pencilled remarks in the margins of library books ('Trash!' 'Call this verisimilitude?').

Our friendship had certainly gone downhill. We hardly ever spoke. She was out every night, visiting her friends in diseased-sounding roads – Listria, Exmer, Ickburgh. I would hear her on the phone to her dinner-party hosts, explaining her special diet. 'No gluten darling, it swells me up. No sugar of course, or dairy. No, I don't miss them at all. I realise now that I've been poisoning myself for years. Now I feel – not just healthy, but *spiritually cleansed*. Listen, I'm quite happy with just a plate of vegetables. Lightly steamed, no butter.'

Her shrieking laughter sounded forced, hysterical. She was 55 and growing her hair. Before, graceful androgyny, a sensual tomboy, now mutton dressed as mutton. Before, six-packs of beer in the fridge, now a lonely tofu packet.

Likewise isolated I lay on my narrow bed, staring at the cobwebby ceiling. I'd decorated this room, plus other bits of the house, on first moving in. Now I wondered, what alien energy had possessed me? Lying there I felt a willingness in myself, a desire. To take something. Or someone. Yet to rape a person, I mused, would be missing the point. You wouldn't get *them*, simply by forcing entrance to their physical selves. Afterwards you'd still be alone, possessing nothing of them, knowing nothing.

Nina's bedroom – the largest and best room in the house, with three sash windows and dark polished floorboards – was off-limits to me. Standing in the shadowy upstairs corridor, I caressed the brass doorknob. It seemed to turn itself in my hand.

I prowled around the room. It smelled of Nina, it *was* her. Family money, the kind of furniture you couldn't get from Ikea or MFI, Turkish silk rugs, Venetian masks, Indian puppets.

Her diary lay on a low table by the double bed. Nina's Diary, it announced in coloured letters, pasted to the cover. Read me, see what I say.

My throat seemed to swell and constrict, as something uncoiled in my chest cavity, between my breasts. At the same time I heard a little voice, sharp as a pin. Far off, yet inside my ear. Choose now. Open the box – box it said, not book – or resist temptation. Either way, remember, you're the one in control. And this moment existed, remember.

My heart beat, eyebrows itched with sweat. Alert, alert! Intruder! – my body semaphored, as though itself being attacked, broken into. I could refrain from action, be the not-doer of this thing. But in that case, who would I be? Nothing, only my vanished former self. Not possible. Alas! – my spirit cried as it fled. And then the voice spoke again, in a different tone, enquiring sweetly why not? She never said you couldn't. Anyway, what's inside? Only words. And words can't be stolen or possessed, words aren't *things*. You're not stealing, only looking. Can't hurt to look.

It felt as though permission had been granted. So, calm now, I picked up the diary. Opened it, started reading.

'Peter Eccles. Friend of M&L. Stand-up com, does market research. Unattached. Consider? Nina Eccles. Nina Hunt-Eccles.

'Adrian Houseman. Freelance journalist, flat (council) Holloway. Hobby exploring prehist. sites. Parents 1 Jewish 1 German – personality conflicts? Unatt. Nina Houseman. Mrs Houseman.

'Mike Jones. Pine furniture shop, Islington. Recent girlf, split...'

But what about me, when would *my* name appear? I scanned through the pages. Not expecting compliments, just something, some snide remark or moan, anything. Then I happened upon a strange drawing, of a worm or snake with human features. It covered two pages. It was me. How did I know that? From the crude shading of hair upon the worm or woman's upper lip – it was true that I'd let my moustache grow, having mislaid the Immac and stopped caring. And from the bulges around its middle portion, the flabby rings of excess flesh. I hadn't realised Nina was such a good cartoonist and disliked – hated – me so much. But why a worm? The iconography was clear – lowest of the low, crawler, etc – rather unfair to worms, I felt, as well as me.

So I stood looking at the nasty evidence I'd wanted to see, I suppose, although hardly expecting such viciousness. 'Is this it?' I said aloud – my audience Nina's one-eyed teddy-bear and Cabbage Patch dolls ranged along the bedspread. Then rage. Having been so long exiled, sidelined, a ghost in this house, I'd forgotten how it felt. Blood filled my cheeks, my eyes bulged. I grabbed a pen and scrawled across the worm, 'This is really YOU, not me.' What I meant, but perhaps didn't clearly manage to say, was that Nina's cruel caricature revealed her own ugliness of spirit.

I flung the diary on the bed and stamped downstairs. How lightly I'd trod in recent years, avoiding the creaky floorboards, almost floating – how careful I'd been to spare Nina any reminder of my presence, what a pathetic, sad, non-person I'd become! Now the floorboards cried out in seeming anguish, the stairs thundered, the front door shivered its stained glass panels. I saw Nina's distorted reflection, heard her key turn in the lock. My old timid self would have slunk away, but now I stood firm to confront her.

'I've read your diary.'

'You read my –' Nina's face turned an ugly colour. A Safeway plastic carrier bag slithered from her fingers. 'You did what?'

'If you want me to apologise, I'm not going to. Now I know the truth. It's you that should be ashamed, not me.'

'Get out!'

'I'm your tenant, not a burglar or a squatter. I've got rights. You can't just chuck me out on the street.'

'Piss off!' Nina spat. 'You're a parasite on my physical and psychic resources. My supervisor agrees with me.'

'Parasite! You encourage parasites, you therapists. Can't do without them. Parasites are your life blood' – this sounded a bit confused, so I moved on quickly. 'How much do you charge, £40 an hour?'

'On the subject of money,' Nina replied disdainfully, 'twenty-five pounds a week is way below the market rent for this area. That's what I mean by exploitation.'

'You're the landlady, you set the rent. It's not my fault if you can't assert yourself.' I'd been shaking when the conversation started, but now I seemed to have pushed through some kind of fear barrier and I felt euphoric. To say what I meant or didn't mean, tell the truth or lies, to hear a voice speaking out of my mouth, unstoppable, wow!

Nina edged past me, flattening herself against the wall in an exaggerated manner, implying disgust at my weight and the amount of house space I was occupying.

'Anyway,' I called, over crashes and bangs from the kitchen as she threw things into cupboards, 'I wouldn't stay here any longer, not if you paid me.'

No reply.

My bravado fading, I started biting my nails. Then I smelled something. An unpleasant smell, like sewage or drains.

Nina emerged from the kitchen, holding a pack of tiny Yakult bottles. She looked aghast at me. 'That smell – you haven't...? You can't have. I don't believe it...'

Oh the horrible, vile imaginings of psychotherapists and houseowners. What did Nina expect and fear to see? Faeces smeared up the walls, furniture pissed on? She ran madly around the house, flinging doors open, peering inside, sniffing. Why should she attribute the as-yet-unsourced problem to me, innocent me, you might wonder? Because I'd become a monster in her fearful imagination. Just one failure to observe 'personal boundaries', as Nina might say, and now anything – anything! – could be either blamed on me or attributed to my malign influence. What would she accuse me of next, murder? I was in a terribly vulnerable position. Best be off, I told myself, before she calls the police!

Nina searched every room in the house before investigating the cellar, where of course she should have looked in the first place. 'Oh Christ! No!'

I slipped into the cellar behind her. It was halfway up the steps. A dark flood. Oily, viscous.

My first thought was, how wise I'd been to store my boxes in the attic. My next thought, serves her right, ha ha. My third...

Not a thought. An action.

I still can't blame myself, though I've searched my conscience. It happened almost without my knowing what I was doing. A push, followed by confused grappling and screams. The splash drenching me too. One little brass bolt on the cellar door – more decorative than practical.

Oh Nina, what went wrong between us? Remember when I first moved in, our long chats in the kitchen? Recipes, problems shared? Wasn't I a valuable friend to you? Through what crack or weak place did mistrust seep into our relationship? Was it my jealousy of that money you inherited, the little sniping remarks I couldn't help but make? When did I become in your eyes a bad, 'crazy' person, while you withdrew among the good, the sane, the psychotherapeutised? How did your view of me affect my behaviour, form the person I became? Did you ever stop to think about that? Or care?

Would you be surprised to hear that I still dream about you?

Last night, for instance, you drove by in a bubble car. You cruelly refused to open the door and let me in, though we were miles underwater, fathoms deep, and I had no car or breathing equipment. 'I'm drowning,' I mouthed at you through the windscreen, but you just laughed, as several turds floated past.

All anyone seems to know (among your legions of former friends, all the women you've intentionally lost touch with) is that you got married. I caught sight of him the other day, sawing at your privet hedge. Is he Mike, Adrian or Peter? Or some other pathetic opportunist?

Yes, I've been watching your house. I've made a temporary home for myself in the cemetery, underneath a stone angel with a broken-off arm pointing to heaven. Your house with all its white stone mouldings looks like an elaborately iced wedding cake, like the witch's house in Hansel and Gretel. A Thames Water van is often parked outside. Three times now they've drained the cellar. It keeps coming back, like pus in a wound.

Your neighbours are having problems too, the foul dark water seeping through their party walls, the infection spreading. Soon all Merde Crescent will collapse and be sucked under, taking other terraces down with it, leaving only rubble and broken chimney pots. Until the very name of Stoke Newington vanishes from human lips and the London street map.

CARTER
Hot

CARTER
Hot

Lennie turned the radiator off and opened the window. The radiator pipe leaked if she turned it down; she checked the plastic tray, then sat on her bed and listened to the slow dripping, waiting for the room to cool down. Her guts ached. She unbuttoned her shirt. She was going to throw up... no, she wasn't. Lennie never threw up; she knew how not to.

'Want a story, Carly?' she whispered. 'Want a Harry Potter?' Carly liked Harry Potter. Harry Potter had to live in a cupboard, even though he was a trainee wizard. Lennie had run out of all the real Harry Potter stories long ago. Now she just made them up, always starting with Harry in the cupboard, and ending up back there too.

Not that Lennie hadn't tried to get Carly out of that blessed cupboard, because she had. Her psychiatrist had said that she should – as if he thought it was Lennie's fault she was in there. For a while, Lennie did everything she could think of to tempt Carly out into daylight, but Carly just wouldn't budge. Lennie thought maybe there wasn't a Carly-outside-the-cupboard. She told the psych that, and he said, so if you let her out you'll lose her? But that wasn't right.

Lennie was sick of trying to explain it to him. He was only pretending to be interested; really he thought she was barking and the only challenge was getting her to admit it. Silly bastard.

'And how old is Carly, I wonder?' he had asked, in that smiley

189

voice they seemed to learn at med school for use with nutters. Lennie had narrowed her eyes, meeting his smarmy gaze until he looked away.

'She's not any age, is she? She's in my head.'

He'd coughed and harrumphed. 'I meant... if you have a sense, maybe, of what sort of age she seems to be?' He'd made his voice less patronising, anyway.

'Eight?' Lennie guessed. 'Or... six?'

'Uh huh.' He'd nodded. 'And I wonder, does Carly want to say anything, to me, now?' He'd used a chummy tone he maybe thought would appeal to a six-to-eight-year-old. Dream on. Carly wasn't around and the only thing Lennie wanted to say to him was 'Fuck off'. But you weren't allowed to swear at them.

They made her go to a group for a while so she could learn to relate better to others. That was where she met Marj. Marj was Unusually Gifted; she'd been studying at Cambridge before her breakdown. She'd been diagnosed with schizophrenia the same as Lennie. She liked to irritate the doctors by reading up on popular psychology and suggesting alternative theories and ideas to theirs, quoting her sources.

Lennie stopped going to the group after a couple of months; she told the psycho nurse that the problems of the other people made her feel depressed and helpless, which was true. Marj also stopped – she told Lennie she was sick of hanging out with a bunch of sad nutters who were miserable boring losers. 'If I have to listen to one more whining cow drone on about her hard life, I'm gonna top myself,' she said, and sighed. 'Why can't they just put up and shut up, huh?'

Lennie shrugged; Marj was a sociopath, so it wasn't surprising she was angry with the group. But she seemed to want to stay in touch with Lennie. She said Lennie was the only one in the group she rated; Lennie thought she might be trying to come out.

Marj said Carly could be a sub-personality. She'd read it in *Subpersonalities – The People Inside Us*. 'This guy says normal people have from four to eight of them – so maybe you should see if Carly's got any mates in there.' She sounded cheerful about it.

'Normal?' Lennie tried out the word.

'Well, you know she's there, so it's not like a *Sybil* situation, is it? Like, multiples... I mean, it's not like you just flip into her...'

Lennie hesitated. 'Psychotic delusion' had seemed to be the diagnosis of choice last time she was on the ward. She mentioned this. Marj flicked through the book.

'Here you are then, this is another guy he's quoting: "If a positive outcome seems likely, and in a low-risk case, the diagnosis of 'Mystical Experience with Psychotic Features' should be considered."'

'Like Joan of Arc or something?' Lennie frowned. 'Carly's not exactly mystical, though, is she?' One of the women on the ward had the Archangel Raphael inside her.

'She is sort of mystical, Len,' Marj said. 'I mean, you don't know where she came from or why she's there, or how to get her out of the cupboard... That's sort of mystical.' She nodded encouragingly.

'I s'pose.' Lennie agreed.

Lennie lived in a tall brick semi in south Manchester. She'd inherited it from her grandparents, and she let rooms through an estate agent, to ladies only. When the second-floor tenant moved out, Marj wanted to move in. She said she was sick of living at home with her parents, she needed her own space. Lennie didn't exactly say yes, but a few days later, Marj's mum brought her round, with a car-load of stuff. Before Lennie could say anything, Marj and her mum had the front door propped open and were puffing up and down the stairs with cardboard boxes of books and black binbags of clothes and bedding.

After her mum had left, Marj strutted round the large bed-sitting room looking pleased with herself. 'Fucking ace!' She grinned at Lennie, and started to unpack.

Marj liked to cook, and on her second night she asked Lennie to eat with her. She was veggie, and used ingredients that seemed exotic to Lennie, like chilli peppers and aubergines and okra. 'Ladies' fingers, Len,' she said, putting a pile of okra in front of Lennie, with a chopping board and a sharp knife. 'Just top and tail 'em, see?' She whacked the blade down at each end of the green, digit-shaped veg, and threw the stump in a pan. Lennie did the rest, slowly. Afterwards she found herself stretching out her fingers uncomfortably, twisting her wrists so her spread hands flicked palms upwards then downwards. She caught Marj's eye and hid her hands under the table.

After they ate the curry Marj rolled a joint. Lennie hung her jacket on the back of her chair, and fanned her face with her hands. She felt sweat running down her back, making patches on her shirt; Carly was getting restless. She drank some more water. Marj didn't seem to notice; she took a drag on the spliff, then passed it to Lennie companionably.

Later, Lennie went downstairs to the dark, wood-panelled hall, and hovered near the cellar door. The central heating control was in the cellar. But she couldn't bring herself to push the cellar door open – she ended up shuffling back upstairs, with sweat dribbling down her spine, feeling stupid and angry, as usual. She'd asked Marj to do it, but Marj said it wasn't all that warm, not in her room, anyway.

Lennie preferred not to leave the house, even to shop. One time she went a few days with no food at all, just drinking ancient green tea and cold water. She only did that once, because Carly didn't like it. As Lennie got weaker, Carly had got more demanding, wanting constant attention, stories and comforting. Soon Carly was frantic, and Lennie could barely cope with her as she staggered round Safeway, coming back with half what she'd normally have carried, so she had to go again soon after that.

Marj said she'd shop for Lennie; she said her mum was picking her up in the car, and they might as well get Lennie's stuff too.

After they'd gone, Lennie went for a look at Marj's room. She could be out in no time if she heard the front door. Marj had a lot of nice things: a computer, an expensive stereo, stacks of CDs; fluffy blue rugs on the floor and velvety purple throws on the sofa and chair; thick green and gold curtains that matched her duvet cover and pillow slips; turquoise cushions on the bed. A long line of ebony elephants walked along the mantelpiece, and a row of brightly painted Russian dolls in descending sizes stood on a shelf.

A book on abnormal psychology lay open on the table. Marj had been reading up on schizophrenia. Yeah, but what did the books tell you? Maybe it was hereditary... maybe it would go away... maybe it was chronic. They had approximate percentages for each possible outcome, but which set were you in? Maybe it started in your dysfunctional family...

Lennie knew it was a problem that she'd been brought up by grandparents instead of parents. Her mother and father had taken off to India in 1970, searching for enlightenment, apparently. Lennie could remember them hazily – she would have been about four when they left. Her mother was 'sensitive', Grandma used to say... like an excuse. Lennie never saw them again. They sent letters and postcards for a year or so. Then they were just gone... Lost, somewhere in India. Never heard of again.

She heard the front door, and scuttled out onto the landing and into the bathroom, but it was only Maya. Maya lived in the attic. Lennie hardly ever saw her, but the last tenant had said she clattered around and played her music too loud. Lennie thought she was pretty, but probably straight – it was hard to tell, as there'd never been any sign of either girlfriends or boyfriends.

The front door rattled again. This time it was the shoppers, hefting many carrier bags which they dropped in the hall. Lennie locked the bathroom door, so she wouldn't have to talk to Marj's mum. The room smelt of pine and lavender. Maya had filled a shelf with soaps and shampoos, bottles of bubble-bath and stuff for scrubbing and gunk for after you got out of the bath, and two translucent blue brushes with black bristles, a small one for your nails and a long one for your back. Lennie had sampled it all, though she hadn't used the brushes – she thought they were unhygienic, like washing-up brushes or toilet brushes. Normally she threw them away if she saw them anywhere, but she made a special effort to ignore these, for Maya's sake.

Lennie emerged when she heard the front door shut on Marj's mum.

'Chinese tonight, Len!' Marj called from the hall; she'd bought a wok. 'Cold beer in the fridge,' she added. She was already slicing veg when Lennie arrived in the kitchen. She waved a sticky hand at the fridge – Lennie got a beer, and saw that Marj had written 'The textual is sexual but the psychotic is erotic' with the fridge magnets. She'd got the 'psychotic' from Lennie's Therapy set: it looked feebler than the chunky words Marj had brought with her.

'Nearly done – it's all chopping with Chinese, the cooking only takes five minutes.' Marj put the chopping board in front of Lennie with a clove of garlic and something gold and jointed that looked like a severed thumb.

'Ginger, Len. Chop it up small, then crush it.' She passed the heavy steel cook's knife to Lennie.

Lennie sat and wiped her sweaty palms on her trousers. The thick knife stuck when she cut into the ginger root – as if it had hit a bone. She had to stand up and lean on the blade before it would slice right through. She chopped the sticky gold fibres with the garlic; Marj came and leant over her, taking the knife and crushing the stuff to pulp with the flat of the blade. Lennie didn't like people getting that close – she could feel Marj's breath on the back of her neck – her body stiffened. Marj moved back to the cooker with the board, and slid the pulp into the wok. 'Jesus, it spits!' She stepped back, then reached in to stir briskly.

The doorbell rang as they finished eating. Lennie peered into the shadowy hall. Normally she preferred not to answer the door but she could see it was the psycho nurse. Sometimes they popped round to make sure she wasn't living in squalor. Lennie tapped her fingers on the doorframe nervously. Better get it over with, or she'd only come back.

It took almost twenty minutes to get rid of the nurse – finally Lennie shut the door behind her, then started back up the stairs. She went all the way up to the attic and rapped on the door.

Maya opened it, wearing a blue silk dressing gown. She raised her eyebrows enquiringly. Lennie looked down and found herself staring at Maya's painted toenails.

'That was the psycho nurse,' Lennie said. 'Apparently, someone – a neighbour I mean – has been complaining about noise.'

Maya folded her arms and leaned back against the doorjamb. Lennie persevered. 'They're on about loud music late at night, and crashing around – they think it's me, okay, because I'm a registered psycho already, so I just apologised and said it won't happen again.'

Maya smiled. Lennie wished she'd say something. 'I don't need any hassle from them, Maya… So can you just, you know, play the music less loud… get some headphones, maybe, yeah?'

Maya nodded. She pushed away from the doorjamb and leant on her door with her left hand, so that it opened slowly and Lennie could see into her room. 'Mary, Mother of God!' Lennie took a step forward and stared into the attic. Maya put her hand in the small of Lennie's back and lightly propelled her in, closing the door behind them.

It was like walking into another world. The air was humid, heavy with flower scents. Plants grew up from pots on the floor and hung down from shelves and sills. Ferns sweltered in corners; a tall palm tapped with green hands on the skylight. And there were a lot of, as in a very great many, cannabis plants.

'Jesus!' Lennie shook her head. 'What if I'd brought the psycho nurse up here, huh? That would've been fucking great, wouldn't it?' She peeled off her jacket and draped it over a chair. Maya put her hand on Lennie's shirt collar and smoothed it absent-mindedly. Lennie started slightly, and Maya patted her shoulder, as if Lennie was a shy woodland creature. Lennie liked it. She went on gazing round the attic.

Wall-hangings printed with women dancing; statues that reminded her of those 70s postcards of Indian temples with dancing goddesses; women holding snakes. Their faces looked out from the hothouse greenery. Lennie stared. 'It's… stunning.'

Maya touched Lennie's face gently. She moved closer; Lennie could feel her breath on her face. She felt frozen, like one of the statues. Maya's lips brushed Lennie's mouth. Lennie's frozen hands moved from her sides and closed around Maya's waist. She leaned in to the kiss – Maya tasted spicy and sweet. Half of Lennie's mind was left behind, thinking stuff about psycho nurses and neighbours and cultivating illegal drugs. Maya moved towards the wide, canopied bed. The other half of Lennie's mind, and the whole of her body, went with her.

'You don't say much, do you?'

Maya was resting on Lennie's outstretched arm. She rolled over and reached down to the floor by the bed, came back with a long tin and a lighter and lit a long spliff. She passed it to Lennie.

'Fuck!' Lennie's eyes widened after the first drag. 'Any tobacco in this?'

Maya's mouth curved in a smile. Lennie touched her lips with a finger, traced the edge of the curve. 'Maya?'

Later, Maya lit candles and made sweet tea that tasted of spices. When Lennie said she was hungry, Maya offered her sugar-glazed biscuits and cake with fruit and almonds and cinnamon at its centre.

'Cin-na-mon.' Lennie rolled the word around her tongue. The tea was called 'chai'.

Lennie touched the pale edge of a candle that smelt of honey. The flame fluttered as she gently pressed the papery wax. Pretty, Lennie thought. Pretty, isn't it, Carly?

But Carly wouldn't answer.

Marj didn't seem too pleased, either, when Lennie told *her* about Maya. She was chopping green and red chilli peppers in the kitchen. She frowned before Lennie had finished speaking, and started to pace irritably, still clutching the heavy cook's knife.

'So, you're what, *shagging* with this Maya?' She sounded amazed, and angry.

'Why shouldn't I?' Lennie asked.

'Dh-ur! No reason, except you don't like anyone standing too near you, let alone touching you.'

Lennie nodded. 'Yeah... I know... It just seems... different, somehow.' She didn't know herself why it was all right.

Marj looked like she wanted to throw up. 'So suddenly it's okay, is it? With *Maya*.' She spat the name.

Lennie stared at her helplessly. Marj paced some more. She kicked the table, turned and strode to the sink, dropped the knife with a clatter onto the stainless steel. 'Fuck off, anyway,' she muttered. Lennie went.

Maya was lying on her stomach on the bed, waving her feet about idly and humming. Lennie ran a finger down her back, and along the ribbon-straps of her silky top. Lennie laid the palm of her hand on Maya's golden skin; traced Maya's shoulder blades with her thumb. 'This is where your wings'll grow,' she murmured. 'Golden angel wings...' She imagined Maya opening the attic skylight, like Gabriel throwing open the gates of heaven.

Maya pulled Lennie down beside her. She smelt of oranges and coffee and spices. Her tongue flicked along Lennie's jawbone; she bit Lennie's earlobe lightly, and rolled herself on top of Lennie. Her hip pressed into Lennie's thigh. She unbuttoned Lennie's shirt, circled a nipple gently with her finger, then with her lips. Lennie moaned, pressed her hand into the arching hollow of Maya's back, drew her thigh up into Maya's wet cunt.

Lennie could have spent all her time in Maya's attic if she'd wanted. Maya only ever seemed to leave the room for long hot baths, though Lennie knew she must go out sometimes, to buy their diet of cakes and biscuits and exotic teas.

But Carly wasn't happy. Carly wanted stories. Carly wanted Harry Potter. Lennie had bad guts half the time, had to keep running down the narrow attic stairs to the bathroom. It wasn't very sexy. She felt as if she needed to apologise for Carly, but she hung back from even mentioning her. She was starting to fall into Maya's wordlessness.

She was starting to lose track of time. They seemed to be always in Maya's bed, smoking dope or having sex, or eating sugar biscuits dipped in chai. Lennie rarely knew what day it was and didn't care.

A couple of weeks after she first slept with Maya, Lennie found herself with Marj in the kitchen. Marj must've asked her to eat, she guessed – maybe she'd got over whatever she'd been angry about. Lennie's guts rumbled and tightened painfully – she was hungry. Carly was murmuring angrily in the background. Lennie put her head in her hands.

Marj hovered uneasily. 'You okay?'

Lennie shook her head.

'Maya dumped ya, huh?' She sat down at the table. 'So, how come?'

Lennie looked up. 'Maya hasn't dumped me. We're fine... It's just... Carly.'

'Maya hasn't dumped you? So, she's just, what, gone away for a while?'

Lennie frowned. 'She hasn't gone anywhere.'

Marj shrugged. 'Okay, whatever.' Marj sounded unconvinced. 'So... what's the problem with Carly?'

'I don't know. I don't know what her problem is. And... I'm tired of looking after her, Marj. She...' Lennie broke off, because Carly was causing such a racket, she couldn't hear herself think.

Marj grunted. 'She's skriking now, right?'

Lennie nodded. Marj got up and started rooting through the fridge. 'Okay, here's the plan: first, we eat. Then we sort out Carly.' She began chopping veg. 'I mean, how hard can it be to suss out a little kid?'

Lennie hesitated. 'It's not like I haven't tried.'

Marj made a dismissive noise through her teeth and threw veg into a pan. 'We'll see,' she said.

When they'd eaten, Marj opened up the abnormal psychology book and flicked through it for a while. 'Problem is, we don't have a clue what we're looking for,' she said after a while. Lennie nodded and saw Maya pause by the kitchen door. She smiled, and Maya walked in. 'We're, er, doing some mental-health research,' she explained.

Marj glanced up, then rolled her eyes. She blanked Maya. Lennie shrugged apologetically. Maya sat down at the table.

Marj was turning pages and muttering. She pushed the book away. 'It's not in the books,' she said with finality. 'It's in you.' She got up and started pacing. 'These books are all just diagnostic. Point is, we don't know what to diagnose because we don't know what happened.'

Lennie sighed. 'The psycho doctor's asked me all that, Marj.

Nothing... nothing happened.'

'Yeah, yeah. They all say that. "Nothing happened", "I can't remember". We got to get underneath that. Something did happen, okay? You've just blanked it out – Denial City, yeah?'

Lennie looked uncertain.

'Bet your grandpa locked you in the cupboard, huh?'

Lennie shook her head.

'Grandma?' Marj prompted hopefully.

'No way. They were fine. Sort of old, and out of touch, I s'pose. They worried about me a lot... and about my parents... never knowing what happened, I mean.'

Marj frowned. 'Enough already. Let's go down to the cupboard in the hall and see if that'll jog your memory.'

Lennie glanced at Maya, who smiled. They all trooped down to the hall.

'Just go in Len... See if you can get in touch with anything.' Marj shut the cupboard door.

Lennie felt the warm, velvety, mothball darkness round her. She sneezed twice. She slid down to a crouching position, and traced the dim, familiar pattern of the lino as her eyes adapted to the lack of light.

The door opened a crack. 'Any ideas?' Marj whispered.

Lennie paused. 'The lino's the same as in the kitchen...' She sneezed again. 'And it's dusty...'

Marj drummed her fingers on the doorframe impatiently. 'Okay, come out then,' she said.

Lennie sidled out, dusting herself off.

Marj paced round the hall. Maya sat on the stairs. Marj stopped by the cellar door. 'How about...?'

Lennie shook her head. 'There's nothing down there.'

'Oh?' Marj raised an eyebrow. 'I think that's yet to be investigated, actually.' She pushed open the door. Lennie's stomach lurched.

A sweet, musty smell wafted up. 'Fancy going down there?' Marj invited. Lennie peered into the darkness. 'No way,' she said.

Marj bristled. 'I'm not asking you, Len, I'm telling you – now get down those stairs before I really give ya something to disassociate about, all right?'

Lennie whimpered, and started reluctantly down the stairs.

'Hey, Len, how's this?' There was a click, and the cellar lit up. Marj came rattling down the stairs after her. 'Dh-ur, there's a light switch at the top, Lennie-baby!' She skipped past. Lennie sat down on a step, sweat trickling down her spine.

'Getting any vibes?' Marj called.

Lennie closed her eyes and leant against the wall.

'I'll take that as a yes.' Marj moved off to look round. 'There's a load of junk here.' She rooted around in tea chests. Lennie opened her eyes.

'Oh, gross!' Marj held up a moth-eaten fox fur.

'Grandma's,' Lennie muttered.

'Yeuch! Someone should give it a decent burial.' Marj moved on to the next tea chest. 'Men's stuff in here... Mm, dinner jacket... thirties original, I should think.'

'Grandpa's...' Lennie said.

'Yeah? So, did *you* pack it all away down here, this stuff?'

Lennie shook her head. 'Next door... they came round... I couldn't face it.'

Marj wandered back to where Lennie was huddled. 'When was the last time you were down here?'

Lennie shivered. 'Not sure.'

Marj shrugged. She climbed past Lennie up the stairs, then turned. 'Er, Len? There's, um, no handle on this side...'

Lennie spoke flatly. 'The door's on a spring – it doesn't open from this side.' Grandpa had shown her very carefully one day, so that she wouldn't ever get stuck in there. 'You have to wedge the door before you come in.'

Marj groaned. 'Hey, thanks for sharing that! Nice timing!' She scowled. 'Still, we're all right, though, because Maya'll let us out, won't she?' She sat down on the step above Lennie. 'Shall I go and call her, huh?'

Lennie stared at her hands. 'She'll be upstairs...' she muttered. 'She can't hear.'

'Yeah, yeah.' Marj prodded Lennie with her shoe. 'I've been here three weeks, Len, and I haven't seen her once...' She sighed. 'Jesus... two psychos locked in a cellar... And only your fantasy-princess Maya to let us out.' She paused. 'How's Carly, anyway?'

Lennie shrugged. 'Carly's gone,' she said.

It had all slotted back into her mind when the cellar light flicked on... The time when the central heating was being fitted; a man working off and on in the cellar; the door wedged open. She'd gone down the frightening stairs with the offerings... her mother's letter, in joined-up grown-up's writing she couldn't read, and a garland of little orange flowers on sewing thread, like the ones round her mother's neck in the photo.

Grandma had read her the letter. She'd kept it under her pillow for a whole year, but still her mother and father stayed away. At Carly's shrine, the letter said. Grandma said Carly was a brave Indian goddess. So she'd crept down the cellar stairs with her best gifts, and made a shrine in a box at the shadowy end of the cellar. For Carly, the goddess her mother was standing next to in the photo, so Carly would let them come home.

Lennie stood up, and went to the dim furthest wall of the cellar. The little shrine was still there. The faded blue airmail letter lay in a dust of dry petals and thread. The black and white photo, curled at the edges, showed her mother grown magically younger than Lennie was now, smiling and tiny between two massive statues. Lennie could read the joined-up writing on the back: 'Caught between two aspects of the Goddess – Kali the Warrior and Maya, Goddess of Illusion.'

It was the man next door who let them out in the end. He heard Marj shouting and banging, and used the key he had for emergencies. When he'd gone, Lennie started up the stairs towards the attic. The door was open – it was cooler than usual. Marj followed her.

'Fuck, Len, this much dope has to be seriously illegal!'

Lennie shrugged. She sat on the bed, feeling empty and cold.

'You don't take your medications, do you?' Marj said.

She knelt down in front of Lennie, stroking her clasped hands lightly with a finger. 'Never mind... You still got me, eh? Plus an attic full of weed...' She stood up. 'Better shut that skylight before it gets too draughty in here.'

She stood on the bed and slammed the window up. Then she jumped down and made for the door. 'I'm starved, Len. Let's go see what there is to cook.'

VG LEE
The Holiday Let

VG LEE
The Holiday Let

'I don't know about those bows,' Pat said.

'They're a honeymoon couple,' I said, 'bows are romantic.' It had taken me over an hour to tie and position the three bows and I was rather proud of the effect.

'Bows are bows,' Pat said firmly, 'and frankly, Lorna, nobody these days has bows tied to their bed rails.'

Pat's new girlfriend, a squirrel-like personage called Devonia, chittered some squirrel-like remark that only Pat could translate: 'Devonia says as far as she knows nobody *ever* did.'

I gave Devonia my best steely glare. Couldn't catch her eye – she was off scrutinising the skirting boards in search of muesli-like dust. Felt urgent need to take Pat aside and say, 'You've picked a rum one there,' but no opportunity.

'What time's this lot due?' Pat asked.

I looked at my watch. 'Fifteen minutes.'

'Well, I wish you luck, hope they're better than the Toronto nuns.'

Devonia shouted something at us from over by the window and Pat nodded and said, 'You're quite right Devonia, they couldn't be worse.'

Devonia stretched out on the newly made bed and bounced her hips up and down several times, then saw how far she could stretch both arms.

'Pat, could you take Devonia home now?' I said and she did;

Devonia smirking and Pat looking aggrieved. I know they'll discuss me later: 'Lorna didn't used to be such a misery guts – it's being dumped that's done it.' They'd be right.

I smoothed the Laura Ashley duvet, adjusted one errant tulip that refused to stand shoulder to shoulder with its sisters, and made a final tour of my flat. All was in order: fresh towels in the bathroom, my Baby Belling cooker was spotless, another small posy of flowers in a jug on the kitchen table. In the sitting room I plumped up the sofa cushions for the third time and looked out of the window. Road empty apart from Mr E, my left-hand neighbour. Loved Mr E dearly, known him most of my life, but couldn't prevent uncharitable thoughts creeping in, as in: wish he would either stay in his back garden or at least develop a minor illness that keeps him indoors. As generous spirited and rabbit-loving as Mr E was, he let Duxford Road down with his open-toed shoes that hadn't been open-toed when bought several years earlier, his ancient baggy trousers and rope-tie waist, the Grateful Dead T-shirt which he'd found in the hedge the previous autumn and worn on and off ever since.

I realise, on the page, you may be picturing a man making a firm retro fashion statement – this was not the case. Sartorially, Mr E was a mess. Also he always had a splintered yard broom about his person and whiffed of rotting vegetables from his sorties in search of rotting veg to feed Alfred the Great, his giant albino rabbit, plus a dozen other flat-eared, grey-furred, twitching-nosed cronies.

Thinks: why are all my friends so unpromising? Why do they all have an affinity with animals? There was Pat and her squirrel girlfriend plus Henry the goldfish; my brother David and his wife Julie and their horses and koi carp – the latter I was supposed to be keeping an eye on while they were in America on a work exchange scheme (not always easy to keep an eye on koi carp); and of course there was my ex, Kate, who fell in love with Tina's Clumber spaniel, Poppy...

So, nobody resembling honeymoon couple Barbara and Sadie in the road as yet. Mr E saluted me with his broom and I gave him a very small smile in return as if I was sucking on a piece of lime. Found myself forced to think of Kate. This letting business had been her bright idea, to distract me from the trauma of our break-up.

'You could live in your brother's downstairs flat while he and Julie are in America and rent out yours. Millions of women would jump at the chance of a holiday in Stoke Newington – it's the lesbian capital of the western world. It will fill the gap of my leaving. You do understand?' Kate taking me by one reluctant shoulder and trying not to look pleased at the thought of leaving me at last. 'About me and Tina? And Poppy? I would die for that dog. She's made me realise a great truth about myself – I'm a canine person and canine persons need other canine persons.'

'How do you know I'm not a canine person?' I'd asked.

'Sorry, Lorna, you're definitely a feline person.'

'I've never had a cat.'

'You've never had a dog either.' She smiled as if scoring some logical point. 'I promise you, you'll meet millions of women.'

'I don't suppose I will.'

'Trust me.'

So far I'd met two women and had a telephone call from one other. On reflecting on Kate's statement, realised she hadn't specified what sort of women, i.e. intelligent, interesting etc. Sisters Louella and Marie had been the Toronto nuns. Ex-nuns, since they'd left their orders, but still liked the 'Sister' appendage. They'd insisted on sleeping on the floor and covering themselves with the rug, had opened every window because they couldn't breathe in such large rooms.

'Too much oxygen, much too much oxygen,' Louella gasped each time she saw me, as if I was responsible for the amount of oxygen getting into the house. They did leave behind a Rosicrucian bible and a note saying, 'Dear Sister Lorna, if you ever feel a need to ask God's forgiveness, we can help.'

The second couple never arrived. Or at least they got as far as the phone box on the corner of Duxford Road from where a Sally telephoned me to say that they didn't like the look of the area. They'd imagined Stoke Newington would be more of a village, it being mentioned in the Doomsday Book; they were really looking for the Garden of England...

However, I privately had high hopes for my honeymoon couple, Barbara and Sadie from just outside Harrogate. I'd had a long and informative handwritten letter from Barbara: 'Sadie and I are looking forward to our holiday in Stoke Newington. This will be a kind of honeymoon for the two of us as we've never been able to get away together before. We can't wait for the chance to walk down your High Street hand in hand and know that we're amongst friends...' and much more. I felt I knew Barbara rather well, had a physical picture of her in my mind: an attractive dark-haired woman of middle height – capable, a baker of bread, a reader of train timetables. I nodded approvingly at my own reflection in the hall mirror – dark hair, middle height, baker of bread and reader of train timetables – attractive, capable Lorna Tree. I would ensure that Barbara and Sadie walked hand in hand unmolested along the High Street even if I had to march along beside them and see off any trouble.

Downstairs, the doorbell rang. I felt a twinge in the heart area. Wished Kate were with me. Don't think of Kate, she doesn't think of you. I opened the front door. 'Welcome,' I said.

Barbara and Sadie were not as I expected. In fact there was no Sadie, only a Barbara. Now in case you're thinking, 'Oh yes, it's one of those predictable stories: Kate leaves Lorna, Sadie's done the same to boring capable Barbara; Barbara and Lorna discover a mutual taste in fine Irish linen tea towels and fall in love' – well, you'd be wrong, although I do personally appreciate a fine Irish linen tea towel.

Barbara was very tall and pale with longish black hair and heavy-framed spectacles. Standing on my front step she seemed somehow to block out the daylight. My smile and fulsome 'Welcome' hit her about chest level. I adjusted my head upwards and said, 'Do come in.' Refrained from saying, 'Mind your head on the lintel/ lampshade/Julie's Japanese lantern mobile,' which might have been construed as 'tallist' remarks. She ducked indoors, thus missing the lintel, but did dislodge the hall lampshade and send the Japanese lanterns flying.

'Sadie couldn't come,' she said. 'At the last minute her mother's feet started playing up. They do that from time to time.'

Didn't know what to reply as had little in the way of feet anecdotes so said, 'Feet can be very tricky.' She looked relieved and said, 'Yes, they can, can't they?'

I led the way up the stairs, fighting the dip in my spirits. Also a little unnerved, as Barbara seemed to be shadowing me as I went from room to room. Tried to get the kitchen table in between us, but no, somehow she'd nipped round behind me again and both of us were wedged between the table and Baby Belling for a moment. Had a nasty image of Lorna being suddenly pinned in a headlock: 'Okay, small fry, there's just you and me in this big empty house, no one's going to hear your screams.'

'Lovely,' she said. 'It's a lovely flat.'

I deeply regretted the bows on the headboard. I turned quickly to catch Barbara also looking at them morosely. 'Lovely,' she said, 'it's a lovely room.'

Barbara in her baggy jeans and oversized check shirt was definitely not a chiffon bow sort of person, but then as Pat said that evening on the telephone, 'Who is, Lorna? Name but one.'

My brother David and I had lived all our lives in the house in Duxford Road. It had been our grandmother's house. She brought us up, as our parents were stationed overseas. It was only after she died and left the house to us that we decided to make it into two separate flats. David married Julie. They had proper well-paid jobs; their flat, our garden, became rather grand. My flat was not grand – I aspired to be a poet and took a number of part-time jobs. At the time of my holiday-let venture, I was working three mornings a week at Green Bees Natural Fertilisers, in Spitalfields. Apart from a broken heart I was reasonably happy. (Pat, my oldest friend, said if I really had a broken heart, I wouldn't be reasonably happy. Pat is a good friend but lacking in imagination.) However, having left Barbara to make herself comfortable, I returned to the lower half of the house feeling anxious, nervous even. As night fell, I began to think there was something of the Hammer Horror vampire about Barbara, which was ridiculous. Rang Pat, who agreed I was being ridiculous. She said I had a problem with tall women that dated back to Mrs Macardle, our sadistic dinner lady at secondary school. Good old Pat to jog my memory re Mrs Macardle, who'd also had something of the Hammer Horror vampire about her. Went to bed cheered and slept soundly.

The next morning the sun shone and I set off to Green Bees, with the intention of making sure all was okay with Barbara when I returned. Got home just after two and made my way noisily up the stairs so she'd know I was approaching – nothing worse than someone banging on your door when you're in a deep meditation or having a snooze. Rapped sensitively on the door – at first silence, then the sound of nose-blowing.

I said, 'Barbara, are you all right?'

'Fine. It's all lovely,' she said, her voice muffled.

'Yes, I know it's all lovely, but are you sure you're all right? Would you like a coffee out in the garden?'

'No, really. I'm reading my book. I'm having an absolutely marvellous time.'

'Okay. If you change your mind, just knock at my door.'

I made myself coffee and took it outside; avoided looking up at what was now Barbara's bedroom window. Tried to act naturally, which meant I began to behave very unnaturally, adjusting the rib of my socks and whistling passages of Cilla Black songs. Did not want to be perceived as a Cilla Black fan, so switched to Joan Armatrading whose songs aren't easy to whistle; within minutes found myself back with Cilla. Saw Mr E mucking out the rabbits on the other side of the wire-netting fence. Had a thought regarding Barbara being a vampire, and how you can't be too careful, and decided to have a word in Mr E's ear.

'Hello Mr E,' I shouted.

'Lorna,' he said without looking up.

I sidled fencewards. 'Mr E,' I whispered loudly.

'Lorna,' he said without looking up.

'Mr E, I want a word, and the word isn't "Lorna".'

Reluctantly he lay down his shovel of rabbit detritus and gave me as much of his attention as anyone who doesn't have long floppy ears and a quivering nose gets.

'Lorna,' he said.

'Mr E,' I said, whispering again, 'I will come out onto the patio every day around 3pm. If you don't see me for several consecutive days, will you come and investigate?'

'Yes Lorna… unless it's raining.'

'No, even if it's raining, I'll be out on the patio.'

'But I won't.'

Two more days passed and still no sign of Barbara, although I could hear her moving around upstairs, running taps, flushing the toilet. Each day I went upstairs to see if she was okay and we had the same conversation through the closed door. She said she was fine and it was all lovely.

'But have you got enough to eat in there?'

'Plenty, thank you.'

I rang Pat. 'Pat, what do you think?'

'I think you're harassing the woman. Leave her alone. Perhaps she misses this Sadie. You made enough wailing and rending of clothes when Kate left.'

'I did not. After the first two days I was controlled and inscrutable.'

'You behaved disgracefully at my Easter brunch party.'

'Only *you* would insist on my coming to a brunch party the day after I'd been chucked.'

'Isn't that what you're doing now? Chivvying Barbara to come and have coffee on the patio with you, on the assumption that your company is better than her own or the errant Sadie's.'

'Well, I'd at least appreciate a visit from you and squirrel face.'

'Her name's Devonia. She looks nothing like a squirrel.'

'Hamster then.'

'We'll see you Saturday for breakfast, same as usual.'

'I may be lying dead in a pool of congealed blood by then.'

'More croissants for us in that case.'

Got the Hoover out. Let Barbara sleep or fall into reflective mood with that racket in the background. I have a love/hate relationship with the Hoover; love the attachments, hate the bulky body of the Hoover that invariably hurls itself downstairs or gets lodged behind items of immovable furniture, almost as if it's saying, 'You can pull that hose as hard as you like, Lorna Tree, but I'm not moving.' My brother said I searched out fluff for the sake of searching out fluff and yes, I had to admit to a gladdening of the heart when I spotted fluff. Acknowledging this made me feel somewhat dejected and a failure. Left Hoover and attachments lying in a heap in the hall and made another coffee. Almost wished Barbara would materialise and we could discuss dispiriting moments in our lives. Found myself mulling over the morning of Pat's brunch party only six weeks earlier; Kate had left the day before.

I'd looked dreadful – exactly like a woman recently spurned – face pale and puffy, eyes dull and watery, hair lank. Downstairs David and Julie were singing, 'We're all going to San Francisco...' at the tops of their voices – which they were, leaving good old Lorna as always to mind the house. Everyone else having fun, not that I wanted to have fun – not easy having fun on your own when you're depressed, worse still in a crowd. The last thing I wanted to do was go to Pat's, but I'd promised and, as my gran had drummed into me and David since we were children, a bloody promise is a bloody promise.

'It will do you good,' Pat had said, 'Kate wouldn't want you to mourn...'

'Kate hasn't died, Pat, she's gone off with a kennel maid. She couldn't care less if I mourn. I hope they both contract hard pad, rabies and/or dysentery.'

'That's the spirit. So you'll come.'

Kate had left loads of her stuff behind. She was a great one for buying ointments, lotions, potions, unguents which were supposed to have a miracle effect on her appearance. In the chest of drawers I found a tube marked Bronzer. On the side it said, 'A light coffee gel giving a realistic natural tan and flawless golden finish.' Just what I needed. I would march into Pat's bloody Easter brunch: 'Kate? Kate who? Oh that Kate. Thank god, she's gone at last. Personally, the relationship had far outlived its sell-by date. Champagne? Yes please, I'm celebrating my singledom.'

I ignored the blob of gel I'd squeezed out onto each wrist for the minute, it was too thick to be going anywhere fast; instead I rubbed the tint onto my face and neck. At the back of my head, flashing lights started signalling, 'Alert, warning, Mayday, Mayday. Stop now, Lorna,' as the front of my head, particularly my nose, red already from crying, became the colour of cooked lobster. The more I rubbed, the worse it looked. No way would it turn into a 'flawless golden finish'. Too late, I remembered my wrists; the immediate goo came off on a tissue, leaving behind two burgundy marks resembling stigmata – most appropriate for an Easter brunch party. Would guests think I'd done it on purpose as an ironic gesture or would they be too concerned about my deep scarlet face?

Put on jeans and light blue, long-sleeved shirt in the vague hope that the blue would counteract the red. Met David in the hall who said, 'Heavens Lorna, what's happened to your face? Julie, come and look at Lorna's face.'

'No, don't bother,' I said sharply, and slammed out of the house.

Pat's brunch was terrible. For a start, nobody was drinking alcohol.

'It's alcohol-free,' said Pat blithely, ignoring my widening eyes but still accepting my bottle of sparkling wine. 'I'll hang onto this for another occasion. Is it hot in here?'

Actually it was chilly. I sat in the only vacant chair, by the open kitchen door. Guests kept tripping over my feet and rucksack on their way in and out from smoking cigarettes in Pat's small garden. Everyone asked, 'Where's Kate?' and when I told them, they hovered uncomfortably for a minute or two before sidling away muttering, 'Must check out the blueberry muffins/blinis/bagel situation. Be right back.' They didn't come back.

'Do try and cheer up,' Pat said, 'You're having a negative effect on my guests.'

'I didn't ask to come.'

'But as you're here, at least make an effort. You're not the first woman to be dumped over a bank holiday.' She switched on a gracious smile and darted off, carrying a small dish of caviar on a large tray. 'Caviar anybody?' she trilled in a false unPatlike voice.

There were Easter eggs everywhere. Why hadn't I thought of bringing an Easter egg? Every time the fridge was opened, I wistfully pinpointed my bottle of wine squashed in between a bowl of cold pasta and a bunch of spring onions. I felt thoroughly dejected. Couldn't decide whether I was being avoided, whether I was being avoided because of Kate leaving, whether I was being avoided because nobody wanted to mention my high colouring, whether I was not being avoided at all per se but might be sending out 'avoid me' signals.

Suddenly I was prompted to shout, 'I'll die if I don't get a Scotch pancake,' and several women turned and stared at me as if I must be mad. Who in their right minds would die for lack of a Scotch pancake? Where was Pat? *There* was Pat, talking animatedly to a short squirrel-faced woman. Typical. What sort of a friend was she, not to be here at my side, being supportive? I watched her making a note in her 'page-a-day' diary, before lifting a saucepan off the stove and pouring liquid the colour of old spinach into a jug. 'That's a date,' she said to squirrel chops and made her way through the crush towards me. 'Lorna, you must have a cup of this – it's a mixture of left-over spinach and seaweed, it will bring your temperature down.'

'I don't have a temperature.'

'Oh, I think you do. You're the colour of a beetroot.'

She poured me a cup. I took it reluctantly and said, 'Pat, I wish people wouldn't keep asking me about Kate.'

'Fair enough. Don't blame you. I'd feel mortified in your position.' Pat put down the jug and picked up a spoon, rapped loudly on the table. 'Everybody, I want to make an announcement.' The room quietened. 'Regretfully, as you probably know by now, Kate has left

Lorna. Very bravely, Lorna has turned up today, and I want us all to make a special fuss of her. Show her it's Lorna we love, Kate was only ever superficially brilliant… and vivacious… admittedly fearless when I had an invasion of flying ants last summer.'

'Thank you, Pat,' I said grimly. I would have said more but suddenly I was surrounded.

'High time you and Kate made the break, so where is she this fine morning?' someone asked.

'She's gone to a barbecue with Tina, her new girlfriend.'

'God, look at your wrists, you haven't tried something foolish, have you? Pat, I think we need two plasters over here, Lorna's tried to kill herself.'

'I have not. They're… they're bruises. I caught my wrists in a… a car door.'

'Of course you did. Pat – plasters, possibly a bandage.'

As my wrists were being bandaged someone else asked, 'I bet this new woman's awful.'

'Kate doesn't think so. I do know she's a Gemini, which is the last star sign Kate should go out with, and she owns a Clumber spaniel.'

Someone else asked me what colour schemes they would have in their new home; someone else told me she'd seen Kate several times in Springfield Park with another woman and a Clumber spaniel and *had wondered*; someone else told me she knew Tina, and she realised the situation must be very difficult but Tina was an extremely witty woman with an almost uncanny rapport with dumb animals. This last someone I pushed hard, my bandages unravelling. The woman staggered back and in an attempt to avoid landing in the dish of caviar, fell instead into the profiteroles.

There was a deep uneasy silence apart from sounds of woman being helped out of profiteroles. I was sorry about these because I'd had my eye on them as a chaser to the Scotch pancakes.

'Have you gone mad?' Pat asked.

'For the time being,' I replied. I unwound the remainder of the bandage and dropped it into the jug of spinach and seaweed. Reclaimed my wine bottle from the fridge and went home.

*

I decided to take Pat's advice and leave Barbara to grieve or do whatever she was doing upstairs in my flat. I kept this up for the next two days. It had become remarkably quiet above me. There was literally not a sound. Had she gone home while I was out at Green Bees? Had she... gulp... killed herself? I decided to leave it one more day but then immediately thought, supposing she wasn't quite dead? Another day could make all the difference. I knocked and called. There was no answer. Not a sound.

Went out into the back garden and stared up at the bedroom window. The curtains were open, they'd been open since she arrived. Lorna is nothing if not inventive. I returned to the kitchen, filled a bucket with warm water, found a cloth and a bottle of Windolene – back outside, manhandled David's ladder from behind the shed and leant it against the wall. Gingerly, because I do not like heights, I climbed up the ladder, bucket in one hand, Windolene tucked under that arm, clutching the ladder with my free hand. Ladder moved slightly and some water slopped out of the bucket and onto my trainers and the rungs of the ladder. I knew I was going to die. I saw the headline in the local paper: Death House Claims Two Lives. I climbed higher. My head reached the bedroom window sill, now my chin rested on the sill and I could see in. Barbara was sitting on the edge of the bed. On the bedside table she'd positioned a mirror. She was looking at her reflection. There was something slightly different about her. I was puzzling over the difference, when she suddenly looked up and straight at me. She looked surprised. I gave her an efficient, someone's got to do these jobs, sort of smile, produced my wet cloth and briskly began to wash the window. I had spotted the difference. Barbara wasn't wearing her spectacles, her hair was tied into bunches – I recognised the ribbons from my headboard. Barbara was not dying from an overdose, in fact she looked remarkably cheerful. When I'd finished, I shouted through the glass, 'Sorry about that. All part of the service. My friend Pat and her girlfriend are coming to breakfast tomorrow morning, I wondered if you'd like to come.'

'That would be lovely,' she said, and I made my careful way down the ladder and returned it to its home behind the shed.

Saturday morning and sunshine. I set the garden chairs and table out on the patio. A few words with Alfred the Great who was munching some of Julie's dahlias through the wire netting.

'Alfred, no,' I said firmly.

Alfred continued munching.

'Alfred, look, delicious dandelion leaves. Yum, yum.'

He batted his white eyelashes at me and telepathised: 'You eat them, then.'

I meandered back to the patio to put cushions on the chairs, then into the kitchen. Dead on eleven, Pat and Devonia arrived. 'I've brought croissants,' Pat announced, dropping a greasy paper bag onto the work surface. Devonia mumbled something like, 'Tail need eating in heaven,' which translated meant, 'They'll need heating in the oven,' and off she scooted to check Julie's bird table for nuts.

'Is it me or has Devonia made up her own language?' I asked Pat.

'It's baby talk. She doesn't use it all the time. I think it's sweet.'

'I think it's weird.'

The light in the kitchen dimmed and there was Barbara, filling the kitchen doorway.

I made the introductions and Pat took Barbara outside to meet squirrel chops, leaving me to make coffee and grill the croissants. A few minutes later Pat shot back in. 'I thought you said Barbara was plain,' she hissed.

'I don't think I said "plain", I think I said there was something ominous about her, quite apart from the vampire element.'

'She has no vampire element. You are so non-empathetic. I tell you, I wouldn't mind having her for *my* lodger.'

'What about Devonia?'

'I'd swap Devonia for Barbara any day of the week.'

'Would you?'

'Barbara's all woman,' Pat said quite loudly, with a smile in her voice: what I call Least Likeable Pat, when she's confident of a sexual conquest. She strutted out into the garden and I followed with a laden tray and a towel roll tucked into my waistband.

Pat was right. This wasn't the same Barbara I'd welcomed in a week ago. She wore the same baggy jeans but with a tight-fitting scarlet T-shirt and a deep V neckline showing off a black lacy bra. She'd put on make-up, just enough to take the pallor from her complexion, to make her eyes look larger and her lips redder. Around her neck she'd tied one of the chiffon ribbons, and her thick black hair was also tied back with one. I looked meaningfully at Pat re the ribbons, but Pat wasn't looking at me, she was drooling over Barbara.

Barbara said, through a mouthful of croissant, 'I'm sorry I've been so unfriendly this week but actually I split up with Sadie just before I came away. I'm still heartbroken.'

She doesn't look heartbroken, I thought sourly. Hadn't affected her appetite. When I split up with Kate I certainly couldn't have managed three croissants, butter and jam, not that there had been anyone on hand to feed me bite-sized morsels. 'Just another tiny bit. Must keep up your strength in times of stress,' Pat was wheedling, almost sitting in Barbara's lap.

'What about Sadie's mother's feet?' I asked acidly.

'Oh, they were the reason we split up. Sadie's mother uses her feet as a weapon, and her bowels. They've ruled our lives for years.'

'That's dreadful,' Pat said, squeezing Barbara's thigh comfortingly.

I thought, 'Pat is so obvious. I despair. What a way to treat a small furry animal like Devonia.'

I looked at Devonia and smiled encouragingly, 'Another croissant, Devonia?'

From next door I could hear the 'crunch, crunch' of Alfred as he started on another of Julie's dahlias. Devonia leant across the table and touched my hand. She said, 'A lack wabbits.'

I said, 'Me too.'

JANE EATON HAMILTON
Hunger

JANE EATON HAMILTON
Hunger

I've done something wrong, I think, except I am still in bed. I scramble up to peer out the window and there she is, in her truck, smashed against the rear of my green car. There doesn't seem to be any damage. From my vantage point high above the street, things look fine. Still, I heard glass break. I open the window, but I catch my fingers so that the window rolls up and over them and the pain is enormous. She drives her truck down Pender and is gone who knows where. There are things between this woman and me and every time she leaves, those things stretch and stretch. Or they feel like smashed fingers, how the pain swells up and is bigger than a basketball or maybe this house, just for a minute, that big and encompassing. But there is no one to cry out to so I don't make a sound.

In an hour, she hasn't come back. She hasn't phoned either. I wonder whether she is going to tell me or whether the first I am to know of it is when the police stop me. I can imagine that clear as day. – Miss, a cop would say, do you realize you have no brake lights? I'd hold up my fingers to see if the bruises would impress him, how the nails are swollen and purple. Officer, I hurt myself, I'd say, but I'd get the ticket anyway, I'd have to come home to her, waving it and shaking my head. I'd say, Seventy-five bucks. That's what I'd say. I'd look from the ticket to her and tell her how much. And then I'd be as good as dead. Around and around, that woman doing circles in my brain, attached in my brain like some elastic she keeps snapping back on me.

*

One day when she came home and I wasn't expecting her, I hid behind the couch. This was in January, when the days are short and cold. Because she was trying to conserve electricity, the house was hardly heated; she didn't care, it wasn't her who was home all day.

– Stupid Bettina, she called, come out, come out. Oh little thick-as-a-brick, where have you gotten to? Where is my supper?

Peeking out as much as I dared, I saw she was in different clothes from those she'd left in that morning. But she was early. It wasn't dinnertime. It was two hours away from dinnertime.

– Here I am! I cried. Catch me if you can! I leaped out and began to run around the living room, up over the couch and coffee tables, into the kitchen and bathroom, then outside even though I was wearing threadbare slippers and there was ice and snow on the steps.

When she caught me, she kissed me. I was right beside a rhododendron bush in the side yard and for a minute it could have been May because I felt like a bloom, hot pink and florid. She kissed me until my lips were broken. I was so grateful. She lifted me light as a memory and carried me back inside the house. – How fast can you cook? she asked me, setting me down beside the stove. Make Spanish omelettes.

I walk out onto our porch, which is now a summer porch, and I look at all our potted flowers. My car is still out there, smashed, but I don't care. She has blue Adirondack chairs and I sit down. Last summer someone stole one, one chair and two footstools and a beach blanket, but the next night she woke me up at three to say the thief had brought them back. There was a note: *I'm sorry I stole your stuff.* She'd believed I'd hidden things so she could paddle me. – Bettina, she'd said, you dickens, you bad girl. Come over here now. Then when the thief returned them, everything was ruined. One slap at a time, she took my spanking back. This year, though, it's the flowers. One too many compliments from strangers passing by is how I see it, because every day there is one geranium gone,

one mallow, one lupin, and one expensive clay pot. I am the one who grows things. It is something I do for her. There are no new plants missing. I look around. She isn't motoring up the street. I take a plant, a big hanging basket full with seedy fuchsia bells, and carry it around the side of the house and under the other porch where she has old, big furniture stored. I hide it inside a cabinet.

Once, early on between us, she sat between my legs, smoking a cigarette. She was wrapped in a white towel fresh from the laundry. Her friend, the friend she'd brought home for me, was lying on my left, but my eyes didn't leave her eyes where all the instructions for my life were written.

– Kiss each other, she said behind her fog of smoke. Thick stick, soupbone, darling, kiss Kirsten while I watch.

Kirsten was a girl like I was a girl. I kissed her but I was shy and slow, I barely brushed her lips with my lips, the merest hint of kisses, kisses that were hardly kisses, insubordinate kisses, really, because it was not what my lover wanted from me. Kirsten was too stoned to know. Kirsten was a girl who would do anything. Kirsten's lips opened and closed while I thought of my lover above us and how I lived in her blue, east end house and how every night she opened my thighs and whispered love into the girl parts of me, words that etched on my tender pink skin so I was scarred, was branded, was tattooed.

– I will never leave you, I told her. Mommy, I said, I will never go.

She moved her fingers hard into me.

– Never! I cried.

She believes it is necessary for me to have a car. It is a car like a preacher would drive, a family car that is boxy and big. I use it to move out onto the streets while she is not at home, to move past the neon signs and over the viaduct. She wants me to stay in Strathcona and Chinatown; she wants me to park in front of downtown churches, seek salvation-to-go, and while God is watching, finger myself. But I cruise further to where men wear suits and soft leather shoes, where women and girls move smoothly in heels, briefcases banging at their nylons. I tell her I like the efficiency, when she asks, that I like the idea of becoming an international financier. I cruise to UBC and SFU and bring home undergraduate application forms which I spread under her hands for her touch.

– My adorable moron, she says. Do you love me, do you love me more than life itself?

    – Yes, I whisper, oh yes oh forever.

    – Don't go to school, she says.

    – Mommy, I won't, I say. I smell her lips, the yellow toxins of her cigarettes, and move underneath her, promising everything.

    – Sweetheart, she says. Darling girl. I will take care of you always.

    – Always, I breathe.

A few weeks ago, there was a knock on the door. When I answered it I found a girl who told me her name was Sue and she'd just moved in next door. The house next door is pink but otherwise exactly the same as this one.

    – Well, she said and smiled over straight teeth, I just wanted to say hello. To be neighbourly and all.

    – Hello, I managed finally.

    – Five of us just moved in, she said. We're film students. Cinematographers.

    – Students? I said, perking up.

    – At BCIT.

The British Columbia Institute of Technology: I've driven past it many times.

    – Three guys and two of us women, she said.

    – Students? I repeated.

    – Sure, she said. I just came over to say hi.

    – Hi, I said. And then I grinned wide and said, Hi, Sue.

*

Sometimes I believe she's a mirage and I am grown, and I have a husband and son. Sometimes I understand she is not my mother and that I have a mother tucked in a dark corner of my brain, a mother who hums as she does dishes, who misses me and jolts alert each time the telephone rings. This mother is everything a mother should be and she has hopes for me, hopes as real and true as a vacuum cleaner, hopes as simple as wanting to know I'm alive. She is in Winnipeg, this mother, waiting. I do not make my lover wait. I torture her with my plans to take a business degree at the university, but I never make her wait. She says she's been waiting all her life for me and now her wait is over.

– Buttercup, she says, holding me like an infant in her arms, rocking me.

I nuzzle close and lose my education. She pulls my education out of me strand by strand until I am a younger girl, a much younger, stupider girl.

– My little snail, she says, bending over me. Tell me what you want. Tell me what to do. Is it that you want a man? Am I not enough?

– I want to go back to school, I tell her.

Her hand is between my thighs. – Turn over on your stomach.

– No! I cry, clamping my legs closed.

She pulls free, falls away and lies on her back. She averts her eyes.

– I won't leave you, I say, relenting.

– School is for smart girls, Bettina, she tells me.

– I won't leave you, I repeat.

– I know about school, she says. School would only fill your brain with thoughts of dead poets. With numbers. With geography. School can't give you a thing.

She is right. I have everything here, with her. There is nothing I need. School could not give me what she's given me, what she gives me effortlessly, what she's filled me with.

But at Simon Fraser University I walk the halls carrying books from her shelves. The university walls are plain and there is a faint smell, a mixture of sweat and fear that students have left behind. This is what I want, what she doesn't understand. When clusters of students pass me, I pretend to be looking at the walls, at display cases, but really I am watching them. When they vanish, I scurry towards the bookstore. If it's closed I press my face against the glass to see the books perfectly aligned on their shelves. Sometimes I kiss the glass to make a grey imprint of my lips.

She owns this house. She tells me she has always owned it but I know there was a time when she could not have, a time before she was a woman. I also know she has lived here for twenty years or more, since before I was born, and that other girls have lived here with her. I make them up. I give them names like Pepper and Godiva and stand them, chewing their fingernails, in front of the dishwasher. Once I tried to find a spare key to my lover's office, a place off-bounds to me, so I could understand these girls and how they came here and how they left. I imagined photograph albums and diaries. I thought of mementos. I turned the house upside down and still, there was no key. But I could not stop imagining my lover bending over these girls, these Pennys and Dots. I saw her face, intent, its crow's feet and full mouth. She is mysteriously wealthy, my lover, yet she lives here, on this bad street, with girls.

One night Sue and the other film students set up their equipment in front of this house. While my lover watched TV, I stood at the window barely cracking the drapes. There were vans from which were hauled huge cameras and studio lights; there were many people, much urgent milling about. Finally Sue stood with a blackboard of sorts, clacking it. A girl rushed up the sidewalk, conferred quickly with another, lit a cigarette and rushed away. I couldn't hear the dialogue, not from indoors, but over and over the scene, which looked intense, was repeated. Over and over. This is what students are like, I thought, full of command and importance, heavy with expensive gear.

– They're shooting a movie, I said to my lover.

She made a noise from the couch. Lackadaisically she said, Bettina, bean sprout, come over here.

– They moved in next door, I said.

– Honey, she said, lifting her head, I can't tell you how many people have come and gone from that house. Come away from the window.

She blew smoke rings that flattened in the light from the TV.

I pulled myself away from the window and slumped beside her.

– You're leaving me, she said sullenly, her eyes on Morley Safer.

I'd met Sue and I'd seen students. Upstairs, under her mattress, I had university application forms filled out and ready to mail.

– After all I've done for you.

She turned to look at me, hard and grey. She stubbed out her cigarette and kissed me. She moved so her hands were covering my breasts then lowered her mouth to tongue my nipple through my shirt.

– Stupid Bettina, she murmured and nipped me.

I was certain the students outside could see her. – Oh! I said and grabbed the back of her head.

– If we only have each other, she said huskily. If we stand together, Bettina. All my life I spent looking for you, all my life. Do you love me? Oh little moron, do you love only me?

She eased my jeans from my hips. I thought of the students, the slight rain, the spotlights.

Today, without being stopped for my tail lights, I drive to Shaughnessy. There are no universities in Shaughnessy, but this is an area of town with educated people. In my preacher's car I have been to all of the good areas, to Kits, to West Vancouver, to the university endowment lands where houses cannot be bought but only leased. I recognize education in the way women and men move. I see algebra in the tilt of women's creamy necks and architecture in men's firm backs. In Shaughnessy, though, not many people are evident. But I understand this means the women and men are at work in their beautiful offices before coming home to their beautiful houses, houses bigger, some of them, than universities.

I stop for stamps.

*

On television I watch *Days of Our Lives*. I watch in spandex in case Michael Easton, the actor who plays Tanner, can see me. I wouldn't know what to do with a boy, what to do with Tanner, but I like to look my best for him weekday afternoons at three.

She sleeps with girls when she is gone from the house. She thinks I don't understand this, she thinks I don't know. But I can smell girls on her fingers; I can tell who's a junkie, who's an alcoholic. She leaves substance traces on my skin.

– Don't get cocky, she told me once. Nothing lasts forever.

I sat at the table copying out recipes she'd brought home. I said, This Alfredo sauce has cream in it.

– I could tell you to leave.

– I thought you were watching your cholesterol.

– Boom, she said. You'd be gone.

I want her. She knows I want her. I want her so badly it starts as an ache in my stomach and moves up and down me, up to the crown of my head and down to my toes. I dream she will let me go to school, that I will go to school and nothing here will change, that after years of school we'll sell this house and move to West Vancouver. She will have her money. I will have my education. I dream we'll be happy.

The first time she touched me I thought I gave birth. I thought her fingers were the head of the baby I once was and I was coming out of myself into the shimmery blue of our bedroom like innocence.

Still, I realize it's as she said, nothing lasts forever. She will grow old. Already when I pinch the skin on the rear of her hand it doesn't sink back into place. Already she's a woman with enough skin for two women.

Sometimes I think the bad streets just past her windows belong to me. Across the way, behind a low-slung group of row houses, a pink condominium grows and grows taller. When I hold my lover mornings, her night-shirted back against my breasts, her smell salty, the big machines start up growling. My lover swears and pulls a pillow over her head, but I am not angry. This condominium, which will block our sunset, will be expensive enough to bring educated people to the neighbourhood. All day I watch from our windows, watch the despairing women and scruffy men who live along our street carrying sacks of groceries, weighted down, and they are mine, as if born of me, as if walking not on the broken sidewalk but inside her house and my body. They are sad or violent. They steal plants as if my nasturtiums will give them what they do not have.

Where we live, there are rats. Though laundry is my responsibility, I am scared to descend into the basement where I hear, and sometimes see, rats skitter along the ceiling pipes. In another house, in another life, in the life my lover took me from, a cat killed rats and I had to lift their warm, inert bodies in paper towels and carry them to the incinerator. I saw their teeth. But laundry is my responsibility, so after my television show I creep down to the basement, a place of darkness and webs. I feel scared she'll arrive home and catch me, I don't know why. I have the hamper in my shaking hands. On top of the pile, her soiled underwear is vibrating. I put the basket down and start to separate whites and colours. I put her panties in the washing machine. I put towels and sheets in the washing machine. I do not see a rat. There are droppings near the dryer but, for today, no rats.

In her fridge are mushrooms, a bag of swollen caps as fresh as I could want. I know she intends me to make a meatless spaghetti sauce, but I decide on mushroom burgers. Sometimes I am reckless with menus; sometimes curious dishes dance behind my eyes and it is all I can do to rid myself of Green Turtle Soup, so vivid does it become. I pull hamburger buns from the freezer. They are plump and covered in sesame seeds. I set them to thaw. While I chop mushrooms and celery I think of education. Education is a drug in my brain, looping through it, startling my synapses.

At seven, I have everything ready. The burgers are in the frying pan ready to cook. The condiments are in the center of the set table. I've even been downstairs; the laundry is dried and folded and put away.

But my lover doesn't come home until a few minutes before midnight and when she arrives she brings a boy, a man, inside with her. She introduces him as Pete.

– It's time, she whispers to me. High time. She slips her arms around me. Take off your clothes, she says.

The boy, the man, is pretty, a young blonde boy with long hair.

– Bettina, sugar, light some candles. Fill the bathtub.

Her voice is hoarse.

After it is over, when we have done it, when my lover and Pete are sprawled on the bedsheets sleeping, I pull free. My body aches. I have done things I never believed I would do and I have watched my lover do these same things. I dress and stand looking at them. The room is steamy. Luckily the application form is at the end of the bed; carefully I slide my hand between the mattresses and pull it free. They don't stir. I take stamps from my jean pocket and adhere them.

I don't clean myself. I know I am messy but I don't use the bathroom, just dress and leave the house with my car keys.

I use the mailbox at Postal Station K, the closest to her house. I am still not stopped by police – I don't know if I have brake lights or not – and when I come home I retrieve the fuchsia, none the worse for wear, from the cabinet.

As I carry it onto the porch she says, I noticed that was missing.

I jump. She is sitting in a corner on one of her blue chairs, her legs curled under her, smoking.

– Bettina, she says, staring right at me. You clod. I know what you've done.

– Is Pete upstairs?

– Don't think you fool me.

– I love you.

For a minute we're both quiet. Then softly she says, I hit your car this morning, you know. My brakes must be going.

Standing on tiptoe I hook the plant on a nail where it sways wildly for a second.

– Nothing matters, she says. She lights a cigarette from the butt of the one she's smoking.

– Some things matter, I say. We matter.

– I tried everything.

– I didn't want Pete, I say, or Kirsten. I wanted you.

– Kiss me, she says.

– I'm not leaving you, I say, it's just school. Maybe they won't even take me. I go across and sit on her lap as I have sat on her lap for months. Her hand smooths the hair from my temples so gently and sweetly I almost cry.

– Bettina, she says. Little puppy, little pussy.

She surrounds me like a bubble; each of my breaths is the stale air from her mouth. She is everything to me. She is my lungs, my heart, every bone in my body.

– Aren't you hungry? I whisper at last. Aren't you starved?

ROBYN VINTEN
How to Grow a New Heart

ROBYN VINTEN
How to Grow a New Heart

I'm growing a new heart. The old one is gone. Ripped out by its roots, torn from its safe little cage and trampled under the size seven Doc Marten of a lying ex. You can probably tell I am without my heart, there are a few tell-tale signs. The red-rimmed eyes; the clenched jaw; the pale face; the sudden leaving of rooms, pubs, clubs for no apparent reason.

Now, for the sake of truth and though not so good a narrative I should probably admit that it may not have been she who tore my heart out, though they are certainly her boot prints all over it. I may have done the tearing myself, in one of my fits of grief/disbelief/rage/despair that went on for months after dark and in the privacy of my own bedroom. Bleeding my misery into her dressing gown. Sitting up watching TV because lying down hurt too much and the TV almost, though never quite, drowned out the slug trails of questions that swirled around and around inside my head. Anyway, it was after one particularly self-pitying night that I woke to find my heart gone, lying on the floor bent and twisted. I put it into a black bin-liner along with the grief-soaked dressing gown and all the other bitter reminders and thoughtlessly given presents, and dumped them bursting from the bag onto her doorstep.

I know that hearts will mend by themselves, given enough time and tears. But this one hurt too much. It held too much pain, had grown too twisted. Even if it had healed it would have been distorted, out of shape. Every other thing it touched would be tainted by its scars. I didn't want that, I didn't need or deserve that. I would rather be without it than have to live with that.

No matter who tore out the heart, it was gone and I was pleased, for a while anyway. The pain that pulsated from it had filled my whole body, weighed me down, pulling every other organ in my body out of synch. The spleen was not absorbing bile, the liver was not neutralising toxic waste, the lungs were unable to take in oxygen.

Now, the relief of having it gone was enormous. I was light, I could laugh again, I could taunt and tease and be as cruel as I liked and feel nothing at all. I could be in the sunshine again, mix with friends, be an almost acceptable dinner-party guest again, except that I was single and that made them nervous/scared/suspicious.

People seemed glad to have me back, thought me recovered, and so did I. I played their games, knew the rules, said the right things, though possibly not in the right way or the right order, but they were so polite/relieved/embarrassed/pleased with themselves for inviting me (a still grieving, recent dumpee) to their parties that they pretended not to notice.

Without a heart everything looked different, things looked both less and more real. The rules became more important than the game, the winning more important than the playing and the whole thing empty, meaningless and boring. Couples whom I knew when part of a couple myself and who had seemed harmless enough, fun even, became tedious. Startled by my suddenly single status, they looked at me oddly. If I still had a heart I would think it was pity, without a heart I knew it was terror.

I could cut through an evening with x-ray vision and see exactly what others were thinking. It was as if my heart had put a veil between me and the world. And when my heart was torn out, the veil was ripped away and my vision cleared. Colours and meanings became bright, feelings and intuitions sharp like a knife, a knife that cut me and made me savage.

This is not the first new heart I have tried to grow. There was the time early on, thinking it was safe, thinking that she who had ripped out the original, or caused me to do it, could do no more damage to me. Thinking even that she might be about to apologise, or to acknowledge that her behaviour had been less than ideal. Thinking that although I did not want her back, maybe we could be friends if only she would admit to the lying and the half truths. Thinking she was on the verge of this after she initiated communication with enquiries about the cat's health and my own, wanting to know if I was okay, and if not, was there anything she could do to make me feel better?

I suggested an apology might be nice. I did not think it was too much to ask; but apparently it was, because she did not respond and has not spoken to me since.

A small heart had already sprung up of its own accord, without any help from me. Self-sown, a stray seed blown there from I don't know where. A little miracle that I had not really noticed until it was too late. I had felt a little something in my still raw rib cage and thought that I would let nature take her course, that I was ready, it was ready, she was ready. That tiny heart, just two small leaves and some tender roots as fine as silken threads, had beaten with hope at first, had started the blood flowing to parts that had been without for some time. It started to work and then stopped dead. Untended, too tender, too, too soon.

So that was a lesson, a hard one but one learnt all too well. It led to more hours in bed, more tears, more late-night TV. More sitting up because lying down was too painful, but at least I didn't have a heart to worry about. It was a thing too pathetic to put out on the compost, not enough nutrients left even for the worms. I could have pressed it flat and framed it, hung it on the wall as a reminder, but it was an ugly thing and I didn't need to see it to be reminded of the risk of too much too soon.

I bided my time then, more savage than before, doubly heartless. Played a little; their games, my rules. I was gay and witty, loud as a hollow vessel is wont to be. I wore bright clothes, I sparkled and shone as cold as a hoar frost. I drank and smoked and didn't feel a thing, stayed sober and dry in public; still and tearless in private. I joked about the break-up, made her look bad but myself look worse. I imagined running razor blades across her corneas, wanting to inflict as much pain on her as she had done on me, knowing that physical pain was the only way to hurt her. If she had a heart it was too well protected or maybe too atrophied for me to hurt her there.

I didn't imagine for a moment that her heart had been torn out; she would never have let that happen, never been that weak. I pictured it surrounded by a hedge of thorns like Sleeping Beauty's castle. A hedge made of loathing but mostly fear. The fear that any sign of possessing a heart would turn her into her mother. (Not such a bad thing, I would have thought, but then *I* wasn't brought up by her.)

I never spoke of hearts in those empty, bright days, just of truth and lies and the dangers of believing anything. The danger of too much therapy, or worse, believing the psychobabble of the therapists and self-help books she had never read but knew by heart anyway. (Not by *heart* of course, for her heart knew nothing, but you know what I mean.)

Meanwhile my first heart lay I don't know where. Still on her doorstep, or lying about her flat in its black bag perhaps (she was never one for tidying up), or maybe thrown out with the rubbish. And my second not-even-heartling had withered to nothing. I did my interpretation of a perfect winter's day, hard and smooth, polished to a razor's finish. Keeping everyone at arm's length for fear that if they touched me I would take their skin off. Disappointed and hurt that no one tried to get close, not noticing those who did – and a few tried. One sneaked up so quietly that she found a way over the cold, marble walls of my defences, past the outer barbed-wire fence, through the wrought iron gates, over the glass drawbridge. (Are you still with me or are my fairy-tale fortresses too mixed?) She risked the broken glass of my desire, stirred only by hers – for without a heart I had no desire of my own. I cut her and she bled and though I was sorry, I couldn't mind very much, not without a heart.

*

You don't really need to know all this, or *want* to know it even. It is all so much fluff; everyone has had their heart broken at some point, many of you will even have had it ripped out and trampled on. I am not telling you anything you don't already know, anything you haven't felt yourselves. Anything that is even very interesting – for the details of these things are never very interesting to anyone other than the broken heartee. So I'm sorry for inflicting it on you and will now move on to what was promised in the title, before you give up on me altogether or report me to the trades description people for false advertising.

So, first you will need a seed for your new heart. A cutting will not work, nor will using a heartling started by someone else. Only from seed will you grow a new heart all of your own that you can be true to. Self-seeded hearts as you have seen are not to be relied on, they have no sense of timing nor can they be trusted to grow exactly where they are needed. You can not buy heart seeds, not at a garden centre. They do not come in neat little packets, two pounds fifteen, like tomatoes or lettuce, filed alphabetically between the geraniums and irises. They are not in pet stores with the poppy seeds nor in supermarkets among the exotic vegetables. Sex shops like Sh! do not sell them either; I looked there among the edible undies and the dolphin-shaped dildos. No signs on the wall, 'Heart seeds for the growing of new hearts to improve your sexual satisfaction and heighten your libido.'

Heart seeds are just not the kind of thing you can buy. I found one seed quite unexpectedly one morning while running in Clissold Park. The sun had just risen, the sky was clear blue, the first daffodil of the year was in flower and two magpies sat side by side and watched me jog past. A second seed came from the sighting of the ex, from finding that I felt nothing at all, and the hope that filled me with. The third floated in from the smile of a stranger, a shy smile that wanted in return so much more than I could give without a heart.

Three seeds then, tucked away in a warm, dark place. Wrapped in cotton wool and watered regularly with purified, gently heated, pH-balanced, filtered, mountain spring water. Not checked more than once a day, so the light and weight of expectation didn't spoil them. Days counted down, hours and minutes, until their first tender shoots sprouted and they could be brought into the light. I left them as long as I could bear it, I knew how susceptible they were to the elements.

Only one can be planted in the heart space, only one transplanted, but you need three to start with, from which you choose the strongest. How to choose? Don't be sentimental; the smile seed I am very attached to, but the spring heart has grown the tallest, though its leaves are a little thin, and the 'ex' seedling has deep roots. It is too early to tell which will be the best. Nature cannot be hurried, no hot-house lamps will speed it up, no super fertiliser, no genetic modification. Time is what it is and can be toyed with only at your own peril. So which seedling? Wait with patience. When the time is right you will know. It will be obvious.

And the timing of the transplant, the first delicate move from warm, damp cotton wool to specially treated seedling compost? Two pale leaves and a couple of roots. If you leave them too long in the dark, the leaves will curl at their edges and stay forever pale; move them too soon and you risk damaging them. So, gently shake them free of the wet cotton wool and move them into a single pot of the best seedling soil. Set them somewhere out of direct sunlight but bright enough. In a warm place but never over 20 degrees centigrade (70 Fahrenheit). Out of the draught, away from the fire, out of view of prying eyes and clumsy hands/feet/bottoms. Out of reach of the cats/dogs/small children. You might lose a seedling in this process; if you hold the leaves too roughly, the roots might rip as you pull them free of the cotton wool or they might not be ready yet. There is always a risk, but you must take it.

Now they are in the light, the seedlings will fill out. The leaves will swell to ventricles, the pale pink colour to red and then to scarlet. They will grow arteries, fine pale tentacles waving in the air searching for other organs to connect with. Their aortas will support and hold the heartlings clear of the soil. They will wobble about slightly, faintly pumping in preparation for when they are larger, stronger, when they are implanted in the body and at the centre of the blood supply and it will be their job to distribute life-giving fluid to the liver, spleen, lungs, brain, clitoris. If you are very clever here, if you know your heart and your anatomy well enough and can find the artery that will link the heart with the head, then pinch it out now (with your nails, sharp scissors, anything will do), near where it leaves the heart, and never mind the squealing. For it is this artery that causes all the trouble.

The heart is a much misunderstood organ. While I was without one there were many things I could not be bothered doing. The washing up, cleaning my flat, putting together the set of drawers I had bought at Ikea. I didn't have the heart for these things. Also a lot of what I did do, I did without enthusiasm, my heart wasn't in it. In me. I was without a solid centre from which I could venture out into the world feeling safe and secure. I did not get excited or nervous, there were no butterflies, no held breaths or fluttering of eyelashes. And sex: while of course it is possible without a heart, there is no blood being pumped to the clitoris, it can be fun but rarely moving. Life was calm, on an even keel, hollow and meaningless. It was barely worth living.

There are many who live their lives like that seemingly by choice. I have already mentioned my ex and will not bore you by repeating myself. I see them out there and in my heartless state I recognise them and they me. There is a look we give each other when we pass in the street, a meeting of eyes across a crowded room, our gazes held just too long. It is a heartless thing, you would not understand.

I wonder at their state. How they got that way. Some I feel were born like that. A heart is not a fully functioning thing at birth, no matter what the doctors say. It is little more than my seedlings are now in their pot growing slowly but steadily towards the light. (You must remember to turn them regularly so they do not grow crooked.) Babies' hearts need light and warmth to grow too. If they do not get it they become stunted and twisted, poor discoloured things too pale or dark and mottled. Unable to function as a good heart should. You can usually pick out these people, there is something dark about their eyes and eyebrows that gives them away.

Some have had their hearts torn out, as mine was, and choose not to regrow them – and who can blame them? Not for them the 'better to have loved and lost...' They would rather not have been born. That any of us choose to go through all that again is one of the great mysteries of the world. Others have just let their hearts atrophy or become grown over. These are harder to spot, but it is worth learning the signs for they are to be avoided as much as any of the above. Sometimes you can pick them by the way any joy is sucked out of the room as they enter it, or if you study their form you can see that they move from one relationship straight into another without a break. These people are to be given the bargepole treatment, preferably near a very deep river, with lead weights in their shoes. (Sorry, there I go again, mixing my metaphors.)

My seedlings are growing. Two better than the other. It is the 'Joy of Spring' one that is floundering. It was never as strong to start with. One ventricle is smaller than the other, its walls too thin, the aorta twisted and drooping. I pluck it out to give the others more room to grow. It is a heartless act, but I do it anyway. It will soon be time to move them to individual pots, put them outside for a few hours in the weak spring sunshine, out of the way of squirrels and robins. Harden them up, darken their colour, strengthen their resolve.

I have to prepare myself too. There is no use planting a seedling in a poorly prepared bed. I rake over my heart space; this is painful though I do it as gently as I can. I turn over the matter there, pick through it. Remove the debris left by the last two hearts. Some clings and will not be shaken loose. I cut through this with a blunt pair of secateurs. Some I find hard to discard, though I know a new heart will not grow with it there. This I rip out and shred before I throw it on the compost heap, lest I grow sentimental over it and try to store it somewhere where it might seep out and poison my new heartlings. I get down to the hard core, the bedrock. This is what keeps me going, the rubble of my life so far, kept together by the sticky residue of lessons learned. Without this there is nothing to build on, nothing to keep me from falling apart.

It is hard work but I am brave and ruthless, heartless even. I clear the space regardless of the pain and then dig in some hope. This can be difficult to find, not for sale at any of the usual outlets. Again I find it in unexpected places: a friend back on her feet after a worse dumping than mine; a present of a charm bracelet from another friend; a decision ball that gives unerringly good answers for whatever questions I ask it. Along with this hope, to earth it, give it weight and substance, I add good wishes and happy memories. I pack it all down, turn it over, water it well and then leave it to settle.

The two remaining heartlings are growing well in their own pots now. I move them to a sheltered place outside, let them feel some light rain. Cover them at night against any late frosts or hungry animals. I whisper to them all the things I want from them, all the joy I hope they will bring. The weight of this expectation proves too much for the 'sighting of the ex and not getting too upset about it' heartling. Or maybe the rain is really to blame, to quote the *Rocky Horror Show*. Whichever, it dies on its aorta. Curls up, loses its colour and crumples into its little pot.

So then there was one. Only one, just a lone little heartling, but a strong one. One that I hope will withstand all the world has to throw at it, withstand it and laugh in its face. I have no room for a heart that would give up at the least shower or the first sign of trouble. I would rather start the whole process over than put anything less than a steely strong, titanium flexible, solid gold heart back into the empty, echoing chamber that is now ready to receive it.

I wait longer than is perhaps necessary. I risk leaving it out at night uncovered – it survives unscathed. I leave it for a whole weekend unattended on a window-sill at the mercy of draughts, direct light and a hungry cat – it thrives. I begin to worry that I am delaying out of fear, that having grown used to the hollow sound of heartless laughter I will not be able to take a new, strong heart.

Ah self-analysis. Don't you just hate it. I fall into it rather too easily, having tried to get someone else to analyse me and watched them fail miserably and expensively. I will stop now but I realise there may be some questions you are wanting to ask me and I know what the first one will be. Why a new heart now? And I imagine you know the answer to that one already. There is someone else. Someone as different from my ex as it is possible to be while still being human (and a woman of course). Someone who wants and deserves a lover with a heart. Someone I do not want to hurt on the sharp edges of my heartlessness. Someone for whom I want to burn down the hedge of thorns, smash the marble walls of my fortress. For whom I want to rediscover desire. Someone I do not want to lose, someone too good to lose, out of the ordinary, out of this world. I am not ready but my little heartling is and so is my heart space.

I was hoping that if I left it beside my bed it would, by some moon magic, find its own way inside me. But all that has happened is that I nearly stood on it in the morning. Clearly, action will be necessary on my part. But there is no manual for this sort of thing, no *Teach Yourself New Heart Implantation*. Everything up until this point has been trial and error. I am sorry if I misled you with the title. I am making this up as I go along.

So here goes. On the kitchen floor surrounded by towels. It's dark outside and I do not have any lights on. I feel this is the sort of thing that should be done in the dark, by touch only. I have a knife out to open up the chest. The heartling has grown bigger than it should, as big as my fist. It is rosy red, translucent, waiting for my blood. Blood and guts – only I do not know if I have the guts to do it. I will need at least a six-inch incision, I will need grippers to pull the ribs apart and I will need a steady hand to lift the heartling, aorta, trailing arteries and all into its prepared place.

I would like some help, an assistant, an aide, but I know I have to do this myself. The knife is sharp, honed on the hard edges of my heartless self. Sharpened to a point. I hold it in my right hand to my breast bone; the heartling is to my left within reach. I have the idea that I can do it in one fluid motion, knife in, ribs apart, heart in, just like that. One swift movement, no pain at all, no blood, no guts. I would be brave, in my imagination, an Amazon warrior slicing her breast off, a cowgirl taking a bullet from her own leg with nothing more than a mouthful of whiskey.

So I lie on the kitchen floor with a knife and a hope and a heart ready to beat in time with another. I lie and lie and watch the clock on the cooker ticking off the minutes. Waiting for my Resolve to build, not dissolve like the hangover cure. Though this is a cure for a hangover of sorts, the hangover of ex-lover, an ex-heart or two.

I am putting it off, you can tell. I can tell. Is this new love worth the pain? What if she breaks my heart, this new, delicate, grown from seed by my own fair hand heartling? What if... I'm still procrastinating, I know it and you know it. I guess I'm waiting for you to get bored and go away, put the book down, move on to another story. Then I can get on with the transplant in peace. Go on, find something else to do, stop watching and I promise I will do it.

There, it's done. It hurt like fuck and I wasn't the least bit brave, I screamed and cried and frightened the cat. The blood wasn't as bad as I thought it might be, though the white grouting on the tiles is now a dirty pink. The heartling needed squeezing to go through the gap but it settled into its bed okay – a little crooked, but what does a lesbian need with a straight heart?

I have to wait now to see if it takes. I have to water it, make sure it gets enough light but nothing too bright. Wait for the artery roots to find their way to their designated organs. But already I can fell them growing, pushing through veins and tissue, tugging my body about. I can feel the organs coming to life, the liver, the lungs, the spleen (all that bile yet to be released). But most of all I can feel that flutter: the nervousness, the breathless excitement, the possibility and uncertainty of a new love.

JILL JAMES
Friday

JILL JAMES
Friday

My favorite thing to do in the world is to go to a boozy, palsy, horsypill party and write short stories in the bathroom while strung-out, smoked-out witch women bang on the door with their flat Scotch-and-sodas on the rocks and wail to piss. And me politely jingling 'Almost all yours!' into a magically impervious little keyhole through which I can just make out the saucy boobs packed into black dresses like slabs of pastrami no one wants to save for later. It makes me feel like those psycho seagulls do when they're flapping around a nude, bald head of pink putty and thinking, 'I'm so high, I could really make a mess. I could really make my mark this time.'

So Friday night I was down at a shindig for Juicy Goldstein's new play 'The Ninth Dildo' which had just been produced by an XXX theater no one had heard of but everyone was very excited by. I knew, tonight I'm gonna really burn, I'm gonna lay a golden egg on that crapper, and even the tiny eggplant and soybean hors d'oeuvres seemed to be twinkling blessings of eloquence and linguistic linguini-like virtuosity. Supple, twisted, naked fictions. Each passage leading someplace better. Everyone else at the party was lighting up and cursing themselves for morons, or cruising ass. I felt bored and like, when am I gonna get to the golden egg crapper to spin my Goldilocks yarns?

So first I squeeze past Vara, Sarah and Tina who are discussing their credit card debt. At a party. Because I can wedge through the cumulative archway of Tina and Sarah's hump-like hips without holding my breath, they applaud. They applaud anything that happens near them. They applaud when the waiter brings salmon bits-on-sticks. They applaud when the fluorescent overhead ceases its flashing dirty-yellow epilepsy. They applaud when Tina says she's consolidating. It's like some sort of dolphin-training, only for cocktail peanuts and white wine spritzers. Eventually I'm in line for the can. I'm feeling myself up to check for my sketchbook and my shoplifted fountain pen, the kind that takes pure peacock blue up its cylinder and doesn't spit, leak, smudge or cake.

In front of me on line is Zabar Goodman. For some reason he's facing *me* instead of the bathroom, which right off is disturbing, and then he's tottering like a tipsy beer-bellied Matryoshka doll. He's a tub. He's got girth. His eyes are like these fermenting oversized olives in heavy cream. I'm thinking he's taking little x-rays of my ribs and pubic bone while greasing up his chubby digits like leather eels. It's making me a little nauseous so I try to be interested in things hanging on a wall. Someone's got a certificate to practice acupuncture. That person is probably nonchalantly prancing around the party sticking little pins in the ears of people who are too drunk to protest. I've seen that happen before, you know. Unsolicited alternative healing. Reiki-rape. Disgusting.

Anyways, this gargoyle Zabar starts up a conversation about Israel. At a party. By now I'm thinking, 'When I get in that bathroom, I will put you in my short story. And buddy, you will not receive good representation.' Later, for no good reason his voice goes all maraschino sweet as he warbles about his website featuring the artistic portraits of seventeen (naked) cashiers he collected in the tri-state area. Finally the shit factory has a vacancy and my new acquaintance backs in, station-wagon style. 'Don't go away,' he mumbles with his hands already in his crotch.

I think that's when Jean Harlow with Dreadlocks arrived in light pink cotton and beaded flip-flops. Have you ever felt like someone suddenly socked you in the stomach so hard that time stopped, and that one moment became this eternal dangling crystal agony? A chandelier hanging dangerous in the back of your throat, all the shiny diamonds cutting up your cheek insides so you can't speak? And you think, If I am in love, why can't I get the right side of my upper lip back down over my teeth, paste on some cherry Chapstick and just behave myself? By this time I had to go to the bathroom legitimately, but Zabar was strangely silent behind the flimsy cardboard door. I could kick it in, I mused through contractions. But instead I studied the female. I could see her urban warrior butterfly tattoo and Kundalini Yoga waistline. I thought about the origin of all beautiful, angelic girls, the ones whose fathers stroked their exotic feline fur, whose mothers made sure they had clean underpanties and fresh crisp socks on their clever kitty feet. I smelled the rose-chestnut bath oil, lavender foot powder, hyacinth-and-aloe face cream. The scent of chick came wafting sweetly over pepperoni, lager and dried semen. I was getting elevated, spiraling up the scarlet bobble of invisible opera-house stairs, sniffing arias and no one guessing. And then there was the sound of Zabar washing up and bizarrely enough, gargling the theme to *Charlie Rose*. I thought, not until Antarctica has a Starbucks station will me and a woman like that get it on. (Implausible. But everyone likes Ovaltine.)

The next fifteen minutes or so is sort of a total blank. I know I began to execute my master plan, locking myself in the bathroom, launching my opening writing routine of casual raisin eating, pseudo-anime drag queen doodling, some snooping around in the cabinet for pharmaceuticals and extraneous lip-gloss. I was about to settle my ass down on the fuzzy toilet tea-cozy, but right then something extraordinary happened. Something that, well, I might have made up if I'd had the time. This girl, the one with the white halo of rasta ropes on her head, starts rattling the handle of the john. I can spot the taut mound of her nipple through the keyhole and some of her face, which is wide and smooth as inside an avocado. Then, before I can scarf my raisins, there's this other opposing eyeball, equally blue, almost pressing against mine through the little keyhole. It's blinking, like a fish pulse in underwater time. I felt my soul wince right then. I felt that I wasn't good enough to write stories any more, that I'd become negligible;

like having glimpsed the eye I couldn't retire, and failing to communicate it properly, I'd been exiled. But to a good place. A witness protection programme in the south of Spain where everyone gets a private villa, laptop and unlimited skim latte.

'Let me in!' said the voice behind the eye. 'I won't look at you. I just have to pee.' It was this voice that turned me into an oblong football and kicked me back centrifugal rotisserie style to a time when I was too young to doubt my body and its raw, agile lust. She had this kind of alchemy over me. I turned the knob and displayed myself between the radiator and the wicker hamper. I waited, inhaling like a fevered teething jaguarundi pup.

When she came in she crushed the door behind her and pressed her fingers to her lips, giggling. She had lemon-yellow polish that was chipping off like candyskin. 'Really I'm hiding,' she whispers. It echoes like the greeting from a volcanic-red pinball arcade. She's acting like we've known each other for twenty years and I don't want to squash this delicate blossoming reunion before we've even met. I look over to the fourth wall to check if I'm breaking out, but I just see her in the mirror and I see myself there too. I look okay – I'm wearing a pea-green velvet jacket and a man's white shirt with pirate's ruffles. But I wish I had a black orchid pinned somewhere on my person. I never had a prom, or a first date, or even an awkward congratulatory hug from a dad, so now I try to direct a wholesome nod of approval into the looking glass, modelled loosely after the mom from *7th Heaven* reruns.

'Do you mind if I chill out in here for a stroke?' she hums. 'Oh please!' I rap back too fast and thin. I've switched onto auto-stewardess, default to robot. I'm operating, moving freely about the cabin, offering her Kleenex, Q-tips, Altoids, tampons, baby-wipes, adjusting the cabin window, maintaining cabin oxygen levels. If they had a little oven where the towel rack was, I would have baked a batch of mini-muffins, whipped up a chocolate fondue. I was considerably wound up. No one this glamorous had ever wanted to share a urinal with me before. No one except Sharon Rosen-Beeker and she had so many metal attachments on her face a giant magnet could have skinned her alive.

I forgot to mention that during most of this I had the foresight to scribble down some notes on a paper towel for potato chips. The notes contained some of the very word clusters found in this actual article. For instance I jotted down 'Jean Harlow w/Dreadlocks' which made the cut. I also wrote 'The Adventures of Yarn Girl on Avenue A', 'buy Polaroid for butt coasters' and 'act 1 turning point – maybe she gets on the game show?' none of which really had anything to do with the party or 'Love in the Ladies' Room'.

'Who are you hiding from?' I ask. It seems like it should be me. I'm giving myself the creeps. I learned this edgy uncomfortable energy from all the park pedophiles who captured me and made me their protégé. I feel like taking a shower. I ease into the spacious bathtub and kneel there in mock piety. The tub is sort of the chaise longue of the restroom, the poor man's waterbed. With the seat down, the potty poop-throne makes a serviceable if insalubrious coffee table.

She squirms a little before following me in gingerly, peering into the porcelain to see if it will hold someone as deep as her. She tweets, 'I'm hiding from conversations concerning unemployment... any Asian spiritual progress, practices, or programs... independent feminist film...' She nuzzles soap-on-a-rope with her chin. It starts mesmerizing us, swinging back and forth between us like a gong.

'That's nice,' I concur. 'I'm hiding from pâté, the executive with the beaver coat, and anyone asking innocently after my mother. Who I'm trying to have "taken care of". It costs a fortune though. And I'm unemployed. Ooops!' I cover my mouth. I slap myself.

She pries my hands off. 'It's okay. Just don't recite a koan.'

'What kind of work do you do?' I'm just saying this to mask a growing concern with kissing and where to put my knees, which are starting to sting, starting to pop like corn. I want to dig for lost objects in her dreads, fish for little plastic gnomes, for supermarket jewelry, for crackerjack key chains.

'I'm a baker. I bake scones, muffins, twists and sourdoughs. And I make the vegan macaroons as well.'

We started making out then. I tasted yeasty bread products the whole time, but I was so happy. I decided to clutch her sleeve. I held it like a salvaged parakeet wing, an antique. I kissed her for maybe twenty minutes straight. I forgot to take any notes. My pretty pen rolled down the drain because I was sitting on it and when I wrapped my legs around the girl, it slipped out and I lost it.

Outside the lavatory laboratory they were blasting a loop of drum and bass, Prince's Greatest Hits and bootleg VU. Then it sounded like someone kept trying to play this crummy Crass cassette and getting rebuked. I quit the tub to clean my face and see if I was more beautiful.

'My name is Gail,' sang Gail. (I felt all choked up by that. She even looked like my AWOL aunt, the divorcée, a schoolteacher who everyone turned against in the early 1980s for falling out of love with my pig of a beef jerky uncle. He had a gun and a pocket full of penknives he was always trying to introduce into everyday situations. You'd have a little trouble buttoning a blouse and there he was with a switchblade muttering 'Need any help?' from behind a mustache of clammy steel wool. I remembered the pumpkin pie I forced down the day Gail left. She'd packed her suitcase in a daze while her stepchildren squatted in the corner of the garage playing Uno, straining their eyes.)

'Gail, we've got to get out of this place.' I helped her stand and stretch her graceful tendril toes. We climbed out onto the fire escape and tiptoed down like acrobats into the concrete garden. It was July. Fireflies were flirting in molten Morse code. There was bright festive garbage in a crate, overflowing with mango crescents, empty beer bottles, smashed firecracker boxes. The night was warm, and if there were rats running, you thought, Good for the vermin. Shouldn't they be in love?

And we escaped out into a New York alley with the reckless alley cats. All the buildings looked like wrapped packages, presents. There was this girl's hand in my hand. I couldn't look at her in case she had to take it back later and maybe it would be crooked, or bent and my fault. Maybe it would be pickled.

It was a good night. I'd had plans. My plans dried into sandy crumbs of unbaked cake mix dandelioning in the wind. I'd crumpled my notes in my fist, fashioning a sparse white egg to pelt at a parked limousine. I hoped someone, some sultry diva behind the opaque turquoise windows with infinite cash and a pan-sexual wardrobe would moan 'You're throwing it all away!' and try to discover me and commission a mini-series for Fox, a novella about my summers in the third world. But I'd say not now, Sophia; I can't talk, Ms Loren. I'm in the middle of actually living. Having actual emotions. Being so alive, I wanted to give back all the paper to the slaughtered, sap-drained trees in exchange for the promise that this virgin July air, resting like lilac silk on our cheeks and skin, would last forever. It was a good night.

ALI SMITH
May

ALI SMITH
May

I tell you. I fell in love with a tree. I couldn't not. It was in blossom.

It was a day like all the other days and I was on my way to work, walking the same way as usual between our house and the town. I wasn't even very far from home, just round the corner.

I was looking at the pavement as I walked and wondering whether the local council paid someone money to go walking around looking at the ground all day for places that needed mending, places where people might trip. What would a job like that be advertised as in the paper, under what title? Inspector of Pavements and Roads. Kerb Auditor. Local Walkways Erosion Consultant. I wondered what qualifications you would need to be one. On a TV quiz show the host would say, or at a party a smiling stranger would ask, and what do you do? and whoever it was would reply, actually I'm an Asphalt Observance Manager, it's very good money, takes a great deal of expertise, a job for life with excellent career prospects.

Or maybe the council didn't do this job anymore. Probably there was a privatised company who sent people out to check on the roads and then report back the findings to a relevant council committee. That was more likely. I walked along like that, I remember, noting uselessly to myself in my head all the places I would report which needed sorting, until the moment the ground ahead of me wasn't there anymore. It had disappeared. At my feet the pavement was covered with what looked like blown silk. It was petals. The petals were a beautiful white. I glanced up to see where they'd come from, and saw where they'd come from.

A woman came out of a house. She told me to get out of her garden. She asked was I on drugs. I explained I wasn't. She said she'd call the police if I wasn't gone the next time she looked out of her window, and she went back inside the house, slamming her door. I hadn't even realised I was in someone's garden, never mind that I'd been there for a long enough time for it to be alarming to anybody. I left her garden; I stood by the gate and looked at the tree from the pavement outside it instead. She called the police anyway; a woman and a man came in a patrol car. They were polite but firm. They talked about trespassing and loitering, took my name and address and gave me a warning and a lift home. They waited to see that I did have a key for our house, that I wasn't just making it up; they waited in their car until I'd unlocked the door and gone inside and shut it behind me; they sat outside the house not moving, with their engine going, for about ten minutes before I heard them rev up and drive away.

I had had no idea that staring up at a tree for more than the allotted proper amount of time could be considered wrong. When the police car stopped outside our house and I tried to get out, I couldn't – I had never been in a police car before and there are no handles on the insides of the doors in the back – you can't get out unless someone lets you out. I thought at first I wasn't able to find the handle because of what had happened to my eyes. They were full of white. All I could see was white. The thing with the woman and the police had taken place through a gauze of dazed white with everyone and everything like radio-voice ghosts, a drama happening to someone else somewhere at the back of me. Even while I was standing in the hall listening for them to drive away I still couldn't see anything except through a kind of shifting, folding, blazing white; and after they'd gone, after quite a while of sitting on the carpet feeling the surprising hugeness of the little bumps and shrugs of its material under my hands, I could only just make out, through the white, the blurs which meant the edges of the pictures on our walls, the pile of junk mail on the hall table and the black curl of the flex of the phone on the floor beside me.

I thought about phoning you. Then I thought about the tree. It was the most beautiful tree I had ever seen. It was the most beautiful thing I have ever seen. Its blossom was high summer blossom, not the cold early spring blossom of so many trees and bushes that comes in March and means more snow and cold. This was blue-sky white, heat-haze white, the white of the sheets that you bring in from the line in the garden dry after hardly any time because the air is so warm. It was the white of sun, the white that's behind all the colours there are, it was open-mouthed white on open-mouthed white, swathes of sweet-smelling outheld white lifting and falling and nodding, saying the one word yes over and over, white spilling over itself. It was a white that longed for bees, that wanted you inside it, dusted, pollen-smudged; it was all the more beautiful for being so brief, so on the point of gone, about to be nudged off by the wind and the coming leaves. It was the white before green, and the green of this tree, I knew, would be even more beautiful than the white; I knew that if I were to see it in leaf I would smell and hear nothing but green. My whole head – never mind just my eyes – all my senses, my whole self from head to foot, would fill and change with the chlorophyll of it. I was changed already. Look at me. I knew, as I sat there blinking absurdly in the hall, trying to simply look, holding my hand up in front of my eyes and watching it moving as if it belonged to someone else, that I would never again in my whole life see or feel or taste anything as beautiful as the tree I'd finally seen.

I got to my feet by leaning against the wall. I fumbled through thin air across to the stairs and reached out for the banister. I got to the top, crawled from the landing into our bedroom and made myself lie down on the bed and shut my eyes, but the white was still there, even behind the shut lids. It pulsed like a blood-beat; dimmer and lighter, lighter and dimmer. How many times had I passed that tree already in my life, just walked past it and not seen it? I must have walked down that street a thousand times, more than a thousand. How could I not have seen it? How many other things had I missed? How many other loves? It didn't matter.

Nothing else mattered any more. The buds were like the pointed hooves of a herd of tiny deer. The blossom was like – no, it was like nothing but blossom. The leaves, when they came, would be like nothing but leaves. I had never seen a tree more like a tree. It was a relief. I thought of the roots and the trunk. I thrilled to the very idea that the roots and the trunk sent water up through the branches to the buds or blossom or leaves, and then when it rained, water came back through the leaves to be distributed round the tree again. It was so clever. I breathed because of it. I blessed the bark that protected the spine and the sap of the tree. I thought of its slender grooves. I imagined the fingering of them. I thought of inside, the rings going endlessly round, one for every year of its life and all its different seasons, and I burst into tears like a teenager. I lay on my back in the bed and cried, laughing, like I was seventeen again. It was me who was like something other than myself. I should have been at work, and instead I was lying in bed, hugging a pillow, with my heart, or my soul, or my mind or my lungs or whatever it was that was making me feel like this, high and light; whatever it was had snapped its string and blown away and now there it was above me, out of my reach, caught in the branches at the top of a tree.

I fell asleep. I dreamed of trees. In my dream I had climbed to a room which was also an orchard; it was at the very top of a massive old house whose downstairs was dilapidated and peeling and whose upstairs was all trees. I had climbed the broken dangerous stairs past all the other floors and got to the door of the room; the trees in it were waiting for me, small and unmoving under the roof. When I woke up I could see a lot more clearly. I washed my face in the bathroom, straightened my clothes. I looked all right. I went down to the kitchen and rooted through the cupboard under the sink until I found your father's old binoculars in their leather case. I couldn't make it out from the bathroom window or from either of the back bedroom windows but from up in the loft through the small window, if I leaned out at an angle so the eaves weren't in the way, I could easily see the white of the crown of it shimmering between the houses. If I leaned right out I could see almost the whole of it. But it was tricky to lean out at the same time as balancing myself between the separate roof struts, so I fetched the old board we'd used under the mattress in our first bed from the back of the shed, sawed it into two pieces so I could get it through the loft hatch, then went back down to the shed, found the hammer and some nails and nailed the pieces of board back together up in the loft.

Birds visited the tree. They would fly in, settle for a moment, sometimes for as long as a minute, and they would fly off again. They came in ones and twos, a flutter of dark in the white. Or they would disappear into the blossom. Insects, which are excellent food for birds, tend to live on the trunks and the branches of trees. Ants can use trees as the ideal landscape for ant-farms, where they breed and corral and fatten up insects like aphids and use them for milk. (I found these things out later that evening on the internet.) Traffic drove unnoticing past the tree. People passed back and fore behind it. Mothers went past it to fetch children from school, brought them home from school past it the other way. People came home from work all round it. The sun moved round it in the sky. Its branches lifted and fell in the light wind. Petals spun off it and settled on a car or a lawn, or fell maddeningly out of range where I couldn't see them land. Time flew. It really did. I must have watched for hours, all afternoon, until you were suddenly home from work yourself and shouting at me for being up in the loft. I came down, went online and typed in the word *tree*. There was a lot of stuff. I came off when you called me for supper, then went back on again after supper, and came off again when you told me that if I didn't come to bed immediately so you could get some sleep then you would seriously consider leaving me.

I woke up in the middle of the night furious at that woman who thought she owned the tree. I sat straight up in the bed. I couldn't believe how angry I was. How could someone think they had ownership of something as unownable as a tree? Just because it was in her garden didn't mean it was hers. How could it be her tree? It was so clearly my tree.

I decided I would do something; I would go round now in the

Ali Smith

dark and anonymously throw stones at her house, break a window or two then run away. That would show her what she didn't own. That would serve her right. It was quarter to two on the alarm. You were asleep; you turned and mumbled something in your sleep. I got out carefully so as not to disturb you and took my clothes to the bathroom so my putting them on wouldn't wake you.

It was raining quite heavily when I went out. I scouted about in our back garden under our trees for some good-sized stones to throw. (It wasn't that our own trees were any less important than the tree I'd seen; they were nice and fine and everything; it was simply that they weren't it.) I found some smooth beach stones we'd brought back from somewhere and put them in my jacket pocket and I went out the back way so you wouldn't hear anything at the front. On my way round to the woman's house there was a skip at the side of the road; someone was putting in a driveway, digging up a front porch. There were lots of pieces of brick and half-brick in the skip and all the smashed-up thrown-away paving slab. I chose as many as I could carry. Nobody saw me. There was nobody at all on the street, on any of the streets, and only the very occasional light in a window.

When I got to the woman's house it was completely in darkness and I was soaked from the rain, and there were the petals plastered wet all over the pavement outside her garden gate. I tucked my piece of slab under my arm, soundlessly opened the gate. I could have been a perfect burglar. I crossed her lawn soundlessly and I stood under the tree.

The rain was knocking the petals off; they dropped, water-weighted and skimpy, into a circle of white on the dark of the grass round the edge of the dripping tree. The loaded branches magnified the sound; the rain was a steady hum above me through which I could hear the individual raindrops colliding with the individual flowers. I had my breath back now. I sat down on the wet grass by the roots; petals were all over my boots and when I ran my hand through my hair petals stuck to my fingers. I arranged my stones and half-bricks and my slab in a neat line, ready in case I needed them. Petals stuck to them too. I peeled a couple off. They

264

were like something after a wedding. I was shivering now, though it wasn't cold. It was humid. It was lovely. I leaned back against its trunk, felt the ridges of it press through my jacket into my back and watched the blossom shredding as the rain brought it down.

*

You sit opposite me at the table in the kitchen and tell me you've fallen in love. When I ask you to tell me about whoever it is, you look at me, reproachful.

Not with *someone*, you say.

Then you tell me you're in love with a tree.

You don't look at all well. You are pale. I think maybe you have a fever or are incubating a cold. You toy with the matting under the toaster. I pretend calm. I don't look angry or upset at all. I scan the line of old crumbs beneath the matting, still there from god knows how many of our breakfasts. I think to myself that you must be lying for a good reason because you never usually lie, it's very unlike you to. But then recently, it's true, you have been very unlike yourself. You have been defiant-looking, worried-looking and clear-faced as a child by turns; you have been sneaking out of bed and leaving the house as soon as you think I'm asleep, and you keep telling me odd facts about seed dispersal and reforestation. Last night you told me how it takes the energy of fifty leaves for a tree to make one apple, how one tree can produce millions of leaves, how there are two kinds of wood in the trunk of a tree, heartwood and sapwood, and that heartwood is where the tree packs away its waste products, and how trees in woods or groves that get less sunlight because they grow beneath other trees are called understory trees.

I fell in love with a tree. I couldn't not.

I am perfectly within my rights to be angry. Instead, I keep things smooth. There's a way to do this. I try to think of the right thing to say.

Like in the myth? I say.

It's not a myth, you say. What myth? It's really real. Believe me.

Okay, I say. I say it soothingly. I nod.

Do you believe me? you say.

I do, I say. I sound as if I mean it.

It takes a little while before I do actually believe that it's all about a tree and of course, when I do allow myself to, I'm relieved. More, I'm delighted. All these years we've been together and my only real rival in all this time doesn't even have genitals. I go around for quite a while smiling at my good luck. A tree, for goodness sake, I laugh to myself as I pay for a bag of apples in the supermarket or pull the stick out of a cherry, flick the stick away, toss the cherry in the air and catch it in my mouth, pleased with myself, hoping someone saw.

I am such an innocent. I have no idea.

This is what it takes to make me believe it. I come home from work a couple of days later and find you gouging up the laminate in the middle of the front room with a hammer and a screwdriver. The laminate cost us a fortune to put down. We both know it did. I sit on the couch. I put my head in my hands. You look up brightly. Then you see my face.

I just want to see what's underneath, you say.

Concrete, I say. Remember when we moved in and before there was a floor there was the concrete, and it was horrible, and that's why we put the flooring down?

Yes, but I wanted to know what was under the concrete, you say. I needed to check.

And how are you going to get through the concrete? I say. You'll never do it with a screwdriver.

I'm going to get a drill from Homebase, you say. We need a drill anyway.

You sit beside me on the couch and you tell me you are planning to move the tree into our house.

You can't keep a tree in a house, I say.

Yes you can, you say. I've looked into it. All you have to do is make sure that you give it enough water and that bees can pollinate it. We would need to keep some bees as well. Would that be okay?

What about light? I say. Trees need light. And what about its roots? That's why people cut trees down, because the roots of them get under the foundations of houses and are dangerous and pull them up. It's crazy to actually go out of your way to pull up the foundations of the house you're living in. No?

You scowl beside me.

And what kind of a tree is it? I ask.

Don't what kind of tree me, you say. I've told you, it's irrelevant.

I haven't actually been permitted to see this famous tree yet; you are keeping it a secret, close to your heart. I know it's situated somewhere over the back, since that's the way the loft window faces and you are spending all the daylight hours that you're home in the loft. I know it's just come into leaf and that before, when you first saw it, it was blossoming, all that stuff about it being white, I've heard it several times now, how you were going to phone me but you couldn't see anything but it, etc. Every night in bed before I pretend to go to sleep it's been you telling me more and more things about trees as if desperate to convince me; on the first night I asked you what kind it was and you went into a huff (probably, I thought to myself, because in your subterfuge, your attempt to screen your affair or whatever it is from me, you'd simply forgotten to pick a kind and I'd caught you out); because what kind it is, you said, waving your arms about in a pure show of panic, is just a random label given by people who need to categorise things, people are far too hung up on categorisation, the point about this is that it can't be categorised, it's the most beautiful tree I've ever seen, that's all I know and all I need to know, I don't need to give it a name, that's the whole point, you said, don't you see?

No, I say, sitting calm and reasonable in front of the wreckage of our room, listen, what I mean is. Some trees can be kept inside and others can't. It'd stunt them. They would die. And it sounds to me from your description and everything, though I haven't seen it myself as you know, but it does sound to me as if your tree is too big for the inside of a house already.

I know, you say. You drop the screwdriver on the undamaged bit of floor at our feet and you lean into me, miserable. I can sense triumph. You are warm under my arm. I shake my head. I keep my sad face on as if I understand.

And probably its roots are too settled now to move it without doing damage, I say.

I know, you say, defeated. I was wondering about that.

And anyway, I go on, but gently, because I know the effect it will have. The thing about your tree is, it belongs to someone else. It's not your tree to take. Is it?

Probably I shouldn't have said that, though it was worth it to find myself holding you so close later that night, a night you didn't leave me, weren't cold and wooden to me. Certainly it is one of the reasons I have to go and fetch you out of the police station the next day where you are being questioned about wilful damage to someone else's property. I've done nothing wrong, you keep telling me all the way home. You say it over and over, and you tell me it's what you repeatedly told the man recording you saying it in the interview room. I notice that you want to go the long way home, that you're keen not to take the shortcut. Once I've settled you in the house, up in the dangerous loft again with a cup of tea I've made you, I sneak out. I head for the streets you didn't want us to walk down. At first nothing is out of place. Then outside a house on a well-to-do street I know I've found it when I look down and see that someone has written, quite large, on the pavement in bright green paint, the words: PROPERTY IS THEFT.

There is a tree in the garden. I look hard at it. But it is just a tree; it's nothing more than a tree, it looks like any old tree, with its early-evening mayflies hovering near it in the shafts of low sun, its leaves pinched and new and the grass beneath it patchy and shadowed. I can feel myself getting angry. I try to think of other things. I tell myself that the correct term for mayflies is ephemeroptera; I remember from university, though I can't think why or how I ever learned such a fact, especially I can't think why I would have retained it until now. There they are regardless, whatever they're called, annoyingly in the air. For an instant I hate them. I fantasise about spraying them all with something that would get rid of them. I think about taking an axe to the tree. I think about the teeth of saws and of the sawdust the different kinds of wood behind its bark would make.

I wonder if an anonymous letter to the person who owns this house about its dangers to the foundations (though it is nowhere near the foundations) might make him or her consider removing it. Dear Sir, I imagine myself typing, before I shake my head at myself and turn to go, and as I do I see the words again on the pavement. The way they're scrawled, how fast and sloping and green their letters are, reminds me of you when we first knew each other, when we were still not far past adolescence ourselves, still knew we'd alter the world.

A woman comes out of the front door of the house. She clearly wants me to stop laughing outside her house. She shouts at me to go away. She says if I don't she'll call the police.

I go home. You're up in the loft. I worry about you up there. It has no floor and you're balancing, passionate, on nothing but thin wood. I imagine you seeing the tree through the thick circles of magnifying glass in the binoculars I used to play with when I was a child; inside your head the tree is close-up, silent, there but untouchable, moving, like super-eight film. I know you; you never compromise; there's no point in calling you down. But you've left me some Greek salad on a plate covered by another plate in the kitchen, a fork neatly beside it. I sit on the couch in front of the dug-up laminate and eat it, and while I'm eating I remember the story about the old couple who are turned into two trees; they let the strangers who knock at the door into their house then find that the gods have visited, and their favour is granted them. I search around in the books until I find the book, but I can't find the story about the old couple in it. I find the one about the grieving youth who becomes a tree, and the jealous girl who inadvertently causes the death of her rival and is turned into a shrub, and the boy who plays such beautiful music in the open air that the trees and bushes pick their roots up and move closer, making a shady place for him to play, and the god who falls in love with the girl who doesn't want him, who's happy without him, and who, when he chases her, is an exceptionally fast runner, being such a good huntress, that she almost outruns him. But since he's a god and she's a mortal she can't, and as soon as she knows her strength is waning and he's going to catch her up and have her, she prays to her father, the river, to help her. He helps her by turning her into a tree. All of a sudden her feet take root. Her stomach hardens into bark. Her mouth seals up and her face mosses over; her eyes seal shut behind lichen. Her arms above her head grow shoots and hundreds of leaves spring out of each finger.

I fold down the page at this story. I get some work things ready for tomorrow and call you, tell you as usual that I'm off to bed, that if you don't come now so I can put the lights out and get some sleep I'm going to leave you.

When we're in bed I hand you the book, open at the story. You read it. You look pleased. You read it again, leaning over me to catch the light. I read my favourite bit over your shoulder, the bit about the shining loveliness of the tree and the god, powerless, adorning himself with its branches. You fold the page down again, close the book and put it on the bedside cabinet. I switch the light off.

As soon as you think I'm asleep, when I'm breathing regularly to let you believe I am, you get up. After I hear the gentle shutting of the door, I slide myself out of bed and into my clothes and I go downstairs and out the back door too. This first night I wish I'd pulled on a thicker jacket; in future I will know to.

When I get to the house with the tree I see you there in the dark under it. You are lying on your back on the ground. You look like you're asleep.

I lie down next to you under the tree.

SUSANNAH MARSHALL
Gasoline

SUSANNAH MARSHALL
Gasoline

The dusty brown car stopped, creating more dust. The guy got out of the driver's seat, walked round to the back door, opened it and pulled my bag from the seat and dumped it on the road. He then grabbed my arm, pulled me from the car and slammed the door. He walked back round to the driver's seat, got back into the dusty brown car and drove off slowly down the straight, shimmering road.

I could see Lullah's face turned to look out the back window. She had breathed on the glass and written my name in the mist: Becky. Then she blew a pink gum bubble, which burst and coated her nose and chin.

I was left beneath the ever-stretching sky wondering what I was doing in the middle of nowhere. I pulled off my Levis jacket and threw it to the road, raising a minor cloud of dust, just to show my annoyance, though there was no one around to see it. I acted out this scene from some movie for no one's benefit but my own. I wished I smoked so I could have a cigarette. A Marlboro or a Camel, or some such brand.

I stooped to pick up my jacket then, raising my head slightly, I found myself at eye-level with a pig. A pig, walking down the straight shimmering road toward me. The pig continued to walk toward me until it was about a foot away where it stopped and we stayed there looking at one another for a short time. I had never looked into the eyes of a pig before.

I was aware how incredibly hot it was. There was sweat running down my back. The sound of an engine broke the moment. Drawing towards us, the pig and me, I saw the dusty brown car returning.

'Come on, pig, get out of the road,' I said as the vehicle neared.

The pig and I stood at the edge of the road, delineated only by dry tufted grass. The car stopped right beside us. This time the guy got out of the driver's seat, and with the same procedure that my own ejection had followed, he turfed Lullah from the car.

'Hi,' she said. 'You want some gum?'

I took the gum and we stood together at the side of the road tufted with grass. Lullah, the pig and I. The car crept away. I was glad to see Lullah.

'May as well walk,' she said.

We looked around half-heartedly, trying to decide which way to go in this big open space, under the arching sky. The pig decided for us. It ambled slowly and we followed, over the rough scrub ground, each step raising a minor cloud of dust.

We walked maybe for a half hour or so. I was still chewing my gum though it had lost its flavour. Every so often we stopped to wait for the pig while it pushed its snout into one of the tufts of grass. It made a loud snuffling sound and then truckled on.

We'd reached a rough track, which looked as though it had been cut by the large tyres of a pick-up when there had been some rain, then the track had dried in the image of tyre treads. We followed the track for a while. The pig ambled along, its snout frosted by dust. Small orbs of sweat were discernible on its back. I wondered whether the pig would get sunburn.

Lullah had taken my hand a while back and we swung our locked hands idly to and fro. Our held palms collected a layer of sweat.

In following the track, which looked as though it had been made by a pick-up, we did indeed come upon a pick-up. It was military green in shade. A guy sat in the front. He had both doors open and a baseball cap down over his eyes. He was listening to something on the radio. A country station.

Gasoline

Lullah uncoupled her hand from mine and climbed into the passenger seat next to the guy. They talked for a while. I could hear the lazy buzz of their voices, blending with the loose twang of country music. I squatted on my haunches in the dust, next to the pig. The pig had its snout to the ground. Its soft ears flopped over its small black eyes, the eyes I had looked into earlier. I had the sudden thought that I'd like to poke its eyes with a stick.

I spat my gum into the dust and watched the wet of my saliva around the gum evaporate in seconds. After some minutes, Lullah returned. She held up a twenty-dollar bill.

'The guy says he'll give us this for the pig,' she said.

I stayed on my haunches for a couple of minutes looking at the pig. The pig looked hot.

'Okay,' I said.

I took the money and folded it into my jeans pocket, stood up slowly and took Lullah's hand. It was warm. We stood at the side of the track. The military green pick-up bumped past us with the strains of country music playing. The pig was in the back.

'Come on,' I said to Lullah in a way that showed I was bothered. I pulled her by the hand along the track faster than I knew she'd want to walk in that heat.

'Slow down,' she said. She pulled her hand out of mine. She stood in the middle of the track cut by the pick-up. She pulled a silver-wrapped gum from her back pocket and unwrapped it slowly. As she did so, she cocked her head and screwed up one of her eyes against the heat. She stared at me through the other. I wanted to poke it with a stick. She folded the gum into her mouth and worked it into a softness before she started to walk again. I realised I'd been wrong to be bothered. I allowed her to fall into walking by my side. She slid her hand into the back pocket of my jeans.

'I can feel your ass moving as you walk,' she said.

I liked that.

'I like that,' I said.

She blew a bubble with her gum. It was almost see-through so I could see her face tinted pink through it.

'Are you tired?'

Lullah let out a quick flute of breath. 'I guess.' She lifted the front hem of her T-shirt and tucked it down through her bra so her T-shirt formed a sort of cropped top. I could see her belly. I could see the slight blonde downy hairs on her skin. They glistened a bit with perspiration. I could faintly smell her sweat. It smelled of blueberries. It made me feel hot.

'Are you hot?' I asked her.

'I guess.'

I picked her up then. I stumbled a bit and couldn't lift her very high. My arms are skinny and I couldn't hold her for long. As I put her down, the action raised a minor cloud of dust.

'We've got twenty dollars,' she said.

'We could get some pancakes and coffee.'

'A whole stack of pancakes,' she said, scraping her hair back behind her ear. Tied-back strands were beginning to loosen from the elastic tie.

There was a small structure ahead. We could see its red roof shimmering in the heat of the distance. It lay on the long straight road, which we were now walking parallel to.

'May not be as near as we think, Lullah,' I said. 'These long roads can play tricks.'

Lullah closed her eyes. Screwed them up tight. 'I'll open them in a bit, then it'll seem nearer.'

I noticed while her eyes were shut, she chewed her gum faster and, the moment she opened her eyes, she stopped chewing altogether for a bit, with her mouth slightly open. As we got nearer to the structure with the red roof, there was something at the side of the road. It was a square of sheet aluminium. About a metre square. Someone had painted in black letters with enamel paint the word GASOLINE and an arrow underlining the letters. It pointed to the structure.

'Gas station,' Lullah said.

'We won't get pancakes there.'

'I know it,' she said turning her face full on mine and pushing her nose to mine so the tips met. She smelled of gum and I could see that there was some sleepy-dust in her lashes. 'You didn't have to tell me that.'

She swung away from me, walking up the road with her head down. She put her hands on her hips like she'd just sprinted and was trying to wind down from the race. I felt far away from her. I didn't know what to say. I didn't know whether to walk a bit behind her, or speed up and walk ahead of her. If I did that, she might go.

I could hear her singing slightly.

'*My* baby,' she sang, 'my ba*by*.' It was no song I knew, and not one I think she knew either. I think she was singing the words as though they were a song. 'My ba*by*.' Each time she sang, there was emphasis on a different syllable. Then loudly she sang 'MY BABEEEE,' and she stopped and turned round in the road. Her action raised a minor cloud of dust. She laughed. She still had her hands on her hips. Her elbows aren't bony like mine because her arms are rounded and soft. I stopped in front of her. Our toes almost met on the long straight road. She leant into me and kissed me. Her mouth was hot and her lips wet, whereas mine were dry in that heat. I stopped the kiss briefly to suck my lips to make them a bit wetter. I tasted salt on them. I leant back to her to restart the kiss. Her lips were wet on mine. She pushed her tongue into my mouth and her bubble gum with it. She pushed the gum round my mouth with her tongue. It was against my teeth, then in the side of my cheek. She dug her hands into the back pockets of my jeans and pulled my hips into hers. I felt her push her abdomen against mine. The zip on my jeans dug into me. The metal was warm. She stopped kissing me but left the gum in my mouth. It had lost its flavour. It tasted of her mouth. She moved away from me and began walking up the road again. I followed her.

'Where do you think the guy in the pick-up went?' she said. 'Where is the pig now?'

I thought about it. 'Some town, I guess.'

'My ba-aby,' she sang.

As we reached the structure, which was a small gas station, we could hear a radio. There was an old armchair set under a porch jutting from the red roof, which was made of corrugated metal. The red was paint. Enamel. It was peeling and flaking in parts. We could hear sound from the radio. It sounded like commentary on a ball game. The radio was inside the structure. There was a small window with some faded checked curtain across it. There was a torn piece of cardboard in the window. It was wedged in the corner. There were a couple of dead crickets on the sill. 'BACK IN TEN' was written on the cardboard.

'No one around,' I said. 'They're "Back in ten."'

Lullah was sitting in the old chair. There was a part-drunk bottle of Coke by the side of it. She picked it up and took a long swig.

'It's warm,' she said. 'You want some?'

I took it from her and had a couple of sips. My mouth was dry and I left some spit on the neck of the bottle. I wiped it on the hem of my T-shirt and handed it back to her. She downed the rest of the Coke and put the bottle back next to the chair. She began to take her shoes off.

I walked round the back of the station. There were some old car parts round there. A rusted fender and a couple of old leather car seats. The upholstery was cut and burst and wadding spilled out. There was a cat the colour of smoke curled up on one of the seats. One of its ears was missing in part. There were a half dozen or so old oil drums. Two of them were on their sides in the dust and tufts of grass edged them. There was a green hose attached to a big tank.

'Lullah, there's water.' I picked up the hose and ran my hands down along its length to find the faucet, which jutted from the tank.

Lullah walked round the side of the gas station with the red roof. 'I could use some water. I'm hot,' she said.

I tried to turn the faucet. It was stuck. I stretched out the hem of my T-shirt and put it over the handle of the faucet. It gave me a better grip. I was able to turn the faucet on. Lullah watched me.

The flow of water was slow at first. The water was a rusty colour. I hosed the dusty ground. The water turned the dust red. The stream of water began to turn clear. I directed the water at Lullah's feet. It churned up the dust so her toes were coated in muddy water. I let the flow move up her legs. She cupped her hands together and, bending, placed the cupped hands between her knees. The flow of water was stronger and curled through her hands like the swillings in a bowl. She caught some in the cup of her palms and brought it up to her face. Droplets of water caught the stray strands of her hair. Her blonde hair turned darker when wetted. She opened her mouth wide and swooped to catch the jet of water in her mouth. It filled her mouth and dribbled out down her chin. Her feet moved on tiptoes in the muddied dust.

I turned the hose away from Lullah and held it over my head. It was like being under a shower. Through the falling water, I could see her in front of me. Her thin clothes were wetted and clung to her.

Lullah walked over to the tank and turned off the faucet. The water stopped abruptly. She peeled off her T-shirt and her skirt. They were wet and slapped on the ground as she dropped them. Her knickers were white with small flowers. I could see the fine blonde down on her body. She removed her bra. Her breasts were white and her nipples like small flowers. She walked over to the old oil drums. She moved from one to the other.

'This one's not long used,' she said.

She put a palm on the top of it. When she drew it away, it was messy with congealed oil. She put both palms on it, wiping them so they were coated. She walked over to me then, with her palms slicked with oil. She wiped one over my T-shirt. Streaks of oil followed the shapes of my chest. I felt her palm rub over my breast. She reached up and rubbed her hand in my hair. I could smell the oil – the thickness of it.

'It makes your hair stand on end,' she said.

With her fingertips, she drew an oily moustache over my top lip. She slapped her palm against my chin and rubbed it back and forth to add a beard. As she did so, she sang softly, 'My ba-aby.' The oil made my skin itch a bit. Where it was slapped on my T-shirt it felt clammy. I watched her eyes as she worked. They were small and bright, like the pig's.

She stood back after a few minutes and studied me. Then she came back and drew her palms down my arms. They were smudged with the remainder of the oil. The hairs on my arms were flattened by its stickiness.

'You look like a guy,' she said. 'This here your garage, hon? You got me some gasoline for my automobile?'

I smiled at her.

'Yes ma'am. Say "Yes ma'am",' she said.

'Yes ma'am, I do have some gasoline and you're looking mighty purty today.'

Lullah laughed. She walked over to me on her tiptoes through the dust, which had almost dried out now, and she kissed me. Her mouth didn't taste of gum any more.

'I love you, you jerk,' she said. She took my hand. 'Come on, let's see if we can catch a ride.'

She picked up her wet clothes from the ground and we walked round the front of the gas station.

'We can get a ride to the next town and go have some pancakes,' I said.

JENNY ROBERTS
Pin Point
A short Cameron McGill mystery

JENNY ROBERTS
Pin Point

'You're an obsessive, Cameron. You know that, don't you?'

Becky was stretched out on the lounger, rubbing Factor 20 onto the pink skin of her generous, sexy belly and shaking her head. She was wearing nothing more than a bright-yellow bikini bottom, and her spiky-blonde hair shone and her round face glowed in the bright Canarian sun.

I glanced down at my black Speedo swimsuit and my still-athletic body beneath it and grunted as I towelled myself down. 'I just like to keep fit, that's all! For Christ's sake – I'm 36 this year, Becks, it's a dangerous age.'

Maybe my eyes lingered just a little too long over my friend's midriff. Or maybe she read some unintended criticism in my voice, but her eyes flashed with irritation. She was, after all, a year older than me.

'Yes, but fifty bloody lengths twice every day! For goodness sake, flower, you're *supposed* to be relaxing!'

I laid out the towel on the sun bed and bit my tongue. We'd been friends since breaking up as lovers in our early twenties, but this was the first time we'd ever been on a holiday like this. Usually we did something active. Walking, touring – something interesting. But this year she'd insisted. I'd just started working for myself; she'd had a difficult few months in court. We both needed a rest and Tenerife would be perfect, she said.

Now, three days into the fortnight, I was already going out of my fucking mind with boredom.

Becky rolled her eyes dramatically as I fell onto the sun bed. 'Bloody hell, you're not *actually* going to sunbathe, are you?'

Sometimes she can really wind me up.

'No. I'm not,' I countered, tetchily, 'I'm going to sit under the parasol, read a book and get pissed, so you needn't disturb yourself.'

I turned away in a huff and buried my head in the latest Saz Martin thriller. I could feel her eyes burning into my back, throwing me that bossy look that she does so well, and I gritted my teeth, waiting for the lecture about the effect of constant stress on your heart, the importance of relaxation...

Yeah, yeah.

After a minute or two, she touched me gently on the leg.

I ignored her.

'Cameron... Aw, come on, love, let's not get ratty with each other.' The soft Liverpudlian cadence in her voice and the let's-be-nice tone somehow made me even more irritable. I stared out over the pool at the hundreds of oily bodies toasting in the sun, and held my anger close in a tight little ball. Don't you just hate it when you pick a fight and no one comes?

Becky rested her head on my shoulder and put her arms around my waist, pulling me into her. I could feel her bare breasts against my back and I knew that she wouldn't give a damn about the looks we were getting from the neat little nuclear families all around us.

'Come on, flower,' she whispered, nuzzling my neck, 'lighten up, please... we're on holiday.'

'And just how am I supposed to do that?' I snorted, nodding towards the mass of sunbathers and, in particular, a rather matronly woman in a puce swimsuit who couldn't take her eyes off us. 'How the fuck am I supposed to relax *here*? Just look around you – the place is crawling with middle-class hets and their screaming kids. They're watching every fucking move we make.'

Becky laughed and stuck her chin into my shoulder. 'You old grouch!' she said, blowing playfully in my ear so that a tingle ran all the way down my spine.

The woman in the puce swimsuit gawped in amazement.

Maybe I *was* a grouch. The hotel grounds were beautiful, after all. There were big old trees – proper trees – with ferns growing out from among their branches as well as the tall palms, dotted all around the lush gardens. The grass and the flower beds were immaculate, and the pool was big and not too warm. It could have been paradise, except the whole thing was messed up by people. Cramming the sides of the pool, wearing their designer leisurewear, their David Beckham sunglasses, drinking their alcopops and allowing their children to terrorise the water.

Becky, as usual, could sense what I was thinking. 'Cam, they're just people enjoying themselves. For goodness sake – chill out, love. I chose this hotel 'cos I thought you'd like it here.'

'Yeah, okay,' I conceded reluctantly. 'It's just... well... they're all so fucking alien, aren't they? We stand out like sore thumbs – I feel like everyone's watching our every move.'

She was kneeling behind me now, her hands on my shoulders, massaging, kneading gently, smoothing away some of the tension and shaking her head good-naturedly. 'They're perfectly okay. It's you, you just can't bear doing nothing – can you?'

She was right, of course – I don't do this sort of relaxation well. It frightens me. It's too easy just sitting around in the sun. You can hear yourself thinking.

I screwed my head round and pulled a face at her, feeling guilty. It was a beautiful day. A waiter was collecting our empty glasses off the table behind us, one of the gardeners was watering a flower bed a few yards away. Parrots with bright blue, red and green plumage were swooping through the trees. And the people around us, in truth, were mostly minding their own business. Sometimes, I admit, I can be over-sensitive.

Sometimes I can be selfish, too. Becky was enjoying herself, just lying in the sun – and I was spoiling it. 'It's okay,' I smiled, trying hard, 'you sunbathe to your heart's content, I'm gonna take a walk down by the sea.'

She stuck her head on one side, and studied me for a moment. Then she reached out for her shirt. 'No, I've lounged about long enough, I need some exercise too.' She smiled ruefully and stuck her tongue out at me. 'Otherwise I might run to seed as well.'

I laughed good-humouredly, picked up my own shirt and stood up – just as Becky froze and the colour drained from her face.

'What is it? What's wrong?' I asked, concerned.

She looked up at me. Even in the intense heat, she was trembling.

'It's gone!' she breathed, desperation spilling from her lips. 'My brooch... I unpinned it from my shirt when I sat down... I was going to clean it...' She shook her head with disbelief, her voice catching in her throat. 'Cam, it's gone!'

'Oh, you probably just knocked it onto the ground. It'll be here somewhere,' I tried reassuringly, getting down onto my hands and knees and combing the ground around her sun bed.

But it most certainly wasn't there. It wasn't a brooch you could easily miss. Quite large and shiny, an ornate silver setting with a bright amber stone. Not particularly valuable. Huh, not particularly attractive either – but it had been Becky's mum's. One of her few prized possessions.

'It must be here somewhere,' I said, moving the sun bed, picking up Becky's bag. 'Maybe you put it in here?'

Becky shook her head irritably, almost shouting. 'No! You don't understand! It's gone, Cameron! I put it back on the table next to my drink. I *know* I did. It was there a few minutes ago! Someone must have taken it while we were talking!'

I sat down on the bed and sighed. A thief? Here? Right in the middle of all these people? Well... why not? Why should Tenerife be different from anywhere else?

We both looked around us. At the wrinkled old gardener, who was mopping his brow with a bright yellow cloth a few feet away; at the waiter who had taken the glasses off Becky's table just minutes before and was now threading his way through the sun beds; at all the people on either side of us, sunbathing, reading, walking around.

Becky was thinking the same as me – any one of them could have walked past and casually taken it while we were arguing. She gripped my arm and looked into my eyes, pleading. 'Cam, you've got to help me. We've got to find out who took it, and get it back.'

I closed my eyes and fell back onto the sun bed. For God's sake, Becky, why couldn't you just be more careful?

Then I sat up again and took off my sunglasses. 'Okay, love, don't worry, I'll go and ask around – someone must have seen something.'

The woman in the puce swimsuit was laid out on her sun bed, and she jumped when I spoke.

'Sorry to bother you.' I smiled, trying to be civil. 'I, erm, I saw you looking across at us a few minutes ago and wondered… Well, the thing is… my friend has lost a piece of jewellery and we wondered if you saw anyone take it. It was on the table behind her.' It felt awkward accusing some unknown person of theft. I felt awkward over Becky's carelessness, too.

She shook her head and replied with a Victoria Wood voice – a sort of clipped, lilting Lancashire. 'Noo love, ah'm sorry if I were staring. I were just gazing around. Didn't see anything though – nowt obvious at any rate.'

Mmm, 'nowt obvious' except Becky rubbing up against me from behind – bet you don't often see that in Chorley.

'I were just watching t'parrots,' she continued, unabashed, like she'd never dream of staring at anyone. 'Lovely, aren't they? Hey, mind out, love!'

I ducked as a large green bird swooped past my right ear and up into one of the trees.

'Nearly had you, that one did!' The woman grinned broadly.

I allowed myself a smile and crouched down next to her, lowering my voice conspiratorially. 'The waiter,' I whispered, meaningfully, 'he took our glasses while you were looking across there. Could you see if he picked anything else up? Or did you see anyone else take anything off our table?'

She looked serious and shook her head. 'Didn't see a soul, love, except t'waiter. He could have teken it for all I know. I weren't looking really. I just saw 'im bend down and pick up t'glasses. I couldn't see what he had in his hand.'

I couldn't take my eyes off her – she was a fascinating shade of pink and if she stayed in the sun much longer, then her face would begin to match her swimsuit.

'Well...' she continued, unnerved by my stare, 'He'd be a right fool if he did, now, wouldn't he? Stealing? With all these people around?'

Yeah. All these people. Except, as I asked around, it became obvious that no one had seen anything. A theft, in broad daylight, right behind our backs, in the middle of a few hundred people. Yet no one had heard or seen a thing – and that included Becky and me.

I began to wonder if Becky had been mistaken. Left the brooch in the apartment, or mislaid it. Then I noticed her talking to the gardener. She was suddenly quite red in the face. And he was waving his arms around in a very Gallic sort of way. Irrationally, I began to worry about what she was saying to him. Then I reminded myself that this was Becky, the lawyer, the woman who preached correctness and respect in all things.

The waiter was at my side of the pool, making his way back to the bar and I ran after him, catching him before he disappeared.

'You speak English?' I asked, thinking that he hardly looked old enough to be out of school.

He nodded almost imperceptibly, his black curly hair bouncing a little as he moved his head.

'A little,' he said, with hardly a trace of an accent. His face was fresh and open, with no giveaway signs of guilt or unease. His eyes looked bright and intelligent, but his body language betrayed his boredom. I didn't think he looked much like a thief, but then again, a bright guy like this must need something to relieve the boredom. Maybe a little excitement – like stealing the odd trinket – made his day go round.

I thought I'd try the direct route.

'My friend put a valuable brooch down on her table a few minutes ago,' I said, pointing over to our sun loungers. 'Now it's gone.' I paused and looked him in the eyes. 'I wondered if you saw it. When you collected the glasses, I mean.'

He furrowed his brow and narrowed his eyes, ignoring the man a few sun beds away who was waving a glass at him.

'Your friend has *lost* her brooch, señora?'

I stared back. 'No, someone has *stolen* her brooch.'

I watched his eyes carefully as I spoke and they didn't flicker in the slightest. 'Stolen!' He pursed his lips and shook his head. 'That is a serious accusation, señora. Are you sure?'

He was young, twenty-one or two. Maybe this was his first job, or maybe he was a student working his way through college. Either way he would be stupid to risk his job with petty theft like this. Besides, he was still showing none of the classic signs of deceit – either he was totally honest, or he was a very, very good liar.

'Yes, I'm sure. My friend put the brooch down on the table. Five minutes later it had gone. It's quite large; silver with an orange-coloured stone set into the base and a stick-pin on the back.'

The man on the nearby sun bed was shouting openly now, offended that he was being ignored. The waiter turned and acknowledged him, then continued, his eyes bright and steady.

'I'm sorry, señora, I saw nothing on the table, except empty glasses and a bottle.' He started to turn away. 'You should report this to Reception at once. If you are right then the police should be summoned immediately.'

I was about to agree with him, when a hush fell over the whole of the garden and I looked out across the pool to see two people standing among the trees, shouting loudly at each other.

Becky Williams – astute lawyer and the one woman who can argue a case better than anyone I know – was going into freefall. Standing with her hands on her hips, shouting at the top of her voice in a thick Liverpudlian accent, she was demanding that the gardener empty his pockets. The old man, clearly much offended, had moved up to within inches of her face and was shouting angrily back at her in Spanish, holding his hat in his hand and jerking it up and down by his side.

It was a close-run thing, but I got there before the waiter and prised them apart, inserting myself between them, taking hold of Becky's hands, pushing her firmly backwards, telling her to cool it.

The waiter put his arm around the old man, who was visibly shaken, and spoke to him softly and reassuringly, calming him down.

By now, even the kids had stopped tearing about by the pool, and every face was turned silently towards us. Breathless in the hot afternoon air.

The waiter's eyes flashed angrily at Becky. 'Señora, you have no right to accuse Francisco of such a terrible thing! He is a good man. And you have upset him greatly.'

'Well, it must have been him!' Becky yelled back, still distraught. 'He was working just behind us when my brooch disappeared! And if it wasn't, it must have been you! You were there as well, weren't you?'

'Becky, please!' I hissed, looking straight into her angry blue eyes. 'What the hell are you doing? You, of all people! I know you're upset, but you can't just go around accusing people!'

Becky stared back at me defiantly, but suddenly went very quiet. She was no doubt remembering all the advice she'd given to me about being too impetuous, how important it was to use the right channels, how you should always let the authorities investigate first. Every time I took on a new case, she seemed to remind me how I should have respect for the law. And now here she was accusing a stranger of stealing, without a shred of evidence.

I gave her one last piercing look and, still holding her tightly by the wrist, turned round, facing up to the two men.

'Please, señors,' I said quietly, 'can we talk?'

They both stood there quietly enough, but their faces spoke volumes.

'I saw him, Cam! I *saw* him put it in his pocket!' Becky pointed her free hand accusingly over my shoulder. The gardener stepped back, shaking his head wildly, speaking rapidly and angrily in Spanish to his companion.

I held her wrist even tighter, trying to stay composed, looking as calmly as I could at the waiter, appealing for a translation, still trying to keep a lid on the situation.

The waiter turned back to me, angrily fingering his tray. 'He says it is all a mistake, señora. He says he does not know how your friend could say such a thing about him. He is an honest man. He is a good Catholic.'

'Tell him I believe him,' I soothed, 'but, just to calm my friend down, ask him if he would mind showing us what he put in his pocket?'

The waiter nodded, still agitated, but spoke to the old man. He grunted with indignation and put his hand in his trouser pocket, begrudgingly pulling out the bright yellow handkerchief I'd noticed him using earlier, and muttering to the waiter all the time. When he began to unfold it, Becky and I held our breath.

But, inside the handkerchief, instead of Becky's brooch, there was a battered silver fob watch.

'He says it is *his* watch. His wife gave it to him many years ago when they were young. Now that she has passed on, he keeps it with him always.'

Becky looked like she was ready to shrivel up. She turned away briefly, composing herself, then stood up straight and held out a hand to the old man.

'I'm sorry, señor,' she said reticently, taking his hand in both of hers. 'I feel ashamed. I can't believe I said such a terrible thing. Please forgive me. It's just that the brooch was special – it was given to me by my mother when she died.'

There was a slight pause whilst the waiter translated, then the gardener's eyes brightened and he smiled toothlessly back at Becky, clasped her hands in his own, and spoke to her in Spanish.

The waiter sighed with relief. 'He says, "Some things are special, God bless you – and may God be with your mother".'

The gardener smiled gently, put his hat back on his head, then returned to his hose pipe. The waiter nodded politely and left. One hundred pairs of eyes turned away in disappointment.

Becky had her head down studying the grass. I didn't say a word.

'Yeah, okay, Cameron!' she mumbled, shuffling her feet. 'You don't have to say it! I know! I'm a lawyer! I've gone on at you often enough, I should know better.'

I shook my head, partly in relief, partly in amazement. At least this made a change – usually it was me who made all the excuses. I put my arm round her shoulders and gave her a hug.

'Yeah, well, just keep cool, will you? We have to go carefully here...'

I stopped in mid-sentence. Sometimes you can sense when you're being stared at and I looked up towards the pool. The woman in the puce swimsuit was there, jumping up and down and pulling faces at me, pointing to a clump of bushes just behind us. I spun round at once, just in time to see a tall, thin man in a grey T-shirt and khaki shorts stumble out of the shrubs and make off across the lawn and through the trees, clasping a black canvas bag under his arm.

Becky and I exchanged glances and hurtled after him instantly, weaving through the trees and around the sun beds, jumping over the sunshades that he toppled over as he passed, chasing him as he headed inside the hotel and ran across the huge marble lobby.

'Stop him!' I yelled desperately, to anyone who might be listening. But the few English tourists by the reception desk just looked uncertain and embarrassed. The hotel staff reacted by pressing some security alarm, which sent out an ear-piercing whine as the man scattered a trolley full of luggage across the floor towards us and disappeared out of the main entrance. I jumped over a big maroon case as it careered towards me, then shot out of the door after him.

When I stopped to get my bearings on the steps, Becky was right at my shoulder.

'He turned right,' I gasped, setting off down the street, searching ahead of me among the scattering of tourists.

'There he is!' shouted Becky, pointing past a couple of market stalls, as the man swerved right and shot down a narrow path between some houses.

He was a good thirty yards ahead of us when we got there, but I was fitter than him, and by the time we'd run uphill for a few minutes and the houses had thinned out, I was close enough to see the layer of sweat on his skin and hear the rasping of his breath as he fought to keep going.

He glanced over his shoulder and when he saw how close I was, he gripped the case even tighter, then scrambled away from me, off the path and down the side of a big dry river bed. I followed him, launching myself from the top and grabbing at his sweaty T-shirt as I landed next to him. He twisted away again and I fell heavily onto the rocky, dusty ground, scraping my bare shins and arms – and cursing loudly. He stumbled off again, careering along the river bed, falling over, scrambling across the rocks on all fours, dropping the case as he went. I got up and ran the last few yards, grabbing hold of his ankle as he made one last desperate attempt to get away up the other side.

Finally defeated, he rolled over onto his back, like a submissive dog, his hands held out defensively in front of him.

'Please!' he pleaded in a high-pitched, pathetic – and very English – voice. 'I didn't mean any harm, please let me go!'

Becky picked up the case and stood behind him, pulling a face at his antics. By now he was almost crying. I looked at her and frowned, she shrugged her shoulders in puzzlement.

'Okay, mister,' I threatened, 'Just give us the brooch and we'll let you go.'

He looked at me like he was confused, then turned and reached out for the bag in Becky's hands. She pulled it back out of his reach.

'The brooch!' I demanded, taking a step towards him.

He drew back and started to shake. 'I don't know what you mean,' he whined.

'The brooch that you stole in the hotel garden. Give it back!' I growled.

He shook his head wildly, looking first at Becky and then at me, his hands held out in supplication, his eyes full of something like despair. 'I don't... know anything... about a brooch.' He gulped. 'Please, can I... have my... camera back? Please.'

We looked at each other, and Becky took a step towards him. The truth was beginning to dawn.

'So this is a *camera* is it?' She looked straight into his face, holding up the bag, taunting him. He nodded and made a weak attempt to smile. Like he was guileless. Just another holidaymaker.

Becky kept her cool this time, speaking slowly, carefully as she unzipped the cover and pulled out an SLR and a *very* long lens.

'You use this for holiday snaps do you?' She held the zoom lens in the air. 'Like, close-up snaps? From the bushes?'

He winced and shrank back. 'I'm... I'm just a... I like photography... It's a hobby,' he tried.

Becky folded her arms and stared calmly at him. A lawyer once again. 'Yeah!' she said, 'I just bet it is.'

'No. No, honestly... it's not like that.' He wept.

Becky walked right up to him and breathed quietly into his face. 'Well, in that case, someone better check out the film, hadn't they?'

It was only a short taxi ride to the police station, and he came without a struggle. But it was nearly two hours before we left. Two whole hours of sitting around in just swimsuits and shirts, submitting to the stares and the whispered innuendo from the twenty or more cops who found some excuse to wander into the waiting room. Even the detective who took our statement couldn't stop himself staring at Becky's thighs. It had been hard work getting through to them, and in the end I wasn't sure who I loathed more: the peeping Tom or the dirty-minded bastards at the cop shop.

'Well, I hope they lock him up!' Becky spat, as we walked back into the hotel lobby. 'His kind really piss me off!'

'Yeah, I know, but I wouldn't hold your breath, love. You saw the way they looked at us, they're no better than he is. Still, if nothing else, we've given him the shock of his life.'

Becky grunted in agreement as we walked back into the gardens, then stopped in the shade of a big tree and turned to me, suddenly tearful.

'Oh... Cam, I'm pleased we caught him, but that doesn't get my mum's brooch back, does it?'

'No, I guess not,' I said, stroking her arm, trying to think of something helpful to say to her, 'but at least you reported it while we were at the cop shop. Maybe they'll recover it.' I did my best to sound hopeful, but I could see from the look in her eyes that she didn't believe that any more than me. 'Tell you what, Becky...' I tried, 'I'll buy you something special to make up for it.'

She smiled back bravely and I pulled her towards me and held her close. Round the pool, people were still enjoying their holidays, the waiter was still serving drinks and the gardener was cleaning his tools ready to finish for the day. Three or four parrots were flying amongst the trees, still swooping down over the sunbathers, their colourful plumage flashing in the sunshine.

I couldn't work it out. How could someone – anyone – steal a brooch from under our noses, in broad daylight, without a single person seeing it happen? I was certain it wasn't the gardener – or the waiter – so whoever it was must have either been invisible or very, very quick.

Suddenly I had an idea.

'You look terrible, Becks,' I said, feeling a bit of a heel because, actually, she looked fine. 'You've got tear stains all down your face and your hair is all tangled and dusty. Why don't you go back to the apartment and have a really nice shower? You'll feel a lot better then.'

She looked at me querulously, like she suspected that I might be up to something.

I shrugged casually. 'I'm not in the mood to sit and read any more, I'm gonna take a walk, be on my own for a while – y'know, just chill out a bit.' Sometimes I think I should get a job on the stage.

She looked at me for a moment and seemed to believe me. Then she nodded and walked wearily back across the gardens and into the hotel. I waited until she'd disappeared before I ran across the grass, catching the gardener as he picked up his old canvas tool-bag.

It wasn't easy, and I knew that I didn't have much time, but with what little Spanish I knew, and a lot of sign language, I managed to enlist his help.

It was a good half hour later when I turned the key in the door of our first-floor room, and the sun was just about at its fiercest. Becky was out on the balcony, sitting cross-legged on one of the sun-loungers, reading a book. She was wearing a flowery shirt and a big straw hat, drinking something exotic with fruit in it.

'Hi, Cam,' she shouted through the open door, sounding much brighter now. 'You're soon back! Are you okay?'

I stayed deadpan, my hands in my pockets and very casual, as I walked through the door onto the balcony, looking around me like nothing much had changed. The balconies were stepped back so that, even outside the room, we could be in full sun nearly all day long if we wanted. Above us, window boxes spilled out waves of bright-red geraniums right back to the twelfth floor. Below us, people were laughing and shouting and several children were crying loudly. Earlier, the noise had pissed me off. Now, as I pulled the big fancy brooch out of my pocket and placed it dramatically on the table, I didn't care about the noise any more.

Becky looked up at me, a mixture of delight and astonishment in her eyes.

Then, right on cue, I sensed the rush of air and the flap of wings, and reached out quickly to scoop it up again.

The big green parrot dived across in front of us, squawked in frustration as it skimmed the empty table, and took off again angrily, over the side of the balcony and out across the pool.

'There's your thief, Becky,' I crowed, unable to conceal a triumphant smile, as the bird alighted among the ferns at the top of a wizened old tree trunk.

Becky's mouth dropped open in surprise as, this time, I placed the brooch in her hand.

'A parrot? The thief was a bloody parrot?'

I grinned back. 'Yep. It suddenly came to me when we were standing in the garden. It's well known that magpies steal bright objects all the time, but I read somewhere that it can happen with any bird and, according to the hotel manager, there have been several instances of kleptomaniac parrots on the island. Once I'd tumbled, it was easy. I just watched the birds and it soon became obvious which one was the thief. Then your friend the gardener got a ladder and helped me retrieve your brooch – plus a diamond ring and a necklace – from the bird's favourite perch, that old tree trunk over there.'

Becky got up, shaking her head in amazed delight, and hugged me hard. 'Thanks, Cam, you're a star.' She was hardly breathing, almost too thrilled to talk, and there were tears in her eyes.

I smiled, pleased that the crisis was over, and Becky hugged me even harder and then laughed in real relief.

'You deserve a drink, if anyone does! Sit down, Cameron McGill, you fabulous private investigator. Take it easy. I'll be back in just a minute.'

Ten minutes later I swallowed a mouthful of ice-cold Campari and orange and lay back on the sun lounger, pulling the straw trilby down over my face and closing my eyes. I could feel the sun slowly turning my skin a deep shade of tan. I had the warmth of the sun, the taste of my favourite drink and the company of my best friend. For the first time in four days I felt content and relaxed.

Becky was laid on her front next to me, happy again, the precious brooch locked away in the safe.

Somewhere over the other side of the pool, two keepers from the island's parrot park were trying to entice the kleptomaniac bird down from its perch in the branches above.

Becky smiled across at me, hardly believing her luck.

'You're amazing, Cam, you know that.'

'Aw, yeah, I know,' I replied immodestly. 'But it's just what us top private eyes do all the time. Gather the evidence, put it all together and draw the right conclusions. I'm just fuckin' brilliant – everyone says so.'

I lifted the hat off my face, waiting for Becky's reaction, expecting her to throw something at me. But before she could do anything, before she could even say a word, the big green parrot swooped from the sky and skimmed over us again, cackling evilly as it flew off.

I groaned deeply.

'Becky...'

'Yes, Oh Wonderful One?'

'Hand me a tissue will you, please – something very wet has just landed on my face.'

KATE RIGBY
Hard Workers

KATE RIGBY
Hard Workers

I'm Bobbles. Bobs for short. I'm one of the workers. We all lie on the bed together, we six, in the quilted valley, wondering whose turn it'll be tonight. Pearl's again, I expect.

Pearl's popular with our employer. A workaday sort with a healthy salmon colour and happy veins entwining her seven inches like ivy. Americans would say she's 'kinda regular' and therein lies her attraction. She's got good proportions. Average height, slim but not skinny.

'It won't be me,' I say, rolling into Shad. 'Ms Locke doesn't like me. I think she wants to throw me out on my ear.'

Shad nudges me. 'Well, I'll be hot on your heels, Bobs!'

Me and Shad, we stick together. Shad is Ms Locke's token black worker. If Ms Locke were black, who would be the token white I wonder? They tell me Ms Locke made a beeline for Shad, paid good money for her but now she's gone off her. God knows why. Shad's kinda regular too. Like Pearl in black, only half an inch taller.

Goldie is to my other side. 'You're a real mover, Bobs. You shake that body. You can do things for Ms Locke like none of us can.'

'But she said I hurt her, Goldie.'

'Ah, she just needs to get used to you, that's all, Bobs. You're her newest recruit.'

'Whereas Pearl's stood the test of time.'

'Exactly. But I've been here a fair old while and I'm not all that hot with Ms Locke, you know,' says Goldie. 'Look at me. Aren't I a bit jaded?'

I'm looking at her. She's solid gold to me. A rock. 'Take a good look, Bobs.'

I look into her tall satiny eight-inch form but all I get is my wonky face refracted back at me. I suppose she's got a point.

'Maybe it'll be my turn tonight,' says Janet, voice soft as jelly. But you can see right through Janet with the gloopy skin. And what you see is glitter glitter glitter. Did you ever see the like anyway? She's not *real*, that one. Mind you, I can talk, covered in all my bumps, looking like a walking disease. Who wants someone like me? It didn't take long for Ms Locke to pass judgement. She screamed at me last week. 'Get out! Get out! Vicious bitch.'

But at least I'm not starting to smell, like Janet. It's that squishy skin of hers. There are traces, residues. Fluids dry all tacky on her and she doesn't scrub up clean.

'None of us is secure,' says Melody, and we all groan. If anyone is the favourite around here, it's Melody. And her such a dinky thing! Half the height of most of us and so slender. Such a small pointed head on her. But she can stand up for herself, can Melody.

'We must stick together,' says Shad. (Melody turns up her nose at the thought of sticking to the reeking Janet.) 'Fight for better conditions. What say the workers?'

'Better conditions?' says Pearl. 'But it's such a cushy number here. Lounging around until she's ready for one of us.'

'Ready for you, Pearl, don't you mean,' says Shad. 'It's not enough. I want work every night. I don't want to be no token black cunt.'

We all laugh. 'That's one thing you're most definitely not, Shad!'

But we can't complain. Okay, so we don't get paid as such and we can be called upon to perform any old time of day or night but it's live-in-all-found and we've been on some exciting journeys since we came here, we six. Even lumpy old me! We've shimmied through lush gardens on our way up to the cave, we've heard incredible animal sounds, it's what we came here to do.

Shh! Shh! It's Ms Locke's girlfriend at the front door. With wine. Offering apologies for the other night. We hear the pop of cork, the glug glug, the chink of glasses. Now they're on the settee in reconciliation, hands in private places. But hang on a sec, they're rowing again, same as Saturday. 'No, I'm not,' shouts Ms Locke. 'Yes, you are,' bawls her girlfriend. 'Oh screw you,' shouts Ms Locke. 'I'm going to let my hair down with Goldie.'

We all look over at Goldie.

'Hard as nails, that Goldie one,' says the girlfriend. 'Well, if you'd rather spend time with that lairy fatso than me, then I'm off.'

'You do that,' says Ms Locke.

'Ah, I've had it anyway,' says the girlfriend, 'sharing you with all and sundry.' We hear the slam of front door, and then the flitting of Ms Locke's footsteps up the stairs.

'Now then, darlings,' she says, lying back on the quilt with us. 'Which is it to be? Pearl? Or Melody, my lady?' Her red-nailed hand takes hold of Melody. 'I only said Goldie to wind *her* up.'

Melody is a good little worker. She loves what she does. She, out of all of us, knows Ms Locke inside out. But even she cannot please Ms Locke tonight. 'You're useless, Melody. Crap! Not one of you has got any balls.' Ms Locke is punching her pillow in frustration. 'Not one of you has got any colour.'

She's going to take it out on someone. Yep. She squeezes me and Shad in her right palm and suddenly we're flying through the air to pastures new. Well, to next door's moonlit swimming pool anyway. Splosh. Cor, Janet could have done with this. A midnight dip to cleanse that skanky body of hers, but it's us. Me and Shad. Floating on our backs. Strictly speaking I'm not supposed to get wet, it might damage my innards, my ability to hum good, but who cares?

Because I'm in heaven, riding the waves with Shad, and when the temperature drops and we're starting to shiver, I say, 'Shad, should we snuggle in together?'

'Ooo yeah,' she says, as I squeeze my bobbles into her with sensual movements until we're stacked together as one.

The following morning, we slip apart, bobbing on the water like buoys. Or should that be boys? We're almost boys, aren't we? We never did understand why we were lumbered with such daft feminine names. Though Shad would probably say, 'You speak for yourself, Bobs. I'm all girl.'

Suddenly we're aware of little-girl feet dangling at the side of the pool, swishing, swashing, making waves. Then the swishing stops as, curious, she watches as we drift towards her. Before we know it we are being trawled ashore in a fishing net and left on the concrete while the child goes indoors, flip splashy flop. 'Cor, this is the life, Shad, eh? Sunbathing on the terrace. Better than next door.'

When the child returns we're mostly dry, except for our private bits. We thought we'd landed a right plum job here too, sun-lounging half the day, but the child's got other plans for us, it would seem. 'Grandma,' she calls. 'Grandma, look what I found! Sausages for my cook set! One is done black like Gramps has them and the other one is still raw!' Grandma peers at us uneasily as though something about us rings a distant bell. 'Oh yes,' she says. 'Funny-shaped sausages though, dear.'

And Shad whispers into my ear, 'That's it, Bobs. I'm ready for the chop.'

CHERRY SMYTH
Suckling Pig

CHERRY SMYTH
Suckling Pig

I blame Wells-Next-the-Sea and a six-berth caravan. At Easter, Androula and I took a trip to the Norfolk coast. We left London at four in the morning to avoid bumper-crush and shared the driving without so much as the hint of a row. She didn't cruise in third like she often does and I took the corners gently, keeping to my side of the road. We drove into a peachy sunrise over the Broads, slipped on our sunglasses and rolled down the windows to breathe real air. I could tell by the way she looked at me, half searching, half having found what she wanted, that we'd have sex as soon as we stepped in the door. I put my foot down.

The caravan park was blank and orderly. Nobody about. We unpacked the car and I lay down on the narrow seat in the little square area that was to become our living room and pulled Androula towards me. I lifted her blouse and began to kiss her torso. She has a thin dark feather of hair that leads down her belly to where my tongue adores and I was just about to – when –

There was a rap at the door and Androula leapt up, straightened herself (as it were) and opened it to a bloke who simply barged right on in. 'Mrs K... Kostopoulos,' he said, 'just wanted to show you how to turn on the gas.' He scanned the room and I stayed quiet, eyes closed, baby waves of lust trickling over me, glad of my shades.

'Tired after the journey, is he?' he asked. Androula and I froze.

She laughed, 'Yeah, but the traffic was fine. We left early.' She didn't miss a beat!

Was my clean-shaven face not enough for him? My ponytail, my hips? My present, pert enough breasts? I couldn't give myself away if I tried.

'Well, have a nice weekend,' and he skedaddled. Androula turned to me, blushing like the first rhododendron. 'Mr Kostopoulos!' she laughed and leant over and kissed at my confusion. She rubbed hard down the side of my thighs, something she always did when she was turned on.

'Pull the curtains,' I whispered, imagining rings of holiday-makers encamping round our caravan for a peep.

'I will, my gorgeous Greek stud.'

'Enough,' I said.

'He didn't see us,' she said, though funnily enough, she was whispering too.

Every time I left the caravan, I wore my sunglasses and tied my hair back. The cat was out of the bag and we had to keep it out. We were a straight couple from Harringay and Mr Caravan Park was watching our every move. I packed a pair of sports socks down my Diesel jeans and Androula, well she was herself – Dior red lipstick, long black hair, tight little Chapel Market teen girl tops. How could she not pass?

And then came trouble. The kids. I started it. God knows why. To make her laugh. She has a lovely put-put of a laugh, my girl. There were two slim rooms with bunk-beds at the other end of the caravan. When dinner was ready the first night, I stormed into one of the rooms and scolded the cooler air.

'Now, that's enough nonsense, you two. No dinner for you, do you hear me?'

I've always wanted to yell 'do you hear me?' in revenge for my father's long-lasting belief in my deafness. I came out with the harassed face of exasperated parenthood.

'That pair, honestly,' I puffed. 'I've had it.'

Androula put-putted. She didn't even participate – at first.

Then I gave them names. 'Sinead! Kostas!' I called as we were getting ready to head to the beach. 'Come on, we're leaving.' I remember pausing theatrically. 'I'll count to three and if you're not out here, you're staying here. One… two… three…' Silence. Of course there was bloody silence. There were no kids. *Nada. Niente.* But I strode off with the stern air of the satisfied disciplinarian.

'You're too hard on them, sweetheart,' simpered Androula, taking my hand. Ah, she'd bitten. I was pleased. My face was dead straight.

Mr and Mrs Kostopoulos went on to have a weekend of wonderful walks, sex, watching stars being born at dusk and plea-bargaining with two bad wee articles. The wind still came with a hint of Siberia, but the sun shone and, in shelter, it was warm enough to roll up the sleeves, undo the top button. Green edged the chestnut trees and the blackthorn hedges were sudsy with blossom. There was a line of Scots pines leading to the shore, elegant but scraggy, like trees left over from somewhere else. Sorrento, Cassis, Essaouira. We were happy and joked about buying one of the wooden beach huts that edged the dunes. Playing second house.

It wasn't till we were leaving that I spotted a change in Androula. She always became a little withdrawn at the thought of going back to the office, her eyes tortured by the screen for eight hours a day, her palm taking on the shape of the mouse. I promised we'd come back soon. I suggested Christmas in Kerala. I even spoke my seven garbled lines of Greek. Nothing worked. She was glum as she got into the car and almost weeping as we drove out of the caravan park.

'What is it, darling heart?' I stroked her thigh. I slowed down.

'I don't know,' she said, looking out of the passenger window – always a bad sign.

'You seem lost.' Not as lost as I was. I didn't have a baldy.

'No, but…' she hesitated.

'What?' My eyes were welling up like hers. I drove slower, could barely make out the road ahead.

Her bottom lip quivered. 'I'll miss the kids,' she said finally.

'Kids?' My voice rose involuntarily. 'What kids?'

'Sinead and Kostas.' She was weeping now with the full force of having named the problem.

The car had crawled virtually to a standstill. I cleared a roundabout and stopped the engine. 'Oh lamb, come here.' I took her in my arms. 'There, there,' I said gently, thinking, what the hell had I begun?

She shook against me. For the first time that weekend, I felt like a father, a husband, and my wife wanted a child. I was solemn and serious, weighted with the pressure of lineage.

'It just felt like our family.' Her words were muffled.

'I know, I know...'

'I never wanted a baby, you know,' she went on, 'but having the two of them this weekend, I realised,' she wasn't crying now, 'they were the children I'd never have.' Her heart was breaking and I'd chucked the first stone.

I suppose being butch had let me off the maternity hook – till now. Not for a nanosecond had I ever wanted children – and no one ever expected me to – and suddenly I wished I had, wished I'd longed to be pregnant, so that I could console Androula with the right words. The two tiny ghosts I'd invented in the back room of a holiday caravan had crept under her skin and I didn't know how to extricate them.

That night, even though I was tired, I wanted to make love, to bring her close and repair the hurt. The smell we'd left in the bed greeted us. Home. We kissed softly for a long time and then I took her breasts in both hands and held them. I lowered myself down and took a nipple into my mouth. As I sucked, I made the noise of a baby feeding and suddenly I was suckling and a bolt of jealousy burned through me for the baby that didn't even exist. Where would it sleep? Between us? *Would* it sleep? Would her nipples be bitten raw? Would we be too fucked to fuck? And the voice gained momentum and volume until it screamed, 'What about me? I'm your baby. Mother me!'

I knew I was in deep and had reached something too nasty to share. Shame shivered up from my stomach and I lost my hard-on. Androula sensed it and unlatched her breast. She stroked my hair and I lay on her chest, listening to her breathe, not speaking, until we fell asleep.

I woke up startled from a dream. I seemed to be fenced in at the top of the stairs and couldn't for the life of me figure out how to get down. I grabbed at the bars and kicked but they held firm. It only dawned on me later that the fence was a child-gate on little hinges, erected to prevent a toddler from falling down the stairs. I didn't mention the dream.

I can see now that it was a time of not mentioning for both of us. The next weekend I came down on Saturday morning to find Androula already up and curled on the sofa watching the Teletubbies. I laughed and she laughed in her cute put-put fashion, but we no longer shared the same joke. When she stood up I saw she was wearing a nightie I'd never seen before. It was pink and puckered and it reminded me of something distant. Then I got it – Jesus, it was *smock-like*. I said nothing, thought everything.

She was grumpy as a gorilla that week and I kept out of her way. I checked the kitchen calendar – she was due on. I stocked the fridge and freezer and bought her two Green and Black organic chocolate bars. Seventy per cent. The way she likes it. Then I waited. Come Thursday, there was no whoop of relief from the toilet and Androula devoured me in bed. I'd never seen her so hungry. *Tidal.* And I was the Netherlands. The sex was the kind that makes you feel athletic and indefatigable and you think you'll start again the minute you've come. But usually you just roll over and go asleep.

Well, there was no sleeping. Androula doesn't always want a dildo, but that night she leant under the bed for the box of tricks and pulled out a purple laddie named Joan. I rolled on a condom, strapped it on and went to work. (Would it were that quick and simple, but you get the picture.)

'Fuck me,' she cried, raising her hips and pushing back against the wall with her hands. 'Deeper. Make a baby!'

Part of me believed I could. How could I not? I was virile as a stallion, insatiable, tireless and hey, forever hard. I crooked my forearm under her waist and held her up towards me.

Then a wave of sadness arrived from nowhere. I wanted a dick, a full-blooded, sperm-filled cock that would unload itself inside her. I wanted my DNA to meet and mingle with hers, our cells to collide, all my atoms to be her atoms, to live within her and grow little fingers and toes. I may not have wanted a baby, but I sure wanted the power of making one. I wanted to feel the soft wet walls of her pussy, wanted the sensation of my penis losing strength and cradled by her until I slipped out, small and sticky and beautifully depleted.

I risked telling her, 'I wish I could come inside you.'

Her eyes were wide and could see for miles, could see into my brain, my heart, my gut. Her lips were crimson.

'Me too.' Her voice was warm and sexy in that moment and we both knew what lack felt like and it didn't scare us or separate us. We were equal and understood.

I remembered one of the times I'd put my whole fist inside her. How I shaped my fingertips into a little fish's head and twisted and turned my way upstream. Then the feeling of curling to move inside her and the sudden balloon she made of herself, like the inside of a drum made bigger with sound. Then the sensation as I began to pull out, Androula's breathing easing me, like something being born. I'll never forget that feeling of being part of her leaving her body. It brought tears to my eyes.

'Shall I come out now?' I asked quietly. She nodded.

I withdrew gently and saw the head of the dildo. Androula had started bleeding.

She looked down and gave a gulpy shudder, then said tearfully, 'All that bleeding – for what?'

'I often think that, believe me.' I tried to sound light-hearted. 'That's no reason to have a baby. Just to make a womb useful.'

'There *is* no reason. I just want one. There's my great-grandmother, my grandmother, my mother and me, and then what? Who?'

I cursed the longevity of that Cypriot female line. She talked like a myth I'd never been told or had closed my ears to. My line stops with me and I feel no loss, no regret. I have no need of duplication, multiplication. I am enough. I tell her this as carefully as I can. I realise it's more than language and sun and a taste for olives that distinguishes us. The word 'descendants' rings like a bell for her. A starter's gun. 'You don't see,' she kept saying. 'You just don't see what I mean.' Her accent became more pronounced as if speaking English added to her sense of injustice.

Suddenly there was a huge part of her desire that I did not recognise. Just as she never saw my childhood home, the place I grew and dreamt and fought for eighteen years. She never saw inside, what I saw from those windows. I tried to see through hers. I took her hand and kissed it and began to listen. Silence wouldn't make it go away, I came to realise with a modicum of maturity that I dredged up from somewhere. She spoke with the passion of the misunderstood, the mocked. And I listened.

'Every time for the past week when I've seen a baby in a pram I've felt terrible. I'm sorry, love,' she bit her lip, 'but I've been browsing in Baby Gap. I bought a book of baby names and named three sets of triplets. What's happening to me?' she wailed.

It was much worse than I thought. The woman I'd made promises to was morphing into something morose, alien. She was hitting thirty-four, which meant, with advances in reproductive technology, that this could go on for another thirty years. I panicked.

'Look at Roberto and Josie, for chrissakes!' I blurted. 'No sex life, in bed by ten, up at six, no nights out. The last time I was in the car with Josie she looked up and pointed, "Der's a lorry!" A baby isn't just for Christm–'

'Stop! I know. I've never understood the biological clock. Never heard its ticking. Never once went gooey-eyed over neonate bundles.'

'And what about the environmental hazards? Those Pampers –?'

'Let me finish.' Androula had sat up and was pulling on that hideous pink nightie. Her breasts wobbled. For a delicious moment I envisaged them rotund with milk, then was snapped back to our argumentative reality.

'I'm as bewildered as you. My body's become this vessel with only one purpose. It pulls me towards mothers with babies on the bus, makes me sit beside them and talk about stages in child development. I went swimming yesterday and the Mother and Toddler Group were coming out as I went in, the kids all swaddled like little seals – I loved it.'

'What about your scorn for lesbian mothers whom you called narcissistic breeders not so long ago? And world population? Adoption? I thought this was settled.' I'd run out of steam. I was tired.

'It was. I was. Now I'm not. I'm stirred up. Agitated.' I sensed this was going to be a long night.

'Basically,' I began, stifling a yawn, 'I made my lifestyle choices a long time ago.'

'Look, this isn't a marketing questionnaire we're talking about. You're the one who wanted to get married, remember? Last year?'

I was hit.

She looked at me with renewed estrangement. 'And when did you start saying "basically"?'

'It's a sentimental, romantic notion.'

'What, having a baby or a wedding?'

'It's a much bigger commitment – you can't divorce a kid.'

'Oh, so you're not committed for the long haul?'

'Not to babysitting, bum-wiping, lifting and laying –'

'I do that already.'

Ouch. I was badly wounded.

'What's one more big baby?' she went on.

'Thanks.' I resolved never to whinge again. Get my whimpering before going to work under control. Pick up my socks.

Androula had opened the bedside table drawer and pulled out a packet of Camel Lights and a box of matches. She lit one up. *In the bed.*

'There'd be none of that,' I said, tight-lipped. 'I thought you'd given up.'

A self-righteous scowl.

'You thought wrong. I still have five a day, open all the windows and brush my teeth.'

Whoa! I don't know this woman. A smoking, breeding liar in my bed. I had to regroup, plan another strategy. It reminded me of a stone hitting my windscreen, how a small star-shaped dent had sent out three tentacle cracks which travelled until they reached a point of contact. The cracks had advanced a little more. Then a spur of proverbial lightning struck. Why on earth would she stop at one? There were *two* little blighters in Wells-Next-the-Sea.

I rallied. 'What about your skin, your hair, your teeth? They sap every bit of juice and gram of vitamin from you. Delete brain cells. Memory.' I almost said, 'You'll age overnight,' but knew even in my anxious state that that was below the belt. Nevertheless, it was my duty to get her to renege – I'd be the one she'd kill when this obsession wore off and we'd be holding the baby, so to speak.

'Haven't you heard of the bloom of pregnancy, the glow?' She hit a return.

'It fades.' Boing.

'Aren't you in the least bit interested in discussing this adult-to-adult?' The smoke blew furiously from her mouth. It smelt strong and bitter.

'Wake me when the adult returns.' I sneered and turned over in bed, my back a big, silent no. It was one-thirty. *A weekday.* What had happened to child-free serial monogamy?

'I was thinking about Gary,' she said loudly.

I shot up.

'Gary? My brother Gary?'

'Why not? Then it would have your genes and mine.'

'And Gary's receding hairline and hairy back. No way.' No part of Gary was going to go where I couldn't. I was one step from sulking, two from hitting the Row Room running.

'If you won't discuss it, I'll choose the father myself.'

'Not Gary. Please, Androula. He's got awful table manners and believes in New Labour. What about Kevin? He's lovely.' Kevin's a gay performance artist we know. Tall, smart and hairless.

'What if he decides to do one of those events in the men's covered in sugar and butter for four days again? Not reliable.' She paused. 'There's Femi.'

'A mixed race baby with two white dyke mothers. I don't think so.'

'It wouldn't be the first.'

I couldn't believe it. It was the middle of the night and she'd got me to consider the whole baby question as a *fait accompli*. The baby father! Goodbye to Christmas in Kerala. I lay down again and counted nine months on my fingers. It could be here by January. I could be a – well, what would I be? Surrogate dad? I'd be its aunt if Gary was the father. I'd rather be the uncle. It would call me Uncle. Uncle Mac. The Man from Uncle. Whatever happened to Ilya Kuryakin?

And Androula, Mama. My sweet little sumptuous Mama. My *shared* Mama. Responsibility, thoughtfulness, moral clarity, here I come. Then I remembered the time our first laptop slipped from my grip, rocked spectacularly and fell on its back on the floor. I'd opened it with great reverence and timidity, even though by then any damage had already been done. I was close to prayer. All Androula's work was stored in it. I switched it on, it lit up, like an eye, alive. What if I dropped the baby? The thought travelled through me like a sharp wind, the kind that makes flesh flimsy, the work of the heart and veins and organs and limbs, nothing. Nothing much. Androula lay down beside me and I watched her body give those little tugs towards wakefulness and then drift off to sleep. I didn't sleep a wink all night.

Androula seemed brighter the next morning. She rang me from the office to tell me she'd been promoted – more outreach, less admin, more time to work from home. Her schedule changed almost at once and I saw her more and at odd times. I love these web-based companies. She relaxed again. We didn't mention Project B for over a fortnight.

Then one Sunday morning, we were reading the *Observer* in bed. I'd made breakfast and brought it up on a tray – napkins and all. The street was quiet and we'd no plans for the day except pruning the garden and an early movie. We could hear wood-pigeons in the eaves. I tried to put the sight of their little green and white circles of shit on the path out of my mind.

'This is bliss,' Androula said. 'Hey, listen to this...'

'Hmmm...' I wasn't listening. She always liked to read me

extracts from the paper that I wanted to discover for myself, in context, silently.

'I've been thinking,' she continued, 'of Aphrodite.'

'Yes.' I turned a page. It flapped and creased.

'For our daughter. Aphrodite Diotima. A goddess and a philosopher.'

'After yourself and me.' I humoured her. There was no way on God's earth this was going to happen. What would that be for short? Aphro? Ditie?

'Yes, not this year though,' she said calmly. 'I like this life as it is.'

I hid my staggering relief in the Review Section. I had months, maybe years, ahead of uninterrupted suckling all to myself.

NORMA MEACOCK
Border Women

NORMA MEACOCK
Border Women

On Saturday night all four of us got thrown out of Offa's disco. Milly, Fay, Jacquetta and me. Ophelia, who runs Offa's, used to be a sergeant major in the WRAC before she retired. And you don't argue with a Chieftain tank.

'I never want to see you lot in here again,' she said, blocking the doorway, arms akimbo. 'Fuck off! Do I make myself clear?'

This expulsion was a serious matter. Not that Offa's is Shangri-La, far from it. But we live in the fields, in the hills, in nowhere country. The monthly Women Only disco beckons like a beacon in the murk of November, lighting up our cold, muddy, hillbilly lives.

As the oldest of our foursome, by some twenty years in fact, which puts me in the same age-group as Ophelia, I felt entitled to an explanation.

'Look here! What's this all about? There must be some mistake.' Etc.

She turned venomously towards Milly like one of those cobras that spits you in the eye.

'You're living with a man!'

'Hang on a minute –'

'You've had a man in your bed for the past two weeks. And I trusted you, you cheap little slag. Piss off! You're banned. All of you.' She heaved her full weight behind the door and slammed it shut.

'Brenda Big Mouth must've told her, bloody cow,' Milly said on our way back to the car park. We piled into the clapped-out Jag and fended off the dogs, who leapt on us rapturously.

Question time!

'So who is he?'

'Who's the poor sucker?'

'Oh, it's only that chap who runs the Tandoori Takeaway.'

Jacquetta screwed her face up.

'God, Milly! How can you let that man near you with his repulsive big salami! Or was it a small one?'

Milly smiled gracefully. 'Look on the bright side. We can get a free curry.'

Our local townette has one Tandoori, one Chinese Chippy and seven pubs, one of which still lets us in. That's where we were heading. The Jag leapt into life. The dogs yauped.

'Those dogs stink,' Jacquetta said. Jacquetta's profile has all the aristocratic disdain you can see in Border Leicester ewes. It's the Cheviot sheep nose.

'But what I don't understand,' Fay began, tapping Milly's shoulder from where she sat behind her, 'is why Ophelia went ballistic. I mean, if she's going to excommunicate every dyke who's ever had it off with a bloke, she'll be able to hold Disco Nite in a phone box.'

Jacquetta swept her profile towards Fay. '*I* haven't. And neither have you. It's bloody disgusting.'

But Fay had a point. Take me, for instance. I'd actually married one. Well, two of them in fact, one after the other of course. And everyone knew it.

Milly isn't secretive exactly. She just releases information on a need-to-know basis. We all stared at her reflection in the driving mirror. It smiled back at us with the insane sociability of Norman Bates after he'd stowed his dead mum in the fruit cellar.

'What's going on? Milly! We need to know!'

'Ophelia was one of my Regular Ladies.'

'Well, you kept that hidden up your knicker-leg,' Jacquetta said – in a jaundiced way, I thought. Jacquetta's temperament is not a sunny one. Tensions boil within, the way volcanoes boil.

You can't always predict when they'll erupt.

So – Milly's Regular Ladies. At twenty-eight, Milly hankers after the kind of lifestyle you read about in biographies of Vita Sackville-West, Violet Trefusis, Jo Carstairs – the kind Jacquetta had before her parents chucked her out. She'll never achieve it. The Regular Ladies idea is proof positive of the befuddled, rackety, drunk and disorderly way she goes about things.

Some six months ago, under the illusion that life must have more to offer, she packed in her job at Kwicks.

'You should've stopped there till they sacked you,' Fay warned. 'You won't be able to sign on.'

'I'm not going to. I shall set up as a Sapphic companion, a hetaera, a geisha, a courtesan, an odalisque. I love that word. I wish I'd been christened Odalisque instead of Milly. I shall be a lady of the night, or day, as required.'

'A tart,' Jacquetta said brutally. Milly and Jacquetta had been lovers once and Jacquetta still tries to humiliate her with a dark possessive power she won't give up.

'I shall offer relaxing, life-enhancing, amorous evenings of wanton romance and sensuous delight, to ladies who desire pampering wickedly. Chocolates, éclairs oozing cream, chilled beaded bubbles of champagne on a tiger-skin rug by a warm log fire, music indolent or passionate to suit the erotic mood…'

'Dream on,' Fay said.

I mean, Milly's house is practically a barn: an old stone hafod, backed against a shale cliff, stuffed with jumble-sale curtains to keep the draughts out and still bitterly cold, with no electricity, no water, no bathroom and no loo.

'I shall play the mandolin by candlelight.'

We shook our heads and shut up. That was six months ago. But the business got off the ground in Milly's haphazard way. We didn't ask questions but every so often she'd say she couldn't come to the pub because it was one of her Regular Ladies' nights. And the following evening she'd pay for all the drinks.

'You could've looked further afield,' Fay grumbled. 'You know Ophelia's a hard-core right-winger about bisexuals. And she's jealous as hell. And her ears are as big as the bloody Echelon satellite-listening system.'

'She had her army pension,' Milly said. 'She was a good payer. It's a survival thing.'

I wanted to hear some spicy details. But Fay was brooding over realpolitik in our small community of leslies: 'It's a witch hunt. All lesbians are equal but Some Very Very Pure hard-liners are more equal than others.'

And Jacquetta's black mood cast a pall. She and Fay were now occasional lovers but it didn't stop Jacquetta from falling head over heels for another bird every few weeks. At the moment that bird was our Judas. Brenda Big Mouth. And instead of dancing the night away with Jacquetta, Brenda was all too probably, at this very minute, jigging to the strains of 'Saturday Night da-da da-da da-da-da' in Ophelia's brawny arms. It was enough to cloud the sunniest temperament.

'Forget it! Let's go down the Six Bells and have a pint and a game of pool,' I said, in a lame attempt to pull things together. We were going there anyway. We had nowhere else to go.

Milly had got us banned from the Fox. She made a pass at the manager's wife, a real stunna, in the loo. Well, how was she to know?

We'd got the heave-ho from the Red Lion one Sunday lunchtime. We'd staggered in from a fifteen-mile, Offa's Dykes-on-a-hike day. Twelve of us desperate for a drink, muddy and ruddy. Okay, our boots leaked water and Fay was carrying a pile of sheep skulls. And the place was jim to the brim with tourists all dolled up for Sunday lunch at 'An historic 16th-Century Inn with a warm and friendly atmosphere'. The head waiter refused to serve us so Ophelia clopped him one.

Jacquetta got us chucked out of the Railway after our last gig there. She ate three *specialité de la maison* venison pasties, drank five bottles of Pils, and refused to pay on the grounds that we were the entertainment. The owner called the police on the grounds that the pub was empty. So he lost money? Whose fault was that? I mean, who pays to go to a pub round here on a Monday night to see a band they've never heard of?

As for the Barrels, the Duke's and the White Horse Hotel – they won't let Fay in at any price. It could be the piercings; it could be the bones; it could be the Burlington Bertie masher drag; it could be the bald head. So, on to the Six Bells.

We'd just come over the moor, across the cattle-grid and onto the back road. It was a long way round but the Jag had no tax and the MOT had run out. A huge pink papery November moon rose above Cofn Coch and floated free. Milly glanced up at it and the Jag swerved.

'Look out you daft cow! You nearly hit that bloody badger.'

We tipped together in the back and the dogs jumped all over us; pandemonium for a minute.

'Hang on,' Fay shouted. 'There's something on the road.'

Milly pulled over. Fay leapt out; the dogs leapt after her.

'Badgers are such a bloody pain,' Jacquetta said. 'That's what smashed the front bumper on my MG.'

Milly peered into the chilly night.

'Roadkill. More like a mink or a stoat. She's bringing it back.'

It was a polecat, thin and slinky, drooping over Fay's palm like a deliquescing Dalí watch.

'It's dead. The front wheel caught it.' She tucked it in the pocket of her dinner jacket, whistled the dogs. They all jumped in and off we went.

'It's for the course,' she said to Jacquetta. 'Sor-ree.' Fay is studying Celtic Shamanism. Her caravan's as full of bones as a kipper.

It was the last straw for Jacquetta. 'I'm not sitting in a pub all night next to stinking dead vermin. As soon as we get into town I'm hitching a lift back. In fact, I might move out, go to London. I've had enough.'

Jacquetta had the power to send waves of darkness flooding into her environment the way a squid squirts ink. It always makes me want to mop it up before it does too much damage, get things back all hippity-hoppity. I know it's a policy of appeasement. If you'd been brought up by my mother, you'd feel my way too.

So I took my little ole blues harp out of my pocket and started to play our latest number, which I really do think is about the best song I've ever written.

'Oh for fuck's sake!'

So we sat in total silence until we got to the Six Bells, eight miles later.

It was a one hundred per cent typical Saturday night in the Six Bells. The rednecks at the bar turned like a row of bullocks doing a line dance.

'Owdo?' 'Ahdo?' 'Owsit goin like?' 'Owdo girls?' 'Awright ladies?' 'Ah's the band?'

Believe me, they'd vote for the Taliban if they could. Shoplifters? No problem. Chop their hands off. They won't do it again. Youngsters who nick your old age pension? Hanging's too good for 'em. Tear them limb from limb.

Don't mention foreigners, immigrants, gipsies, hippies, crusties or living on the dole. In this town you have to pass for straight. I mean, *you* try living here with a bird.

Milly got squeezed by three farmers on our way to the table in the corner and I got a kiss from two OAPs. Sexual harassment? Forget it. Every man in this dust-mote of the cosmos takes any chance to kiss, grope, groin and whisker any woman within reach.

Okay. A slight exaggeration. Nobody approaches Jacquetta or Fay. Jacquetta's got her vitriolic force-field. Fay's got a bald head and a face bristling with rivets. But is that the price you have to pay?

We were settling down for a night's serious drinking and a chunter about future gigs (if only), the state of our finances, our relationships, our prospects in life, when Kev launched himself into our chat-room. He was sitting at the next table with Bob and Dirty Harry.

Everybody knows everybody here. We know the entire life history of people we've never met. Kev's got fat arms, short legs, a beer belly, and whatever subject comes up he's an expert on it. He carries his copy of the *Sport* wrapped inside the *Guardian*.

Bob the Bull's a farmer: padded check shirt, jeans, bug eyes and an intermittent dribble. He's a bachelor. Most women would sooner marry his sheep.

Dirty Harry looks like one of those shrunken heads the Jivaro Indians used to pickle. Probably sixty, could be eighty. Insults his wife in public and talks sex to other women; the younger they are, the worse it gets.

Three real cool dudes. You can imagine how glad we were to have them butting in on our Saturday night.

'I saw your Jag in town parked up by the Midland Bank, on Thursday about 2.45. I expect you were in the bank.' Kev-on-the-pull stalking Milly.

'Last year were a good year for lambs though, Harry boy. Only ten born wi' big 'eads, like.' Bob to Dirty Harry.

'Those P-reg. Jags are good on bodywork, not rustbuckets like that Dagenham dustbin I saw your cousin driving through town. They cost you though, the 1975 Jags. Ten miles to the gallon. And you're talking top whack for the parts.' Kev the Creep to Milly again.

'The fat old cow split 'er knickers this morning. Ugly great bloomers... I bet you're wearing something a bit different.' Dirty Harry leering at the four of us.

'I see you're drinking Prout's November Sparkler, Milly. It's a local brewery, fair do's, but a lot of the pubs round here won't stock Jeremy's beers. He doesn't condition them long enough in the cask. Pass me your glass and I'll give you my opinion.'

No, Milly, NO! He'll be offering to buy us all drinks next and we'll be stuck with the wankers for the rest of the night. But Milly will listen to anybody for as long as it takes if they'll offer to buy the drinks.

'What're you all drinking? I'll get the next round in. Milly? Fay? Jacquetta? Alice?'

Next thing they'd dragged their chairs to our table and were all over us like horse-flies.

'Christ Almighty! I can't take much more of this.' A couple of pints had sweetened Jacquetta's ominous mood but now it was coming back with a vengeance.

'If I had an eighteen-year-old in bed with me tonight instead of that old sow...'

'The young Speckled Beulah's just the teaser to bring the ewes on all at the same time, see. I kicked his arse out of it last week and put the tups in.'

'Strictly speaking, Milly, they're not Indian, not Indian you know, in the Tandoori. They're Sylhetis from the independent state of Bangladesh. It used to be East Pakistan until 1971. It was the Moguls who brought the tandoor to the sub-continent.'

'I'd make her wet her panties, I would. You know what I'm talking about, like.'

And Dirty Harry pudged his fingers into Jacquetta's thigh.

She reared up, hissing like Medusa. 'Fuck off, you fucking scumbags. We came in here for a drink and a private conversation. Butt out! Piss off! Leave us alone!'

You city slickers may wonder why it took us so long. Well, it's completely against pub etiquette round here to tell men who invade your space to bugger off under any circumstances. Especially if they've bought you a drink. It just isn't done.

They gawped at us. They shuffled off wordless, defeated and humiliated. Fay and Jacquetta clashed fists triumphantly. 'Yesssss!' Milly and I raised eyebrows with an uncomfortable sense of foreboding.

'Brilliant!' Fay said. 'Now, first on the agenda: any chance of a gig any time, any place?' looking at me. I'm songwriter, harmonica player and manager of our band, Miss P's Collar and Tie. Jacquetta's on drums. Milly and Fay are lead and bass guitar.

Great name, don't you think? I expect you remember Miss Peters from Malory Towers, 'tall, mannish, with very short hair and a deep voice,' who hates wearing skirts?

We're on the way up. Well, we must be. From where we are, it's the only way.

The next round of drinks talked us through Ophelia. The one after that got us started on Brenda Big Mouth. Fay offered to try out an ancient Hud curse with a horse's skull as a bit of practical course work. We were getting well into the spirit of this – concocting all manner of fabulous shamanic vengeance and whispering wickedly – when the D word coming from the next table entered our ear-space.

'She's had many a drink off me, like. You know what they say about her –'

'One of those dykes.'

'You mean a piece of crap that's lying in the street.'

'Needs a bloody good shagging.'

'They all do. That'd sort 'em out...'

Fay leapt up, all five feet of her, bald head glinting, studs shining, like a sword blade sprung from its sheath.

'No dyke would touch you bunch of stinking arseholes with a bargepole. I'd sooner shag a dead polecat!'

She reached in her pocket and slapped the aforesaid in the middle of their table.

Suddenly, unexpectedly galvanised back into life, the polecat sprang up with a snarl of blood-curdling ferocity. I've never seen men jump so fast. Splattering beer and clutching their trouser-legs, they fled like greased pigs. The creature capered through the pub with bared teeth and cleared the place quicker than the American Werewolf in Yorkshire.

Eventually it found the open door. I think the Jag must've clipped its foot, because it moved with little limping pounces as it pranced off into the night.

Brian came from behind the bar swinging a knout of bar towels towards us. He was not a man you would describe as having a GSOH.

'You must be bloody mad, the lot of you, letting that bloody ferret loose in here. I'm banning you until further notice, see? Go on! Get out! Bloody trouble, that's what you are.'

Outside, the frosty air skinned our noses. The car glittered.

'Hey, Milly, has that Tandoori got a licence? Can we get a drink?' It hadn't. And the Spar, with its Eight Till Not Terribly Late policy, was shut.

'Anyway, I need my kip,' Fay said. 'That's enough malarkey for one night.'

We drove out of town.

We dropped Jacquetta off at her aunt's bungalow on the far side of the village. It's temporary and she's restless. She spends half her time at Fay's anyway. It wouldn't surprise me if she did move to London.

Fay lives a couple of miles further on, under the forestry. As soon as the dogs scented home ground, they flung themselves at the car windows.

'There's some oak-leaf wine at the cottage,' Milly said. 'The elderflower's probably ready too.'

'Yeah, but I've got to feed the dogs. And I'm knackered. I'll see how I feel. I might come up later on the bike.'

We watched Fay make her way down the bank and across the stream, the dogs streaking ahead up the opposite slope towards her caravan.

I blessed the full moon when we got to the hafod. While Milly parked the car I climbed through the back window – she's lost the key – and rooted round for candles.

'What about the Raeburn? Worth lighting it now?'

'I can't be arsed. Pour us a glass of wine.'

I poured the wine, rolled myself a joint and went out for a pee. Fay had constructed a loo of sorts out of a bucket under a bender, with a tarp over the top, and a palisade of bones round the outside that makes it look like Baba Yaga's hut. It's a New Ruralist installation, I grant you that, but I prefer the grass. The brittle oak leaves made a soft patter like sand in a rainstick as they fell off the trees.

After a while, Milly came out and we both stood there. You could feel winter coming on in the cool air, but pleasantly, as if, for this moment, the world was perfectly balanced. She pressed her warm lips against mine. And when she opened her mouth I felt her neat cool teeth.

RACHEL SUTTON-SPENCE
Small Change

RACHEL SUTTON-SPENCE
Small Change

I want to explain why I did it. Time will tell if I got it right. Or maybe there wasn't a right or a wrong. I just did what I believed was right.

It all started one very ordinary Saturday morning. I had just taken an apricot pie out of the oven and Helen was washing up. There was a knock at the door and I opened it to a smartly dressed man with a briefcase.

'Patricia Bartlett?' He wore a professional smile.

'Yes,' I replied, with that knee-jerk obedience that comes when a bureaucrat uses your full name. He showed his identification and I asked him in. We sat in the front room – him, Helen and me – and he turned my life upside down.

When he'd gone, we sat in the kitchen and discussed our options.

'What should I do?' I asked desperately.

'Whatever you decide, my darling, you know I'll support you.'

'What if the papers get hold of it?' I babbled, as I poured tea into the milk jug. 'What happens if our friends find out before we tell them?'

Helen gently took the teapot from me. I put the tea cosy over the jug.

'Can't I pretend it never happened and it will go away?'

She shook her head kindly. 'That might not be the best tactic, sweetheart.'

She was right, of course.

'We need a plan,' I said decisively. 'Help me make a plan.'

We talked for hours and eventually agreed on a plan: to tell no one until we had a plan.

And we ate our way through the pie.

The next week I was noticeably distracted at work. Being a tree surgeon (or an 'arboricultural consultant' as my business card says) carries some basic responsibilities and I've always found that there's nothing like a buzzing chainsaw to focus the mind. But all the same, I was as distracted as you can be when roped in the canopy of a hundred-foot lime tree.

'Are you okay?' asked Matt, my ground-worker, as I fumbled with my butterfly harness and nearly dropped the rack brake.

'Just domestic worries,' I replied, confident this would fob him off. When a lad's boss, twenty years his senior and a known lesbian, mentions 'domestic worries', he soon changes the subject.

'Oh. Pass the pruning saw, would you?'

They were not so much domestic worries, actually. More like financial. I've never been bothered by money before. Helen and I came out at college in the early 1980s and absorbed the feminist politics of the time. We rejected the traditional ideas of consumption and capitalism, along with the accepted norms of physical beauty and feminity. Our goal was to live simply and honestly, respecting women and nature. It all seemed so easy back then – by re-using carrier bags, eating lentils and wearing our hair short we would overthrow the oppressive patriarchal society.

Two decades later, we've mellowed a bit, and our political flames have died to glowing embers. We're settled in our work, bumbling contentedly into a peaceful middle age. We've realised we're not going to save the world but we do our best not to destroy too much of it either. We have modest aspirations and so long as we have each other we are totally content.

But thirty years ago a well-meaning aunt bought me a

handful of premium bonds for Christmas. I barely gave them a thought until that civil servant knocked on our door and told me I'd won the million pound prize.

Like I said, I was worried about money.

On Friday evening, Mel dropped round on her way out clubbing. She's twenty-two and lives in another world. Mel's dad was my first – and last – boyfriend. Our short relationship came to an amicable end when we discovered that we both fancied Miss Walker, the new biology teacher, but he and I have stayed good friends ever since. When Mel was seventeen, he found her in the garage, locked in an uncompromisingly carnal embrace with her best friend Jasmine on the back seat of the Nissan. That was when he called me, and Helen and I have been Mel's godparents ever since.

As we sat chatting over Helen's particularly fine rhubarb pie, an alien possessed my mouth and I heard myself asking Mel, 'If you had a million pounds, what would you do?'

She rolled her eyes despairingly. 'That's so boring. We went through all that when they started the lottery.'

'Humour me, Mel. I'm just interested.'

Mel's not rich. Last year she graduated from college with a degree in ceramics and psychology and for the last six months she has worked at the covered market, selling olives. It's a steady job even if it doesn't pay so well. Still, Mel believes that money's for spending, and if you haven't got any, credit will do. You could build a house from the cards in her purse.

'I'd pay off my debts and then I'd buy things.'

'What things?'

'Lots of things – CDs, a new phone, a computer, a DVD player. Get some really good clothes.' She thought a while longer. 'Oh, and buy a house, of course. Get a car. Buy some nice clothes.'

Mel likes clothes a lot. Helen and I buy ours from Millets and we wear identical trainers. Mel is deeply ashamed of us.

'Don't you buy all those things, anyway?' I asked. 'Even without any money?'

Mel's sunny disposition temporarily went behind a cloud. 'It's my life,' she said, reminding me in an instant why I never had children. 'Everyone whacks it on plastic these days.'

Bravely, Helen ventured, 'Is all this credit-card debt wise when you're up to your ears in student loans?'

'If God had meant us to spend our own money, he wouldn't have invented credit cards. Debt keeps this economy running.'

'Such wisdom in such a youthful frame,' I muttered.

'When capitalism collapses, my debt goes with it. And so would any hypothetical million pounds.'

You couldn't argue with that. I was fairly sure that Mel could cheerfully spend her way through a million and then start to rack up more on her credit cards.

Helen smiled brightly. 'More pie, anyone?'

Our encounter with Mel gave us an idea. We invited our friend Joanne over on Saturday. Joanne works absurdly hard at something impenetrably financial and as a direct consequence has the biggest income of anyone in our acquaintance. She came out at college at the same time as Helen and me, and she's a feminist, too. She strongly believes that women have the right to earn as much as men do. We sat her down with a cup of black coffee (Joanne doesn't eat pie) and asked her what she'd do if she had a million pounds.

She pondered silently for a while and then said, 'I think, all told, that I almost have.'

I was glad we weren't eating pie. I'd have choked.

'If you consider the equity in my London flat and the house here, my pension scheme, my company share options, and various bits and pieces, I can't be far short of it.'

Come to think of it, her jacket alone would have made a sizeable contribution towards the final sum.

'So, isn't a million enough?' I asked, carefully. 'Do you still have to work so hard? What do you have to spend it on?'

'I like good things,' she answered honestly. 'I like eating in good restaurants and going on holidays to faraway places and staying in quality hotels. I save quite a bit for a good pension, too. We won't have children to look after us in our old age. And, of course, living alone is always more expensive.'

She hasn't got a steady partner and never has had. Perhaps she can't fit one into her busy schedule.

'Besides, I like working. I'm good at my job and I'm worth the money.'

Suddenly I realised that Joanne *lives* for her job. Her work and the money she makes from it are the focus of her life. She'll never have enough of it, just like I could never have enough of Helen.

Dame Cynthia Bishop does like pie. We served her an old-fashioned apple pie when she came over on Sunday evening. Helen's mum and Cynthia were at grammar school together. Helen's mum got married and worked as a traffic warden, once coming third in the national hunt for Traffic Warden of the Year. Cynthia did not marry. She went into the civil service and the year before she retired, the Queen made her a DBE for services to public drinking water. After forty years of ensuring safe water in every tap in the nation, it is well known that Cynthia takes each bottle of Evian as a personal insult. It is considerably less well known that for 18 years she lived with her secretary, Shirley. Shortly after Helen and I met, Helen gave her 'Mum, Dad, I've got something to tell you' speech. When she finished, her mum just said, 'Time to ring Cynthia.'

We were young, arrogant and ignorant. Cynthia was gentle, wise and infuriating. And very good for us. She's been our guiding star for 21 years and now we were ready to face her with our uncomfortable truth.

'Cynthia,' Helen began, 'what would you do if you had a million pounds?'

'Nothing that I don't do now,' she replied. Then, with the clarity of thinking that kept drinking water safe and earned a royal investiture, she asked, 'What would you do?'

The uncomfortable silence that followed spoke volumes.

'What's the matter, girls?'

We love Dame Cynthia very much. No one else could call us 'girls' and live.

'Tell her,' said Helen.

So I did, and her reaction was a great comfort.

'Oh, you poor dear. How dreadful for you.'

Cynthia lives at peace with the world. She's not had a partner since Shirley died in 1978 and she doesn't live a lavish lifestyle. 'I'm content knowing I've done some good in this world,' she said. 'My generation was brought up with clear ideas of duty and service. My life's work has been my small contribution to society. I certainly didn't do it for the money. People put too much importance on money these days.'

'We all need *some* money, though,' I reasoned.

'I'm not advocating poverty, you silly child.' Silly child? Me? 'I've seen poverty that would make your hair curl. Of course money is important. But I would rather leave clean water as my legacy than a bulging bank account.'

'So, are you saying I should give up my job and take up voluntary work?' I asked desperately.

'Is that what you want to do?' She really could be infuriating.

'What do *you* think I should do?' I wailed.

'Do what you believe is right, dear. And what will make you happy. When the two coincide, you will know. Helen, how about some tea to go with this delicious pie?'

On Monday Matt and I finished taking down a beautiful and very dangerous cedar and I decided to buy Helen a new car. But then I realised there was nothing wrong with the car she already had. On Tuesday we shored up a split oak and saved it for another generation and I almost booked Helen and me on a cruise to the Caribbean. But then I remembered she gets seasick on a houseboat. On Wednesday high winds kept me in the workshop maintaining tools and preparing invoices. I bought her a bunch of flowers and went home early, in need of some loving comfort.

To cheer me up we had my favourite evening – a chip supper and *Desert Hearts* on the video. It gave me an idea.

'We could go to Reno and put the whole million on a single game of blackjack.'

'If you like, my darling,' she replied equably. 'But you might win and then what would we do?'

We watched as far as the kiss in the rain and then got distracted. Well, anyone who has seen *Desert Hearts* knows it is easy to get distracted after the kiss in the rain.

Later, as I lay awake thinking about everything and listening to Helen's soft breathing, it suddenly became clear. It was so obvious what to do with the money. I turned over and slept better than I had in weeks.

Last night, we had all three of them round – Mel, Joanne and Cynthia. I had spent the afternoon creating a masterpiece of a lattice-topped blackcurrant pie for the occasion.

When we told Mel and Joanne about our win, they both reacted in the same way – with a carnival of colourful language.

'What are you going to do with it?' asked Mel, once they had absorbed the news.

Helen smiled encouragingly at me and I took a deep breath. 'Give it all away.'

Mel and Joanne uttered some more choice expletives. Even Cynthia raised a quizzical eyebrow, but said nothing.

Mel said, 'What, all of it?'

'It has to be all or none. If I start creaming off little bits for this and that, I won't be able to stop.'

'I don't get it,' said Mel. 'Why don't you want it?'

'I'm not daft. I know that having some money makes life easier, but we already have enough for that. And I get my true happiness from Helen, not from money. Doesn't that sound gruesomely schmalzy? I'm sorry, but it's a fact. More money couldn't make me any happier than I am already.'

'You really mean that, don't you?' asked Mel in astonishment.

'I was surprised too, when I worked it out,' I confessed.

Joanne said, 'You need to think about your future, though.'

I parried: 'I often do and my future has never included a million pounds before. I don't see why it should start now.'

Joanne persisted: 'But tree surgery is a young person's game and you're getting on. What will you do when your tree-hugging days are over?'

'Arboricultural litigation consultancy. I've done some already and it pays well. You'd be amazed what people try to blame on a tree.'

'What about you, Helen?' Joanne wasn't going down without a fight. 'Are you going to let her chuck it all away?'

'She's just told you she thinks I'm worth a million quid,' Helen said. 'What more can a girl ask for?'

'Mental,' said Mel. 'Both of them.'

Joanne nodded.

'What do you have in mind?' asked Cynthia gently.

'Helen and I have shortlisted 792 charities and voluntary groups of different sizes – local, national and international. £990,000 divided equally between them will give them £1,250 each.'

There was a long, long pause. Joanne nibbled absent-mindedly on a blackcurrant.

I could tell they were all desperate to ask, and eventually Cynthia gave in: 'What about the other £10,000?'

'Someone has to send the cheques out. We thought we'd ask Mel if she'd do it, for that fee. It might make a dent in her overdraft.'

Mel nodded in acceptance.

Cynthia nodded in approval.

Joanne shook her head in disbelief.

Helen cut us all some more pie.

SUSAN STINSON
Crease

In the middle of Maryland, I shoved the bus window open as far as it would go, knelt on the seat and stuck my head and shoulders out the window. Wind crackled in my ears and nested in my hair. I held my mouth in an O, inhaling rings of fast-moving air until I had to laugh, giddy with mist and speed.

I was in a valley far from home, passing white barns and big houses as I leaned into emptiness, heavy breasts bouncing in my high-compression nylon/lycra motion-control bra, one of two passengers on a corroded city bus with loud exhaust and soft brakes rattling south to Texas to be sold for salvage. As we left behind a sign that said, 'Pick your own pumpkins,' I tried to think of recipes. Instead, pressed into the sharp edge of the window frame, I looked down past the shivering flank of the bus to the jittery road streaming beneath me, and grabbed hard onto another kind of joy: Lilian.

Lilian, in a crinoline and a beaded body suit, is reading aloud to our friends. Jen, Sarah, everyone is here. We've already had homemade crackers, Waldorf salad and wine. We've all been sitting in the living room, eating and flirting in a neighborly way, talking about pellet- versus wood-burning stoves and the threat of Wal-Mart coming to town. It's a party in honor of Emily Dickinson's birthday. Lilian is reading:

If your Nerve deny you –
Go above your Nerve –
He can lean against the Grave,
If he fear to swerve –

I'm lingering in the kitchen, putting a cherry pie in.the oven. I set the timer and watch through the doorway. Lilian's big thighs are visible under the audacious slip she's wearing as a skirt. I made it for her.

Technically, crinoline refers to petticoats stiffened with horsehair thread, but, for Lilian, I didn't even use starch. Her slip is all soft fullness: three yards of blue tulle, nylon thread. I wrapped her bare waist with the tape measure and marked the correct quarter inch with my thumb. The slip had to fit tightly, or it would sag under its own weight. I folded a strip of organza between two layers of cotton, and sewed three rows of stitches to guide me in attaching the translucent skirts. I felt tender as I gathered and pinned the tulle, which made a tiny ruffle along the inside of the waistband that only she would feel. The balls of my fingers became pricked and tender from bunching the fabric, but then hummed with vibration as I fed my work under the needle of the Singer. I loved the motorized stitches streaming over bumps of gathered tulle.

She's finishing the Dickinson:

If your Soul seesaw
Lift the Flesh door –

She has asked my permission to read the piece she's been working on about me. I looked it over last night at the kitchen table, and felt a little ill. 'What does this have to do with Emily Dickinson?'

Lilian chewed on a fingernail. 'Adrienne Rich called Dickinson "Vesuvius at home". She has that in common with you.'

I didn't try to deny my volcanic qualities, but fiddled with my earrings, thinking about times I'd seen her pause in writing to reach under her T-shirt and take both breasts in her hands. She would hold them for a moment or two, then pick up her Dr Grip pen and go on. Picturing that, I said, 'Okay.'

Everything Lilian writes matters, even if it makes me want to fill the sink with water and put my head under until it is over. She offered to change my name, but I chose notoriety. That may surprise those who know me, but I am more proud of my lover than afraid of anything, even the truth. So now she lifts the page and reads:

When compelled by a persuasive idea at a meeting, Carline fingers her belly. Once I volunteered for the finance committee of a food bank about to go bankrupt just so I could watch across the table for that gesture, strangely invisible to others. She loves to chair and take notes, both; refuses to do one without the other. She's not always popular, but she's effective. When she shows me a brochure she has written, she puts it down and opens to the middle, smoothing the pages back, creasing the binding to give me the heart of it before she'll let me wander. She built our bed.

I've tried to get Carline to show a little flesh at the monthly tea dance on a Sunday afternoon. I brought her a camisole to wear under the double-breasted butterscotch jacket she uses for big presentations, but she doesn't want to flaunt anything, not even for a staid bunch of lesbians still doing the macarena. I gave her a rhinestone evening bag, but she said it wasn't practical enough to be her serious purse.

People see me, but Carline gets missed. She puts on one of her pantsuits in a durable fabric, and becomes a fat lady waiting for a bus, a woman whose inner life is of interest only to the truly adventurous. Of course, my friends, I count you among them. I tried to get her to be Elvis one Halloween, could imagine the shrieks of delight if she greased her hair, wore a leather jacket and baggy trousers, offering her hips in performance. I knew she had the concentration to pull it off, but she rolled her eyes, mildly offended, and went as Marie Curie, instead.

I've been asked what I see in her. It's a question beneath the dignity of an answer, but in this company, I will say that Carline is present in the sweetness of her body, in its pain and its raunch. She would never speak of this, but sometimes she falls backwards off the edge of the bed until her shoulders rest on the floor. Her heels try to hook the far rim of the mattress while her hips hold their ground. She's stretched, belly suspended above the warm split where I press with one hand, using the other to keep a thigh on the bed. She gives up noise, modest apartment cries that open to bigger rooms. She groans. Her neck bends at a difficult angle, but she takes more weight on her shoulders, arches her back. Four fingers in, I watch the underside of her belly ripple, curving lewdly, fat with abandon. I kiss the crease at its base.

Lilian puts the sheet of paper down. Our friends are hushed, gathering breath to praise and tease. Before I can recover, Lil takes my hand and pulls me into the room. 'Your turn, Carline. Tell us about your trip.'

Without letting myself stop to think, I begin:

In the middle of Maryland, I shoved the bus window open as far as it would go, knelt on the seat and stuck my head and shoulders out the window...

CONTRIBUTORS

CONTRIBUTORS

Kathleen Kiirik Bryson is a novelist/actor/painter who was born and raised in Alaska. Her first novel, *Mush,* was published by Diva Books in 2001, and she is just finishing her second, *Girl on a Stick*, a pitch-black comedy about rebus puzzles, Catholicism and Americans. Kathleen hopes to be co-directing the low-budget digital feature *The Viva Voce Virus* in the summer of 2003 (for which she's also written the screenplay). It too is a surreal dark comedy.

Elizabeth Carola divides her time between working, Saving the World, interacting (when lucky) with offbeat females and bemoaning the Death of serious literary fiction. She has published stories, journalism and poetry; and her play *Cut* was produced in 2002 at the (Hackney) King's Head.

Carter won the Scotch 3M Record Your Poem competition in 1976, back when tape recorders were as big as houses with giant spools of tape that had to be loaded by industrial cranes. Since then, she has published a few more poems and a textbook on communication for GNVQ, and written and performed comedy for dykes with Mindy Meleyal. She comes from Devon and lives in Manchester where she works for the council, NACRO and Relate, and is a shop steward. She's also a member of Northern Gay Writers Workshop at Commonword and this is her first story.

Emma Donoghue is an Irish writer, born in Dublin in 1969, who spent eight years in England before moving to Canada. Her fiction includes *Slammerkin* (winner of the Ferro-Grumley Prize for Lesbian Fiction), *Kissing the Witch*, *Hood* (winner of the American Library Association's Gay and Lesbian Book Award) and *Stirfry*. She has also published two works of lesbian literary history, two anthologies and two plays, and writes drama regularly for BBC Radio 4. Her latest book is a sequence of historical short stories, *The Woman Who Gave Birth to Rabbits* (Virago, 2002). For more information, check out www.emmadonoghue.com

Frances Gapper has written one novel for adults, *Saints and Adventurers* (Women's Press, 1988), and one for children, *Jane and the Kenilwood Occurrences* (Faber, 1979). Her short story collection *Absent Kisses* was published by Diva Books in August 2002.

Jane Eaton Hamilton is the author of a new collection of short fiction called *Hunger* (Oberon Press, 2002); a children's book, *Jessica's Elevator* (Press Porcepic, 1989); poetry – *Body Rain* (1991) and *Steam-Cleaning Love* (1993), both from Brick; and an earlier story collection, *July Nights* (Douglas and McIntyre, 1992). She has written for newspapers and magazines including the *New York Times* and won many awards for both fiction and non-fiction. Stories have appeared in the *Journey Prize Anthology* and *Best Canadian Short Stories* and, most recently, in Tarcher Putnam's *The Spirit of Writing: Classic and Contemporary Essays Celebrating the Writing Life*. For more information, see www.janeeatonhamilton.com

Jill James is a freelance writer who lives and works in Brooklyn, New York, where she was born. Her talent emerged early with the elegant poem 'Percilla's Crazy Gorilla', which was the most prominent item posted on the refrigerator in the 1980s. After a serious bout with Ben and Jerry's Syndrome, she began writing for magazines and the internet, most recently the NYC lesbian zine *She's Out All Night*. Her electr-opera about a drag king and his wheelchair-bound, femme alter-ego is coming soon to theatres everywhere. Ms James is extremely pleased to be included in the Diva anthology after her story 'Mockingbirds' was published in *Diva* magazine last November.

Jackie Kay was born in Edinburgh in 1961 and grew up in Glasgow. She has published three collections of poetry, the first of which, *The Adoption Papers* (Bloodaxe 1991), won the Saltire and Forward prizes. The second, *Other Lovers* (Bloodaxe 1993), won the Somerset Maugham Award. *Trumpet*, her first novel, won the Author's Club First Novel Award and the Guardian Fiction Prize. Her collection of short stories, *Why Don't You Stop Talking*, was published by Picador in 2002. She lives in Manchester with her son.

VG Lee, having lived, worked and had fun in London for many years, has recently moved to Hastings. She lives in a house at the top of a hill, equidistant from the supermarket and the sea. Her first novel, *The Comedienne*, was published in 2000, and her second, *The Woman in Beige* (starring Lorna from 'The Holiday Let'), is due out in the spring of 2003, both from Diva Books. VG Lee was a founder member of All Mouth, No Trousers literary cabaret group and her poems and short stories have been widely published in anthologies and magazines.

Rosie Lugosi has an eclectic writing and performance history, ranging from singing in the 80s Goth band The March Violets to her current incarnation as Rosie Lugosi the Vampire Queen, electrifying performance poet and host of the Creatures of the Night Poetry Slam at The Green Room, Manchester. She is also Organisatrix of the infamous fetish event, Club Lash. As well as two solo collections of poetry (*Hell and Eden* and *Coming Out At Night*), her short stories, poems and essays have been widely anthologised. Her chilling story 'You'll Do' appeared in the first *Diva Book of Short Stories*. *Host*, her first novel, is with an agent. She won the Erotic Oscar Award for Performance Artist of the Year 2001.

Jane Marlow was born in Hertfordshire in 1966, grew up in Dorset and lives in London, where she studied French at the University of London before going on to drama school and working as an actress. Now a journalist and writer who has also exhibited her photography, she has an MA in women's studies from the University of Westminster. Her novel *Maddie and Anna's Big Picture* was recently published by Diva Books.

Denise Marshall lives in a state of domestic chaos with her patient lover, son and dog in north London. She has given up cooking and all household chores in order to devote more time to writing.

Susannah Marshall was born in Zambia in 1968, the Year of the Monkey. She has had a variety of day jobs, teaching English and working in community arts, and currently works in mental health, but throughout she has written stories and poems and produced paintings. She has had work published in *Iron*, *Mslexia*, *Acclaim*, a collection of lesbian erotica and, most recently, *City Secrets*. She lives in Rochdale with her dog, Juliette Binoche, Kate Bush and Nigella Lawson (part of that sentence is not true). She was a pirate in a previous life.

Norma Meacock (b. 1934) has had several stories published as well as two novels. The short story form is her favourite. Her jobs include much casual work: in cafés, on the buses, potato picking, cider apple picking, thistle weeding. She has also taught English to adults and tutored creative writing classes in London and Powys. She is a mother and a grandmother. Most of the time she lives in rural Shropshire on the Welsh border where she is founder and organiser of Knighton writers, but she is often found in London where she works as volunteer kitchen help for The Food Chain.

Kate Rigby was born in Crosby, Liverpool, in 1959. She lived in Bournemouth for many years before moving to Devon where she lives with her sister, an artist. Kate is a psychology graduate who has worked variously in hotels and with drug addicts. Her book, *Fall of the Flamingo Circus*, was published in hardback by Malvern (1988) and in paperback by Allison & Busby (1990). An excerpt appeared in the second volume of *Pretext* (2000), an anthology of cutting-edge literature published by the University of East Anglia. She received a Southern Arts bursary for her novel *Where a Shadow Played* (1991) and has a couple of other novels desperately seeking publishers.

Jenny Roberts lives in York, and with the help of her partner and the excellent women who work for her, she manages to combine running the Libertas! Women's Bookshop with writing. She has two Cameron

McGill mysteries in print with Diva Books – *Needle Point* and *Breaking Point* – and is working on the third, *Dead Reckoning*, which she hopes will be published in 2003.

Helen Sandler edited the first *Diva Book of Short Stories*, which won the Lambda award in the States for best anthology. Her tale in that collection then grew into a novel, *The Touch Typist*, also from Diva Books – where she works and where she has been so absorbed in other people's writing this year that she has not come up with a story of her own for *Groundswell*. But she *has* finally moved in with her partner and stopped writing about bedsits.

Ali Smith was born in Inverness in 1962 and lives in Cambridge. Her collection of stories, *Free Love* (Virago), won the Saltire First Book Award and a Scottish Arts Council Award in 1995. Her first novel, *Like* (Virago), was published in 1997; and a further collection, *Other Stories and Other Stories* (Granta), two years later. Her second novel, *Hotel World* (Hamish Hamilton, 2001), was shortlisted for both the Orange Prize and the Booker Prize.

Virginia Smith was born in London in July 1968. She grew up in Essex, studied in Liverpool, and now lives with her family, and a lurcher called Ruby, in Southampton. Her first novel, *The Ropemaker's Daughter*, was published by Diva Books in 2002.

Cherry Smyth is an Irish writer living in London. Her debut poetry collection, *When the Lights Go Up*, was published by Lagan Press in 2001. Other fiction appears in *The Anchor Book of New Irish Writing* (2000) and *Hers – Brilliant New Fiction by Lesbian Writers* (Faber & Faber, 1999). She wrote the screenplay for the short film *Salvage* which was broadcast on Irish TV. She has just completed a two-year residency at a women's prison and edited a collection of inmates' poetry called *A Strong Voice in a Small Space* (Cherry Picking Press, 2002).

Susan Stinson has published two novels – *Martha Moody* and *Fat Girl Dances With Rocks*. *Martha Moody* won a Benjamin Franklin Award in Fiction from the Publishers Marketing Association in the US and has been published in British and German editions. Her book of poetry is *Belly Songs: In Celebration of Fat Women*. Her work has been featured in many journals and magazines including *The Kenyon Review*, *The Seneca Review*, *Curve*, *Sojourner* and *The Women's Review of Books*. Stinson lives in Northampton, MA, where she has recently completed a new novel, *Venus of Chalk*.

Clare Summerskill is a writer, actress, musician and stand-up comedienne. She has written several commissioned plays for theatre companies such as Age Exchange and Women In Theatre and she wrote and performed in *An Evening With Katie's Gang* at The Oval Theatre, a cult lesbian musical comedy shortlisted for the Drill Hall's New Playwriting Award. She has also written for several sketch shows on Radio 4, including *So What If I Am?* and the last series of *Weekending*. This is the second short story that Clare has had published. 'Single Again' appeared in the first *Diva Book of Short Stories*.

Rachel Sutton-Spence was born in Liverpool in 1964 and spent a formative part of her youth in Brazil. She now lives in Bristol, with her partner Kerry and their guinea pigs. After years of writing non-fiction (about sign language, mainly, especially sign language poetry) she has started writing short stories again, and would like to thank Julia Green for her help and encouragement. While cycling across America – somewhere in Kansas, or was it Missouri? – she decided to give up her job to enjoy riding and writing. She hasn't regretted it for a moment. Although 'Small Change' is not autobiographical, she does think our nation should eat more fruit pie.

Louise Tondeur was born in Poole in 1972 and grew up in Bournemouth in self-catering holiday flatlets owned by her parents. She did a degree in drama at the University of East Anglia and, while back there studying for the MA in creative writing, she won the Curtis Brown Literary Bursary. Her work has appeared in *Firsthand*, *The Rialto* and *Pretext*. Louise's first novel, *The Water's Edge*, will be published by Headline Review in March 2003. She is currently working on her second novel. She lives with her girlfriend in Cambridge.

Sue Vickerman long ago lived as a *sannyasini* in an Indian ashram, researching for her MPhil on women's spirituality. Her quest subsequently took her to a separatist peace camp in upstate New York, and ultimately across four continents. Finally, equipped with no answers as to the meaning of life, she started to write fiction. Her stories and poems have appeared in a number of anthologies (Virago, Diva Books, Diamond Twig) and magazines (*Orbis*, *Staple*, *Mslexia*). Sue has written a novel, *Special Needs*, and two plays, and is currently working on a poetry collection. She lives in a lighthouse near Aberdeen.

Robyn Vinten came to England in the mid-80s and forgot to leave. She lives in a rapidly becoming fashionable part of north London with her cat. She plays football, tennis and softball despite her advancing years. She had a short story published in the first *Diva Book of Short Stories*.

Christine Webb is a Midlander by birth, but lives in Buckinghamshire with her partner of more than 35 years. She has worked in education all her life, and has been writing as long as she can remember, in both prose and poetry: at eight, hearing of Shakespeare for the first time, she determined to rival him. This has not happened. A collection of poems is, however, to be published next spring by Peterloo Poets. She is an intermittent gardener, disorganised cook and occasional traveller, but is tireless in her criticism of our political scene. She is currently working on a historical lesbian romance.

Polly Wright is an actress, writer and lecturer, noted for her portrayals of Vita Sackville West, Violet Trefusis and Virginia Woolf all in the same play! (*Vita* by Sigrid Neilsen.) She was a founder member of the Birmingham-based company Women and Theatre, with whom she co-wrote and performed more than fifteen plays and numerous cabaret sketches. She joined the Tindal Street fiction group in 1999 and published her first short story, 'Tutte Bene', in the Tindal Street Press anthology *Her Majesty*. Head of the creative studies department at Fircroft College of Adult Education, she runs workshops in drama, literature and creative writing as well as organising and reading at literary events.

Also from Diva Books

Absent Kisses
Frances Gapper

Short stories from a unique imagination

"Frances Gapper is such a brilliant writer that it's surprising she
doesn't already have the ubiquitous Orange/Booker nomination,
a fan club and her own battalion of stalkers"
Rainbow Network (five-rainbow rating)

"Frances Gapper writes with humour and imagination... an
unsettling mixture of the earthly and the ethereal" *Shout!*

"An extraordinary and wonderful read" *Ali Smith*

RRP £8.99 ISBN 1-873741-78-2

The Diva Book of Short Stories
edited by Helen Sandler

Groundswell's big sister

"Look out for *The Diva Book of Short Stories*" *Observer Magazine*

"[A] wonderful collection... Recommended!" *Gay's The Word website*

"Introducing fresh voices alongside established names, Sandler has
gathered together an indispensable collection of contemporary
lesbian fiction" *City Life*

RRP £8.95 ISBN 1-873741-47-2

How to order your new Diva Books

*Diva Books are available from bookshops including Libertas!, Silver Moon
at Foyles, Gay's the Word, Prowler Stores and Borders,
or direct from Diva's mail order service:
www.divamag.co.uk or freephone 0800 45 45 66
(international: +44 20 8340 8644).*

*When ordering direct, please add P&P (single item £1.75, two or more
£3.45, all overseas £5) and quote the following codes:
Absent Kisses ABS782, Diva Book of Short Stories DVB472,
Groundswell GRO774.*